Praise for *Insidious Intent*

"A highlight of novels written by Val McDermid is the tight control she maintains over her complex plots that are enhanced by believable and complicated characters . . . McDermid brings something special to the table as she shows in her latest novel . . . The intense plot moves briskly. McDermid keeps each twist believable . . . The author's expert exploration of the human experience has never been better."

—*Associated Press*

"The narcissistic, controlled killer is engaging quarry and McDermid's procedural details are as on point as ever. But, as usual, this story's true center is the evolution of Tony and Carol's relationship . . . The final twist is both shocking and fitting, a must-read for series fans."   —*Booklist* (starred review)

"Back on the job as head of the newly formed Regional Major Incident Team, DCI Carol Jordan is tested to the max by the Wedding Killer . . . McDermid . . . rais[es] the heat in agonizingly tiny increments, until she's ready for a finale guaranteed to leave you reeling."   —*Kirkus Reviews*

"McDermid puts both her characters and the reader through the emotional wringer with *Insidious Intent* . . . Both a terrific individual read and a culmination of ongoing character arcs throughout the books. McDermid is a maestro still at the top of her game, and adroitly balances shock and inevitability as events for beloved characters take a dark turn."

—*Mystery Scene*

"Thoroughly pleasing, engaging, indeed compelling, a very fine piece of craftsmanship."   —*Scotsman* (UK)

"Val McDermid, known as the queen of psychological thrillers, surp   ne of the most surprising twis   iding."

Irish Independent (UK)

INSIDIOUS
INTENT

Also by Val McDermid

A Place of Execution
Killing the Shadows
The Grave Tattoo
Trick of the Dark
The Vanishing Point
Northanger Abbey

TONY HILL/CAROL JORDAN NOVELS

The Mermaids Singing
The Wire in the Blood
The Last Temptation
The Torment of Others
Beneath the Bleeding
Fever of the Bone
The Retribution
Cross and Burn
Splinter the Silence

KAREN PIRIE NOVELS

The Distant Echo
A Darker Domain
The Skeleton Road
Out of Bounds
Broken Ground

LINDSAY GORDON NOVELS

Report for Murder
Common Murder
Final Edition
Union Jack
Booked for Murder
Hostage to Murder

KATE BRANNIGAN NOVELS

Dead Beat
Kick Back
Crack Down
Clean Break
Blue Genes
Star Struck

SHORT STORY COLLECTIONS

The Writing on the Wall and Other Stories
Stranded
Christmas is Murder(ebook only)
Gunpowder Plots (ebook only)

NONFICTION

A Suitable Job for a Woman
Forensics

INSIDIOUS INTENT

VAL McDERMID

Grove Press
New York

First published in Great Britain 2017 by Little, Brown

Published simultaneously in Canada
Printed in the United States of America

First Grove Atlantic hardcover edition: December 2017
First Grove Atlantic paperback edition: November 2018

Library of Congress Cataloging-in-Publication data is available for this title.

ISBN 978-0-8021-2865-2
eISBN 978-0-8021-8928-8

Grove Press
an imprint of Grove Atlantic
154 West 14th Street
New York, NY 10011

Distributed by Publishers Group West

groveatlantic.com

18 19 20 21   10 9 8 7 6 5 4 3 2 1

This one's for Professor Dame Sue Black and
Professor Niamh Nic Daied – for the friendship,
the fun and games and the forensics.

A black scene of calumny will be laid open; but you, Doctor, will make all things square again.

'On Murder, Considered as One of the Fine Arts'
(Second Paper)
Thomas de Quincey

PART ONE

1

If Kathryn McCormick had known she had less than three weeks to live, she might have made more of an effort to enjoy Suzanne's wedding. But instead she had adopted her usual attitude of resigned disappointment, trying not to look too disconsolate as she stared at the other guests dancing as if nobody was watching.

It was just like every day at work. Kathryn was always the outsider there too. Even though the title of office manager wielded very little in the way of actual authority, it was enough to set her apart from everyone else. Kathryn always felt that when she walked into the kitchenette to make herself a coffee, whatever conversation had been going on either stopped altogether or swerved away from the confidential to the inconsequential.

Really, it had been stupid to think today would have been any different. She'd once seen a quote that had stuck with her – the definition of insanity was, doing the same thing over and over again and expecting different results. By that standard, she was definitely insane. Sitting on the fringes of a wedding reception on a Saturday night but expecting to be at the centre of conversation and laughter fell smack bang at the core of repetitive behaviour that never produced anything but entirely predictable failure.

Kathryn sneaked a look at her watch. The dancing had only been going for half an hour. But felt like a lot longer. Nikki from accounts, hips gyrating like a pole dancer, opposite Ginger Gerry, slack-jawed with delight. Anya, Lynne, Mags and Triona in a neat shamrock formation, elbows tucked in, bodies twitching and heads bobbing to the beat. Emily and Oli, feet shuffling in sync, eyes locked, grinning at each other like idiots. Idiots who would probably be going home together at the end of the night.

She could barely remember the last time she'd had sex. She'd split up with Niall over three years ago. But it still stung like a razor cut. He'd walked into the house one evening, the sharp sour smell of lager on his breath, a faint sheen of sweat on his skin. 'I've been headhunted for a job in Cardiff. Running my own design team,' he'd said, his excitement impossible to miss.

'That's great, babe.' Kathryn had slid off the stool at the breakfast bar, throwing her arms around him, trying to stifle the voice in her head shouting, 'Cardiff? What the *fuck* am I going to do in Cardiff?'

'Big salary increase too,' Niall said, his body curiously still, not responding to the hug.

'Wow! When are we moving, then?'

He disentangled himself. Kathryn's stomach clenched. 'That's the thing, Kath.' He looked at his feet. 'I want to go by myself.'

The words didn't make any sense. 'What do you mean, by yourself? You're just going to come home at weekends? That's mad, I can get a job down there, I've got transferrable skills.'

He took a step back. 'No. Look, there's no good way of saying this ... I'm not happy and I haven't been for a while

4

and I think this is the best way for both of us. For me to move away, start again. We can both start again.'

And that had been that. Well, not quite. There had been tears and shouting and she'd cut the crotches out of all his Calvin Kleins, but he'd gone anyway. She'd lost her man and she'd lost her dignity and she'd lost her home because half the lovely terraced house in her favourite Bradfield suburb had been Niall's and he'd insisted they sell it. So now she lived in a boxy little flat in a 1960s block too close to where they'd lived together. It had been a mistake to move somewhere so near the place she'd been happy, the house she had to walk past to get to the tram stop every morning. She'd tried making a ten-minute detour to avoid it, but that had been worse. An even sharper slap in the face, somehow. Every now and then, the couple who had bought the house emerged as she walked past and they'd give her a little wave and an embarrassed half-smile.

Since then, Kathryn had made a few tentative attempts at getting back to dating. She'd signed up for an online dating site and swiped her way through dozens of possibles. When she pictured herself standing next to them, none of them seemed remotely credible. One of Niall's old workmates had texted her and invited her out for dinner. It hadn't gone well. He'd clearly thought she'd be up for a pity fuck, and had been less than happy when she'd told him to sod off. At her cousin's fortieth, she'd hooked up with a sweet lad from Northern Ireland. They'd ended up in bed together, but it hadn't exactly been a raging success and he'd escaped back to Belfast with a broken promise to call her.

That had probably been the last time she'd had sex. Fifteen months ago. And this was supposed to be her sexual prime. Kathryn stifled a sigh and took another swig from her glass of Sauvignon Blanc. She had to stop feeling so sorry for herself. All the magazines she'd ever read were agreed on that point – nothing was a bigger turn-off for a man than self-pity.

'Is someone sitting here?' A man's voice. Deep and warm.

Kathryn started and jerked round. Standing with his hand on the back of the chair next to her was a stranger. A not bad-looking stranger, she noted automatically even as she stammered, 'No. I mean, they were but they're not now.' Kathryn was used to sizing up potential clients. Not quite six feet tall, she thought. Thirty-something. Mid-brown hair with a few silver strands at the temples. Full, well-shaped eyebrows over pale blue eyes that crinkled when he smiled. Like now. His nose looked a bit thick around the bridge, as if it had been broken at some point and poorly set. His smile revealed slightly crooked teeth, but it was an engaging smile nevertheless.

He sat down beside her. Suit trousers, brilliant white shirt with the top button undone, blue silk tie loosened. His fingernails were square and manicured, his shave close and his haircut crisp. She liked a man who took care of his grooming. Niall had always been meticulous that way. 'I'm David,' he said. 'Are you with the bride or the groom?'

'I work with Suzanne,' she said. 'I'm Kathryn. With a y.' She had no idea why she'd said that.

'Nice to meet you, Kathryn with a y.' There was amusement there, but not in a piss-taking way, she thought.

'Are you a friend of Ed, then?'

'I know him from the five-a-side footie.'

Kathryn giggled. 'The best man milked that in his speech.'

'Didn't he, though.' He cleared his throat. 'I noticed you sitting here by yourself. I thought you might like some company?'

'I don't mind my own company,' she said, regretting the words as soon as they were spoken. 'But don't get me wrong, it's really lovely to meet you.'

'I don't mind my own company either, but sometimes it's nice to talk to an attractive woman.' That smile again. 'I'm guessing you don't much like dancing? So I'm not going to suggest we strut our stuff on the dance floor.'

'No, I'm not much of a dancer.'

'I'm a bit fed up with the music. I prefer conversation, myself. Do you fancy going through to the bar? It's quieter there, we can talk without having to shout at each other.'

Kathryn couldn't quite believe it. OK, he wasn't exactly George Clooney, but he was clean and polite and attractive and, extraordinary though it seemed, he was acting like he was interested in her. 'Good idea,' she said, pushing back her chair and getting to her feet.

As they weaved through the tables to the ballroom door, the man who called himself David cupped her elbow in his hand in a solicitous gesture. Kathryn McCormick's killer was nothing if not solicitous.

2

Detective Chief Inspector Carol Jordan shrugged into her heavy waxed jacket and pulled a thermal hat over sleep-tousled hair. A black-and-white collie danced around her feet, impatient to be out into the morning chill. She tied the laces on her sturdy walking boots and stepped out into a flurry of rain. She shut the door of the converted barn behind her, letting the tongue of the lock click softly into place.

Then they were off, woman and dog cutting up the moorside in sweeping zigzags. For a few blessed moments, concentrating on what she was doing drove the turmoil from Carol's head, but it was too insistent to be kept at bay for long. The phone call that had come from out of the blue the night before had stripped her of any chance of a restful night and now, it seemed, of any peace this morning. There had been no running away from the blame her caller's bitter voice had directed at her.

Years of policing at the sharpest of sharp ends had provided Carol with ample cause for regret. Every cop knew the acrid taste of failure, the tightness in the chest that came with delivering the worst news in the world. Those cases where they'd failed to bring any kind of consolation to people who had a sudden gap in their lives where a loved one should be – those cases still rankled, filling her with a sense of raw inadequacy when she drove down certain streets, crossed particular landscapes, visited towns where she knew unspeakable things had happened.

All those things were generic, though. All cops everywhere who had an ounce of sensitivity to what they were doing carried these loads. But this was different. This latest quantum of blame was a personal burden.

She'd thought she could escape these outcomes that twisted inside her like a tightening rope when she walked away from the job, from the badge and the rank. Her relentless pursuit of a multiple murderer had cost the life of her brother and his wife. What possible reason could there be for staying? She'd wanted nothing more to do with a job that demanded such a high price.

But other people had known only too well the buttons to push to draw her back to policing like a moth to a flame.

#1: Boredom. She'd spent six months stripping her brother's barn conversion to the bare bones then rebuilding it, learning the skills she needed from YouTube videos and old men in the local pub. She'd been driven to erase all traces of what had happened there, as if by remaking it she could convince herself Michael and Lucy's death had been a hallucination. She'd been close to the final stages of the project when her rage had finally cooled enough for her to understand she was growing bored with her choice. She was a detective, not a builder, as the man asleep in her spare room had forcibly told her.

#2: Loneliness. Carol's friendships had always been inextricably linked to her job. Her team were her family, and some of them had made it past her barriers to become her friends. Since she'd walked away, she'd pushed them all to arm's length and beyond. One of her neighbours, George Nicholas, had tried to breach her defences. A generous man, he was the reason she had the dog. Flash was the offspring of his own sheepdog, an anomalous pup who was afraid of sheep. Carol had taken the misfit because she thought they belonged together, somehow. George had seen that as a signal for a closer connection, but he hadn't been who she wanted. George could never be home for her. A return to policing, though? That would take her back into the orbit of people who made her believe she belonged somewhere.

#3: Pride. That had been the killer vulnerability that had left her open to an offer she should have refused but couldn't. Pride in her skill, pride in her smarts, pride in her ability to find answers where nobody else could. She knew she was good. Believed she was the best, especially when she had the right hand-picked team around her. Others might have thought her arrogant; Carol Jordan knew she had something to be arrogant about. Nobody could do this job better. She had doubts about all sorts of things but not about her ability as a guv'nor.

And finally, the killer button to press. #4: Temptation. They'd held out so much more than the simple chance to return to a job that had defined and rewarded her for so long. They'd invented something new, something bright and shiny, something that might change the future of the way they did policing. And she was their first choice to lead it. A regional Major Incident Team – ReMIT – that would scoop up all the sudden violent deaths, the most vicious sexual assaults and the sickening child abductions from six separate police forces. The first tentative step towards a national agency like the FBI, perhaps. Who else could do it if not Carol Jordan?

But she'd screwed up before they could even ask her.

A screw-up so breathtakingly stupid that the only way to rescue her was an audacious act of noble corruption that she should never have considered accepting for a nanosecond, never mind buying into heart and soul. She'd been blinded by the vote of confidence in her abilities, flattered that a man of honour should risk his integrity to place her where she belonged, and, at the last ditch, doomed by the demands of her own ego.

And now there was more blood on her hands and nobody to blame but herself.

Carol drove her body harder against the gradient, making her muscles complain and her lungs burn. Flash quartered the hill in front of her, a sudden flurry of rabbits scattering before her, dirty white scuts bouncing across the moorland grass like a random release of old white tennis balls. Carol didn't even break stride, registering nothing around her, locked into the fury she was directing entirely towards herself.

What was she to do now? The one principle she'd always clung to was her drive for justice. It had taken her to dark places and forced her down reluctant paths but it had never failed her. To deliver criminals to judgement had always fulfilled her. That sense of restoring some kind of balance in the world also gave balance to her life. But there could be no justice here.

If Carol admitted the conspiracy she'd been part of, she'd only be a tiny part of the damage and destruction. It would kill ReMIT before it was even up and running properly. And that would improve the chances of serious criminals escaping the consequences of their actions. She'd have screwed up the careers of other officers who had counted on her. She'd likely go to jail. Worse still, so would other people.

The guilt was hers. The blood was on her hands. There was only one road to redemption. She had to make a success of ReMIT. If she could turn it into an elite team that really did deliver arrests and convictions in the most exacting of circumstances, if they could put killers behind bars before more lives were needlessly taken, if she really did make a difference ... She'd still owe a debt for those other deaths. But at least there would be something to put on the other side of the balance sheet.

3

'I'm worried about Torin,' Detective Sergeant Paula McIntyre said as the teenage boy walking away from the car sketched a farewell wave without actually turning round.

Dr Elinor Blessing muted the radio. 'Me too.' It had been on her mind for days. The last thing on her mind as she let the oblivion of sleep overtake her, the first thought on waking.

Earlier that morning, she'd groaned at the invasive ringtone from her partner's iPhone. Bloody cathedral bells. How could such a small slab of silicone produce so much noise? At this rate, she was going to end up as the Quasimodo of the A&E department. 'Paula,' she grumbled sleepily. 'It's my day off.'

Paula McIntyre snuggled into Elinor and gave her a soft kiss on the cheek. 'I know. But I've got to get me and Torin showered and breakfasted and out the door in good time. You go back to sleep. I'll be so quiet, you won't even know I'm there.'

Elinor grunted, unconvinced. A tremor shuddered through the mattress as Paula bounced out of bed and headed for the shower. Combined with the niggle of worry about Torin, the rattle of the extractor fan and hiss of the shower were too much. Any prospect of sinking back into sleep had been booted far into the long grass. Accepting the inevitable, Elinor made a guttural sound of disgust and got up.

Wrapped in her dressing gown, she climbed the stairs to the loft conversion their fourteen-year-old ward had turned into his wannabe man cave. Knocking first – because taking on Torin so recently had meant they'd dutifully read up on how to survive parenting an adolescent – Elinor stuck her head round the door. 'Morning, Torin,' she said, sounding a lot brighter than she felt. 'Sleep well?'

His grunt echoed her own waking, though an octave lower.

'Time to get up.' Elinor waited till one long thin hairy leg emerged from the duvet, then retreated downstairs to the kitchen. Coffee. A bowl of fresh fruit for Torin. Toast for Paula. Two eggs standing by to be poached for Torin, baked beans already in the pan. Juice for everyone. All set up and ready to roll without a moment's thought. What occupied her mind was not the breakfast but the boy.

He'd fallen into their lives by chance. Neither woman had felt the biological pull towards motherhood but after Torin's mother had been murdered, he had refused point-blank to move away from Bradfield to live with his aunt and grand-mother, distant relatives in terms of emotions as well as miles. His father worked offshore and hadn't been around to any significant degree for years. 'I need to stay where my friends are,' he'd insisted, stubborn but not unreasonable, in Elinor's view. The combination of Elinor's friendship with his mother and Paula's professional involvement in the investigation had somehow ended up with Torin in their home and in their care. Neither was quite sure how it had happened. But neither was willing to reject a boy who had lost his anchor.

And so their life together had expanded to include an adolescent boy. It hadn't been an obvious match-up, but for months it had appeared to have worked. Elinor had been amazed – and, if she was honest, a little concerned – that Torin seemed to have coped so well with his mother's death. Their friend, clinical psychologist Tony Hill, had reassured her. 'Grief is individual. Some like it public, some like it private. For some, it's complicated because their relationship with the dead was complicated. For others – like Torin, apparently – it's relatively straightforward. He's sad, he's bereaved, but he's not in the grip of anger or resentment that he can't come to terms with. No doubt you'll get unexpected outbursts that seem to come from nowhere. But I don't think he's internalising some fucked-up reaction that he's not letting you see.' Then he'd smiled his crooked smile and undercut himself. 'Of course, I could be totally wrong.'

But on the face of it, he'd been right. Torin and the women had adjusted to each other. Elinor and Paula had rediscovered that board games could be fun and that there was a whole new generation of them waiting to be purchased and played. Torin had sat through movies he'd never have considered worth watching. Slowly and carefully, they'd learned what they needed to know about each other.

His schoolwork had recovered from the sudden dip provoked by the shock of his mother's death and he seemed unworried at the prospect of impending exams. Paula had fretted that he didn't seem to have much of a social life. At his age, she'd been one of a group of girls who hung around together for hours on end in each other's bedrooms, experimenting with make-up, comparing the snogging techniques of the boys they'd kissed – for Paula had not yet found a way to explain herself to herself – and gossiping about everyone who wasn't in their charmed circle. The boys had the same tight knots of friendship, though she had no idea what they talked about except that it was different.

Torin's life wasn't like that. He occasionally met up with friends on a Saturday to mooch around the expensive designer shops that cluttered the streets behind Bellwether Square, but mostly he seemed to prefer his own company. Though he was never far from the umbilical connection of one screen or another. But Elinor, whose colleagues at Bradfield Cross Hospital covered a wide range of ages and backgrounds, assured her that this was what teenagers were like these days. They communicated through selfies and Snapchat, through tagging and Twitter, through images on Instagram. And by the turning of the season, it would be another thing altogether. Face to face was so twentieth century.

But over the past two or three weeks, something had shifted. Torin had descended into a moody silence, barely acknowledging their questions or comments. He'd become the grunting, uncommunicative teenager of cliché, contributing nothing to conversation at mealtimes, escaping to his room as soon as he'd finished shovelling food into his mouth. When Elinor asked him if he wanted to talk about his mother, he'd startled as if she'd slapped him. 'No,' he said, dark brows drawn down in a heavy frown. 'What's to say?'

'I wondered whether you were missing her more than usual,' she said, stoic in the face of his hostility.

He sighed. 'I'd only be a disappointment to her.' Then he'd pushed his chair back, even though there was still a slice of pizza on his plate. 'I've got homework.'

And now Paula was admitting what Elinor herself had been concerned about. There were good reasons to worry about Torin. As Paula eased the car into the slow-moving morning traffic, Elinor chose her words carefully. 'I think something is bothering him. More than his mother, I mean. Something we can't guess at because it's outside our experience.'

'So what do we do?'

'Do you think there's any point in talking to the school? His form teacher was pretty helpful after Bev died.'

Paula joined the queue of traffic turning right. 'It's worth a try. Do you want me to get Tony to come round for dinner, see if he can loosen Torin's tongue?'

'Let's hold that in reserve for when we hit the brick wall.' Elinor tried not to let despondency take hold. 'Maybe it's all about being fourteen and not having a man around the place to talk to.'

'He can FaceTime his dad any time he wants. And he usually talks non-stop to Tony. I don't think we have to go down the self-flagellation route, Elinor.' Paula sounded sharp. Elinor hoped it was nothing more than the traffic getting to her.

'If you say so. But . . . '

Paula broke the silence. 'But what?'

Elinor gave a wry smile. 'Carol Jordan always says you're the best interviewer she's ever seen. And you can't get him to open up. So I reckon it must be serious.'

Paula shook her head. 'He's not a suspect, El. He's a hormonal adolescent boy who's gone through a major tragedy. I worry that he's bottling stuff up, not that he's hiding criminal activity.'

Elinor pushed her long black hair back from her face, enjoying the sensation of having it loose instead of tightly coiffed for work. She chuckled. 'You're right. That's me put in my place. Thank you, you always reassure me.'

Paula scoffed. 'Even when I don't reassure myself?'

'Especially when I sense that little niggle of doubt that tells me you're human.' She stroked Paula's arm. 'What have you got on today?'

'Well, we're only getting properly into our stride in ReMIT now. The internet trolling case, that was an accident rather than something we were formally tasked with. So we'll just have to wait and see what lands on Carol's desk. I'm looking forward to it.'

Elinor smiled. 'I know it.' She shifted in her seat, craning her neck to see what she could of the road ahead. 'Pull up after the lights, I'll cut through to the shops from there, save you going round the block and getting snarled in the Campion Way traffic.'

Paula stopped, and leaned across to give Elinor a parting kiss. 'It'll be something and nothing,' she said. 'At that age, it always is the end of the world. Except it never is.' She sounded confident but Elinor read the doubt in Paula's blue eyes.

As she walked through the morning crowds, Elinor told herself to accept her partner's words at face value. 'Something and nothing.'

Even though she didn't believe them for a moment.

4

No matter that Carol had closed the barn door almost silently; Tony Hill had spent so long living alone that even in his sleep he was aware of subtle changes in his environment. The section of the barn that Michael Jordan had built as a guest suite had also doubled as his software lab and he'd made it virtually soundproof. But still Carol's departure managed to rouse Tony from his perennially light sleep. Some delicate disturbance of the air, some faint disruption of the soundscape of his dreams. Whatever it was, he woke knowing instantly that she had left the building.

He lay there for a few moments, wondering how they remained held in each other's orbit. They'd both tried to put distance between them at one time or another, but it never persisted. And now here he was, under her roof. Here, though neither could quite bring themselves to admit it, because she needed him to help her through the process of renouncing alcohol and because he needed her to make him feel his humanity was real rather than a mask. Which was why he'd been there when the phone had rung with its dark message.

He'd known at once the call was trouble. Carol's grey eyes had darkened and her face tightened, exposing fine wrinkles he'd never noticed before. She'd run a hand through her heavy blonde hair, the low lighting in the barn revealing more silver than there had been a few months before. A poignant moment of realisation that she was visibly ageing.

It was odd how these moments stood out in sudden relief. He'd noticed it with his own face. Months would go by without any change impinging then suddenly one morning in the mirror, he'd catch a sideways glimpse and understand that what had once been laughter lines were now permanently etched in hollow cheeks. Sometimes when he got out of bed, his body protested. He remembered Carol laughing at him for making what she called 'old man's noises' when he'd pushed himself to his feet from a chair the other day. He'd never thought much about either of them ageing; now he'd become aware of it, he knew his thoughts would loop back there till he'd figured out what it meant to him. The burden of a psychologist: a job with no downtime.

What he had to figure out now was how to help Carol hold it together in the wake of this latest trouble. He knew her well enough to suspect she'd use it as a spur to push herself even harder. Her own self-worth would be bundled into the success of ReMIT like the double helix of DNA, the two things completely interdependent. And that was a dangerous strategy. Because however good a detective she was, she couldn't control the outcome of every case.

Before he could descend further into introspection, the faint rumble of an engine caught his attention. The rare traffic on the quiet lane running past the barn was usually audible only for a few seconds, but this vehicle was hanging around, the sound not receding but growing louder. It seemed they had a visitor.

Tony scrambled out of bed, almost falling back again as

he struggled awkwardly into his jeans. He grabbed the thick fisherman's sweater he'd taken to wearing on his boat and headed through the main barn towards the front door, hopping as he registered the cold stone flags under his feet. The engine had stopped, he realised. He opened up as a closing car door made the expensive soft click of German engineering. The man who straightened up to face him was all too familiar.

'John,' Tony said, not bothering to hide his weary resignation. The arrival of John Brandon, Carol's former chief constable, the man who had engineered her return to policing, did not come as a shock. Not after the previous evening's news. 'You'd better come in.'

Brandon approached, his resemblance to a miserable bloodhound even more pronounced than usual. 'I'm guessing from your expression that you've heard?'

Tony stepped back to let him enter. 'She's got plenty of enemies, John. Did you really think none of them would have picked up the phone?'

Brandon sighed. 'Bad news always travels fast.' He looked around, and Tony clocked his practised copper's eye taking in the details of the newly refurbished space. The exposed beams, the perfect plasterwork. Spare, simple furnishings and a massive stone fireplace piled with logs ready to be lit. No pictures on the walls yet, no rugs on the flagged floor. Japanese screens that closed off a sleeping area; a squared-off corner that Tony knew hid a luxurious bathroom. 'She's made a good job of it,' Brandon said.

'That should come as no surprise.'

'Where is she?'

'Up on the hill with the dog. Taking it out on the landscape.'

Brandon sat down on one of the deep tweed-covered sofas. 'Who told her?'

'DCI John Franklin from West Yorkshire. You could say he took a kind of savage pleasure in it.' The mere memory of Carol's stricken expression was enough to bring a mutinous cast to Tony's features. 'It pretty much devastated her.'

Brandon sighed. 'I wish he'd kept his mouth shut.'

'Why? There's no way to spin this that wouldn't have the same result.'

'I wanted to tell her. I wanted to explain that it wasn't her fault. That what happened falls into the category of the law of unintended consequences.'

'What?' He pushed his fingers through his dark curling hair in a gesture of frustration. 'You and your powerful friends corrupted the system to have Carol's drink-driving arrest thrown out on a technicality. Only, that meant another three drivers walked free too. Then one of them gets behind the wheel again, but this time he's so drunk he kills himself and three other innocent people in a late-night crash? And you think you can shrug that off as an "unintended consequence"?' Tony made a sarcastic quotation mark gesture in the air.

'Nobody's shrugging it off. But if anyone has to shoulder the blame, it's me and the Home Office team who thought it was a good idea in the first place. Not Carol.'

Tony shook his head, impatient. 'Good luck with getting her to see things that way. You'll be lucky if you get to close of play today with her still in post.'

Brandon shifted awkwardly, twisting his lanky legs around each other. 'I was hoping you might help me persuade her there's no point in resigning now. What's done is done. ReMIT is bound to have a live case sooner rather than later and we need her running the team.'

'I've not spoken to her this morning. But she'll do what she thinks is best, regardless of what either of us has to say, John.'

While he was speaking, the door opened and Flash bounded across the room, washing Tony's thigh with a welcoming tongue, then wheeling to face Brandon, ears alert, head forward, scenting the air.

'She will,' Carol said, taking a handful of steps towards them. 'I told you at the time it wasn't a good idea to interfere with a righteous arrest, John.'

'You didn't put up much of a fight, as I recall.' The words were defensive but Brandon's tone was regretful.

Carol sighed. 'You calibrated my weakness perfectly. And I gave in to temptation and flattery.'

'It wasn't flattery,' Brandon protested. 'You were the best person to run ReMIT. You still are.'

Carol slipped out of her jacket and hung it on its peg. 'You're quite possibly right. And that's why I'm going to work now.' She turned back to face them, her eyes blazing cold with anger. 'You've done a terrible thing to me, John. Four people are dead because you and your pals decided I needed to be whitewashed. You can hide behind your conviction you did the right thing. But I can't. I let myself be talked into taking the job at ReMIT out of vanity and ego.' She ran her hands through hair flattened by her walking hat, letting it reassert its natural shape. 'I let myself believe my motives were pure, but honestly? They weren't. So I've got to live with that guilt. I'm ashamed now that I agreed to be part of your shabby deal. And the only thing I can do that comes anywhere near redeeming myself is to get out there and do a job that might save other people from dying.'

Tony felt pride and pity at her words. 'That's no small thing,' he said softly.

'Four lives, John,' Carol said. 'For all our sakes, you'd better hope nobody unravels what really happened at Calderdale Magistrates Court.'

5

Paula was surprised to find she was first in the office. Usually, DC Stacey Chen was already ensconced behind her protective carapace of half a dozen computer screens when the rest of the team arrived. But today the self-contained office where she practised the black arts of digital investigation was dark, the door closed and, Paula assumed, locked. She hung up her coat but before she could fuel up from the team's high-spec bean-to-cup machine, the phone in Carol Jordan's office rang out.

The door was open. When Paula had been part of Carol's old MIT team in Bradfield, the house rule was that no phone went unanswered. So she hustled across the room and snatched the handset on its fourth ring. 'ReMIT, DS McIntyre,' she said.

'Is DCI Jordan there?' An unidentified female voice she didn't recognise.

'Who's calling?'

'Detective Superintendent Henderson from North Yorkshire.'

There were still few enough women at that rank for Paula to know Anne Henderson by reputation. She was one of the quiet but deadly ones. Never raised her voice but was never knowingly outflanked. 'Behind the door when they handed out a sense of humour,' had been the verdict of a Bradfield sergeant who had started his career on the North Yorkshire force. Paula didn't think that made you a bad person, though black humour was often what got MIT detectives through the horrors they routinely confronted. 'I'm sorry, ma'am,' Paula said. 'DCI Jordan's in a meeting right now. Can I help you? Or take a message?'

'We've got something we think you might like to take a look at,' Henderson said abruptly. 'How do you proceed with these handovers?'

'I'm not sure of the protocols yet,' Paula said. 'But I imagine DCI Jordan would like to bring a team out to the crime scene.'

'That won't be possible.' Henderson's voice was clipped, annoyance in her tone. 'The officers at the scene did not consider the death suspicious.'

'So, what? They didn't preserve the scene?'

'It's complicated. Perhaps the best thing is for the local SIO to email you the details? Then take it from there?'

Paula didn't know what to say. What would Carol Jordan want? If the crime scene was a bust, they'd need to start somewhere else. 'That's probably best,' she said.

'I'll get that organised. Once she's had a look, DCI Jordan can give me a call and we'll progress things.'

And that was that. As Paula replaced the phone the squad room door opened and Stacey Chen walked in with DC Karim Hussain at her heels. Stacey looked glum but Karim had all the bounce of a puppy who's been thrown a brand-new tennis ball. 'Morning, skipper,' Karim called. 'Shall I make us all a brew?'

Stacey rolled her eyes and made for her office. 'Earl Grey,' she muttered, unlocking the door.

'I know,' Karim said brightly. 'No milk, the same colour as Famous Grouse.' There was a miniature of the whisky in the cupboard below the kettle for the purposes of quality control. 'I learn, Mr Fawlty.' He batted his ridiculously long eyelashes in a parody of a flirtatious waiter. Nobody paid any attention. He shrugged and carried on making the brews. Just as well his sister couldn't see him now. She'd love to take the piss out of him, the big detective reduced to chai wallah.

Paula followed Stacey. 'You OK?'

'I'm fine. I did what needed to be done.'

'How did he take it?'

'I have no idea. I've blocked him from all my comms.' Stacey settled in behind her screens, their ghostly flickers mapping random colours on her face and her white blouse. Her expression was blank and uninviting. Most people, Paula thought, would relish the opportunity to have a good rant about an ex-boyfriend as treacherous as Sam Evans had turned out to be. Stacey wasn't most people, however.

'DSI Henderson from North Yorkshire was on a minute ago. They're pinging details on a case over to us.'

Stacey's smile was grim. 'Good. Something to get our teeth into.'

Paula retreated, glad of the coffee Karim plonked in front of her. She logged on to the system and checked the ReMIT cloud storage. North Yorkshire hadn't wasted any time. Their designation, NYP, began the serial identification of the only file folder in the 'Immediate Attention' section. Paula felt her pulse quicken. For the first time, ReMIT was faced with a case from an outside force. This was where they began to prove themselves.

By mid-morning, the small team was assembled in a horse-shoe round a pair of whiteboards. DCI Carol Jordan stood in front of them, shoulders tight, hands fists at her side.

Apart from Karim, only DI Kevin Matthews looked raring to go, Paula thought. Carol Jordan had dark smudges under her eyes, Stacey resembled a convincing understudy for the Grim Reaper and Tony Hill, their first best hope for hitting the ground running in terms of what they were looking at, hadn't stopped frowning since he'd walked in ten minutes before. The final member of the team, DS Alvin Ambrose, was impressively impassive, arms loosely folded across his chest in a 'wait and see' pose, his shaved head gleaming under the strip lights, his dark suit giving him the air of a nightclub bouncer nobody would want to argue with.

'We've got a completely corrupted crime scene,' Carol began. 'It's far from the ideal way to start our ReMIT role. But we're not going to let that stop us.' She turned and wrote 'Kathryn McCormick' in firm capitals at the top of the board. 'Three nights ago, a motorist driving on a back road from Swarthdale to Ripon came on a burning vehicle in a lay-by. He parked twenty metres further on, then he and his passenger walked back. The fire was blazing inside the vehicle and they could see the outline of a figure in the driving seat. The driver, a thirty-six-year-old engineer, tried to approach but was driven back by the heat.' Carol wrote 'Simon Downey' on the board in smaller letters. Under it, she wrote 'Rowan Calvert'. 'Rowan called the fire brigade while Simon ran back to his car for the fire extinguisher.'

Kevin snorted. 'That'd have as much impact as a fart in a thunderstorm.'

'Indeed,' Carol said. 'By the time the firefighters arrived seventeen minutes later, the flames had begun to subside but the interior of the car – a Ford Focus – was a shell. A shell with a very badly burned body in the driving seat. The assumption was that the car had somehow caught fire, the driver had pulled over but been unable to get out. The conclusion was accident, with an outside possibility of suicide.'

'Did the witnesses see the driver attempting to get out?' Paula asked.

'They couldn't see much through the flames and smoke, but according to their statements, they saw the person making some jerky movements,' Carol said.

'That's pretty unlikely,' Kevin said. 'An intense fire like that? You're not going to survive long enough to make any serious attempt to get out.'

'But the connective tissues contract in a fire, don't they? That's how burned bodies end up in the pugilistic pose. Maybe the witnesses saw that happening and thought it was spontaneous movement, not the effect of the flames,' Paula mused.

'Probably.' Carol took a quick glance at the folder in front of her, checking what the printout from North Yorkshire said. 'The scene management seems to have been cocked up from start to finish. A couple of the car windows had popped or melted because of the intensity of the fire, so the interior of the car and the body were pretty much doused in chemical foam and water spray. And in the morning, when the car had cooled down enough, they stuck it on a low loader and took it to the fire service warehouse to be examined.'

'What about the body?' Alvin asked. 'When did they recover that?'

'Back at the warehouse. Thankfully, they had the pathologist there to supervise the recovery and removal, or who knows what we'd have ended up with.' Carol sighed. 'The fire investigator didn't start work on the car right away because he was already working on an arson over in Harrogate, so it was left in the warehouse.'

'Where presumably anybody could have interfered with it?'

'Not quite anybody, Kevin, but yes, I take your point. Because they thought it was an accident, it wasn't a high priority.'

'What changed their minds?' Tony asked.

'What the duty pathologist discovered when he carried out the post-mortem yesterday evening. Whatever happened in that car, it wasn't an accident. Or a suicide.'

'How come?' Karim blurted out without thinking. He caught the amused glances that Kevin and Paula exchanged, the barely suppressed eye-roll from Stacey and Alvin's sudden interest in the floor.

'Because murdered people don't kill themselves,' Carol said.

6

Less than half an hour later, the main ReMIT office was empty again. Stacey was in her office with the door closed, making a start on tracking Kathryn McCormick's online footprint. With luck, Paula and Karim would return from their search of the victim's home with a tablet or a computer that would unlock Kathryn's life. But until then, Stacey would use all the official access points and unofficial back doors at her disposal to start building an outline that a piece of hardware would help her to colour in.

At the opposite end of the squad room, Carol and Tony were facing each other across the desk behind the closed door of her office. He knew her well enough to realise she had the lid clamped down so tight on her feelings that she'd have been hard pressed to manage a question about her coffee preferences. He was supposed to be in his office at Bradfield Moor Secure Hospital, managing a supervision session with a postgraduate student, but he'd put her off. Whether Carol liked it or not, today he planned to stick by her side, no matter what.

'Sounds like the pathologist did a decent job at least,' Tony said.

'Well, he picked up on the lungs right away. No signs of smoke inhalation, no scorching from breathing in hot gases. So she was definitely dead before the fire started.'

'But it still could have been an accident, right? She could have had a brain haemorrhage or an aortic aneurysm or something instantaneous like that and dropped a lighted cigarette. The absence of damage to her lungs isn't conclusive, is it?'

'Were you not paying attention in there?' Carol's tone was sharp, accusatory.

'Sorry, I had a text from the student I cancelled this morning, I had to deal with it.'

'I don't know why you cancelled in the first place. I'm not a child, I don't need a nursemaid to keep an eye on the one thing in the world I feel competent to do.' She sounded weary, her tone a match for the dark smudges under her eyes.

'I thought you might appreciate someone in your corner.'

Carol scoffed. 'That's what that lot out there are. My team. Whatever goes down, they have my back.'

Tony wasn't sure whether Carol was trying to convince him or herself. An all-too-recent betrayal – a leak from inside to the press of the dismissed charges against her – was still raw. It had happened once; the awareness that it could happen again must be humming away like a low background noise in her head. And given what was still hidden, another revelation would be a flash-bang grenade so loud it might drown out everything else she'd achieved. 'We all do,' he said mildly. 'But the others have their own tasks to focus on. There's not much for me to go at yet, so—'

'Anyway,' she interrupted. 'What ruled out the kind of accident you're suggesting was what the pathologist found when he took a more detailed look. Kathryn McCormick's hyoid bone was snapped in two. Now, in itself that doesn't prove she was strangled. Notoriously, the hyoid bone can be broken in a car crash, if the seat belt crushes the throat. But there was no indication of any accident or emergency stop here. Stacey double-checked the pics North Yorkshire sent over and there are no skid marks in the lay-by, no signs of hard braking. And the exterior of the car is undamaged, as far as we can tell from the pics. So the broken hyoid combined with the clean lungs makes it pretty clear that the fire was set to cover up a murder.'

'It didn't work very well, as cover-ups go, then.'

'No.' Carol gave a sarcastic laugh. 'This obsession people have with forensic science and true crime these days makes them all think they know how to outwit us. They've seen the TV series, they've listened to the podcasts, they've read the books. But when it comes down to actually killing another human being and trying to dispose of the body . . . Well, it's not so easy. Then the wheels come off and they start to make critical mistakes.'

'Hmm,' Tony murmured. 'You're probably right. They were quick off the mark on the ID, weren't they? Was that down to the pathologist too?'

Carol shook her head. 'Good old-fashioned policing. Well, more or less. The cops at the scene ran the car number plate on the PNC and it came up with Kathryn McCormick's name and an address in Bradfield. Then some poor sod had to call round the dentists' practices till they found the one where she was registered. They did the dental comparison earlier this morning and came up with a match.'

'So the ID hasn't been released?'

'Not publicly. We've not tracked down next of kin yet.' Carol sighed. 'It's a weird one, though.'

Tony nodded agreement. 'Most killers who go to the trouble of trying to cover up their crime want the body to disappear, not light up the sky like Bonfire Night. I know it was a back road. But all the same, he couldn't have shouted louder if he'd tried.' He jumped up from his chair and started quartering the small room, talking as he walked. 'Was he trying to burn her so badly that nobody would suspect murder? Was he making absolutely sure she was dead, a macabre kind of belt-and-braces job? Or was it all about the fire? Killing her was incidental, burning her, was that the real thrill?'

'Or was he only making sure he got rid of forensic traces?'

Tony stopped, rolling his eyes in a dumb show of stupidity. 'That's probably it. Sometimes I forget that the simplest answer is the most likely one.' He dropped back into the chair. 'How are you feeling?'

'I'm fine,' Carol shot straight back. 'You know I'm always OK when I'm working.'

He knew that was what she always told herself. 'Do you think the press will find out about—'

'I don't know, and right now, I'm trying not to think about it. I'm trying not to wonder whether John Franklin and his mates in West Yorkshire CID hate me enough to risk the consequences of leaking the story to the press. I'm trying not to imagine the headlines. And I'm trying to convince myself that the answer is not an industrial quantity of vodka.' She pulled a wry smile. 'So please, if you're going to play "Me and my shadow" today, shut the fuck up about it.'

The smile saved him from panic. Her anger was still turned against herself. And while that wouldn't be without consequences, at least he'd be around to help her through the worst of them. 'Fair enough,' he said. 'So, what's the plan?'

'I thought I might take a run out to North Yorkshire. The crime scene isn't going to yield much in the way of forensics, but I'd like to see the reality, as opposed to video and stills. And I know you like to poke around and see things for yourself.'

'I like to get a feel for the killer's preferred terrain.' Tony stood up again and reached for his battered brown anorak. There had never been a nanosecond when it had flirted with fashion, which was the least of his concerns. But even he had to admit it was starting to blend in a little too well with the city's homeless population. 'Do you think I need a new coat?' he asked Carol as they walked out.

'Always,' she said drily. 'Let's swing by one of the outdoor shops on the way out of town.'

'That's a bit . . . precipitate, isn't it?'

Carol chuckled as they waited for the lift. 'Strike while the iron's hot. If I wait till tomorrow, it'll have turned into your most prized possession, the thing without which you can't imagine writing another profile.'

She stepped into the lift ahead of him. Tony swallowed hard. Maybe it was going to be all right after all.

7

For a cop, Karim was a surprisingly sedate driver. He stayed under the speed limit, even in the twenty-miles-per-hour streets of suburban Harriestown. He paused at junctions, he waved pedestrians across the road and he slowed as he approached traffic signals rather than speeding up to make sure he caught the light. It reminded Paula of being driven by her mother, who had given up her car with an obvious relief when she turned sixty-five and retired from her bookkeeping job. She wasn't sure if Karim was that kind of anxious driver, or whether he was trying to impress her with how law-abiding he was.

Once they reached Harriestown, Paula took over the directions. She'd worked in Bradfield all her adult life and the job had brought her to the southern suburb several times. Starting out as a beat bobby, it had mostly been small-scale street crime, drugs and burglary. But over the years, the area had become gentrified, its terraced streets desirable acquisitions for young professionals. The pubs had been tarted up, featuring gastropub menus and occasional live music. There was a wholefood emporium and the scrubby little parks had sprouted kids' play equipment that made Paula wish she was a child again. But the spit and polish that had raised the average income of the area hadn't immunised it from crime. During her years as a major incident squad detective, Paula had investigated three murders that had intimate involvement with a Harriestown postcode. And now it looked like number four.

Kathryn McCormick hadn't lived in one of the terraced streets that spread out in a grid around the park that sat between the grand Victorian edifices of the former Reform Club and Conservative Club, both now converted into allegedly luxury apartments. Kathryn's flat was altogether less distinguished. Karim turned into the grounds of a boxy 1960s block that had probably replaced a pair of substantial semis. He hesitated, staring at a sign that read, PRIVATE. RESIDENTS PARKING ONLY.

'Ignore it,' Paula said. 'Just find a space.'

'What if they clamp it?'

'They won't. I can always nick them for failing the correct use of the apostrophe.'

Karim gave her a mistrustful look, then a cautious smile. He parked neatly in the nearest space then followed her to the main door of the complex. There were fifteen numbered buzzers with an entry intercom system. 'Damn,' Paula said. 'I was kind of hoping for a caretaker.' With no expectation of a response, she pressed the buzzer for Flat 14, the address where DVLA had the car registered. No reply.

Starting with Flat 15, Paula worked her way down the buzzers. She struck lucky on 9. It was hard to tell much about the person on the other end except that they were probably female. Paula identified herself and explained that they needed access to the building.

'How do I know you are who you say you are?' the voice demanded.

This was what came of filling people with trepidation about the likelihood of being conned, robbed and murdered on their own doorsteps. 'You could come down to the door and check our ID,' Paula said.

'I'm not dressed,' the voice complained. 'I was on a late shift. You woke me up.'

'I'm sorry about that. If you want to buzz us in, we could come to your door and you could check us out.' She shook her head at Karim, who grimaced in return. 'We are the police.'

'I'm on the first floor,' the voice said, then the door buzzed loudly.

The door to Flat 9 was open a crack, a bleary-eyed face surrounded by a cloud of bright aubergine hair visible in the gap. Its owner was fighting a losing battle against the years, judging by the smudged make-up round her eyes and mouth. 'ID?'

Both officers held up their shiny new warrant cards.

'ReMIT? What's that? You not from Bradfield Police?' The woman frowned in suspicion.

'We're a regional squad,' Paula said repressively. 'Do you happen to know your neighbour in Flat 14?'

The woman snorted. 'Lives above me, she does. I had to complain when she first moved in. High heels on a wooden floor is about as anti-social as it gets in a block like this.'

'And how did she take it?'

'She said she was sorry,' the woman said grudgingly. 'And to be fair to her, she took her shoes off at the door after that. But I never had anything else to do with her.'

'Did she have any other friends in the block?' Karim asked.

The woman looked him up and down, eyebrows raised. She probably didn't consider his black jeans and black Barbour jacket to be proper police attire, Paula thought. Unlike her own navy pegs and the boxy blue jacket that

Elinor said looked disturbingly like a Mao jacket from the eighties. 'I've no idea, son. We keep ourselves to ourselves here.'

Pointless, Paula thought as they took their leave and headed for the top floor. There was no reply at any of the flats. 'What are we going to do, skip?' Karim looked worried.

'We can call BMP and ask them to send a car round with the big red key.' Paula rummaged in her bag. 'Or we can try these.' She brandished a small leather case, flipping it open with her thumb. 'So much more discreet than a battering ram.'

'Is that legal?' Again, Paula was reminded of her mother. She wasn't sure whether his general enthusiasm was going to be enough to overcome that particular problem. She reminded herself that she'd been the one to recommend him to Carol, on the basis that he was a grafter who could be a lot tougher than he looked when he had to be. And that he was smart enough to hold his own on this ReMIT team. He'd learn that sometimes the rules could be tweaked a little. Otherwise he wouldn't last long on Carol Jordan's team.

'We need to effect entry. This causes a lot less damage than the ram. And it means we can secure the flat after we leave.' She was already crouched by the door, studying the mortice lock and selecting the picks to try. 'I've only had this kit a few months,' she said absently as she concentrated on the feel of the lock under her fingers. 'There's some good videos on YouTube and I've been practising round the house. But this is the first time I've done it on the job.' She slowed her breathing and adjusted the tension bar, slipping a different rake into the lock. Her hands were starting to sweat, but before the picks slid disastrously out of control, there was a satisfying click and the lock yielded to her. Paula stood up and grinned at Karim. 'We bring a different skill set to policing in this unit, Karim. You'll get the hang of it.'

He brightened at her words. 'I hope so.'

The door opened into a square hallway with four doors off it. A rack of coat hooks was fixed to the wall, a two-tier shoe rack beneath it. A grey wool winter coat hung alongside a dark green rain mac and a hip-length brown leather jacket. The shoe rack contained four pairs of nondescript low-heeled shoes, a pair of Nike trainers and two pairs of smart leather boots. So far, so ordinary.

A quick sweep of the doors revealed bathroom, kitchen, bedroom and a surprisingly spacious living room with a view of trees and back gardens. 'I'll take the living room, you take the bedroom,' Paula said, faintly amused to see Karim flush at the prospect of so much intimacy with a strange woman. But credit where it was due, he didn't protest. She was starting to think he might be a fast enough learner to carve out a place for himself in their tight little team.

The living room smelled strongly of lilies. A bunch of the white trumpets sat on a side table near the window, specks of orange pollen littering the surface. They were fully open but not yet starting to decay. Paula estimated they'd probably been there for five or six days. A day or two before Kathryn had been killed, then. She crossed to the flowers to see whether there was a card but was unsurprised to see none.

The room was plainly but harmoniously furnished. Nothing seemed old or worn and Paula surmised that it had all been chosen to furnish the flat when Kathryn had moved in. Presumably two or three years ago. She vaguely remembered seeing that sofa in IKEA when she and Elinor had been moving in together. A mirror above the fake marble mantel over the fake coal fire, a framed print of Monet's water lilies on the opposite wall.

She stood in the centre of the room, taking it all in. There weren't many places to search. Kathryn had lived a life in plain sight. A small bookcase revealed a dozen fat paperbacks; suspense thrillers, family sagas and Elena Ferrante's novels of Neapolitan friendship. The rest of the shelves were occupied by framed photographs. A few Mediterranean views; a couple who looked in their early sixties and were presumably her parents; a graduation photograph that resembled the one on the driving licence DVLA had pinged over to them; and some group shots of women having a good night out. No apparent boyfriend.

The most promising potential source of information was a desk in the far corner with a stool tucked underneath. Half an hour later, she was beginning to feel a little sorry for Kathryn. There wasn't much sign of a vibrant social life in her desk drawers. Presumably she dealt with her utility bills and banking online, for there was no evidence of them here. There was a Christmas card list, which someone would have to go through later. A folder of recipes torn out of newspapers and magazines. Another folder containing payslips, which at least confirmed that she still worked at the company listed on her dental practice details. And a third containing the paperwork for the flat purchase. She'd got a decent deal on the place, Paula thought.

The bottom drawer yielded the only stash that might prove relevant. A large manila envelope was stuffed with cards, bits of paper and photographs. Paula tipped it out on the desktop and discovered Kathryn's personal life.

His name was Niall. A big lad with auburn hair and, occasionally, ginger stubble. His broad open face gave him the look of a farmer but he had been a designer for a small Bradfield business that planned and built home offices. There were invitations to company functions, the most recent dated a little over three years before. And right at the bottom of the pile, a business card that had been torn in half then sellotaped together. Niall Sullivan now, apparently, led the office design team of a company in Cardiff. You didn't have to be a detective to draw a picture. He'd left her behind. If she'd been the one doing the choosing, she'd have chucked away the valentines and the birthday cards and the little notes with the hearts drawn on them asking her to pick up a loaf of bread or a bottle of milk on her way home.

It wasn't beyond the bounds of possibility that Niall Sullivan had reappeared in her life. He'd have to be checked out. But unless Kathryn had been a deranged stalker making his life a misery – and Paula could see no trace of that – then there didn't seem much in the way of motive.

Paula replaced the material in the envelope and put it in an evidence bag. As she closed the drawer, Karim walked in.

'Talk about leading a blameless life,' he said. 'There's nothing there to raise an eyebrow, never mind a suspicion. She's got five business suits, one for each day of the week. Half a dozen dresses you might wear to a night out. Jeans, smart trousers, blouses, a couple of T-shirts and some jumpers. It's like she's one of those women who goes through her wardrobe every six months and weeds out everything that she hasn't worn. Even her underwear's totally dull. Marks and Sparks, matching bras and pants, all of it respectable.'

'What?' Paula was amused. 'No ratty old pants or bras gone grey in the wash?'

'No, nothing like that. She's not even got a shoe habit. Nothing more exciting than a couple of pairs of high heels.'

'Zero indicators of a secret life,' Paula sighed. 'Looks like she had a live-in boyfriend till about three years ago, but no signs of anyone since then.'

'Well, if her clothes are anything to judge by, she wasn't going out on the pull.' Karim picked up a snow globe from the windowsill and shook it idly. 'You done in here?'

'I think so. You take the bathroom, I'll do the kitchen.

Maybe we'll get lucky and find a stash of illegal drugs.'

Karim snorted. 'You'll be lucky if you find an out-of-date yoghurt.'

Paula shrugged. 'Something got her killed. We just haven't found it yet.'

8

He'd thought the murder would lift the burden. That it would remove what felt like a physical weight from his shoulders. It had made sense in the planning. He wanted to kill Tricia. He wanted to kill her so badly he could feel the blood pulsing in his ears, a dull tattoo of rage whenever he thought about her. He wanted to kill her but he knew he couldn't. Not least because he didn't know where she was hiding.

So he killed someone else instead. Surely that would work? Surely if he imagined her face while he was doing it, there would be some relief? But it hadn't worked like that. Killing Kathryn hadn't taken the pain away.

What it had done, however, was to give him a feeling of power and control that had taken him back to how he used to feel every day. How he used to feel before she stripped him of everything that had defined him. And that was a start. It wasn't enough, but it was a start. It might keep him going till he could make her answer for what she'd done to him.

She had told him in a lay-by. She'd asked him to pull over. Said she had something to say, something that was pressing on her, something that wouldn't wait any longer. He'd had no idea what was coming. Not a fucking clue.

She'd gone to Ruby's wedding on her own the weekend before. He could have gone with her, but Ruby had always irritated the living shit out of him and her husband-to-be was possibly the most boring man on either side of the Pennines, so there was no reason to expect their wedding guests to be remotely interesting. So he'd given her his blessing to go without him. He'd even told her to have a good time.

He hadn't anticipated quite how good a time.

She'd been distant and fidgety since the weekend. He thought it was because the wedding had made her broody for one of her own. How stupid could he be? Really, how stupid? So they'd ended up in a lay-by where she'd told him she'd slept with a man she'd picked up at the wedding.

'It's not that he's Mr Right,' she'd said. 'But he made me realise that you're Mr Wrong.' Every word a slap in the face. 'You're too volatile. Too angry. I spend half my life scared of you.'

He'd felt sick then, not angry. What did she mean, scared? Everybody knew he didn't suffer fools gladly. That he had high standards. But he wasn't a bully. He just wanted to get things done right. Her accusations baffled him as much as her admission that she'd slept with a stranger she'd picked up at random at Ruby's wedding.

That had been bad enough. But there was worse to come. Not only was she leaving him, moving out of their beautiful flat with its panoramic views over Manchester city centre to the Derbyshire hills. She was also walking away from the business they'd built together. A partnership, like their life. It had been his business first, but she'd helped turn it into a success, and to show how he appreciated that, he'd given her a slice of the company. And now she'd turned her back on what they'd made and not even returned what was properly his.

The company published a series of locally targeted glossy magazines. She dealt up front with the punters, organising copy and writing some of it herself, drumming up advertising, sorting out the distribution. He dealt with the technical side – design, layout, working with the printers. Without either of them, there was no business. Since she'd walked away, he'd limped along with part-timers and freelances but he knew he wouldn't be able to fool the advertisers much longer. Either he'd have to make a quick bargain-basement sale or the business would collapse under him.

She'd taken everything from him and he wanted to kill her. But he wasn't stupid. Even if he managed to track her down now, if she died he'd be the obvious prime suspect. Mr Wrong, dumped in love and in business. But if someone else died in her place, who would be any the wiser?

All he'd wanted was to take his pain away. To burst the boil of his rage and frustration. When Kathryn had passed out thanks to the GHB he'd slipped into her champagne and he'd known it was game on – he'd relished that moment of mastery over her. She lay sprawled on the sofa, snoring softly, barely stirring when he straddled her. Then he had his hands round Kathyrn's soft warm throat, squeezing the life out of her, imagining it was Tricia. It had been surprisingly glorious. The first time since the bitch had left that he'd felt comfortable in his own skin. That feeling of being in charge of his life again flooded back as Kathryn's face grew purple and her tongue poked out between her ugly blue lips. The more she lost, the more he gained.

Within twenty-four hours of killing Kathryn, he knew he'd found something that would divert him till he could figure out how to take his proper revenge.

Which was why he would be spending Saturday at another stranger's wedding.

9

Tony squared his shoulders, still trying to adjust to the down jacket Carol had talked him into. 'It's warm, it's waterproof and it's in the sale,' she'd insisted.

'It's purple. I look like a blackcurrant on legs.'

'You look good in purple. I know it's a radical experiment for you to wear anything that isn't a shade of grey or blue, but you need to live a little.' She'd scooped up the jacket and headed for the till, waiting impatiently for him to catch up and produce a credit card.

It was all right for her, he thought. Carol had the knack of choosing clothes that suited her. Even though the shape of her body had changed as a result of the hard physical work the barn restoration had demanded, she still managed to find jackets that flattered her new broad shoulders, and trousers that emphasised the length rather than the musculature of her legs. And she seemed to do it effortlessly, without spending days trawling shopping malls. He had no idea how that worked.

He'd spent the rest of the drive to Ripon squirming and fiddling with the various zips and poppers, working out the best pockets for keys and wallet and phone. It was a relief to both of them when they came upon the lay-by.

They hadn't needed the detailed directions from the North Yorkshire team. The police tape fluttering in the late morning air was more or less redundant; the tarmac scorched black and the hedgerow burned brittle told their own story. When Carol cut the engine, Flash whimpered with delight, sensing the possibility of a walk. 'Stay,' Carol said briskly, opening the door. The dog subsided with a sigh.

As soon as they stepped out of the car, the lingering chemical smell left by the fire and its extinguishing hit them. Even three days later, it still teased the nostrils and caught at the throat. 'Looks like it was pretty intense,' Carol said. She stood, hands on hips, breathing deeply, as if the air might tell her something.

Tony walked the length of the lay-by, pausing every few steps to look around. He carried on walking down the lane. 'Why here?' he muttered under his breath. 'What's special about this place?' This crime felt planned and prepped. What little they knew about it suggested a killer who had worked out how to cover his tracks. The use of the victim's car. The intensity of the fire inside the car that had burned the forensic traces. The victim sitting in the driver's seat – was that a bid to push lazy investigators towards suicide or accident? It certainly looked that way. Tony called back down the lane to Carol, who was still prowling round the lay-by. 'Are there cameras on this road?'

'No. If you know what you're doing, you can criss-cross the Dales on lanes and back roads without being picked up by ANPR or speed cameras.'

'And you knew what you were doing, didn't you?' Tony said under his breath. He walked as far as a farm gate. It led to a field full of sheep. He opened the gate and slipped inside, careful to close it behind himself. He took a zigzag path across the field, sheep scattering before him. He wasn't sure what he was looking for, just that he was looking.

But there was nothing remarkable. A drystone wall marked the far side of the field. On the other side, another field. In the distance he could see a footpath fingerpost but that wasn't anything to get excited about around here. The national pastime of dressing in sophisticated technical gear and wandering round the countryside meant that every National Park was criss-crossed with paths. From the air they must look like elaborately patterned knitwear, he thought. Not that he was opposed to walking. He did it all the time. It helped him think. And now he had a purple padded jacket, he'd fit right in with the other ramblers.

Tony turned full circle. There was no human habitation in sight. He could make out a dilapidated stone sheepfold in the distance, and a couple of well-established copses broke up the grey and green of walls and fields. But there was nothing here that spoke to him. He headed back, making sure his route took him past the other side of the lay-by hedge. The heat had penetrated all the way through, leaving the twigs charred and brittle. Just as well there had been plenty of rain recently or the whole thing might have gone up.

He found Carol leaning against the bonnet of the car. 'Anything strike you?'

He shook his head. 'No. But there must be something. If you're right, there are plenty of places in this area where he could have done it without much chance of being caught in the act. So why here? Why this lay-by in particular?'

Carol pulled a wry face. 'More questions than answers. As usual at this stage.'

'At least we've got questions.' He rolled his shoulders again. 'And a purple anorak.'

10

As far as DS Alvin Ambrose could work out, there was no clue in the name to suggest what RSR Solutions did. He had to Google the company that Kathryn McCormick had listed on her dental records as her employer. Its website revealed it was a recruitment agency with premises a few streets away from ReMIT's office in the Skenfrith Street police station.

RSR Solutions was one of a dozen companies in a new smoked glass and polished concrete building in the Woollen Quarter, the area of the city where once merchants had traded wool and fine worsted cloth. Most of the old buildings had decayed to sagging shells in the eighties, but over the past half-dozen years, speculators had been buying up the sites, demolishing the old and jacking up shiny new replacements so they could pretend it was the entrepreneurial heart of twenty-first-century Bradfield. Even a newcomer like Alvin could see that was at best disingenuous; at worst, plain dishonest. To Let signs sprouted like weeds in every other set of ground-floor windows.

There was no security in the foyer of RSR's building so he walked unchallenged to the lifts. RSR was on the sixth floor and they at least had a receptionist who sat under the company slogan: 'Square peg or round peg, we've got the right hole.' It didn't inspire confidence in Alvin. But he mustered his best smile for the pretty young woman behind the desk. He was good at smiles; he'd learned the necessity of defusing the impact of his substantial bulk and the colour of his skin. Big black men had to confound expectations depressingly often. 'I'm Detective Sergeant Alvin Ambrose,' he said, producing his ID.

She looked startled but studied it closely. Her smile was tentative. 'How can we help you?'

'It's to do with Kathryn McCormick. I need to speak to her manager.'

'Kathryn? She's not in today.' She was already tapping her computer keys.

'I know. But it's her manager I need.'

She had the phone in her hand, manicured nails poised above the keypad. 'Can I ask what it's in connection with?'

Alvin shook his head. 'You can ask but I can't tell you. Sorry.'

She raised her eyebrows. 'Very mysterious.' But she made the call. 'Lauren, I've got a police officer here at the front desk who needs to speak to Kathryn's manager. Would that be your responsibility?' Pause. 'OK, I'll tell him.' She replaced the phone and folded her arms across her body, hugging herself. 'So, Lauren from HR's coming down. Kathryn's the office manager, so she doesn't really have a direct supervisor.'

'Thanks for using your initiative,' Alvin said. There were no chairs in the reception area so he took a stroll round the perimeter, pretending an interest that he didn't feel in the corporate photographs. A couple of minutes drifted by then a squat woman with the biggest hair he'd seen for years emerged from a door behind the reception desk. She advanced with her hand out.

'I'm Lauren Da Costa, I'm in charge of HR here at Right Shape Recruitment Solutions. And you are?'

Alvin introduced himself again. 'Can we go somewhere a bit more private?'

'This is about Kathryn, right? You know she's not in work today?'

'Like I said, can we go somewhere more private?'

Lauren Da Costa's expression could have served as a template for shocked incredulity. For a long moment, she was beyond speech. At last she spoke, stumbling over her words. 'Kathryn? Are you sure? She's the last person ... Suspicious death? That makes no sense.'

'There's no room for doubt,' Alvin said, his voice a gentle rumble. It always settled his children to sleep and it had a similar soothing effect on witnesses. 'I'm very sorry. And I know the last thing you feel like is answering questions, but I'm afraid we need to find out all we can about Kathryn.'

Lauren gave a shaky nod. 'Of course. But I really can't help you beyond the factual stuff – where she lived, the CV she brought us when she came here. We weren't close at all. I never saw her outside work. She was a good manager but she wasn't the most sociable of people.' She seemed to be recovering, physically gathering herself together, straightening in her chair and starting to reveal her interpersonal skills. 'The person you need to speak to is Suzanne Briggs – sorry, Harman. Our office newly-wed. Today's her first day back from her honeymoon. I know Kathryn was at her wedding, they've always got on well.'

'That sounds about right. Can I see her?'

Lauren stood up. 'I'll fetch her. Do you want me to break the news to her, or ... ?'

'No, please,' Alvin said quickly. He didn't relish telling Suzanne her friend was dead, but it was always worthwhile

51

to see the reactions of a witness when they heard bad news for the first time.

Lauren was gone for almost five minutes. She brought with her a young woman with the kind of identikit looks that would have made Alvin struggle to pick her out of a line-up. Slim, with long blonde hair tied back in a ponytail, make-up that blanded out difference, perfectly manicured nails. Her clothes were formulaic too – narrow-legged black trousers, a magenta top that clung in the right places and a couple of others that Suzanne would have been less happy about had she realised. And of course, heels that made her awkward gait verge on the ugly. Alvin loved women but he didn't love this look.

Lauren made the introductions then backed out, murmuring something about being in her office if . . . Suzanne's expression hadn't changed from puzzlement since she'd entered, and now she said, 'I don't understand. Why am I here? I thought at first something had happened to Ed. My husband, Ed.' A momentary flash of something like triumph. 'But Lauren said no, it wasn't Ed. So what's going on?'

'You're a friend of Kathryn McCormick?'

Suzanne's frown deepened. 'I suppose. I mean, she was at my wedding but we're not what you'd call close.'

'Lauren seemed to think she's closer to you than anyone else at work.'

Suzanne twisted her hands in her lap, fiddling with her wedding and engagement rings. 'She isn't really best friends with anybody. With her being office manager, she sort of has to keep her distance a bit. But yeah, we get along fine, Kathryn's OK. Why? What's happened?'

'I'm sorry to have to tell you that Kathryn is dead.'

Suzanne's eyes widened and her mouth fell open. She was clearly shocked but there was a gleam of excitement in her eyes too. 'No! What happened?'

'Her body was found in a burned-out car three days ago. We believe her death may be suspicious.'

'Oh my God. We were still on our honeymoon. You mean, while we were lying on the beach and drinking cocktails, Kathryn was being murdered? That's terrible!'

'I'm very sorry. But what we need to do now is build up a picture of Kathryn's life. Who her friends were, what she did in her spare time, whether she was seeing anyone. Whether she'd fallen out with anyone.'

'God.' Suzanne crossed her legs and rubbed her left arm as if it had grown suddenly cold. 'She never fell out with anyone. She was a great boss. She had the knack of sorting things out without upsetting people, you know?' Alvin didn't. He'd been a copper all his working life. Compromise and conciliation wasn't really how working relationships operated in his world.

Suzanne continued. 'She hadn't had a boyfriend since Niall moved to Cardiff without her. Niall, her ex. That must be three years ago now. We were always trying to persuade her to come out with us in a gang so she could meet someone, but she wasn't much of a party animal. I don't know what she did in her spare time but she always joined in when we were talking about TV programmes. So I guess she watched a lot of TV.' She gave a thin smile, as if she was well aware how scant was her knowledge of a woman she'd invited to her wedding.

'Was she on her own at the wedding?' Alvin felt the weight of depression in his shoulders. Was there really so little to know about the short life of Kathryn McCormick?

'Well, she didn't bring anyone, if that's what you mean. But I don't know if she met anyone on the day. I mean, it was my wedding. I wasn't paying much attention to anyone except Ed. My husband.'

Alvin thought she'd better be careful not to wear those

words out. 'So you weren't in touch at all while you were on your honeymoon? You didn't check out social media?'

'Well, obvs,' she said, her eyebrows rising in a narrow arch. 'I wanted to see all the pics people had posted on Facebook and all the lovely congratulations. Kathryn posted a couple of pictures. I think I "liked" them, but I didn't exchange any messages with her.'

He'd get Stacey to check Kathryn's Facebook account but he wasn't holding his breath. It looked like he'd hit a dead end. He stood up, nothing left to ask. 'Thanks for your help.' He fished a card out of his inside pocket. 'If you think of anything at all that might give us some insight, call me on this number. Maybe you could ask around, see if any of your other guests remember Kathryn talking about anyone she met or spoke to on the day? I'd appreciate it.'

She looked eager. 'I'll get on to it right away. People are going to be really sorry. God knows who we'll get running things now Kathryn's gone.'

Not much of an obituary, Alvin thought as he waited for the lift. Killing Kathryn didn't seem to have made much of an impact on those around her. So far, he'd not seen anything approaching a tear. As far as he was concerned, that was all the more reason to find who had done this. It was part of the reason he'd become a cop in the first place: to defend people who didn't have anybody else to do that for them. The world had failed Kathryn McCormick in life. It was up to the ReMIT team to make sure that didn't happen in death too.

11

Oddly, Kathryn McCormick's kitchen probably revealed more about her than any other room in her flat. Judging by the battery of equipment that filled her cupboards and drawers and hung from wall hooks, she was a serious cook. A knife block held half a dozen razor-sharp Japanese knives that Paula couldn't help envying. The food processor and blender on the counter were top of the range and a bookcase was crammed with cookbooks with cracked spines and dog-eared corners. The question of what Kathryn did with her spare time was answered here.

On the side of the fridge was a supermarket calendar, featuring a monthly recipe and a glossy photo of the result. But it wasn't the pumpkin-and-sage lasagne that made Paula unhook it and lay it down on the worktop. If there was a clue to what had led Kathryn to her death, it might well be here.

Methodically she flicked back through the previous months and found little of interest. Hair appointments, a couple of work-related nights out. A weekend visiting Mum and Dad. A check-up with the dentist, a date with her GP and a couple of theatre trips to see musicals in nearby

Manchester. No companion's name on the calendar though there was room enough to accommodate one.

Finally, Paula checked the current page. Saving the best till last, she hoped. Just over two weeks ago, on the first Saturday of the month, Kathryn had written, 'Suzanne & Ed's wedding.' Three days later, 'David, Pizza Express, 7.30'. Paula drew her breath in through her teeth and stretched her lips in a grim smile. 'David,' she sighed softly, running her finger along the calendar dates. On the Saturday, a week after the wedding, David appeared again: 'David, Manchester Palace Theatre, *Funny Girl*.' And again the following Tuesday: 'David, Tapas Brava, Bellwether Square, 8pm'.

The final entry for the current month started on Friday, with a line drawn through till Sunday: 'David, Dales weekend'. And this time, there was a phone number scrawled underneath. Paula never liked to jump to conclusions but it was hard to escape the conviction that a man called David had connected with Kathryn at Suzanne and Ed's wedding. And two weeks later, he'd murdered her. She gave an involuntary shiver.

She took her phone out but before she could call Stacey and present her with David's phone number, Karim came in carrying a box of condoms. 'This is the only thing out of place in the bathroom. She's got matching Clinique everything except deodorant and toothpaste. Electric toothbrush with one head in the holder. One bath towel, one face towel on the rail. And then in the bathroom cabinet, these.'

He passed the box over to Paula. A dozen Intimate Moment condoms, the box said. 'Probably should have bagged it, Karim. He might have touched it. Scrabbling around to get a condom in the heat of the moment . . . ' She took out a pen and flipped the box open and tipped the contents out on the worktop.

'Looks like they're all there,' Karim said.

'Lucky for you.' Paula turned the box over. 'Sell-by date's nearly three years off. If my memory serves me well, condom shelf-life is three to five years. So it looks like this box isn't a hangover from the boyfriend who legged it to Cardiff three years ago.' She pointed to the calendar. 'Looks like she might have hooked up with someone at this wedding she went to a fortnight ago. We need to check that out when we get back to the office. But before we go, let's do a quick look through the drawers in here. Everybody's got an "all drawer".'

'What's that?' Karim asked, turning and opening the drawer behind him.

'You know. The drawer where you put everything that doesn't have a home anywhere else. String. Fuses. Those clips you fasten bags with. The little daggers you stick into sweetcorn. Batteries.'

'Right.' He pushed the drawer closed. 'This is cutlery.' He opened the next.

'But most importantly, keys. Your spare front door set and all those odd ones that don't fit any lock in the house but you don't want to bin them in case they turn out to be important.'

'Dishtowels and dusters.'

Paula opened the end drawer on her side. 'Aha. Now, when the fairy godmother turned up at my christening and asked whether I'd rather be lucky or beautiful, I chose lucky. And even after all these years, I have no regrets. Look, Karim. The "all drawer".' She pulled it out to its full extent. 'Even the obsessively tidy have to keep their crap somewhere.' She raked around among the random detritus of things Kathryn had inexplicably hung on to. In the far corner, she found three bunches of keys, each with a plastic label on its ring. 'House, Parents and Flat,' Paula said. 'Well, that'll make locking up after ourselves a lot easier.'

Karim looked over her shoulder. He was careful to keep

out of her personal space, she couldn't help noticing. Unusual in a man, extraordinary in a copper. 'Good find, skipper.'

Paula gave the contents of the drawer one last shuffle then pushed it closed. 'I don't think I've ever done a search with so little to show for it,' she grumbled. 'Come on, let's see what Stacey can make of our mysterious David. If she did pick him up at that wedding, somebody must have snapped them.'

Karim groaned. 'Why do I see an endless trawl through somebody else's wedding pix on Facebook and Twitter and Instagram?'

'Don't forget WhatsApp.'

Another groan. 'And then there'll be the official photographer.' He trailed after Paula as she made for the door.

'Still glad you signed up for the elite squad?' she asked as they descended the stairs.

He snorted. 'The thrill of the chase, skip. You can't beat it.'

12

They found the fire investigator in a tiny office off his lab in a private forensics facility a stone's throw from the A1 in a business park landscaped with struggling trees and low hedges darkened by traffic pollution. From the outside, it had the anonymous air of a call centre or the administrative arm of an internet retailer. But as soon as they left the car park, it was clear this was a different sort of set-up. The building was surrounded by a tall chain-link fence that was almost invisible against the greys and greens of the foliage. They had to wait by the electronically controlled gate while someone in a distant security office checked the ReMIT IDs they held up to the camera.

When they finally arrived at the reception desk, a man with iron-grey hair and the muscular build of someone twenty years younger frowned at them. 'You're supposed to book an appointment ahead of time, not just turn up on the doorstep,' he grumbled, pushing a visitors' book towards them. 'Sign in here. And I need to scan your ID.' He held out a hand.

It took another five minutes before they were escorted to

Finn Johnston's office. The fire investigator looked too young to have such a senior post. He had fine mousy hair draped limply across a narrow head. His face seemed to be in retreat from a sharp nose, as if he'd been caught in the teeth of a gale at birth. But his expression was alert and he had an air of stillness that inspired confidence even though Carol estimated he couldn't be much past thirty. Under his white lab coat, he wore a T-shirt that proclaimed 'Firefighters don't work from home', which made her want to roll her eyes and groan.

'Well, this is an unexpected honour,' Johnston said in a broad Yorkshire accent. 'They still talk about you in East Yorkshire, DCI Jordan.'

She wondered momentarily what they said. It hadn't been her easiest posting and she didn't think she'd made many friends. A good detective had died under her command; it had been one of the heaviest burdens she'd had to carry. 'I guess they've not seen much action since,' she said coolly. 'But we're not here to reminisce about ancient history. I need everything you can tell me about the car fire on Sunday night.'

He leaned forward in his chair, elbows on the desk, hands clasped. 'How much do you know about fires?'

'Let's pretend we're absolute beginners,' Tony said.

Johnston raised his eyebrows at Carol, wanting to know whether Tony was allowed to take the lead.

She nodded. 'What he said.'

'When we attend a fire, we kick off by looking externally. When there's a body involved, we automatically start from a place of suspicion. And that's what I did on Sunday. There wasn't much point in trying to establish a forensic cordon around the car because of the entirely legitimate activities of the firefighters, so I concentrated on the car itself. The first question I always ask myself is which part is most damaged.

Whether it's a house or a car. Now, your car, that consists of separate compartments. The engine. The boot, if it's a saloon. And the compartment where the driver and passengers sit. You don't often find a car with equal damage to all three parts.'

'And in this case, it was where the people sit,' Carol said. 'We've seen the pictures.'

Johnston smiled. 'Right. And the area of most damage is usually the indicator of where the fire started. Now, most people, what they think they know about cars going on fire is what they see on the telly or in films. Somebody throws a match in the petrol tank, and boom! Up it goes like an explosion in a fireworks shop.' He shook his head, an expression of amused pity on his face. 'Your petrol tank is full of petrol vapour but it won't go up unless it's got oxygen present as well, to feed it. It's even worse with diesel. You can actually put out a match or a fag in a puddle of diesel.' He mistook the blank look on his listeners' faces for interest and continued. 'Now if you stick a rag in with a bit of space around it and set fire to the rag, you will get a fire to start but that's just like a torch and it's unlikely to set the whole car on fire.'

'So, let me get this right,' Tony interrupted, sensing Carol was losing her patience and not wishing that on someone who seemed mostly harmless. 'For the passenger compartment to burn the way it did, the fire would have had to start there?'

Johnston beamed at his star pupil. 'Exactly. Now, sometimes you get kids wanting to burn out a car after they've nicked it and what they often do is stick a box of firelighters in the footwell. And that does a right good job, except that it leaves the chemical signature of the kerosene behind. Which is a dead giveaway to any investigator worth their salt. I've not found that telltale here, which, if I'm honest, made me lean more towards the idea of some kind of bizarre accident.

An electrical fault in the dashboard maybe. But I couldn't find any evidence of anything like that. Or a dropped cigarette. So it's not at all clear at this point.'

'And then you discovered she was dead when the fire started,' Carol cut in. 'With that in mind, what do you have for us?'

'I know it's tempting to think about the fuel tank, but forget the petrol. With a fire like this, you're looking at the inside of the cabin for all your fuel sources. So I started thinking about that. And I've been doing all sorts of chemical analyses over the past few days.' He cleared his throat and turned to face his computer screen. 'I can show you . . . '

'That's fine,' Carol said. 'Send it to me. But for now, give me the headlines.'

Crestfallen, Johnston turned back, the slope of his features even more pinched and pronounced. 'I think there was a plastic bag full of packets of crisps under the victim's legs.'

'Crisps?' Tony looked startled. 'You mean, like salt and vinegar, cheese and onion?'

'The flavour doesn't matter. The bags catch fire easily and the crisps themselves are loaded with oil. They're like dozens of miniature firelighters but they don't leave a kerosene residue. It's a completely different chemical signature.'

'Who knew?' Tony muttered.

'Fire investigators, obviously,' Carol said. 'So this whole fire started from someone setting light to a bag of crisps?'

'A bag of bags of crisps,' Johnston corrected her. 'There must have been quite a few to really get it going. And there's lots of traces of other flammable stuff that looks perfectly reasonable to find in a car. Newspapers. Glossy magazines. What looks like the remains of a couple of plastic bottles of spirits.'

'And that's all it took? It doesn't sound like much,' Tony said.

'You'd be surprised. Don't forget the interior of the car

itself is another fuel source. Upholstery, foam padding, plastics, the victim's clothes – it all adds up. And if the perpetrator left the window open a few inches, all the oxygen you need to feed the flames. But we can't be sure about that, because windows start to deform at five hundred degrees centigrade. Anyway, that's beside the point. What happens is, you get off to a vigorous start, you have enough of a fuel load – and oxygen – to maintain that and then you get what we call flashover. The point where a fire in a room, or in this case, a car, becomes a room on fire. That can happen inside a minute if the conditions are right. And a flashover is not a survivable event.'

There was a long silence while Tony and Carol digested the information. Then Carol said, 'So he knew what he was doing.'

Johnston nodded vigorously. 'Oh yes, he knew his stuff. Once upon a time I would have been sitting here telling you that your perp was likely a firefighter or someone with a professional knowledge of chemistry. But these days, half an hour on the internet and everybody's an expert. There's nothing here that a lay person couldn't work out for themselves with a bit of online research. And nothing specialist in the way of ignition sources or accelerants. It helps if you know a bit about chemistry, but honestly? Anyone with half a brain could come up with a strategy to turn a body to ash without leaving a clue.'

13

He'd chosen Leeds for his second outing. He'd always had an eye for detail; it would, he thought, be a mistake to look for all his victims on the same ground. Apart from anything else, it increased his chances of someone recognising him. Weddings in the same circle of acquaintance often happened in a cluster. And there were only so many hotels big enough to host the scale of wedding where an interloper wouldn't stand out. Eventually a waiter or a barman might clock him on a return visit, especially if the police ever came asking. Going back to the same city time after time would be taking too much of a risk.

It wasn't hard to crash a wedding. Most hotels of a certain size had at least one every Saturday. He'd worked out not to go too posh because chances were they'd have some form of control on the door. A guest list or someone checking the gilt-edged invitations. But he also knew not to go too far downmarket because he wouldn't fit in. He'd be exotic enough to be noticed. Somewhere in the middle, that was the way to go.

He'd already discovered how easy it was to find out the

names of the happy couple. Catch the florist delivering the table arrangements. *Are these the flowers for Mary and Paul's wedding?* 'No, they're for Jackie and Darrel.' Bingo. Or the bakery delivering the cake. Same routine. There was always someone to blag. People were so trusting. Like he had been once.

The secret of successful infiltration was not to turn up too early. He had to time it perfectly. Wait till they'd finished the meal, when everyone was milling around, going to the loo, staking their claim to the tables round the dance floor. Then he'd make his move. Shirtsleeves, top button undone, tie loosened. A man enjoying himself among friends. He'd head for the bar. Get himself a drink, strike up a casual conversation with another bloke. Then scope out the room. This was the most exciting part of the day. The adrenaline buzz, the knowledge that he'd made it this far, and now he was on the high board, teetering on the edge of a spine-tingling dive into action.

It didn't take long to identify the likely candidates. Once the dancing started, couples and little knots of friends coalesced and the outliers became obvious. The table where he'd spotted Kathryn McCormick had initially been colonised by a mixed group of women and men. Half an hour in, and she'd been the only one left, alone at the table, toying with a half-empty glass of wine. Over the next hour or so, some of the others had returned briefly to finish drinks, hang jackets over chairs and grab vapes before slipping outside. They exchanged a few words with Kathryn. One even made a determined attempt to get her on to the dance floor, but Kathryn had resisted.

She wasn't unattractive but she would never have stood out in a crowd. Hell, she wouldn't have stood out in a couple. She was, he thought, pretty much perfect. And so he'd made his move. And it had gone perfectly. She'd been wary for a few minutes. She probably knew he was out of her league.

But he was good with people, he knew that. He'd learned over the years how to pay attention to what they said, how to interpret their body language, how to win them over with a few well-aimed quips. And so Kathryn had allowed herself to be drawn to him. He'd neatly extracted her from the body of the wedding and escorted her to the bar on the pretext of being able to talk more readily.

Three dates and she was ripe for the plucking.

It had gone without a hitch. And it wasn't beginner's luck. He'd proved that by already acquiring his second surrogate. Amie McDonald – 'That's Amie with an i e, not a y, not like the singer.'

'The singer?'

'You know, the Scottish one. "This Is the Life".' She burst into song. '"Where you gonna go, where you gonna sleep tonight?"'

He smiled and shook his head. 'Sorry, passed me by.'

'Anyway, she's Amy with a y, and I'm Amie with an i e.'

What was it with these women and their insistence on spelling their names in ridiculous ways? Did they really think it made them special? Though in a way, of course, they were special. Because they were his.

And they were his because he'd done his homework. He'd put in the hours online, researching what he needed to do to avoid leaving a trail for the cops to follow right to his door. Once he started looking into ways to subvert investigative tools, his contempt for criminals who let themselves be caught grew incrementally. If you were going to commit a crime, why on earth would you not prepare as thoroughly as possible? It wasn't rocket science. When you really started looking, there were no shortage of strategies to avoid detection.

For example, he'd set himself up with a bundle of pay-as-you-go phones, bought with cash in a scruffy hole-in-the-wall shop on a recent trip to the West Midlands. He'd used a new one the day before the wedding, in Leeds. If the cops ever connected the dots and started looking into the victims, they'd find messages from him. Well, from Mark to Amie. And they'd contact the network providers to gain info about the phones. What numbers they'd called, where they'd been calling from. But he wasn't stupid. He'd only ever put the battery in the phone he'd used with Kathryn in and around Bradfield. He'd called restaurants and the theatre box office to give them more wild geese to chase.

So next time, they'd find themselves chasing Mark whose phone only ever showed up in Leeds. He wondered whether they'd be convinced it was the same killer or whether they'd come up with some mad, convoluted theory about a bunch of different men carrying out murders in the same way. A sort of League of Gentlemen Killers. He was sure one of the newspapers could be lured into some mad speculation of the sort.

Tonight, he was meeting Amie for dinner. He'd booked a table in an Ethiopian restaurant outside the city centre in an area that wasn't well endowed with CCTV. He'd checked out where to park so he'd have a clear run to the restaurant door. Just one camera and that would only catch his profile for a couple of seconds. He'd pretend to vape as he went past, avoiding the possibility of the camera capturing a recognisable image. He'd worried whether he could be identified from his walk, but a brief research trip round the internet had convinced him that so-called forensic gait analysis was pretty much junk science. It wasn't ever going to convict him on its own. And he'd made damn sure there was no other evidence to tie him to his actions.

He'd be the perfect gentleman over dinner. His cover story was a beauty. His wife of seven years had died from breast cancer a year ago. She'd made him promise not to shut himself away like a hermit, but it had been hard to get out in the world again. Finally, he'd started to come out of his pit of grief. The wedding had been the first proper social occasion he'd taken part in since the funeral.

So imagine the mixture of emotions he'd felt when he'd seen her sitting at the table. Because she could be the sister of his dead wife, so strong was the resemblance. At that point he'd give a wry, pained smile and tell her he thought he was dreaming.

By that point, Kathryn had been eating out of his hand. She wasn't thinking of him as out of her league now; she understood why he'd been drawn to her. It was a masterstroke.

He glanced at his watch and sipped his caramel crunch latte. He drew his decoy phone from his pocket. Time to draw Amie in even tighter. This was, after all, a kind of courtship dance. A little text for now, to keep her on the hook, to make sure she knew he was thinking of her.

She'd never guess what his thoughts really were.

14

Alvin was crammed into the corner of the tiny seating area in a Thai café halfway between RSR Solutions and the office, wolfing down a generous helping of Pad Khing. He was a big lad, he reasoned, so he needed to refuel at regular intervals. And in this job, you seized your moments when you could. He was almost finished when he felt the vibration of his phone against his thigh. Elbowing the man next to him out of the way, he put his container on the table and fished out the phone before it went to voicemail.

Before he could even identify himself, the woman on the other end had launched into speech. 'You are Detective Ambrose? Suzanne said I need to talk to you about Kathryn. It's terrible, what has happened to her—'

'I am Detective Sergeant Ambrose,' he said firmly, pushing himself to his feet. 'And you are?'

'I'm Anya. Anya Lewandowska. I work with Kathryn and Suzanne.' Her accent was faint but discernibly East European.

Alvin shoved past the people between him and the door,

ignoring their protests and complaints and burst on to the
pavement like a projectile from a catapult. 'What is it you
wanted to talk to me about?'

'You ask Suzanne if Kathryn had a boyfriend?'

'That's right.'

'She just started going out with a man called David. She
met him at Suzanne's wedding.'

A surge of excitement set Alvin's adrenaline flowing. 'Did
you see him?'

'Only the side of his face. They went through to bar, I
think to talk. I saw them when I went to bathroom.'

'Are you at work now? At RSR?' He was already barrelling
down the street towards his car.

'Yes, I am in office.'

'OK. I'm coming back right now, I need to talk to you.
And can you ask Suzanne not to go out for lunch because
I'll need to talk to her again too.' He unlocked the car and
squeezed behind the wheel. 'I'll be there very soon. And if
anybody's got pictures from the wedding on their phone or
their Facebook page, I'll need to see them too. Sit tight, Anya.
And thanks for phoning.'

'I like Kathryn. She hired me, she was always fair to me. I
see you soon.'

Now that was a better epitaph, Alvin thought. He'd heard
a lot worse.

This time, Lauren was waiting for him in reception. She
led him back to the room where he'd spoken to Suzanne.
Anya was already there, seated by the window, one black
stocking-clad leg crossed over the other. She looked in her
mid-thirties, her hair in a neat brown bob, her dark eyes nar-
rowed in concern. Her mouth was a full-on scarlet bow, her
lips fixed in a straight line.

Alvin introduced himself and asked if she'd mind him

recording their interview. Anya frowned and nodded with an air of reluctance. He took her through the formalities of name, address, date of birth and how long she'd been working at RSR. 'I came to England in May 2011, and I started work here eighteen months later. Kathryn was deputy office manager then and she was promoted two years ago when Becca left,' she said. Her reluctance seemed to have evaporated as soon as she started speaking, Alvin thought with relief.

'So, you called me to tell me Kathryn McCormick had a boyfriend called David that she met three weeks before her death at Suzanne Harman's wedding?' Clumsy, but he wanted to make sure the details were on the recording.

'That's right. Like I told you. I went to the bathroom beside the hotel bar because there was a big queue for the one beside the wedding room. I know this hotel, I worked there for a few weeks when I first came to Bradfield. I saw them sitting in the bar together when I went past. She was very smiley, like they were having a good chat.'

'What time was this?'

'I'm not sure. Maybe about seven o'clock? After the meal and the speeches, and the dancing had started maybe half an hour before. Maybe more, I don't know. I had a few drinks.' She shrugged, her lips quirking in a rueful smile.

'And Kathryn introduced you?'

'No, I don't think she even noticed me.'

Alvin's turn to frown. 'So how did you know this man was called David?'

Anya gave him an indulgent look. 'Because I ask her. On Monday, at the coffee machine. "Who was that I saw you with at the wedding?" And she went pink all over her face and neck. "His name's David," she said. "I'm meeting him for a pizza tomorrow." Like she was really pleased with herself. I think she didn't have a boyfriend for a long time.' She raised one shoulder in a half-shrug. 'That's all I know.'

'Can you describe him?' Alvin wasn't holding out much hope and it turned out he was right not to.

Anya spread her hands in a gesture of frustration. 'Not really. Like I said, I only saw him from the side. He was quite slim, I think. His hair was dark, quite thick, with a bit of grey at the sides.'

'Any idea of age?'

She shook her head, dubious. 'I don't know. Not young, not old. Maybe thirty-five, forty? I wasn't staring at him, I wasn't that interested.'

'Do you remember anything about what he was wearing?'

She looked up at the ceiling. 'Pale blue shirt, I think a blue tie. Grey suit trousers. Nothing special at all.' Again the one-shouldered shrug. 'I wasn't paying attention, I wanted to get back to party.'

Alvin took a deep breath. Bloody witness testimony was a nightmare. Notoriously unreliable even when they were adamant, with one as uncertain as Anya, the chances were that the man called David had been wearing blue trousers, a grey shirt and no tie at all. 'Did you take any pictures at the wedding? On your phone?'

Anya looked surprised. 'Only selfies with my friends.'

'Do you mind taking a quick look, see if there's any with this man David in the background?' He knew it was a long shot, but he had to try.

Anya took her phone out of her skirt pocket and brought up the photo album. She thumbed through a few shots, shaking her head. 'There is nobody in background, only us making faces.' She turned the phone so he could see she was telling the truth.

'Let's get Suzanne in and we'll go through whatever pictures she's got from the wedding,' Alvin said wearily. 'We'll need a laptop in here with a decent-sized screen too.' He wasn't a glass half-empty kind of man, but this felt horribly like a waste of time.

An hour and a half of scrutinising official and unofficial photographs of Suzanne and My Husband Ed's wedding snaps and Alvin's eyes felt like someone had blown sand into them. To be fair to Anya, she'd stuck with it, studying every shot from the wedding photographer and the ones that friends had shared on Facebook.

Suzanne clicked forward to the next one. Two men clinking pint glasses together, the now-familiar banqueting suite bar in the background. She clicked again, just as Anya said, 'Wait!' Shocked, Suzanne went back to the previous shot.

Anya bit her lip. 'I think that's him. There, at the bar. In the background.' She pointed at a man in not quite full pro-file who appeared to be talking to his neighbour. 'It looks like him.'

Suzanne zoomed in on the man's face but the definition wasn't good enough and his features were a blur. 'He doesn't look like anyone I know,' she said. 'He must be one of Ed's guests.'

'I need you to email that picture to me,' Alvin said. 'Highest possible resolution.' He waited while she opened an email program then typed in his address. He'd ping it across to Stacey as soon as possible. 'I'm going to need copies of all the photos of the wedding that you can track down. And we'll need to talk to your husband Ed about this man, to see whether he can identify him. Can we do that later, do you think?'

'You want to come round to our house?' Suzanne sounded almost excited.

'Either me or one of my colleagues.' With a bit of luck and the following wind of Stacey's digital expertise, by morning they might be much closer to a prime suspect. For once, Alvin thought, it would be sweet to wrap a case up so straightforwardly.

But straightforward wasn't what ReMIT was for.

15

It wasn't so long ago that Torin McAndrew had enjoyed morning break and the dinner hour. Ironically, it was one thing that his mother's murder had made better. When the truth had first emerged about her abduction and death at the hands of a psychopathic killer, there had been one or two dickheads who'd thought it was smart to slag her off. Make out that it was somehow her fault that a nutter had picked her as a victim. Torin had been too shattered to front them up himself, but even through the fog of his grief, he'd registered the support he'd had from his schoolmates. Not only his mates, either. People he barely knew existed weighed in on his side. And a handful of the older lads from the sixth form, the ones that everybody wanted to be like, they'd stepped up too.

The bastards had backed off double fast, and Torin had found himself in possession of a posse of pals to hang out with. They kicked a ball around at break if it wasn't raining, huddled under the library porch if it was. They swapped gaming tips and cheats, made gauche comments about girls, complained about teachers and made tiny plans for the weekend. At lunchtime, they queued for lunch together and talked about football and music as they necked their school dinners, barely paying attention to what they were shovelling down.

He'd never quite managed to belong to a group like this before. Somehow, he'd never quite fitted in. Torin had always hung around the fringes, torn between the desire to belong and a vague contempt for their concerns. But now he was grateful that he had their companionship. His mother's death had left him lonely and stranded. Paula and Elinor had been amazing, taking him in and giving him a home. But they'd never had kids. They were lesbians and they didn't have a clue what it was like to be a teenage boy. So there were holes inside him they didn't even know existed, never mind that they could come anywhere near filling. Having mates at last made those holes smaller. He'd begun to feel less lonely, less lost.

But now all that was under threat. Now, it was being in class that was safe. In class, he could pretend nothing bad was happening. In class, they had to turn their phones off; it was a rule that all the teachers stuck to, no exceptions. If you accidentally forgot to turn your phone off and you got caught out with the buzz of a text or the chime of a new post on social media, you got your phone confiscated till the end of the school week. No arguments. They'd all had to sign up to the policy, their parents too.

So the first thing everybody did when the bell went for break or lunch was to turn their phones on. He remembered a movie he'd seen where there were rows of lifeless automata that suddenly straightened up and became animated at the flick of a switch. He sometimes thought he and his mates were a bit like that. You got through class with a bit of your brain completely switched off. And then you turned on your phone and it was like the light of the screen turned you on too.

Until a couple of weeks ago, he'd been like everybody else, eager to get plugged back in to the digital world. Who'd posted a mad video, whose meme had gone viral, what new app was getting everybody enthused. They'd share the things that tickled them. Sometimes they'd get into a heated discussion about whether something was sick or not. But mostly, it was a quick catch-up then they'd move on to whatever concerned them that day.

Not any more, not for Torin. Now, his phone felt like an unexploded bomb in his hand. It had betrayed him and every time he turned it on, he felt it brought him closer to disaster. Sometimes he thought he could hear his mum's voice saying, 'Don't turn it on, then.' But that would be worse. Because then he wouldn't know when the bomb went off.

But that wouldn't save him from the fallout.

16

Telford wasn't DI Kevin Matthews' cup of tea, he decided within minutes of turning off the M54. He reckoned it wouldn't have met with the approval of its namesake, the great engineer, who had managed to make the functional attractive in a way that had escaped most new town planners in the sixties and beyond. It wasn't the aesthetics alone that bothered him. There were elements of the layout that made villainy a lot easier. The swift access to the motorway network made for an easy getaway for any toerag with seriously evil intent. And with his petrol-head world view, Kevin knew the dual carriageway that cut the town in half would be the perfect drag strip for boy racers to burn rubber in their pimped-out hatchbacks, the roar of their phat exhausts splitting skulls till gone midnight every weekend while the traffic cops avoided trouble by picking on drivers further down the motorway. For the residents of the shoebox houses nearby, it would be a perpetual source of misery.

But mid-morning on a weekday, the boy racers were either in bed or at work. The roads were half-empty and Kevin had no difficulty following his satnav's directions through the dispiriting centre, past identical houses in labyrinthine clusters until he came to what had obviously been an older village surrounded and swamped by the new town's development. Here, red-brick cottages clustered round a scrubby triangle of green with a whitewashed pub on one corner. As he arrived, a uniformed PC got out of a car parked outside the pub. Kevin assumed she was the Family Liaison Officer assigned by the local force to support the McCormicks. He pulled up behind her and introduced himself.

PC Seema Bradley appeared to be a calm and sensible woman in her mid-thirties. 'I've been an FLO for a couple of years now,' she said as they walked back to the McCormicks' house. 'My mum's Asian and my dad's from Birmingham so I know how to fit in anywhere round here. The brass like to keep their boxes ticked,' she added, a wry twist to her smile.

Kevin laughed. He touched his hair, faded a little with age but still indisputably ginger. 'Whereas I don't fit in anywhere except Scotland and Ireland.'

'Fair enough. Is there anything I need to know before we do the knock?'

Kevin told her what little he knew and together they opened the gate and prepared to blow a hole in two people's lives.

Jeremy and Hannah McCormick lived in a neat little terraced house with a minuscule front garden that was home to a couple of variegated euonymus bushes trimmed to geometric precision. Not Kevin's kind of gardening, but there wasn't much else you could do with so small a space. He took a deep breath and squared his shoulders. There was no job in policing worse than the death knock. He rang the bell and took a polite half-step backwards, nearly colliding with Seema on the narrow path.

The man who opened the door leaned heavily on a stick. His body was stooped and hunched, though he still had a thick head of light brown hair. His face didn't match the frailty either. It was as if a sixty-year-old's head had been stuck on the fragile body of a man in his late eighties. He peered up at them through strong glasses. 'You're not the chiropodist,' he said, sounding disappointed.

Kevin took out his ID. 'Mr McCormick?'

The man nodded. 'Yes. Who are you?'

Kevin held the slim wallet closer. 'I'm Detective Inspector Kevin Matthews and this is PC Seema Bradley. Can we come in, please?'

'What's this about?'

'We'd rather not discuss it on the doorstep. If we could step inside?' Seema said, her voice quiet but firm.

From inside, a woman's voice. 'Is that not the chiropodist, Jeremy?'

He turned with difficulty and said, 'It's the police.'

'The police?' Now she appeared behind him, a trim woman with her hair in a neat silver bob. She frowned over his shoulder at the two officers. 'What's this about? Has something happened to Kathryn?' She clearly saw something in Kevin's face, for her eyes widened and she put a hand on the wall to steady herself. 'Oh my God,' she gasped. 'Something terrible's happened. Jeremy, something terrible's happened to Kathryn.'

Kevin wasn't quite sure how she managed it, but Seema steered the McCormicks down the hallway to the living room. They clung to each other as if they were afraid of being swept out to sea on a current of fear. They subsided on to a sofa and stared at Kevin with a mixture of horror and disbelief. 'What's happened?' Jeremy McCormick kept saying.

Kevin sat down opposite them. 'I'm very sorry to tell you that your daughter Kathryn is dead.'

Hannah McCormick shook her head. 'That can't be right.

Not Kathryn. I spoke to her Friday teatime, she was going off for the weekend with a friend. There must be some mistake.'

Her husband, his face twisted in pain, gripped her arm. 'They don't make mistakes about people being dead, Hannah.'

Kevin's toes curled tight in his shoes. He hated these confrontations with shock and grief. Nothing he could do or say would mitigate the hell he'd brought down on these people's heads. 'I'm very sorry,' he repeated. 'But there's no mistake.'

Seema pitched in. 'I know this is a terrible moment for you both and it's very hard to take in. Kathryn died on Sunday night but it's taken us till now to make a positive identification. But that identification is quite clear.'

Tears spilled from Hannah's eyes. She seemed not to notice. 'What happened?' she said. 'Was it a car crash?'

Christ, Kevin thought. *Where do you even begin with this one?* 'There's no easy way to say this,' he began, but Jeremy McCormick cut him off.

'Say what?' he demanded, anger in his voice. 'You've already told us our only child is dead. What in the name of God could be harder than that?'

'Kathryn's death is being viewed as suspicious,' Seema said calmly. 'We believe someone killed her.'

'No!' Hannah wailed, her body racked with terrible gulping sobs. Jeremy raised his frail arms and cradled his head, rocking to and fro. There was nothing to be done but sit out their initial anguish. Eventually, the first storm passed and they leaned against each other, exhausted.

'What happened?' Hannah asked.

'We don't know exactly,' Kevin said. 'Her car was set on fire and her body was inside it.'

Hannah whimpered.

'She wasn't alive when the car was set on fire,' he added hastily. 'We believe she was strangled earlier. We think the fire was set by the killer to cover his traces.'

Jeremy moaned. 'Why would anyone do that to our Kathryn? She was a lovely girl. A good worker. She never did anybody a bad turn.'

'It's shocking, I know,' Seema said. 'Now, I'm going through to the kitchen to make us all a cup of tea. I'm sure you want to help Inspector Matthews as much as you can. I know this is the last thing you feel like doing, but the more we can learn about Kathryn, the sooner we can make progress with the investigation into her death.'

'I do have some questions,' Kevin said. 'If that's OK?'

Shakily, Hannah nodded. 'Can we see her? To say goodbye?'

One of the most dreaded questions. 'I wouldn't recommend it. She was very badly burned.'

'It's best that we remember her as she was,' Jeremy said, reaching for her hand.

Hannah flinched away and shot him a dark look. 'She's my baby. I want to say goodbye.'

'Honestly,' Kevin tried again. 'It's not a good idea. Sleep on it. And if you still feel the same, we can arrange it. But your husband's right. Better to think of her as she was in life. Though I do understand you want to say your farewells.'

'It's not that,' Hannah said. 'If I don't see her for myself, my imagination'll run away with me. I'll be picturing all sorts of terrible things happening to my lovely girl.'

She had a point, Kevin thought. But really, what kind of peace could there be in seeing the incinerated remains of your child? 'Kathryn was already dead before the fire,' he tried. 'Anything you see now won't reflect her last moments. She was gone long before that.'

'He's right, Hannah,' Jeremy said. 'We need to hold on to the good memories, not torture ourselves.' His voice cracked. 'And we need to help the police. I need to know how this terrible, terrible thing happened to our girl, and we're not going to find that out by staring at what's left of her.'

A long silence, broken finally by Hannah clearing her throat. 'We'll do everything we can to help. But I still might want to see her.' She looked at Kevin with piteous eyes. 'She was our only one.' Her hands tormented the tissue that had wiped her tears.

Jeremy patted her arm. 'So you'd better ask your questions, Inspector.'

Kevin took a deep breath. He didn't want to imagine how he'd feel if this had happened to one of his children. Keeping his emotional distance was the only thing that made this job possible sometimes. 'Thank you. Now, Mrs McCormick? You said you spoke to her on Friday teatime? About what time was that?'

'About half past six. She'd just got in from work, she said. But she couldn't talk long because she was going away for the weekend.'

'Did she say who she was going with?'

Hannah's brows furrowed. 'She didn't say a name. Only that it was a friend from work.'

'You're sure? A friend from work? Did she say whether it was a man or a woman?'

'I assumed it was a woman. She's not had a boyfriend since she and Niall split up. And that was, what? Three years since.'

'Would she have told you if it had been a man?'

'No, she wouldn't have,' Jeremy said sadly. 'She wouldn't have said anything in case we got our hopes up that she'd met someone she could be happy with. We were so upset when Niall left her, you see. She wouldn't have said anything until she was sure.'

'I see. Did she say where she was going?'

Hannah pinched the bridge of her nose between finger and

thumb, concentrating. 'She said this friend had the loan of a cottage in the Yorkshire Dales.' She sighed in frustration. 'But she didn't say where. Not even where it was near.'

Seema came through with four mugs of tea balanced on a chopping board. 'Sorry, I couldn't find a tray,' she said, distributing the mugs. 'I couldn't see any sugar either.'

'We don't take sugar,' Hannah said firmly.

Kevin made no complaint even though he usually had a spoonful to make tea palatable. 'Can I ask which of Kathryn's friends she might have confided in?'

They looked at each other blankly. 'I don't know,' Hannah said. 'She talked about the women she worked with a lot, but I don't think there was anyone in particular that she would have considered a close friend.'

And so it continued. Kevin asked every question he could think of, but nothing provoked a useful nugget of information. Not until the very end. 'Had Kathryn been anywhere recently where she might have met a new man?' He expected nothing.

But her father had something to say. 'She was at a colleague's wedding a fortnight or so ago. She said she'd been talking to lots of people. She mentioned a friend of the groom's. Just in passing, you understand. A man called David.'

'Did she say anything more about him?'

Hannah frowned. 'No. Only that it was nice to go to a wedding and not have a nasty surprise.'

Kevin felt a prickle on the back of his neck. 'What did she mean by that?'

Hannah and Jeremy exchanged a look. Jeremy took the lead. 'The last time she was at a wedding, her ex-boyfriend was there. Niall. It gave her a shock, that's all. She didn't think he'd have the brass neck to show up somewhere he knew she'd be.'

17

By the time Paula and Karim made it back to base, Stacey had already made impressive inroads into the history of the number on the calendar. She barely looked up from her array of screens as they approached. 'Pay-as-you-go, obviously. Everybody knows how to make my job harder these days.'

'What else—' Karim began eagerly before Paula jabbed her elbow into his ribs.

'It was bought in a hole-in-the-wall shop in Dudley, in the West Midlands.' Stacey tapped a key and one of the screens changed to a Google Street View of a down-at-heel street. She zoomed in on the phone shop frontage, flanked by a kebab takeaway and a Marie Curie charity shop. 'The usual sort of thing. Phones unlocked, laptops repaired. Buy your throwdown phone here, no questions asked.'

'But it's worth paying them a visit, right? Even if they don't keep proper records, they might have CCTV?' Karim asked.

Paula shook her head. 'Waste of time. They'll have complete amnesia and if they have cameras, they'll have wiped all but the most recent data. He chose this shop for a reason. He won't fall into our hands that easily.'

'He's a planner, this man David,' Karim said.

'The ones we get usually are,' Paula said. She'd spent years in Major Incident Teams. Enough to know that the random attackers who hit flashpoint and lost control usually hadn't thought anything through. But killers who had a mission in their head, they took care. They worked out their options and the odds and made plans.

'I suspect the phone's been destroyed now,' Stacey went on. 'There's been nothing since Friday evening at 6.23. I tried calling it and it didn't ping on the network.'

'How do you—'

'Don't ask,' Paula told Karim firmly. 'What happens with Stacey stays with Stacey.'

The data analyst looked up momentarily and a quick smile flashed across her face. She clicked her trackpad and a list of numbers appeared on a screen. 'All the calls made from this phone originated in the Bradfield area. He called various restaurants, an indie cinema, the theatre. But the only individual he called or texted from that phone was Kathryn McCormick.'

'Which means it'll be a waste of time to follow up on the other calls.' They hadn't noticed Carol Jordan arrive until she had spoken, so intent were they on what Stacey was showing them.

'You don't think he was booking meals or tickets?' Karim asked.

'No. I think he was doing two things,' Carol said. 'I think he was deliberately trying to waste our time by having us chase around all over Bradfield checking out bookings and CCTV footage for Kathryn and him out on the town. I'd bet a month's salary that wherever he took her for a meal, it wasn't anywhere this list. And that he paid in cash and booked the table in a false name.'

Paula nodded. It made perfect sense. 'You said two things.'

'He wants us to think he's Bradfield-based. That's where he wants us to focus our attention. I suspect that means that wherever he lays his hat, it's not Bradfield.'

There was a glum silence for a moment, broken by an angry roar from the main squad room. 'Where the fuck are you hiding, Stacey?'

Everyone except Karim recognised the sound of an enraged Detective Constable Sam Evans, formerly of the Bradfield Metropolitan Police MIT that Carol had run before the murder of her brother and his wife had pushed her into walking away from the job. As far as Carol knew, he was also Stacey Chen's boyfriend. What Paula and Stacey knew was that description had been redundant since the night before. What only Stacey knew was that she had, with a few deft keystrokes, destroyed his digital existence. Credit cards withdrawn, bank account emptied and frozen, mortgage messed with, council tax transformed to a debt, social media accounts erased and phone service suspended.

Just because Stacey had never ravaged anyone's life before didn't mean she couldn't do it with precision and thoroughness.

What she hadn't bargained for was him turning up at the ReMIT office. She'd half-expected him to attempt to confront her at home. If she'd understood Sam half as well as she understood her machines, she'd have known he'd always take the easy path. Why try to blag his way past a doorman she'd undoubtedly have told to refuse entry to her ex, when his police ID would grant him access to Skenfrith Street cop shop and thus to their office?

'Stop hiding behind those bloody screens,' Sam roared. The muffled barking of Flash, secured in Carol's office, answered his shout. Before anyone else could respond, he had barged into Stacey's office, pushing past Carol and looking around wildly. 'Great,' he shouted, his face flushed with anger. 'The gang's all here. Has she told you what she's done to me?'

Carol rounded on him. 'What do you mean by this? How dare you barge in here, shouting the odds? You need to keep your private life private, Sam.'

His lips tightened and he snarled, 'Don't you fucking "Sam" me. You're the one who started all this, dissing me like you did.'

'If you mean my not choosing you for this squad, you've proved my point.' Carol's voice dripped contempt but Sam was too far gone in anger for the insult to give him pause.

'And you—' He pointed at Stacey. 'I couldn't figure out what the hell was going on last night when I couldn't get any money out of the hole in the wall. Then this morning, I realised there's only one person I know who has the skills to do this to me. Why? All because I went for a night out with my mates? That's mental, Stacey. You need to fix this.'

Stacey opened her mouth to speak but before she could say anything, Paula charged in, determined not to let this become worse than it already was. 'You really think Stacey would do something like this over a lover's tiff? Think again, Sam. Cast your mind back over the crap you've pulled lately. The crap that really would upset Stacey a lot more than anything you could do to her personally.'

Her words stopped Sam in his tracks. He gave Carol a quick glance, obviously checking whether she knew what Paula was referring to. But they'd kept the full extent of his treachery from Carol and she looked startled enough for him to believe that. Which might be enough for him not to drag his betrayal into the light of day. 'It doesn't matter what her so-called excuse is,' he blustered. He stabbed his finger in Stacey's direction again. 'You better fix this and fix it now.'

Stacey stood up, leading with her chin. 'Or what, Sam? You can't prove a single thing you're alleging against me.

Whereas I . . . ' She gave a little shrug, her perfectly tailored jacket moving sinuously with her.

His eyes widened as he took in the implications of what she was saying. But Carol butted in before he could reply. 'Is anybody going to tell me what the fuck is going on here?'

Paula stared Sam down. 'I think Constable Evans was just leaving.'

A long pause. Then Sam turned on his heel and barged out of the office. A few seconds later, the door to the main squad room slammed shut. Carol shook her head like a dog emerging from water.

'Is there any chance you could pretend that didn't happen?' Paula asked, less tentatively than she felt.

'Would there be any blowback if I did?' Carol was slowly learning to be more wary of deals, even deals from people she'd count as friends if the chips were down.

Paula and Stacey exchanged looks. 'I don't think so,' Stacey said.

Carol ran a hand through her hair. 'I'll be in my office. Paula, come and talk to me in five.'

And she was gone. Karim unpeeled himself from the wall he'd been trying to disappear into and followed Paula back into the main office. 'Do I have to pretend that didn't happen too?' he asked cautiously.

Paula chuckled. 'No. Don't take this the wrong way but you're too far down the pecking order. If we told the boss, she'd have to do something about it. If Stacey had wanted to go down that road, she'd have done it herself.'

'So what happened?'

Paula leaned against her desk. 'You remember that story in the papers last week, about the boss's drink driving charge being dropped because of a faulty breathalyser?'

'Yeah,' he said. 'Man, they made it sound like the whole set-up was totally bent.'

'Exactly. It nearly scuppered ReMIT before we got started. And it had obviously come from a leak, because there was no reporter in the magistrate's court when the cases were dismissed. So we did a little bit of detective work and discovered the story had come from Sam.'

'How did he know about it?'

'Stacey had told him. She thought she could trust him, not just because he was her boyfriend but because he's one of us. You know the principle – kick one and we all limp. Except Sam was apparently wearing shin pads. He was furious with Carol because she didn't choose him for the new squad even though he'd worked for her in Bradfield. So he thought he'd screw her over.'

Karim drew his breath in sharply. 'That's a shit's trick.'

'Some of us were less surprised than others. But it was Stacey's call on how to deal with it.' Her expression revealed a rueful respect. 'Never ever mess with Stacey. That's your life lesson for today.'

'What'll happen now?'

Paula pushed herself off the desk and headed for Carol's office. 'If Sam's got any sense, nothing. He'll tell his bank he's been hacked and sort it out.' She had her back to Karim so she didn't see the anxiety on his face. Even if she had, it wouldn't have given her pause.

Carol's door was ajar, so Paula walked in. Flash raised her head and gave a little yelp of welcome. 'Where's Tony?' she said as Carol nodded her to a chair.

She looked up from the notes she was writing. 'I dropped him off at Bradfield Moor. He's got a couple of patient sessions this afternoon. What was that all about?'

'The story in the paper about your case being thrown out of court? It was Sam who leaked it.' Paula tried for a smile but it came off as a grimace. 'Stacey may have delivered her personal idea of justice.'

Carol groaned. 'Well, as long as this is the last I hear about it, good on her. Obviously not having him on the squad was the right call. So, any progress on Kathryn McCormick?'

Paula reported what little they knew. 'Alvin's got them going through the photos from the wedding, Kevin's confirmed he was using the name David, and that's about it,' she concluded. 'And Kathryn may have had a run-in with her ex at another wedding a while back.'

'Interesting, we'll need to follow up on that.' She reached for a notepad and scribbled a reminder. 'The fire investigator was helpful but we didn't get anything there that moves us forward. Tony's muttering under his breath, but that's par for the course at this stage.' Carol shifted in her chair, leaning on the desk and smiling. 'I wanted to talk to you about something else, though.'

Paula hoped they weren't going to return to Sam's outburst. She returned the smile, albeit nervously.

'You need to get your inspector's exams out of the way,' Carol said. It was the last thing Paula had expected.

'You don't need another inspector on the squad,' she protested. 'You bumped Kevin back up to his old rank. I'm happy where I am.'

'Kevin only came back on condition that it was temporary. Until I found another inspector I rated to fill the slot. And I think you're that officer. You know how we work here. You're the best interviewer I've ever worked with and you're a smart detective. I want you to step up, Paula.'

'I'm not ready for this. And I'm rubbish at paperwork.'

'No worse than anybody else on this squad. So start swotting for your exams. It's time, Paula.'

18

By the end of the afternoon, Alvin felt his brain had turned to mush. Suzanne and Ed's wedding guest list ran to over ninety people and he'd communicated with all but a handful of them. Phone calls, texts, messages and face-to-face conversations had all led to one irresistible conclusion. Whoever David was, he wasn't an official guest. Ed had confirmed what Suzanne had already told him. The only David on the guest list had been his sixty-two-year-old uncle who was overweight and bald.

Still, Alvin had checked all the other guests on the off-chance they hadn't brought a David along as a last-minute substitute for a boyfriend or spouse. They all sounded bemused, amused or confused by his questions. But none of them admitted to having been with a man called David.

'He was a crasher,' he told Carol when he arrived back in the office with a 64GB SD card crammed with as many photographs of the wedding as he'd been able to garner. He took off his jacket and threw it over a chair with an air of disgust, then loosened his tie. 'Nobody admits to knowing him. The one definite photo ID that Anya Lewandowska made, with him standing at the bar talking to another bloke? I spoke to him. He's called Andy Swift and he was there with his girlfriend who works with the groom. He said he'd never seen the guy before, that they were having the kind of non-conversation you have at the bar. His description was even more vague than Anya's.' Alvin raised his voice an octave and aimed at a Northern accent. '"What, you think I'm a poof or something? I couldn't be less interested in what some geezer at a bar looks like."'

As he spoke, Tony wandered into the squad room with a distracted air. 'He went there with the specific intention of acquiring a victim,' he said, dropping wearily into a chair. 'The only question is whether he was specifically looking for Kathryn or any random victim.'

'Does it matter?' Alvin asked.

'If he was stalking Kathryn, he might show up in her shadow. There must be some CCTV coverage of her route to work, or where she did her shopping,' Carol said.

'Isn't it more likely that he was stalking her specifically?' Alvin rubbed his temples, trying to shift the headache that was starting to trouble him. 'I mean, isn't a bit speculative? Who's to say he'd have found anyone willing to be picked up?'

'I'd have thought he was in with a good chance,' Tony said slowly. 'A wedding, love in the air? It makes people think about being with someone. Weddings are a notorious catalyst.'

'What? People decide it's time they got hitched just because they've gone to a wedding with their partner?' Carol sounded sceptical.

'That,' Tony said. 'But also the opposite. It makes people question their relationship. Do you want to marry me? Why don't you want to marry me? If we're going to be together forever, we might as well get married because it makes all the legal stuff less complicated if one of us dies. If we're not going to get married, what's the point of us?' He shrugged. 'One of my colleagues once told me that six couples had split up within two weeks of his wedding.'

'Bloody hell,' Alvin said. 'I had no idea. So you think the whole lovey-dovey atmosphere might have made Kathryn an easier pick-up?'

'I think it might have made her more susceptible to an approach from a stranger than if she'd been in the pub with her mates, yes.' Tony struggled out of his purple anorak and dumped it on the floor next to him. He caught Carol's eye. 'What? It's too bulky to drape over a chair.'

'Did I say anything? I'm not your mother.'

Tony shuddered. 'Don't even put that image in my head. Vanessa's bad enough.'

Alvin stood up, rolling his massive shoulders inside his jacket. 'I'm bloody stiff. I'm not used to being hunched over a phone all day. I'll pass these pics on to Stacey, then if there's nothing else for me right now, I'm going to call it a day.'

'You might as well. Go home and read your kids a bedtime story for once. I'm calling it a day myself soon,' Carol said. But she couldn't keep herself from clicking through the investigation reports the team had uploaded earlier.

Stacey showed no signs of knocking off. She was intent on one of her screens, fingers flying over the keyboard. When Alvin walked in she raised her hand, palm out; half greeting, half injunction. She drew her eyebrows together in concentration, clicked the trackpad then turned her eyes to him. 'Sergeant Ambrose,' she said.

'Alvin,' he corrected her for the ninth or tenth time. Paula had said she'd be formal till she felt relaxed around him. Obviously he was still not doing whatever it took to break down her barriers. 'I brought you all the wedding pics I could get my hands on. Somebody said you had software that could compare faces?'

Stacey allowed a tiny smile to twitch the corners of her mouth. 'I wrote some code that improved on the standard facial recognition software that was available to us. So what we've got here is at least as good as anything else on the market. Probably better than most.' She held her hand out and he dropped the SD into her palm. Her slender fingers closed over it; he couldn't help notice the French manicure, perfect but short enough not to interfere with her keystrokes. She was always immaculate. Her clothes were clearly expensive and fitted her as if they'd been tailored for her alone. Her hair and make-up were always unruffled, making her hard for him to read. He'd assumed she came from money till Kevin had told him she'd made millions from the software company she ran in her own time. 'She likes the licence to be nosey that the job gives her,' he'd said, not entirely approvingly.

Good on her, Alvin thought. 'There's one definite ID,' he said. 'I've saved it in a separate folder, called David.'

'Thanks,' Stacey said, already slotting the SD card into a slot in a MacAir.

'Good luck,' he said, turning to go.

She chuckled. 'This is the part of ReMIT where luck doesn't come into it, Alvin.'

19

Amie McDonald stood, hand on hips, surveying her wardrobe. All she knew was that they were going for dinner. Mark had asked her if she liked spicy food and she'd told him she wasn't scared of hot stuff, so at a guess they'd be going for an Indian or a Thai. There were plenty of those to choose from in Leeds but none that were really dress-up places. The city boasted a few high-end restaurants, but none of them were noted for the chilli content of their food.

Dissatisfied with what she saw, she raked through the contents of the rails, the hangers rattling as she quickly discarded various possibilities. She wanted to look good, like she'd made an effort. But not needy. Because she wasn't needy. Amie had never had any trouble attracting men. It was keeping them that was the problem. Her standards were too high, that was the top and bottom of it. She couldn't be doing with the way they colonised her flat, leaving their clothes draped over chairs, their shoes kicked off in front of the telly, their dirty mugs always on the kitchen worktops and never in the dishwasher. One had even had the nerve to mansplain that he didn't want to disrupt her personal dishwasher loading system. That had been his firing offence.

Maybe Mark would be different. Amie didn't hold out too much hope; she'd been caught like that before. But he was well groomed and well dressed, which was a big step in the right direction. His hair was well barbered, swept back from his forehead in an understated quiff, though the colour was a bit too uniform and she wondered whether he dyed it. Still, why shouldn't he? She'd been everything from platinum blonde to raven black via chestnut and aubergine since her teens. It had only been in the last year or so she'd finally settled on glossy brown with highlights. So, good on him for taking care of himself. His clothes fitted well, and she'd spotted the designer logo on the stylish black frames of his glasses.

Amie pulled out a shimmery red tunic that fell mid-thigh and held it against herself. It was a bit unforgiving around the hips but she'd be sitting down with the table for cover. The curving V of the neckline flattered her breasts, which was probably a good tactical move at this point. It was, after all, technically a first date. You couldn't count being picked up at your friend's wedding as a date.

She hadn't been looking forward to going to the do. Not because she didn't love Jamie and Eloise, because she did. She'd worked alongside Jamie in the council tax office for five years now, and he was always the one who could make people laugh, even on a rainy Monday morning. And Eloise was a sweetheart. Just right for him. Not like that bitch he'd been seeing when Amie had first got to know him. She'd even thought about making a move on him herself after he'd ditched the bitch, but much as she liked him, she couldn't fancy him. As far as Amie was concerned, Jamie had all the sexual charisma of a wellington boot. She'd been genuinely happy when Eloise had said yes.

But when the wedding invitations had gone out, Amie had still been seeing Steve. They'd been invited as a couple. For the sake of appearances, she'd tried to swallow her increasing irritation with him till after the wedding, but five days earlier, she'd snapped and chucked him out with no room for reprieve. So there she was, stuck without a date for the office wedding of the year. She'd even thought of inventing a tummy bug rather than front up at the celebrations without a partner, like Billy No Mates. But in the end, her desire to be in the thick of things had won out and she'd gritted her teeth, put on her glad rags and pitched up at the swanky reception.

The irony was that if she'd hung on grimly to Steve for the sake of appearances, she'd have missed out on Mark. He'd spotted her sitting at the table on her own while the dance floor pulsed with sweaty humanity and he'd whisked her off to the hotel bar where they could hear each other speak. It was clear he wasn't just after an easy pick-up. He actually did want to talk.

Five years of listening to people's pathetic and ridiculous excuses for why they hadn't paid their council tax bills had instilled a weary cynicism in Amie. But in spite of that, she'd been touched by Mark's story. Losing someone you loved to cancer was a tough thing to get past, and she could see why he didn't want to be in a room full of people getting pissed and having a laugh without a thought for tomorrow.

She'd even felt vaguely honoured that he'd picked her out as someone who looked like a friendly face. It turned out his late wife had been a mate of Eloise's from school. He thought he'd only been invited out of pity, he'd admitted towards the end of the evening. But – and he'd gone all shy, like a schoolboy – although he'd been drawn to Amie because she reminded him of his wife, he'd been amazed to find a kindred spirit in the last place he'd expected it.

So when he'd asked to see her again, she'd jumped at the chance. They'd swapped phone numbers. He told her he worked for Marks and Spencer, that his job entailed being on the road a lot because he had to do undercover checks on the displays in individual stores, to make sure they were properly installed and in line with policy. But he'd promised they'd meet the first evening he could be back home in Leeds.

Which was tonight. Amie tossed the red top onto the bed and picked out a pair of flattering black trousers to go with it. Three-inch black patent stilettos and a matching clutch bag completed the ensemble.

Mark might have been the perfect gentleman after the wedding, but Amie was determined to do whatever it took to snare him. This time, she convinced herself, she might actually have found Mr Right.

20

Two things were not as they should have been when Carol opened her front door. Firstly there was no confusion of black-and-white fur cannonballing into her the moment she stepped inside. And secondly, a dense aroma of venison braising in a sauce of red wine and onions and juniper filled her head. It was overwhelming and current, not a hangover from a previous meal. Disorientation slithered through her before she realised Tony must have prepared dinner then gone out with the dog. It came as a shock. She had been living on her own, completely self-reliant, for so long that this still felt like ceding control and she wasn't sure she was ready for that.

Particularly not in the wake of Tony pushing her into a place where giving up drink had become her only real option. Although the new case that had landed on her desk had been absorbing and perplexing, the desire for a drink had never been far from her consciousness, humming underneath the demands of the day like the low rumble of distant thunder. However hard she might deny it to Tony, Carol couldn't pretend she was in control of her drinking. She had allowed it to creep in from the wings glass by stealthy glass until it occupied centre stage.

Most alcoholics – there, she'd said it, even though it was only inside her own head – killed only themselves in the end. Yes, they screwed up the lives of everybody who cared about them, but the only fatality was usually the one who'd chosen that particular form of slow suicide. But Carol's drinking had cost lives. However you cut it, she thought, there were deaths that lay at her door. Their blood on her hands. Their blurred faces in her nightmares.

Letting the thoughts bubble to the surface made her crave a drink. Instead she opened the simmering oven of the Aga and took out the heavy casserole dish. She lifted the lid and savoured the smell. It obviously hadn't been in the oven for very long for the wine was still a distinct element in the aroma. It was, she thought, an act of faith on Tony's part to use wine when cooking for her. She hoped he'd used the whole bottle. She gave the thick stew a stir and put it back in the oven as the doorbell rang.

Assuming Tony had forgotten his keys in a typical moment of absent-mindedness, she didn't even bother to check the spyhole. The enormity of her error was obvious to Carol the moment she opened the door. There, wrapped up in an elegant shearling coat and matching hat was the woman who had brought her and her team so much grief over the years. Nine times out of ten, when something had appeared in the paper that disadvantaged an investigation, the byline on the story was this woman's.

And yet, Penny Burgess, crime correspondent of the *Bradfield Evening Sentinel Times*, smiled at Carol with all the warmth of a woman coming face to face with her best friend. All the years of knock-backs and put-downs from Carol might never have happened. 'DCI Jordan,' she said in a tone of delighted surprise.

'Who else were you expecting on my doorstep?' Carol said sourly, wishing she could take back the words as soon as they'd left her lips.

'I wouldn't presume to guess,' Penny said. 'I hear you've done wonders with the place. Are you going to invite me in to show it off?'

Carol's bark of involuntary laughter echoed across the yard. 'What do you think, Ms Burgess?'

Penny shivered theatrically. 'I think it's bloody chilly out here. Anyone with an ounce of pity would bring me into the warm.' She moved one foot forward. Carol leaned more firmly against the door.

'Consider me pitiless. What are you doing here? You're a long way off your patch.'

'No more Ms Nice Guy, eh? OK, I'll cut to the chase, Carol. Dominic Barrowclough.'

Carol had to fight to keep her stare level and her breath under control. She shook her head. 'Sorry, not one of ours.'

'Dominic was driving a souped-up Vauxhall Astra last night. You know the kind of thing. All flared wheel arches and a spoiler like a snowboard on the back. He was hammering down the road from Barkisland to Greetland and he took a bend on the wrong side of the road. Unfortunately for everyone concerned, he met a Mini coming the other way and the resulting impact drove the Mini into a Ford Galaxy travelling behind it. Maybe a bit too close behind, but nobody's casting blame in that direction.'

'All very unfortunate, as you say. But I'm not sure what an RTA on a West Yorkshire back road has to do with me.' Carol clamped her teeth tight shut and gripped the door so tightly she could feel the edge of the lock biting into the base of her thumb.

Penny cocked her head to one side, her eyebrows rising. It was not an expression that conveyed belief. 'Dominic and his girlfriend Casey died instantly. The driver and the passenger in the Galaxy – Perry and Lisa Davidson from Pontefract, married couple in their thirties with two young children – they died too. The Mini driver – a young woman from Halifax, they haven't released her name yet – is in intensive care, hanging on by her fingernails.' She paused, expectantly. Carol managed to hold her tongue and Penny shrugged.

'Are we going to keep pretending you haven't a clue what I'm on about when we both know somebody from West Yorkshire will have been on the phone to you within ten minutes of them identifying Dominic Barrowclough?'

For once, Carol couldn't decide which way to jump. Keep playing dumb, or acknowledge what she knew without admitting any kind of responsibility? 'And what would this notional phone call have said?'

Penny shook her head, a pitying expression on her face. 'That Dominic Barrowclough was one of the other people who got off their drink-driving charge because of an alleged faulty breathalyser. The same faulty breathalyser that let you off the hook so you could take up your shiny new job at ReMIT.'

Carol felt a chill move through her, as if she'd swallowed a freezing cold stone. 'If that's the case, you should be talking to West Yorkshire Police about their faulty breathalyser. Not to an innocent motorist.'

'Not quite what I'd heard,' Penny said with a knowing look.

'I can't help that. Now, if that's all ... ?' Carol moved to close the door.

'I've only just begun, Carol.' There was steel in her voice. 'I'm told you were out to dinner on the night of the broken breathalyser.'

Carol said nothing but she could feel her heart thudding against her ribs. What was coming next? And where was

Tony? She couldn't decide whether she wanted him to stay far away from this interrogation or to thrust himself into the heart of it, taking the fight to the enemy.

Penny waited for the non-existent response, then her lips curled in a sly smile. 'Out to dinner at the table of a man who's renowned among your neighbours for the quality of his cellar. Not to mention his generosity.'

'And you've got a witness who says DCI Jordan was drinking, have you?' A familiar voice cut across Penny's words. Tony was invisible in the darkness behind her, but Carol could see the ghost of the white of Flash's coat. As Tony moved into the light, she could see he was holding on to the dog's collar, keeping her close to his side. 'No? I thought not. Because anybody who tried to stir it like that would be abusing their host's hospitality, which around here is pretty much a capital crime.' He'd rounded Penny Burgess's shoulder and was in the doorway. Carol moved without thinking so they stood shoulder to shoulder. 'They'd also be lying,' Tony continued. 'Which would expose you and your paper to all sorts of legal pitfalls, were you to be daft enough to rely on some vindictive bastard's falsehoods.'

'We all know you're putting up a smokescreen, Dr Hill,' Penny said, glaring at him. 'There are too many people who know what really happened that night to keep the lid on it.'

Tony gave a dry chuckle. 'What? Three can keep a secret if two of them are dead? But that only works if there's a secret in the first place. Carol has nothing to hide. Maybe you should be writing a story about the financial pressures that mean the police can't afford to maintain their equipment.' He pulled a face. 'But that wouldn't be very sexy, would it? Quarter page in the middle of the paper. Not like a front page accusing senior cops of corruption. Even if that's nothing more than a fantasy.'

Penny's lips were a tight straight line. He was right, Carol thought. He'd exposed Penny's weakness. She had nothing but a couple of shreds of rumour she was taking a flyer on. 'So if that's all,' Carol said sweetly, 'we've got dinner to eat.' She stepped back, preparing to close the door. But she'd underestimated how quick the reporter was when it came to fancy footwork.

'So you're living here now, Tony,' she said. 'That's a happy ending, isn't it? After all you two have been through together.'

Tony squeezed his eyes shut momentarily. 'A working dinner, Penny. My boat's still moored up in the Minster basin.' He released Flash, who immediately leaned into Carol's leg.

'I'm sure it is. But if you're moored up here, walking the dog . . . Well, my readers love a heart-warming happy ending. God knows you deserve it.'

'Go away, Ms Burgess,' Carol sighed. 'You're really starting to piss me off.'

'Fair enough. You can't say I didn't give you a chance to rebut the version of events that's gaining traction. There are four people dead whose relatives want answers to the question of why Dominic Barrowclough was driving around West Yorkshire when he should have lost his licence weeks ago. They need somebody to blame, and I don't think you can count on West Yorkshire Police to keep covering your back.' She gathered her coat more closely around her in preparation for leaving.

'I have done nothing wrong,' Carol said, her voice low and steady.

Penny scoffed. 'That's not what I'm hearing.'

Tony stepped forward quickly, forcing her to retreat. 'You of all people should know how committed DCI Jordan is to justice. You know the work she's done, the cases her teams have resolved down the years. Is making life easier for criminals really what you're after? Because that's all you'll achieve if you join the fake news brigade. These are alternative facts, Penny. The truth is that Carol catches criminals and puts them away.'

Penny glared mutinously. 'It's a shame not everybody makes it to the glory day, isn't it? This isn't the first time you've left bodies in your wake, is it, Carol?'

Abruptly, Carol turned on her heel and disappeared inside. 'Good job,' Tony said sarcastically, stepping back into the doorway and closing the door firmly in Penny Burgess's discontented face. From the far side of the barn, Carol watched him take off his jacket and hang it up in silence. The last thing she felt like was a post-mortem, but she couldn't ignore the scene that he'd walked into.

'I'm sorry,' she said as he went across to the kitchen area.

Tony paused by the oven, his back to her, and said, 'Bloody Sam Evans. Paula told me all about it. If he hadn't wanted to make you pay for not choosing him, none of this would ever have surfaced.'

'But it has. And Penny Burgess is like a terrier who gets a whiff of a rabbit. She'll quarter the hillside sniffing the bloody air till she finds where the truth's gone to ground. I've barely got ReMIT up and running and already I'm living on borrowed time.'

He took the casserole out of the oven and stirred it enthusiastically. The smell was amazing. 'Nobody who sits around George Nicholas's dinner table is going to talk to a scummy hack like Penny Burgess.'

'He had staff working that night.'

'Bet they couldn't make a venison casserole like this.'

'Where did you get the recipe?' Carol asked, momentarily diverted. Cooking was not one of Tony's core skills.

'On the internet. I did exactly what it said, except you didn't have any juniper berries.'

'Shame you dumped the gin down the sink,' she said wryly.

Tony replaced the casserole. 'Half an hour, I think. George Nicholas's staff won't rat out a friend of the house. And even if they did, their evidence is meaningless. They weren't in the room all evening. Even Penny Burgess wouldn't take a chance on something so fragile. Or if she did, her editor would kick it into the long grass. They don't want to make an enemy of the cops unless they're on rock-solid ground.'

Carol moved away from him, trying not to show the fear and anger churning inside. 'How dare she come here? This is my home.' In spite of herself there was a catch in her voice.

'Should have set the dog on her,' Tony said.

Carol laughed. Shaky and spluttering, but a laugh never-theless. 'Death by a thousand licks.' She turned to face him, eyes sparkling with unshed tears. 'Do you want to talk about Kathryn McCormick?'

He shrugged and began to pace. The dog eyed him uneas-ily, her eyes following him. 'I've nothing to say. There's nothing to get hold of so far. The only interesting thing is that the killer picked her up at a wedding. But we've no way of knowing whether he went there to pick up Kathryn specifi-cally or just to acquire any random victim. We can't even say whether he went to the wedding to find a victim or whether he seized a passing opportunity. So there's really no point in talking about it till we know more.'

'What about the body dump?'

Tony stopped by the window that looked up the black moorside. 'He chose it carefully. No cameras. A quiet road, so not much risk of witnesses. But that's a description that fits a lot of places in the Dales. Why that one?'

'OK. Why that one?'

He threw himself down on a sofa. 'I have no bloody idea. I can't profile a single instance, you know that. I need more.

So as far as I'm concerned, this would be a good time to teach you how to play FIFA 17.'

'I hate football.'

He grinned. 'Trust me. This isn't football, it's fun.'

21

The drive from Telford to Cardiff had been a nightmare. An accident on the M5 had brought traffic to a standstill for almost two hours and by the time Kevin had crossed the Severn and entered Wales, all he was fit for was a pint, a pizza and bed. But he still managed to be on Niall Sullivan's doorstep at half past seven next morning in the teeth of a fine drizzle that was doubling the weight of his leather jacket.

He took a moment to assess where Sullivan was living before he hit the bell. It was on the edge of what were called executive developments when they were jacked up in the eighties but this one hadn't worn well. The brickwork looked dirty and pockmarked. Several of the houses betrayed their shoddiness with watermarks and stains on the stucco of the upper storey. Sullivan's home, a two-storey detached house, looked in decent repair, though. A bit tired and dated, but cared for. In the drive, a new BMW 4-series convertible and a Mini. Looked like Niall had replaced Kathryn, Kevin thought. Which bumped him down the suspect list.

But still, the hoops had to be jumped through. Kevin pressed the bell, letting a long peal ring through the house.

Through the door he could hear the sound of feet clattering down stairs and the door opened on a frowning bear of a man with a thatch of damp auburn hair. He was dressed in suit trousers, a navy shirt with the top button undone and a pair of Chelsea boots, which explained the noisy descent of the open-plan staircase Kevin could see over his shoulder. 'Yeah?' he demanded. 'What?'

'Niall Sullivan?' Kevin produced his ID and held it up. 'I'm Detective Inspector Kevin Matthews from the Regional Major Incident Team based in Bradfield.' He couldn't help it, but it still gave him a buzz to use the rank he'd been stripped of years before. Carol had dangled its restoration in front of him as a bribe to get him to come out of retirement and he'd leaped at the chance, not merely to up his pension but to redeem himself in his own eyes. He was as proud of it now as when he'd first won the promotion.

Sullivan tightened his mouth in an expression of distaste. 'This is about Kathryn, right?'

'You've heard about—'

'This is 2017, not 1917,' Sullivan interrupted. 'I've lost count of the number of messages I got yesterday. As soon as you lot turned up at her office, the word spread faster than Ed Sheeran's downloads. Look, I'm sorry she's dead, of course I am. We were together a long time. But I don't know what you're doing here. I moved down more than three years ago and I've only seen Kathryn twice since then.'

'You didn't keep in touch?'

He scoffed. 'Hardly. Once she realised I was serious about moving without her, things got pretty frosty between us.'

A woman's bare legs appeared on the stairs behind him. 'What's occurring, Niall?' Kevin could hear the Welsh accent even in those few words.

Sullivan glanced over his shoulder. 'It's nothing, just get in the shower.'

The rest of her appeared wrapped in a dressing gown that stopped in the middle of her tanned thighs. She had a tousled mane of blonde hair and a pert face bare of make-up. 'Who's this, then?'

Kevin introduced himself again as she descended.

'I'm Pippa,' she said. 'Niall, invite the nice man in. It's bloody draughty with that door wide open. Come on, Inspector, I'll make you a cup of tea.'

'Pippa?' Sullivan protested but he'd already lost and he knew it. He sighed and stepped back, pointing down the hall to where Pippa had disappeared into the kitchen. 'Let's keep this quick and to the point,' he muttered at Kevin's back as he followed him. 'I've got a busy day ahead of me.'

Like Pippa herself, the kitchen had all the right stuff in the right places but it lacked any sense of cosiness. It resembled the set-dressing of a show house. One that Kevin definitely wouldn't have bought. His Stella would have roared with contemptuous laughter at it.

Pippa made the tea, managing to invest that simple job with a look-at-me performance. Kevin leaned against the counter and smiled at Sullivan. 'So when did you last see Kathryn?'

Sullivan studied the ceiling. 'Let me see ... It must have been October. We were both at the same wedding. Gayle Thomas. She used to work for me. She got to be pals with Kathryn.'

That chimed with what the McCormicks had told Kevin. So far, Sullivan appeared to be telling the truth. 'How did the meeting go? At the wedding?'

Sullivan shook his head in frustration. 'It wasn't a meeting. We didn't speak. I saw her across the room. That's all. She didn't even catch my eye. I don't suppose she wanted to talk to me any more than I did her. Look, we were over. Done. There was nothing left between us.' He was, Kevin thought, protesting a bit too much. Was that for Pippa's benefit, or was Sullivan hiding something?

'She was no match for you,' Pippa stated firmly as she handed Kevin a mug of tea with too much milk. Baby tea, he thought.

'We do have to explore every avenue,' Kevin said.

'Are you saying she hadn't had a boyfriend since Niall left? I mean, if there were other men in her life, you wouldn't be here, would you?' Pippa's smile was malicious.

'I can't discuss the investigation with you, sorry. I do however need to ask, sir, where you were on Sunday evening.'

'He was with me,' Pippa said. 'We went for a curry down the Brewery Quarter with four of the team from work.' She squeezed Sullivan's arm as she handed him his tea. 'Then we went clubbing. So he wasn't setting fire to his ex in Yorkshire, was he?'

It sounded very much as if she was right. 'I'll need their names and contact details,' he said, knowing as he spoke it would be a waste of time. But then, so much of what they did in a murder investigation was a waste of time.

Sullivan nodded. 'Give me your phone number, I'll ping them over to you.' As Kevin fished in his pocket for a card, the man continued. 'I had no hard feelings towards Kathryn. I didn't hate her. I just got bored. She didn't have any—' He waggled his hands, searching for the word. 'Get up and go. She wanted everything to carry on the way it was. Me, I wanted more.' His smile was rueful. 'I'm not a bad man, Inspector. We weren't right for each other, me and Kathryn, that's the top and bottom of it. No way did she deserve this. She was a decent person.'

'No enemies? Nobody bothering her at work or among the neighbours?'

Sullivan shook his head. 'She wasn't the sort to make enemies. She didn't really rouse strong feelings, Kathryn. When

I was working up to leaving, I couldn't even remember how we ended up together in the first place.' He patted Pippa's backside and his face lit up. 'Not like with you.'

There was nothing more for him here, Kevin thought, his heart sinking at the prospect of the long drive north. 'Thanks for the tea,' he said.

As they walked back down the hall, Niall said, 'I hope you catch the bastard who did this. I totally don't understand how it could have happened. Truly, Kathryn wasn't the sort of woman to provoke a reaction on that scale from anybody. We were out one night in town, and we ran into somebody she'd sacked a few months before. And this lad she'd given the bullet to, he couldn't have been nicer to her. When she told me afterwards that she'd been the one to give him the elbow, I couldn't believe it. I'm not saying she'd win a popularity contest. She didn't have charisma. But she was genuinely inoffensive.' He shook his head. 'Whatever happened to kick this off, I'd lay money that it wasn't anything Kathryn did.'

They shook hands on the doorstep. 'We'll do our best,' Kevin said. He walked back to his car, pondering what Niall had said. What if Kathryn's death truly was nothing to do with her? What did that mean for the investigation?

That, he reckoned, was one for Tony Hill.

22

Kevin wasn't the only member of the ReMIT squad making an early start. But what drove Paula out of the house before Torin had even descended for breakfast was nothing to do with Kathryn McCormick's murder. Procrastination had never been one of her faults, but if it had been, living with a teenager would have given her pause. If you put things off, before you knew it, you'd missed the bus and it was too late to achieve the pay-off you hoped for. Nothing stayed in the same place for long with adolescents; even when it looked like all Torin was doing was vegging out, things were constantly changing in his world.

So after the conversation she'd had with Elinor the previous morning, she'd emailed Torin's form teacher and asked for a meeting. Paula still hadn't quite got her head round the way communication between teachers and parents had changed. When she'd been a kid growing up in Manchester, the only time the two groups ever met was parents' evening, when the teachers basically laid down the law and parents nodded obligingly. Because obviously the teachers knew best. Otherwise they wouldn't be teachers, would they? Parents were only ever summoned to the school when their child had committed some heinous offence and the notion of a parent taking the side of their child against the monolithic phalanx of the educational establishment was laughable.

But these days, parents and guardians were expected to take an active role in their children's education. It was all a bit novel for Paula. But at least it meant that when a problem did emerge, she wouldn't have to start from scratch with a total stranger. Still, she'd taken care with her appearance that morning, keen to make a good impression. She'd even dried her hair properly and rubbed styling paste in to give some shape to her dirty-blonde bob. Linen suit fresh out of the dry cleaner's bag and a scoop-necked navy top underneath. Silver earrings like fingerprints and a thin silver chain finished the job. She wasn't going to put the fear of death into any bad guys looking like this, for sure.

Lorna Meikle had been Torin's form teacher when his mother had been murdered. She'd been supportive and concerned, taking his change of circumstances in her stride but never for granted. Elinor and Paula had warmed to her when she'd worked with them to develop a strategy for helping him recover the ground he'd lost in his grief at Bev's death. There had been no problems since and they hadn't seen her for a while except for the last parents' evening, where the focus had been Torin's potential choice of A Level subjects. But when Paula had messaged her, she'd responded immediately and agreed to meet before school began.

The traffic was heavy, but Paula knew all the back-doubles and she cut through the narrow alleys between streets like a teenage joyrider trying to evade capture. She made it to the school with ten minutes to spare. Lorna Meikle was pulling up in her car as Paula locked up and they walked to the building together, making small talk till they turned into Torin's form room.

Lorna was a matronly woman in her late forties. She'd taken a career break to have her own three kids and she had the air of someone who took in her stride whatever the world might throw at her. But there was a steely edge there, and Paula had seen from the first that the kids respected her. Sometimes that respect was grudging; there were plenty of pupils who could never be described as students, kids with no realistic aspirations or ambitions, who saw school as a battle they had to survive then escape. But still, as Torin said, 'Nobody messes with Mrs M.'

In the classroom, Lorna subsided into her chair, settling her comfortable bulk with a sigh. 'I swear every year here puts five years on me,' she grumbled genially.

'You should try my job.' Paula perched on one of the desks. 'Though mind you, I'd rather have mine than yours or Elinor's.'

'Indeed. So, Paula, what's going on with Torin? I presume that's why you're here and not out of some professional concern?'

'I was hoping you could answer that question,' Paula said.

'How are things at home?'

'He's been ... different the last two or three weeks. Very quiet. Hard to communicate with, which isn't like him. It's not like he was after his mother died. There's something quite—' Paula paused for a moment. 'Edgy, almost. Stressed. Have you noticed any change in his behaviour?'

Lorna nodded. 'Like you, I find it hard to put my finger on what it is. Something is clearly bothering him. It's as if there's something he keeps glimpsing out of the corner of his eye that he doesn't want to look at, if that makes any sense?'

Oddly enough, Paula thought it captured exactly how Torin had been. 'We wondered if he was being bullied?'

Lorna sighed. 'It's the obvious assumption, I'll grant you that. But I really don't think it's bullying. He's not isolated.

He has a group of friends who seem to be quite protective of him. And he's not doing that thing bullied children do, where they want to stay around the grown-ups at break and lunchtime.'

'What about cyber-bullying? Could that be happening?'

'It's always a possibility, but again, I think his behaviour would be different. We've talked a lot to the students about cyber-bullying and trolling. We have a zero-tolerance policy, and there is evidence that it works.'

'What kind of evidence?' Paula wasn't about to let a state-ment like that go past her without having it backed up.

'We've had several instances where trolling and bullying have been reported to us. Either by the student themselves or by someone from their peer group.' Lorna gave Paula a reassuring smile. 'We do encourage them to protect each other as well as themselves.'

Paula shook her head. 'That doesn't mean it works every time. If it's happening outside school—'

'I believe it would show up on their social media and their friends would pick it up. If Torin was a loner, a boy without friends, I'd say it might slip past. But that's not who he is, Paula.'

'So if it's not bullying, what is it?'

Lorna frowned. 'I don't know. It's true that his work is suf-fering. It's as if he can't focus. As if something's distracting him.'

'Something that's worrying him to the point where he can't concentrate?'

'Yes, that's how I'd characterise it.'

Paula hesitated for a moment then went for it. 'Has he got a girlfriend? Might that be what's going on here?'

A swift bright smile lit up Lorna's face. 'I don't think so, no. He's not, forgive me, as sexually and emotionally pre-cocious as some of them. He does hang out with a mixed group, boys and girls. But I don't see any evidence of him pairing off with anyone.' She raised an eyebrow. 'We can usually tell.'

'But what if it was someone he didn't want to acknowledge for some reason? What if they had to keep it hidden and that's what's stressing him?'

Lorna shifted in her chair, her expression troubled. 'I suppose that might produce the effects we've both noticed. But I know the girls in that group and I can't imagine why he would be secretive about any of them.'

'What if it's not one of them? What if the secrecy's not about him but about her? Maybe she's somebody else's girlfriend? Maybe her family wouldn't like her seeing someone like him?'

'Maybe she's pregnant,' Lorna said. 'I think that would trump either of your scenarios.'

Paula couldn't keep the look of horror from her face. 'I hadn't even thought of that.' She swallowed hard. It made a terrible kind of sense. 'You don't think . . . ?'

'I'm not trying to panic you, Paula. As I said, I don't think he's got a girlfriend, so my suggestion was purely academic. But the way he's acting would be what I'd expect if it was something of that order troubling him.'

'There's no evidence of a girlfriend.' Paula spoke slowly, thinking aloud. 'No sudden attention to grooming or fashion. And he hardly ever goes out, even at weekends. But what else would have the same emotional impact as getting a girlfriend pregnant?'

Lorna shrugged. 'I can't help you there. But we need to work out what's troubling him. I don't want him blowing his GCSEs and his future chances over it.'

'Do you think it's drugs?' It was the obvious question. It was also obvious that Lorna wasn't going to introduce the subject. Schools were always reluctant to acknowledge the problem to parents. Never mind to a parent who was a police officer.

'I'd be surprised.'

'What? This is the only school in Bradfield that doesn't have drug issues among its students?'

Lorna sighed. 'Look, I won't deny there's a small but significant level of drug abuse among our students. But there's a definite demarcation line between habitual users and the rest, and Torin doesn't appear to have any social connections that would lead me to believe he's using recreational drugs.' Her expression twisted into a bitter smile. 'I've seen enough kids in the classroom who are clearly under the influence of drugs or coming down after they've been high. I know the markers and the symptoms and I would have no hesitation in telling you if I thought Torin's using. For his own sake, I'd tell you. But I don't think he is. You're going to have to look somewhere else for your answer, Paula.'

'Well, I am supposed to be a detective,' she said wearily, checking her watch. 'And I need to be on my way. Thanks for your time, Lorna. And if anything does occur to you . . . '

'I'll be in touch.'

Frustrated at the lack of answers, Paula headed for her car and the morning briefing. Time to put Torin to one side and concentrate on a different set of frustrations.

23

He studied his reflection in the mirror, paying particular attention to his hair. The temporary dye had promised to wash out in two to three shampoos, and he was pleased to see the familiar threads of silver had reappeared at his temples. Attention to detail, that was what survival was all about. If he took care to protect himself, he'd evade capture and he could carry on with his plans for as long as it took to make him feel right with the world again.

If anyone had caught him on camera at the wedding in Leeds where he'd picked up Amie – and he thought he'd avoided that – they wouldn't have a snap of the man called David who had swept Kathryn McCormick off her feet. They'd see Mark. Dark brown hair swept back from his forehead, round gold-rimmed glasses, the shadow of designer stubble along his jaw. It was amazing how little it took to look very different. The glasses seemed to change the shape of his face; the hairstyle and the stubble created a very different image from clean-cut David. If by some outrageous coincidence anyone had attended both wedding parties, he thought they'd have struggled to make the connection.

Because the hair dye washed out so effectively, he didn't have to worry that anyone he was in regular contact with would see these shifts in appearance. Colleagues he could confidently bluff. If a journalist or one of the advertising and marketing team commented on the stubble, he'd laugh it off as a new look he was trying out. And in a couple of weeks, he'd let the stubble grow out into a goatee for the next round of shape-shifting.

He was almost beginning to revel in the challenge. He needed the buzz he got from playing these women, practising for the real thing. When he managed to track down Tricia and make her pay, he'd know exactly what he was doing. There would be no mis-steps, no clues left behind.

Tracking her down, that was his other priority. She'd done a good job of disappearing. Her phone was dead, her email address defunct, her social media accounts closed down. The lawyer who had contacted him on her behalf wouldn't even say whether she was still in the country. And the bank wouldn't tell him where she'd last drawn out money on the joint business account. He'd asked around all their friends but either they didn't know or they weren't prepared to tell him. He was sure he'd find her, given time. But she'd set him a challenge.

Which was not something he could call Amie. She'd been eager from the moment he'd spoken to her in the crowded, noisy ballroom. Whisking her away to a quiet corner had been a bit harder; she was a good few years younger than Kathryn, and unlike her, Amie was a woman who enjoyed the dance floor, with all its opportunities to show herself off. But he'd played the quiet guy, the one who wanted to get to know the real Amie. And the line about how she reminded him of his poor dead wife had been the sucker bait that drew her away from the hubbub and into his conversational web. She was all over the idea of a date, though she'd clearly been leaning more towards clubbing than chatting. But still, she'd been willing to let him lead the dance for now.

He'd spent half an hour on the internet, checking out the Indian restaurants in Leeds before he'd settled on one on the edge of the city centre that had plenty of positive reviews for the food but also, if the photos on the website were to be believed, a modern ambience a million miles away from paper tablecloths and cheap red napkins that disintegrated at the first sign of liquid.

His research paid off. Amie had never been there, but she knew people who swore by it. And the reviews had got it spot on. The food was South Indian, subtle and delicious in its flavours. The paper dosa had been a little greasy; he hated that slick of oil that fried food left on the fingers. But apart from that, it had been a success. A few glasses of wine and Amie had become more garrulous, telling him how she kept looking for someone to share her life with but none of the men she'd been involved with had been willing to put in the effort that a partnership demanded.

It hadn't been too hard to indicate that he was different from them. The odd word here and there, the occasional remark that made him look like a good catch. A considerate nod, a conspiratorial smile; that was all it took.

She'd been completely on the hook by the end of the meal. So much so that she'd invited him back to her place. There was no doubting what was on offer, and he had to admit, he'd been tempted. She wasn't bad looking and it had been weeks since he'd fucked anyone. It was only after he'd been left high and dry that he'd realised how much the sex meant to him. Plenty of it, and plenty of variety. They'd been great in bed together, him and Tricia. And not just in bed . . .

But he knew he'd be crazy to respond to Amie's come-on. He couldn't go to her place and fuck her without leaving a forensic trail a mile wide. And then when she turned up dead, his DNA would be in the mix. OK, he'd never done anything to earn a place on the national DNA database so it wouldn't lead the police to his door. Better safe than sorry, though. If he ever crossed swords with the law, he didn't want to risk Amie McDonald showing up like a big flashing light in his past.

So he'd fallen back on the dead-wife scenario again. 'I'm very touched,' he'd said when she suggested going back to hers for a nightcap. 'And I really like you, Amie. I want to see you again. And I want to get to know you properly. You see, I haven't slept with anyone since Tricia died—' He let his voice catch as if in grief. Really, it was more like delight, killing off his ex with his words the way he couldn't chance doing in reality. 'So I want it to matter. To both of us.'

She'd looked taken aback. As if she wasn't used to men saying no to the chance of bedding her. Then she'd laughed softly. 'You're a very unusual man, Mark,' she'd said.

'That's nice of you to say so,' he said. *You have no idea.* 'So, what are you doing on Friday?'

So they'd arranged to meet for another dinner. This time, he offered to drive out to a country pub where they could relax over a good dinner. Somewhere he could readily pay in cash, as he'd done in the Indian restaurant. Another way to avoid forensic traces.

He was the invisible man. He chose his targets, he struck and he disappeared back into his unblemished life.

Nothing could touch him now.

24

It was soon clear that the morning briefing was to be a report of the absence of evidence rather than its presence. One by one, the ReMIT team reported the scant results of their inquiries. Finally, all eyes turned to Stacey, sitting demurely at the far end of the table, immaculate in a teal blue suit and a shimmering navy silk shirt. Carol gave her a tired smile. 'So, Stacey, we're all counting on you.'

Stacey smoothed her already perfect hair and nodded. 'I have something, but not much, I'm afraid. And what I have is pushing the technology to its limits.' She took a clicker from her pocket and activated the white screen mounted on the wall behind her. Half-turning in her chair, she brought up the shot that featured the man Anya had identified as being the one she'd seen with Kathryn. 'This is the raw phone-camera file. Not very clear, as you can see. When we enhance it and use the predictive pixel software, we get this.'

The screen dissolved to reveal an isolated image of the man's quarter-profile. It was sharper and clearer than the original but still not a shot they could credibly use to identify someone. 'So, what I used next was facial recognition software. Like I said to Alvin, I've tweaked the original to make it more powerful. I ran all the pics we have from the wedding through it.' Another dissolve and three photos appeared side by side. None of them was full-face and all of them had been blown up from figures in the background.

'He did a bloody good job of staying out of sight,' Alvin muttered. 'These days, everybody's a photographer, especially at big occasions like weddings.'

'Was that deliberate, do we think? Or just that he wasn't in the room for very long?' Carol asked.

'Both, I suspect,' Tony said. 'We already know he's a careful planner. There's no reason to believe he'd throw caution to the wind before he's even acquired his victim. I think we have to assume everything is calculated in this approach.'

Stacey nodded. 'But even the most tech-savvy person probably doesn't realise how far the technology has come. Even with scant resources like this, the latest algorithms can predict a full-face image of our man.' This time, a single image appeared. It had the slightly unreal look that CGI often produced, but it looked recognisably like a person.

'That's amazing,' Paula said. 'So I guess we can show this to the wedding guests who remember seeing Kathryn with him to see whether it's a decent likeness.'

'That makes sense. Alvin, you've already established a relationship with these women. Go back and show them this image. Stacey, make up a six-pack for Alvin so nobody can accuse us of skewing the ID towards a suspect further down the line.'

'I'm on it,' Stacey said, getting up from the table and heading back to her den. Alvin shook his head ruefully and followed her a moment later.

'It's a good lead,' Kevin pointed out.

Tony, who had been staring intently at the image since Stacey had first summoned it, chewed the end of his pen. 'It's suggestive,' he acknowledged.

'It's more than suggestive,' Carol said. 'It's got the potential to be a key breakthrough.'

'You think?' Tony dropped his pen to the table with a clatter.

'Don't you?' Carol looked puzzled.

'That thing I know you do when you meet someone new, Carol? That thing where you automatically catalogue how you would describe them to the rest of us,' Tony said. 'So how would you describe this man?'

Carol considered, tilting her head to one side. 'Mid-thirties. Brown hair going grey above his ears, side parting, floppy fringe. Eye colour probably blue. Though it's hard to tell. Rectangular black framed glasses, very much on trend. Thick eyebrows, large nose.'

'And which one of those characteristics is fixed? Which of them couldn't you change quite readily?

The others looked at each other, troubled. 'He's right,' Paula said. 'They could all be altered without too much trouble.'

'His nose?' Karim wasn't convinced.

'Remember Nicole Kidman's nose in *The Hours*?' Paula said.

Karim scoffed. 'I think I was ten when that came out, skip. Twelve, maybe, at the outside.'

Paula rolled her eyes. 'She had this false nose that you couldn't spot, even in close-up. It completely changed the way she looked. When they showed it to preview audiences, people didn't even realise it was Kidman.'

'That's movies. They can make anybody look any way they want,' Karim protested.

'The fake nose Kidman had was so realistic she wore it out in public to avoid recognition,' Paula retorted. 'It fooled people in the street, it fooled the paparazzi.'

'How do you know this stuff?' Kevin chuckled.

Tony held up a hand. 'The nose might be the real thing. Having a prosthetic nose made might be a step too far for our man. But apart from that, all we have are a collection of features that could be altered without much trouble.'

'You're saying this photo is a waste of time.' Carol sounded grim.

'I'm saying we'd be making a mistake to rely on it.' Tony looked around at the glum faces and gave a hesitant smile. 'You know I'm right.' The look they shared told him they agreed, much as they hated to admit it.

'Still,' Carol said. 'A nose is better than nothing. Let's see what we can sniff out, eh?'

25

There were three branches of Pizza Express in Bradfield and no way of knowing which one Kathryn and David had visited on the Tuesday after the wedding. Karim looked at the app on his phone that stuck little purple pins in the map to show their locations. He remembered what Tony had said at the briefing about the caution and planning already evident in their killer's behaviour and considered what he knew of the CCTV cameras that covered the city centre. Not enough, he decided.

He glanced across at the closed door of Stacey's office and took a deep breath. He was the new boy on this team and still the outsider. Nobody had deliberately made him feel unwelcome, but it was clear that everyone else knew each other and trusted each other's way of working. Nobody had that level of confidence in him yet; sometimes in his peripheral vision he caught his colleagues cutting their eyes at him when he'd stepped out of line or asked a stupid question. Even Paula, the friendliest of the lot, sometimes rolled her eyes when he didn't know something he had no way of knowing. He didn't think any of it was meant unkindly, but he didn't feel anyone was cutting him much slack.

As for Stacey? She terrified him. She appeared to know more about data systems than any human should and she didn't waste her time interacting with carbon-based life forms like him. She dressed the way he thought an AI office robot might, in impeccably fitted suits and blouses made of fabric that seemed to have a life independent of its wearer. As if that wasn't enough, word was that she'd turned her skills to profitable use. Stacey Chen could buy and sell the lot of them if she felt like it.

Altogether it added up to a recipe for terror for a nice boy like Karim, who still sort of lived at home, in the granny flat above the garage that his mother had reluctantly let him move into after his actual granny had died. His mother still behaved like he was twelve, checking up on what he had in the fridge and how full his laundry basket was. All his life he'd been under the thumb of women and it seemed like ReMIT was designed to be more of the same.

So he really shouldn't be scared of Stacey, should he? She didn't have the power over him that his mother or the aunties had. How much scalding contempt could she pour over his head?

Before he could change his mind, Karim jumped up and hustled through to Stacey's office, not waiting for a response to his knock. Stacey was encased in her ergonomic chair behind her screens, Alvin at her side, peering over her shoulder. Stacey didn't even look up but Alvin glanced his way. 'Hey, Karim. You after the human computer here?'

Stacey tutted, not taking her eye off the top-right screen. Her fingers darted back and forth over the keyboard. 'There,' she said. 'Number six. Now go forth and put your witnesses to the test.'

To Karim's ears it sounded more like an invitation to put the witnesses to the sword. 'Have you got a minute, Stacey?' he asked, trying not to sound timid.

Stacey leaned back and rolled her shoulders to loosen her back. 'What do you need?' she asked, her voice neutral.

'I'm trying to prioritise the Pizza Express branches that David might have taken Kathryn to,' he said. 'Bearing in mind what Tony said about him being careful about forensic traces, I thought he might have chosen the venue based on the number of CCTV cameras that could pick up him or his car.'

Stacey flashed a smile so swift he wondered whether he'd hallucinated it. 'Good thinking. You want me to map the restaurants on to the CCTV maps, is that it?'

He nodded, relieved that his idea hadn't been dismissed. 'Please. If that's possible?'

Already her fingers were dancing, her eyes shifting between screens. 'Come round here,' she said.

Obediently, he rounded the IT set-up and stood at her shoulder, keeping his distance. Stacey pointed at the middle screen in the top row. 'That's your restaurants. On the left are the traffic cameras. On the right, Bradfield Council street cameras.' She clicked her trackpad and the maps on either side flowed to the central map, overlaying the original. 'I'll send it to your terminal,' she said.

He grinned. 'That's brilliant, thanks.'

'Not quite finished yet,' she said absently, scrolling through another menu. 'OK. This is inevitably incomplete and probably not entirely accurate, but it shows the private CCTV systems we're aware of in the city centre. Banks, shops, takeaways, that sort of thing.' She clicked again and the new map overlaid the original composite. 'I'm sending that to you as a separate file, just for reference in case you get a positive ID and need to attempt a backtrack on his movements. Good luck.'

It was a dismissal. Stacey was already on to the next task before he'd even left her side. Karim went back to his desk and printed out both maps. On the first one, he also marked the location of the tapas restaurant where Kathryn and David had gone for their second meal together.

While he was poring over the printout, Tony pulled up a chair and sat down beside him. 'What are you trying to figure out?' he asked.

Karim explained his theory and Tony nodded approval. 'It makes sense that he'd scout out possible destinations. This one, for example.' He pointed to a Pizza Express in the middle of Temple Fields, an area of the city centre known for the vibrancy and variety of its nightlife. 'All the streets round there are bristling with cameras because of the levels of street crime.'

'And drug dealing,' Karim added. 'They've stepped up patrols because of the amount of people getting off their heads on spice down the bottom end of Temple Fields, down towards Campion Boulevard. So I'd put that at the bottom of the list of possibles.' He traced a line on the map with his finger. 'But this one ... You come off High Market Street which, OK, has lots of cameras, but it's still crowded even at that time on a Friday evening. Into the lane down the blank side of Debenhams and all you have to do is turn the corner and you're there.'

'Looks good. What's this you've circled in pen?'

'Tapas Brava. I was a bit surprised he took her there, to be honest. It's smack bang in the middle of Bellwether Square and that's got to have more cameras per square metre than anywhere in Bradfield.'

'But most of them are private ones. They tend to be focused on the shopfront or the cash machine or whatever, not so much on the street. And actually, Tapas Brava is a pretty clever choice. Look. You can hardly see it on the map, but that's Raddle Alley. It's too narrow to walk two abreast, and it cuts through from Groat Market, down the road from Central Station.'

Karim followed Tony's finger. 'I see it. I don't know how I've missed it. I couldn't count the number of times I've been in Bellwether Square but I've never even noticed it was there.'

'It's a shortcut from town back to where my boat's moored up in Minster Basin. That's the only reason I know it. And it's right next to Tapas Brava.'

Karim stood up, folding the printout and putting it in the inside pocket of his jacket. 'I'd better crack on then,' he said, feeling more optimistic than he had when the actions for the day had been handed out.

By lunchtime, Karim had to admit that optimism had been unfounded. Nobody at any of the busy Pizza Express branches remembered serving Kathryn and David. One of the duty managers had pointed out that they served hundreds of customers every day and unless they were a Bradfield Victoria footballer or some minor celebrity, or they'd kicked off about something, there was no chance the waiting staff would remember the faces.

Karim had asked about the possibility of checking their credit card receipts for the evening in question and the manager had laughed at him. 'No chance, mate,' he'd said. 'Even if you could get a warrant, it'd be useless. People don't just use personal credit cards. They use company cards, joint account cards. It'd be a total needle-in-a-haystack job. And besides, they might have paid cash. You still get some people that do. Because they're old-fashioned or' – he winked – 'they don't want it showing up on their credit-card statement.'

He'd saved Tapas Bravas till last because it was a much smaller establishment. There were only a dozen tables and a further fourteen seats at the long zinc counter. It was dimly lit, the dark wood of the furniture and the floor balanced by bright modern prints by artists Karim couldn't even begin to guess at. He'd arrived at the height of the lunchtime rush and, realising it wasn't the right time to gain the full attention of the staff, he swallowed his guilt and took the last available stool at the bar. He was entitled to a meal break, he told himself, while also recognising that on this squad nobody paid any attention to things like overtime and regular breaks. Karim told himself it was a legitimate way to ingratiate himself with potential witnesses and ordered a plate of chipirones and half a dozen fish croquetas.

By the time he'd slowly worked his way through the small plates of unfamiliar but delicious food, the place had more or less emptied out and he snagged a passing waitress. He showed her the pictures of Kathryn and David, explaining why he was there. She shrugged her lack of recognition but sent her colleagues over anyway.

One waiter, a young Spaniard who'd been working at Tapas Brava for five months, seemed less absolute than the others in his lack of recognition. When Karim reminded him of the date, he nodded. 'I think, but I'm not sure.' He pointed to a corner table behind them. 'I think maybe table eight.'

'What do you remember about them?'

'If it was them, he paid in cash. And she said, and this is what I remember, "Do the staff get the tips?" So I tell her, we keep the cash tips but we only get half of the ones that go on the credit card.'

'Is there any way of finding out the name the table was booked in?'

He shrugged. 'We can look.'

Karim followed him to the computer screen where the bookings were managed, his heart beating a little faster. With the date and the time and the table number, it was easy to locate. 'It is here,' the waiter said. 'Eight o'clock. It was booked in the name of David and here is the phone number.'

Karim's face fell. He didn't have to check his notes to

know that this was the same pay-as-you-go number that Kathryn had had for David. A further twenty minutes questioning the waiter and his colleagues took him no further forward. Nobody remembered anything about the couple on table eight. Not what they were wearing, not how they had behaved towards each other. Nothing.

It looked like Tony had been right. The man who had killed Kathryn McCormick had done nothing on impulse.

26

A few hours later, on the other side of Pennines, Amie McDonald was putting on her glad rags, ready for another date with Mark. He was bloody lovely, she thought. A true gentleman; not a 'wham, bam, thank you, ma'am' merchant. He listened when she talked, he paid attention and responded to what she said. Obviously he was still holding a bit of a candle to his ex, and it wasn't easy, going head to head with the dead because they could always trump you simply by being dead. But even though she was quite a bit younger than him, he'd obviously taken to Amie, otherwise he wouldn't be taking her out again. It stood to reason. And age difference was no big deal these days, not now men had learned to take better care of their looks and their figures like women did.

She carefully applied her most expensive mascara, the one that claimed to double the volume and never to smudge. If she was going to get him into bed tonight, she didn't want to wake up with panda eyes and black smudges all over the pillow. With a final touch-up of her lippie, she was ready to go.

Amie picked up her phone then, as she was about to put it in her bag, she had a sudden thought. Jamie would be chuffed to bits to know she'd got so lucky at his wedding. She tapped out a quick text message.

Hiya Gorgeous. Hope you and El are having a fab time. You weren't the only ones who struck it lucky at the wedding. I'm off on a second date with El's dishy friend Mark, a million times more fab than scuzzy Steve!!! Wish me luck!!! xxx

It really did feel like the start of something big. Amie had been convinced she'd found Mr Right before but there was something different about Mark. Something special. She had a funny feeling that he was the one.

And in a way that wasn't funny at all, she was right.

One of the many things Tony liked about Carol was that she didn't speak for the sake of hearing her own voice. She talked when she had something to say. Sometimes she had questions she thought he might be able to help her answer. Other times she had observations she wanted to test against his experience and understanding. Occasionally she wanted to think out loud, throwing the bones of a theory in the dirt to see what shape they might make. Very rarely, she opened up some seam of information about herself, almost against her will.

But if she had nothing to offer, she didn't feel the need to fill the space with noise. Mostly, silence between them was easy. Lately, however, there had been too many occasions where it had been electric, crackling with the tension of the things unsaid. Her fight against alcohol had made for contentious exchanges and, if that were possible, even more contentious silences. Tony, empathetic to the point of self-harming, felt the pain of her abstinence as powerfully as anything he'd ever endured personally.

That evening, they'd exchanged barely a word on the drive back from Bradfield. It was an early finish for them and Tony suspected Carol felt an unreasonable guilt at leaving ReMIT while there was still light in the sky. Habitually, when she was working a murder, she was seldom away from the case for more than half a dozen hours of snatched sleep at a time. And even then her phone would be on the bedside table next to her, the ringer turned up full.

But there was nothing more to be done in the case of the murder of Kathryn McCormick. North Yorkshire officers on the ground were carrying out routine inquiries to try to track down how the car had ended up where it had, but Tony suspected they were wasting their time. This man knew what he was doing.

The forensic specialists would do their thing and deliver their results in due course, but none of Carol's team truly believed that would take them any further forward. The fire had destroyed any chance of DNA. The firefighters had destroyed any possibility of fingermarks on the bodywork of the car. There might be some toxicology results from the largely incinerated organs of the dead woman, but even if there were, the chances of that producing something so out of the ordinary that it would have any probative value were infinitesimally small. The only outside chance was that the forensic chemists might find a chemical signature among the charred remains that would be distinctive.

What that might be, none of them could imagine.

Normally the victim would lead them towards the killer. Most murders were domestic affairs. Spouses, partners, children, friends. The webs that connected the two people whose lives had collided fatally were generally obvious, even if the motives were sometimes obscure or apparently trivial. Even when strangers attacked, there were usually markers of where their paths had crossed.

So far, they appeared to have mapped the point where Kathryn McCormick met her killer. From all Tony had read and heard, she had been a slightly dull, pleasant woman. Even the people who worked under her were unwilling to speak critically of her. She seemed to have no gift for friendship but equally no talent for creating enmity. She wasn't unattractive but it seemed she lacked any charisma when it came to attracting men. He saw her as someone determinedly making the most of very little. The telling detail for him was Paula's mention of Kathryn's apparent love of cooking. Even though she had nobody to feed, she'd devoted a lot of time and money to what could be an adventurous and challenging hobby. She was trying to do something that marked her out as special. The kind of thing that a certain type of magazine promoted as a way to keep a man satisfied. That she'd chosen that route rather than the obvious Fifty Ways To Satisfy Your Man In Bed did tell Tony something about her killer.

The man who called himself David had made a clever and deliberate choice of victim. He hadn't gone for an easy pick-up. If all he'd wanted was sex and violence, he could have picked up someone in a club who was too drunk or high to care who she went home with. He could have found someone desperate for a substitute for love in a late-night bar. But this man had something else in mind. He needed something different for his satisfaction. He needed somebody who was looking for love and was in the right frame of mind to find it.

'He needed to be able to believe she'd fallen for him,' he said out loud when they were almost back at the barn.

'What?' Carol sounded startled, as if she too had been lost in thought.

'It's important to him. What he did with Kathryn, he

courted her. He chose her because he thought he could make her fall in love with him. He picked her carefully. Everybody at a wedding is in a state of heightened emotion. A woman on her own, chances are she's in a vulnerable state. She sees happy ever after all around her. But she's on her own. On the outside looking in. Then out of nowhere, Mr Well-Groomed Nice Guy whisks her away from the noise and the in-your-face confection of romance to something like the real thing.'

'You think that's what this was? A romance?' Carol sounded curious rather than dismissive. She'd been on the end of his explorations and explanations for long enough to trust his insights. Not always right on the money, but seldom far off. She signalled the turn that took them on to the back road leading to her barn, the road where all her recent troubles had started.

'A simulacrum of a romance,' he said thoughtfully. 'You know I hate to jump to conclusions on the basis of one murder, but that's the only obvious theory that fits the facts we have. I might be completely wrong but it makes sense. He's got a story in his head, and he wanted to make Kathryn fit it.'

'Why?'

'So that when he kills her it means what he wants it to mean.'

Carol frowned, saying nothing for a long moment. 'Sometimes I wonder how you come up with these ideas.'

'A lifetime of looking through the wrong end of the telescope,' he said. 'You've met my mother.' He gave a mirthless laugh. 'She was my training wheels. I've spent my whole adult life dealing with messy heads and now I can only see the world through that prism.'

'That'll be why we get on so well,' Carol said ironically. 'But right now, your theory is as good as anything else out there. We've barely begun and I can't see how we move forward. I can't believe we're this stuck this early.'

'That's because this one's very good. I'll be honest, Carol. The best we can hope for is that one's enough. Because if he gets a taste for it, we could really struggle here.'

PART TWO

27

The blazing car was a beacon in the velvet blackness. There at the heart of the Yorkshire Dales where light pollution was trivial, the flames were an assault on the eyes. Halfway between Snazesett and Burterbusk, a narrow twist of single-track road with passing places, there were no casual passers-by to see it, however. The nearest town of any size was Hawes, which formed the apex of a triangle with the two hamlets, five miles a side. The small local inferno registered only as a faint red glow along the ridge, which went unremarked by everyone except a woman from Leeds who thought it might be the Northern Lights.

The fire had passed its zenith when Anselm Carter left his cowshed, having seen to the trouble-free delivery of a bull calf to one of his Highland cattle. All he was thinking of was a cold can of Guinness to take away the taste and smell of the past couple of hours, but he knew his landscape too well not to notice the flames down the hill on the road that bordered his best pasture. There were no beasts on that piece of land at the moment, but Anselm didn't want his valuable grazing damaged by a wildfire.

Sighing, he went inside the farmhouse, where his two teenage daughters were snuggled like puppies on the sagging kitchen sofa watching some American adolescent nonsense on the telly. 'Tell your mam I've gone down the road, there's a fire and I need to check it's not threatening our land,' he said, reaching for the Land Rover keys.

One daughter looked over momentarily. 'A fire?'

'Aye.'

'What's to go on fire down there?'

'Nowt that I can think of. Best take a look, though.'

Her attention was already back on the screen and Anselm stepped out of the cosiness of home into the chilly dark. The fire was still going strong and it pulled him along the rutted farm track like a lodestar. By the time he reached the main road, he could see it was about half a mile on towards Snazesett. Nothing there but a passing place and a grit bin, he thought.

But as soon as he turned onto the road, he could see the outline of a burning car, the interior an inferno of red and orange and yellow. His headlights illuminated gouts of greasy black smoke spiralling into the night sky.

Anselm pulled up twenty metres away, turning on his hazard lights. Not that anybody was likely to be down here at this time of night on a Sunday. He jumped down and walked towards the car. As he approached, heat engulfed him. He'd had a sauna once, when he'd got his brother to look after the farm for a weekend and he'd taken Nell to a fancy hotel in Harrogate. He couldn't see the point of it, getting all hot and bothered from choice. Nell had liked it, though. She'd seen a home version in IKEA once, pointed it out wistfully to him, but he thought it was a waste of money that could be better spent on a new bathroom with a proper shower.

This wall of heat felt like that sauna, though it smelled nothing like the herby miasma in there. This smelled of burned plastic and grease, the sort of thing that would make you sick if you breathed in too much of it. Anselm couldn't see anything inside the car, and although flames were licking out of the holes where the windows should have been, they soon vanished in the night. The council grit bin had melted into a shapeless yellow blob streaked with black, but apart from that, it all looked pretty localised. The odd spark was landing in his field but he didn't think there was any prospect of one catching hold.

He walked back to the Land Rover, pondering. He could call out the fire brigade and the police, but there didn't seem much point. There was no danger to life, limb, livestock or land; nobody would thank him for being pulled out to the back of beyond on a Sunday evening over some joyriders setting fire to a stolen car, which was what this likely was.

Anselm drove back up the track towards the smudge of light that was his home. Morning would be soon enough to talk to the local bobby.

28

The mood in the ReMIT squad had descended into gloom. Kathryn McCormick had been their first major case and they were comprehensively stuck, their wheels spinning in a spray of mud. And everyone was acutely aware that their impasse was being scrutinised from all sides. John Brandon had taken to calling Carol every other day to discuss what leads her team were chasing. But even he, with all his years of experience, hadn't been able to come up with any suggestions they hadn't already done to death. Although he affected a casual air, she could tell he was feeling pressure from his political bosses at the Home Office. She wasn't the only one whose reputation was on the line here.

Apart from Brandon, who was technically retired and thus professionally immune, the command levels of all the six forces who had committed to the setting up of ReMIT had the most powerful vested interest in a successful outcome. But even there, the unit had its enemies. Senior officers whose fiefdoms had been inevitably diminished. Ambitious men and women whose clear promotion paths up the ranks had been made complicated. The mean-spirited whose faces were set against any bright moves towards change. Carol and her team felt the pressure of all those differing expectations from above.

Then there were the detectives who'd been confident in the capabilities of their own CID departments, whose noses had been put out of joint not only by losing the most serious reputation-defining cases but also from not having been chosen to walk among the elite. Carol could imagine the glee in a dozen CID watering holes throughout the region as they pored over the lack of progress in what was one of the highest-profile cases in recent memory.

And at the bottom of the pile, the foot soldiers. The uniformed lads and lasses who did the grunt work on every investigation. Nobody liked the endless door-knocking, searches of grim council estates or muddy woodland, PNC checks on the registered owner of every car that had gone through a particular set of traffic lights, the monitoring and guarding of crime scenes, or dealing with members of the public who were obstructive, grumpy and nosy by turns. It was annoying enough to have to do it for their own detectives, but when outsiders came in with their demands for even more tedious drudgery, it generated a burning desire among some for them to fail.

Luckily, there were others who wanted to shine, to take the opportunity to impress someone outside a chain of command that had probably already made its mind up about them. But they would be equally fed up at the lack of success. No chance for them to make a splash if nothing was happening. No way out of their dead ends if ReMIT failed.

Even their friends were anxious. Carol had grown to dread John Brandon's name popping up on the screen of her phone. Every night when she'd gone home, the desire for a drink had all but overwhelmed her. Most nights Tony had been there to game with her or keep her company, which meant on a point of principle she couldn't break her word and drink. But on the nights when he wasn't there, when an early start or a late finish at Bradfield Moor meant it made sense to stay on his barge in town – those nights had been a titanic struggle that left her drained and depressed. The lack of progress in the case was dragging her to her knees.

On the Monday morning three weeks after the discovery of Kathryn McCormick's body, Carol had been confronted on her way to the ReMIT office by her old boss, James Blake, chief constable of Bradfield Metropolitan Police. Their relationship had been antagonistic from the first, and he could barely hide his glee when they came face to face in a corridor in Skenfrith Street station. 'Not going too well, is it, Carol?' he'd drawled. He was flanked by a pair of uniformed superintendents who both looked as if they were barely suppressing a smirk.

Her stomach tightened. 'Early days, sir.'

'Three weeks in and no viable suspect? Not what I'd call early days.'

'Some cases are more difficult to crack than others. That's why we were set up.' She felt a muscle in her eyelid twitch and hoped he didn't notice.

'You were set up to solve the difficult cases, not flap around like headless chickens. From what I hear, you're completely bogged down.'

Carol forced a smile. 'We'll get there, sir.'

Blake chuckled. 'I admire your optimism. Shame it's not matched by your team's abilities.' And he swept past, leaving her quivering with a mixture of rage and fear. She ducked into the nearest ladies' toilet, rushed into a cubicle, slammed the lid down and collapsed on to it. Her hands were shaking, her stomach churning, her legs trembling. She wanted to scream, to whimper, to howl. She was doing her best, but her best just wasn't enough. Not any more. She couldn't sleep, she didn't want to eat and she couldn't give in to the one thing she craved. She didn't even want to close her eyes in the dark because all she could see then was the horrors of past cases stuttering through her mind like old Super 8 home movies.

Carol leaned against the wall and tried to breathe steadily. She had to pull herself together for the sake of her team. She'd chosen them. She'd plucked them out of their careers and made them targets. She couldn't live with herself if she let them down. She clenched her fists and rubbed her knuckles over her head. The pain took her mind off the turmoil in her brain.

Five minutes later she walked into the squad room with a brave attempt at a spring in her step. But it was clear from her first glance that nobody had any optimism left. They'd followed all the obvious lines of inquiry, then the less likely, till finally they were reduced to acknowledging there was nowhere left to go other than to retrace their steps in the hope of finding a different answer. They'd even put out an appeal on one of the online recipe forums Kathryn had used, looking for anyone she'd developed a friendship with who might know something – anything – about the mysterious David. But still they had no idea where she had been killed or the reason for her murder. Or why her killer had chosen to set her car on fire with her in the driving seat in an obscure lay-by in North Yorkshire.

They'd barely sat down at their conference table when the phone rang. Karim, who had learned that this job fell to the lowest on the totem pole, jumped up to answer it. 'Regional Major Incident Team,' he said, surprisingly brightly. Pause. 'Yes, she's here. One moment, please.' He put the call on hold and said, 'Guv, it's DSI Henderson from North Yorkshire.' He tried to smile but looked as if he wanted to burst into tears.

Expecting a bollocking in one shape or form, Carol took

the phone and visibly braced herself. 'I'll take this in my office.' The team watched her get up and go. As she closed her door behind her, there was a collective letting out of breath and an exchange of worried looks.

Once she was in her own space with the door firmly shut, Carol gripped the phone tightly and closed her eyes. 'DSI Henderson,' she said, her tone brisk and businesslike. How bad could it be?

'DCI Jordan, I have some news for you. Last night, a farmer in the Dales spotted a burning car. He took a closer look and saw no cause for immediate concern so he didn't bother reporting it till first thing this morning. When the local patrol car checked it out, they saw what looked like a body. Your team appears to have a repeat offender. And a second chance.' Crisp and to the point.

A wave of dizziness hit Carol. Henderson's words felt like a reprieve. Dear God, how rubbish a human being had she become that she saw a suspicious death as an opportunity? 'That's very interesting,' she said.

'And this time you have the advantage of not having had the crime scene destroyed by the firefighters,' Henderson added. 'I've got a full forensic team on their way and I've given instructions everything is to remain in situ until ReMIT says so. I'll have our SIO ping you all the details we have.'

'Thank you, ma'am.' Carol tried to keep the relief from her face. 'I'll brief the team and we'll be at the scene as soon as we can.'

'Let's hope you manage to produce a result this time.' The line went dead. Carol leaned back in her chair and breathed deeply. They'd been hampered from the start by the compromised crime scene on Kathryn McCormick's murder. This time, there would be no excuses. But this time, hopefully, there would be no need for excuses.

*

The Land Rover wasn't the ideal vehicle for getting anywhere in a hurry. Not to mention the heavy rumble of the diesel engine that made conversation difficult. But Carol had grown used to it over the past year and she liked the sense of security it gave her. And there was plenty of room for the dog, who was sprawled out along the floor in the back, her head on Tony's feet. Paula was riding shotgun, her laptop open on her knees and tethered to her phone so she could give a shouted commentary as information came in from North Yorkshire's team.

'Where exactly are we going?' Tony asked as Carol keyed the postcode into her satnav.

'Heading for the middle of nowhere, turning right at the back of beyond and keeping going till we see a white scene of crime tent,' Carol replied.

'The names sound like something out of *Lord of the Rings*,' Paula said. 'Snazesett and Burterbusk. Are they having a laugh?'

'Probably from the Vikings,' Tony said. 'They left more than red hair genes when they did their raping and pillaging round Yorkshire. So where is it near?'

'Nowhere, by the looks of it,' Paula said. 'And according to what Stacey's just sent me, you'd have to backtrack a long way before you find a road with an ANPR camera. Same as before, he's chosen somewhere he's not going to be readily logged in and out of.'

'He knows the terrain,' Tony said. 'This isn't random.'

'You think he's local?' Carol chipped in.

'It looks that way. Either that or he's a keen walker who's spent a lot of time there. What else have North Yorkshire got for us, Paula?'

'The car is a two-year-old Peugeot 108 cabriolet. For the car illiterates among us—'

'That'll be me,' Tony said.

'—it's one of those diddy little ones with a canvas sunroof that folds back rather than a full cabriolet hood.'

Carol groaned. 'Does that matter?'

'It might affect the way the fire burned,' Paula said. 'If the roof caught, it'll have provided more oxygen for the fire so it will have burned more fiercely. Over the past couple of weeks, I have become something of an expert on fires in cars,' she added ruefully. 'Fire investigators are very eager to share.'

'Any ID from the car? Are the licence plates readable?'

'It's registered to an Amie McDonald at an address in Cookridge, Leeds. West Yorkshire officers attending say there's nobody home. Next-door neighbour says Amie works for the Leeds City council tax department, so the Westies are off to the council offices to try and track her down. Though if it's the same guy and he's following the same procedure, she's not going to be sitting in her office waiting for us to drop by.'

'We need to check, all the same,' Carol said. 'Even though it's her car, it doesn't mean it's her body. She might have lent it to someone. Or it might have been stolen. We'll probably have to fall back on dental ID if it's anything like the last one.' She nudged the car into a gap at a roundabout and turned on to the main artery that led towards Burnley and onwards to the Dales. 'What else?'

'Local farmer called Anselm Carter called it in at six-thirty a.m. Apparently that's when he starts milking. He saw the flames yesterday evening around nine when he came out of the cowshed. He went and took a look, didn't see the body so he thought it was just a burning car that was no risk to his land or his livestock so he thought he might as well leave it till morning to phone it in.'

'I can't say I blame him,' Tony said. 'If I had to get up at six to milk cows, I don't think I'd be that keen on having the police and the fire brigade doing their thing and needing cups of tea till the small hours.'

'So the local patrol car took a run out first thing and of course, they could get close enough by then to see there was a body in the car. They reckoned the seat belt must have burned through and the body slumped down across both front seats. There are some pretty grisly pictures, if you're interested, Tony?'

He grimaced. 'I'll wait till I can see the real thing. Once is sufficient.'

'It's the same killer, isn't it?' Carol turned on the flashing blue light attached to her dashboard. 'I know we don't theorise ahead of data, but it's hard to imagine a scenario that doesn't come back to the man who killed Kathryn McCormick.'

'I'd have to agree,' Tony sighed. 'I'm trying not to sound too perky about it, but this is the best thing that could have happened from our perspective. Kathryn's murder didn't give us enough data. With an untainted crime scene and a whole new set of witnesses, we might just start to make some forward progress.'

'I hear what you're saying, Tony, but for Christ's sake, don't say that outside this car.' Carol's exasperation was obvious. 'For a man who's supposed to be the soul of empathy, sometimes you have a tin ear.'

'I can't profile properly on a single case, you know that,' Tony said huffily.

'Not everyone understands you like we do, Tony,' Paula said. 'Most people would struggle to see any positive side to a murder.'

'Maybe so,' Tony said. 'Nothing we can do changes the fact that someone died last night. But the dead are out of reach. I save my empathy for the living, Paula.'

29

The smell was the same, but stronger because the fire had been more recent. The acrid notes of burnt plastic mingled with something more primal. Carol, Paula and Karim stood in a tight knot on the outside of the fluttering plastic tape that marked out the province of the forensic team and the fire investigator. Kevin was on his way up to the farmhouse to see whether Anselm Carter had anything to add to what he'd already told North Yorkshire.

And Tony was walking a grid that only he understood. The passing place on the single-track road was separated from the grazing by a ditch and, beyond that, a single strand of barbed wire. It didn't seem much to keep cows corralled. He walked along the road in the direction the car had come from, seeing nothing of interest. A hundred metres along the road, he stopped and assessed the ditch. It was about a metre deep and about a metre and a half wide. He reckoned he could get across without too much trouble. Tony backed up a couple of strides and took a short run at it. He cleared the ditch but his momentum almost took him into the barbed wire fence. He teetered on the lip of the ditch and just managed to save himself from toppling backwards into the muddy trench. Now he was on the other side, he could see that the flimsy strand wasn't the only precaution against wandering cattle. Beyond it was the thin filament of an electric fence. When it was switched on, it would give the cows enough of a jolt to divert them away from the road.

Tony studied the barbed wire apprehensively. He wasn't the most dextrous of men; this was precisely the kind of scenario that could end in torn trousers and blood running down his legs. He could get Karim to do it. But Karim wouldn't read the scene in the same way he did. There was nothing else for it. He'd have to take a chance.

Gingerly, he pushed the wire downwards and stepped over it. Luckily there was enough clearance and he let out a long sigh of relief as he cleared it. There was no tell-tale hum coming from the electric fence but he touched it with the back of his hand to make sure. Nothing.

He crossed the electric fence and walked slowly back towards the burned-out shell of the Peugeot, alternately staring at the ground and the distant horizons. He wasn't sure what he was looking for but he knew there had to be something that connected this setting to the scene of Kathryn McCormick's immolation.

And it was a setting, he was sure of that. This wasn't a random passing place on a random road. It had been chosen for reasons that were at the very least practical but which might have a deeper emotional and psychological significance. What that was, he had no idea yet. But everything he learned at this stage had the potential to open doors in his head further down the line.

It was a striking landscape. Low hills that swept in curves to valleys where sheep and cattle grazed. Stands of trees that dotted the slopes. Drystone walls that straggled up the gradients and crossed at angles that were everything but right. It was greener than the moorland around Carol's barn and the views were more dramatic. But he could see the genetic link between the two landscapes.

As he drew nearer, he could see the activity around the car itself. White-suited figures in their protective suits, masks across their faces, taking photographs and samples. Just as he had his own grammar for reading a crime scene, so had they. The things that mattered to them would never attract his attention, and vice versa.

He carried on past the crime scene, still not happy that he had found what he was looking for. Whatever that was. He paused and looked around again. Nothing out of the ordinary. But twenty metres on, he came upon something that stopped him in his tracks. Right in front of him, on the field side of the fences, something had scraped a scar in the surface of the grass. About a couple of feet square, there was a deeper indentation on one side. It looked fresh; the grass that it had uprooted was wilted rather than dead. Something had recently been tossed into the field.

Tony turned and cupped his hands round his mouth. 'Carol,' he shouted. Her head lifted and turned towards him. 'You need to see this.' He pointed extravagantly at the ground.

She walked up the road towards him, Paula and Karim at her heels. 'What is it?'

He indicated what he'd found. 'I was looking to see if maybe he'd jumped across the ditch to get away.'

'Why would you do that in the dark when there's a perfectly good road?' Karim asked.

Tony grinned. 'Now that is the kind of question I ask. And I don't know the answer, but I do know that somebody chucked something into this field from somewhere near where you're standing. You can tell by the direction of the skid mark and the flattened grass,' he added.

'I'm glad to see you've been picking something up from the forensics techs,' Carol said drily. 'Paula, can you get one of the crime scene specialists up here? I want this processed.' She looked up at Tony. 'Nice work, Tony.'

He shrugged. 'You lot would have found it eventually when you considered the wider scene. I got lucky, that's all.' He turned away and scanned the horizon. Without saying anything more, he set off across the field at an acute angle, dodging cowpats and sheep droppings. He kept his eyes on the ground; if there were any traces of someone else having passed this way, he didn't want to compromise them.

At the far side of the field, he stopped by a metal five-barred gate with a sturdy spring-fastener latch. 'You're not going to have left any traces on this gate, are you?' he said aloud. 'You're far too savvy for that. But I'm not going to take a chance on messing up the forensics just in case. I mean, it was dark when you came here. You might have made a mistake.'

He contented himself with checking out what lay beyond. A rough tractor track led back towards the Carter farmhouse through another pasture where sheep dotted the green. Beyond that was a drystone dyke. Where the wall met another, he could make out the fingerpost for a footpath. 'Was that what you were looking for?' he mused. 'Did you literally walk away from what you'd done?'

Carol watched Tony wander off across the field, wondering what bee was buzzing in his bonnet. Given their lack of progress so far, anything was worth pursuing. She briefed the white-suited CSI tech who muttered darkly about amateurs messing with his crime scene. Nevertheless, he started scrutinising the bank on both sides of the ditch to see whether he could find any signs of a crossing.

Carol left Karim with the CSI and walked back to the focus of attention with Paula. 'One thing strikes me,' Paula said.

'What's that?'

'If our cars say anything about our personalities, I bet Amie's a very different kind of woman to Kathryn. The Ford Focus is exactly the kind of car you'd associate with a woman like Kathryn – a bit staid, reliable, nothing to frighten the horses. But the Peugeot 108 – that's a very different message. It's a sporty little number. A bit racy, even, you might say.'

'Interesting,' Carol said. She chuckled. 'Everybody's channelling Tony today, apparently.'

The fire investigator was stripping off his gloves and dropping them into a paper bag when they reached the car. The white pointed hood made him look like a cartoon of a man in a wind tunnel. Carol introduced Paula to Finn Johnston then asked what he had for them.

'Well, it's definitely a human body in there.'

'What else would it be?' Paula wondered.

'You have to keep an open mind. Round here, people have been known to transport sheep and even pigs in their cars.' He gave her a boyish grin. 'You're not in the city now, Sergeant.'

'Can you tell whether it's a man or a woman?' Carol asked.

'Hard to say. Not my field. But because of the way the body's canted over, the midriff has been somewhat protected, so when they move the body, the medic might be able to give you a quick answer. What I can tell you is that it's either a woman or a man with small feet.'

'You can tell that from charred remains?' Paula asked.

'No. I can tell that because I can see the trainers. And I can tell you the victim was wearing jeans with some kind of stretch material incorporated in them.'

'That's different from the previous victim,' Carol said. 'Why is that?'

'The sunroof. The best way of thinking about a body in a

158

fire in a contained space like a car is to imagine your Sunday joint roasting in the oven. A nice leg of pork with plenty of skin for crackling. If you leave it in long enough, the surface skin will blacken, it'll split and it'll char. Then the fat under the skin melts and as it's released, it catches fire and burns away. And eventually you get down to bone. And bone has very well defined stages of thermal decomposition. Colour changes, cracks and fractures appear. If the fire burns long enough, you get ash. Like at the crematorium. Time's the key. Regardless of how high or low the temperature is, the result will be the same if you leave it long enough.'

The images his words conjured up made both women feel slightly queasy. Carol didn't think she'd be serving roast pork any time soon. Good communicators like Finn with his vivid comparisons almost made her wish for the nerds who blinded her with science. But it was those very comparisons that made the case come alive for Carol and her team. Those word pictures were impossible to forget, long after they'd forgotten the detailed scientific explanations for what they'd seen. They made her care because they made the events real.

'So what's the difference with the sunroof?' Paula persisted.

'When the sunroof burns, it funnels the fire upwards. The hot gases are drawn out of the hole so the lower parts of the interior may not be too badly damaged. So here, although everything above mid-shin is pretty well incinerated, the lower calves are less badly damaged. I've obviously not disturbed the body but I can see enough to tell you that the trainers are superficially damaged but more or less intact. Which means the feet probably are too.'

'So we'll get DNA?' Carol asked.

Finn shrugged. 'I'd have thought a definite maybe. That'd make it easier for you, I guess?'

'We still have to have something to compare it with,' Carol said. 'If it's her car and the DVLA details are right, we might be quicker finding a dental comparison. Any chance of getting evidence of someone else inside the car this time?'

He looked dubious, puffing his cheeks and blowing out air through pursed lips. 'I doubt it. Though we'll hopefully get more detailed results about the cause and progress of the fire this time because we've not had the hoses and foam all over it.'

'Which is a good thing,' Carol said.

'Indeed.' His sharp nose twitched. 'I'm not getting any of the obvious accelerants on smell alone, but that doesn't mean they weren't present. Just that they've dissipated in the fresh air. What I can tell you is that it looks as if it started in the same place – in the driver's footwell. And this one went even faster and hotter because of the fabric roof. Once that went up, the oxygen supply increased massively and the fuel load inside the car burned faster and hotter.' He pulled a face. 'You'd have to hope your victim was already dead when the fire started.'

Carol liked him better for that brief moment of humanity. 'That's what we all hope. When will you have something to tell us?'

'Two or three days,' he said. 'If we're lucky, we'll get something more distinctive this time.'

Carol shook her head. 'I wouldn't count on it. This guy knows how to cover his tracks. So far, he's not put a foot wrong.'

30

Sam sucked down a third of his pint in one go. He'd spent three weeks in a bubble of hot rage that nothing seemed capable of cooling. It had taken him days to sort out his bank account and credit cards. His mortgage was still suspended and he kept discovering new things that Stacey had done to his digital footprint. He'd had to close down his Facebook account because every day it filled up with cute GIFs of cats. His Instagram was infested with puppies and his Twitter feed was a constant retweet of stupid bigoted comments from football fans of every stripe. It was vengeance out of all proportion to his offence. All he'd done, for God's sake, was to tip off a journalist about Carol Jordan's miraculous escape from her drink-driving charge. From Stacey's overreaction, you'd have thought he'd taken up paedophilia as his latest hobby.

Everything had been going so well up until then. He'd got his feet under the table, Stacey was buying him expensive presents and she thought the sun shone out of his arse. And it wasn't an effort. He'd been out with women who had a lot less going for them. She wasn't bad looking, the sex had been better than OK and frankly the fact that she was loaded had been a great incentive. Sam had reckoned he was on to a good thing and he'd planned to make it last. Why did she have to lose it over a stupid newspaper story that was nothing more than the truth? OK, the paper had kind of insinuated that the rules had been bent for Jordan's benefit, but that wasn't his fault.

He sighed and took another swig of his beer. And now he was stuck drinking on his own because nobody on his new squad wanted to be his friend on account of they thought he had airs and graces because he used to be on an MIT.

Just as he reached that low point in self-pity, a fresh pint appeared on the table in front of him, followed by an attractive well-groomed woman whose age he estimated at somewhere between forty and forty-five. Not that Sam thought a few extra years disqualified a woman if she had other satisfactory attributes. And this one definitely had some of those. Lustrous dark hair, stylish coat with a casually knotted velour scarf, expertly applied make-up. He thought he'd seen her before but he couldn't remember where.

She slid into the booth opposite him and gave him a mega-watt smile. She had good teeth, he couldn't help noticing. 'You don't mind if I join you?'

He smiled. 'Not if you come bearing pints. Have we met?'

'Not as such. I've seen you at press conferences. My name's Penny Burgess. I'm the chief report—'

'I know who you are.' He curled his lip in a scornful smile. 'You're the one got Kevin in trouble years back.'

She smiled, a lazy smile that held all sorts of promises. 'Kevin got himself in trouble. But that was a long time ago, and I think he's forgiven me now that he's back at his old rank.'

'I wouldn't bank on it,' Sam scoffed. 'That lot in ReMIT don't forgive anything or anybody.'

'Had a bit of bother with them, have you?'

He shook his head. 'None of your business,' he said roughly.

'Hard to believe Carol Jordan didn't pick you for her swanky new team.' She ran a finger round the rim of what looked like a gin and tonic.

'I'm happy where I am,' he said, with more conviction than he felt.

'All the same.' She let the words hang in the air between them.

'All the same, what?'

'Did you hear about the fatal car crash a couple of weeks ago up near Halifax?'

'I may have done,' he said, wary now. Penny Burgess's reputation was unsettling for someone in his position.

'Five dead. It was four initially, but the fifth victim gave up the ghost yesterday.'

'That's too bad.'

'The driver who caused it, Dominic Barrowclough? He was one of the other people who got let off the hook along with Carol Jordan. The allegedly faulty breathalyser. But you know all about that, right?'

Sam gave her a level stare. 'I don't know what you're talking about,' he said flatly.

Penny laughed, her eyes sparkling with humour. 'Don't try to kid a kidder, Sam. I know you were the source for the story that revealed Carol's "lucky break".' She made quote marks in the air with her fingers.

He drained his first pint and pushed the glass violently to one side. It was a gesture that could have been taken as a threat. Equally, it was entirely deniable. 'I've got nothing to say to you.'

'I think you do,' Penny said. 'You leaked once, you'll leak again, Sam. Next time it'll be easier. And it'll go on getting easier. I want to make sure it's me you leak to, that's all. And I won't leave a paper trail. Cash, Sam. In traditional brown envelopes. Absolutely no blowback.' From her bag, she took a folded copy of that evening's paper. She pushed it over to him and with one finger, he flipped the fold open. There was no envelope. Instead, four crisp red fifty-pound notes. He twitched and hastily closed the paper again.

'What do you take me for?' This time there was an aggressive note to his voice.

'A source who likes to be well paid. That's just some beer money, Sam. Look, they hate you already. What have you got to lose?'

He shook his head. 'My job?'

'I would never betray one of my personal sources. And as long as you don't pass on anything to me that only you could know, you're covered.'

A long silence. The burn of anger fought with Sam's sense of self-preservation. The bargain she was offering made sense. 'How do we communicate? How do I protect myself?'

Penny took out a notepad and scribbled a number. 'We meet in the dark. In the indie cinema in Kenton Vale. When you've got something for me, call this number. It's a hole-in-the-wall dry cleaner's. A one-man operation. Put it in your phone under "dry cleaning". Tell him the name of the film and I'll see you in the back row at that evening's screening. You don't even have to watch the film, Sam.'

The paper sat on the table between them. 'It's a criminal offence, to corrupt a police officer,' he said.

'You already committed a criminal offence when you leaked that story about the breathalyser. If someone passed that paper trail on to the IPCC, you'd be fucked.' She shrugged prettily. 'You know you want to, Sam. It's eating you up. I can see it in your eyes.'

He snatched up the paper and downed the beer she'd

bought him in one. He wiped his mouth and stood up, flushed. 'Carol Jordan is a drunk,' he said. 'The woman running the ReMIT can't get through a morning without hitting the vodka bottle.' He started away from the table.

'How do I stand that up?' Penny said, urgency in her voice for the first time.

'That's your problem,' Sam said, walking away. 'I thought that was what you were supposed to be good at?'

He hit the street at a good pace. For the first time since Stacey had fucked his life over, the burn of rage had receded. Not by much. But it was a start.

31

Carol had left Paula in the North Yorkshire HQ canteen while she talked to DSI Anne Henderson about the division of labour now it looked as if they might have a repeat offender working their patch. Paula had taken advantage of the break to search online for a birthday gift for Elinor. She wasn't good at presents. Her intentions were generous and loving, but she always struggled to come up with the right offering for the woman she loved. It frustrated her that even though she had no doubt how well she knew her partner, she couldn't track down something special and unexpected.

But this time she was on a mission. When Torin's mother had died, he'd inherited all her jewellery. A few months previously, Elinor had decided that since Torin was staying, they should inventory Bev's jewellery to keep the house insurance straight. He'd brought down the polished wooden box that held Bev's necklaces and rings and bracelets. Most of it was pretty undistinguished but there were a few more valuable pieces that Bev had inherited from her mother and grandmother, whose husband had been a successful fish merchant in Hull. Elinor had exclaimed with delight over one piece, an antique garnet pendant flanked by two pink pearls. Paula knew she couldn't find exactly the same piece but she was determined to track down something so similar it would provoke the same delight.

Paula wasn't going to be suckered into buying something mail order that she couldn't inspect personally. So she opened her laptop and chose haystack.com, an auction and direct selling site whose search results were geographically focused. 'Garnet and pearl' gave her four results, only one of which was a pendant. The thumbnail looked very similar to the one Torin now owned, and Paula couldn't keep from smiling at the prospect of early success. She clicked on the thumbnail then drew her breath in sharply. This pendant didn't just look similar. It was, she thought, identical.

As well as making a note of the jewellery, Elinor had insisted they photograph it. Paula had snapped the pieces on her personal mobile, so she quickly scrolled back through her photo album till she found what she was looking for. Still there, which demonstrated that sometimes it was OK to ignore Stacey's insistence on backing things up and not cluttering her phone. Paula compared the two images. There was no doubt about it. The two pendants were identical.

Either this wasn't the unique piece they'd believed it to be or something more disturbing was going on. But there was nothing she could do about it for now. Paula bookmarked the page. After all, it might still end up as the answer to her present-giving problem.

For the rest of the day, it niggled at the back of her mind like a damaged tooth that twinges at unpredictable intervals. She barely registered that they'd established Amie McDonald wasn't at work or at home. But until they could be certain hers was the body in the mortuary, nobody was going to talk to her family or her workmates in connection with the burned body on the moorland road. At this point, Amie wasn't officially a missing person. Unless someone reported her to the police, they could afford to keep the lid on the possible identity of the victim. Officers from North Yorkshire were working their way through dental practices in Leeds, so far without result. The morning, everyone hoped, would bring an answer.

When Paula arrived home around nine, the house was empty. Elinor, she knew, was the senior doctor on call in A&E and wouldn't be back before midnight. Torin had left a note on the kitchen table that read, 'Gone to Harry's to revise.' It was a regular get-together, though Paula thought it had fallen into abeyance lately. She was glad they'd picked up the reins again.

And it gave her a chance to take a look in the box that sat on the top shelf of the IKEA Billy bookcase in Torin's room. Just to check, she told herself. Paula ran up the stairs and paused on the threshold of his room. The only time either of them entered without invitation was when Elinor changed his bedding. But the need for answers trumped Paula's respect for Torin's space.

She pushed the door open and walked in. The room had the familiar musky smell of teenage boy and sweaty trainers. His bed was unmade, the duvet a scrunched mountain range in the middle of the sheet, pillows for foothills. School books were scattered over his work table and his laptop, folded shut, was propped against a table leg. The walls featured a couple of posters for console games and one for *The Walking Dead*. Paula imagined there were bedrooms like this all over the country. Apparently innocuous, giving nothing away of what was going on inside the heads of their occupants. Fourteen was old enough for all sorts of threats to the equanimity of parents and guardians.

She crossed to the bookcase and reached for the box. She paused for a moment with it in her hands before she set it down on the bed and lifted the lid. The interior was divided into sections, each section occupied by particular items: earrings, rings, brooches, bracelets. Necklaces and pendants were in separate black velvet boxes. Paula opened them one by one, convinced every time that the next one would contain what she was looking for. But none of them held the pendant.

So engrossed was she in her search that she didn't hear the soft footfalls on the stairs. It was only when the light changed that Paula realised she wasn't alone any more. She turned to face Torin, a jewellery box still in her hand. 'What the fuck are you doing in my room? With my stuff?' His consternation was obvious, in spite of the forced outrage in his voice.

'I was looking for something,' Paula said.

'So I see. This is my stuff now. My mum left it to me. You've got no right.' His heavy brows lowered over a frown. He advanced towards her and for the first time, Paula took cognisance of his size. He was a few inches taller than her now and his shoulders had broadened over the past months. There was nothing threatening in his demeanour, but she realised that if he chose to be, he might be very frightening indeed.

He held his hand out, demanding the box. Paula gave it to him without hesitation. She took her phone out and swiped to the open image in her photos. 'I was looking for this,' she said. 'But I couldn't find it.'

He backed away, his expression horrified. 'Why are you raking through my things? Where I keep things, it's none of your business.'

'I wanted to get one like it for Elinor. For her birthday.' Paula was determined to get to the bottom of this. She was, after all, supposed to be good at interviewing people.

'So buy one. Don't go trying to nick my mum's jewellery.'

It was a suggestion so outrageous that Paula almost laughed. 'I can't nick what's not there,' she said calmly. 'I went looking online for something similar, and lo and behold, there it was on haystack.com for £800.'

He was startled. 'Eight hundred?' Then he recovered himself, almost. 'So, what, that was more than you wanted to spend? So you thought you'd have mine?' He was red-faced and blustering now.

'Torin, I spend my working life catching out liars. I know when people are bullshitting me. Your mum's garnet-and-pearl pendant isn't where it was when we catalogued her jewellery. And its double is on sale online. Now, what's going on here? What do you need £800 for?'

'It's not me selling it. Try and buy it and you'll see for yourself. But even if it was, it still wouldn't be any of your business what I do with my own things. You've got no right to be in here going through my stuff.' Now he sounded whiny. Paula could see that he was as much scared and upset as he was angry. She didn't want to corner him and escalate this to a place it would be hard to recover from.

She raised her hands, palms out in a placatory gesture. 'You're right. I should have waited till you were home and asked you where the pendant was. I shouldn't have just barged in and started poking about.'

He nodded fiercely, his chin jutting out. 'Yeah. You should have.'

'So where is it?'

He slammed the flat of his hand against the wall. 'Did you not hear me? My stuff. My business. I'm not one of your criminals that you can bully. Now get out of my room. Leave me alone.'

It was the impassioned cry of adolescents down the ages. There was nothing to be gained by confrontation, Paula realised. She couldn't afford to burn bridges with someone who would be sharing her home for the foreseeable future. Getting the truth out of people you shared your life with was apparently a lot harder than squeezing confessions out of criminals.

It was a lesson she wished she hadn't had to learn. And it was one she didn't know how to share with Elinor.

32

The North Yorkshire foot soldiers had triumphed. Some bright spark had uncovered the fact that Amie McDonald had grown up outside Leeds in nearby Morley and decided it was worth checking dental practices there as well as in the city. The second call hit the jackpot and by ten the next morning, the ReMIT team were on their way to interview the friends, colleagues and family of the woman they now knew to be Amie McDonald.

The council tax office where she worked was in an imposing and ornate Victorian red-brick building on a busy corner. Alvin followed his guide, a shocked section leader, through municipal corridors with high ceilings and the faint smell of institutional floor polish. 'I'm going to put you in here,' she said, opening the door of a small meeting room with a central table and six chairs. 'I'll go and fetch Jamie Taylor, he worked with Amie and they were great pals.' Her hand went to her mouth. 'He's going to be gutted,' she added as she left.

She was back with Jamie in a matter of minutes. 'There you go,' she said, patting him on the shoulder, almost pushing him towards Alvin.

Alvin sized him up. He was slightly built with a head that was small for his body. His mousey hair had a close undercut and a floppy top that made him look like a mushroom. He had the on-off anxious smile of a man eager to please but uncertain of how to. 'I'm Detective Sergeant Ambrose. Take a seat, please, Mr Taylor.'

Jamie settled in the chair furthest from Alvin, folding then unfolding his arms. 'Is this about Gary and the champagne bucket? I didn't even know he'd taken it till we got back from our honeymoon on Sunday.' His voice was high and light, verging on the camp.

'No.' Deep breath. 'I'm afraid I've got some very bad news for you. Your friend Amie McDonald is dead.'

Jamie physically recoiled, horror on his face. 'N-no,' he stammered. 'Y-you must have made a mistake.' He shook his head. 'That can't be right.'

'I'm afraid there's no mistake.' Alvin softened his voice.

'But how? She's fit as anything, Amie. Was it an accident or what? What happened?'

'There's no easy way to say this, Mr Taylor. We believe Amie's death to be suspicious.'

'What? You mean – somebody *killed* her?' He shook his head, incredulous. Then his eyes widened. 'Was it Steve? Did he come after her?'

'Who's Steve?'

'Her last bloke. She dumped him a few days before Eloise and me got married. She was really pissed off about having to come to the wedding by herself, but she just couldn't put up with him for another day. I can't believe it.' He shook his head again. 'I mean, I know he's a dick, but to kill her?'

The mention of Amie going to the wedding alone caught Alvin's attention. Just like Kathryn McCormick. Was this chance, or was it part of the killer's MO? 'At this point, we don't know who killed Amie,' he said. 'We're in the very

173

early stages of our inquiry. But obviously Steve is someone we're going to have to talk to. So if you can give me his details . . . ?'

Jamie nodded vigorously, pulling out his phone. 'Steve Standish.' He turned the phone to Alvin, displaying a phone number. The detective copied it into his notebook. 'I can't get my head round this.'

'What was she like, Amie? You knew her well?'

Jamie smiled. 'She was, like, my best mate. Amie and Jamie, the nearly twins, she called us. Our desks faced each other and we used to make each other giggle all the time. There's not much fun in our job – we spend our days talking to people who can't pay their bills, whose lives are falling apart half the time. So you need some light relief or you'd go off your head, frankly.'

'So she was a lively person?'

'Oh yes. Never a dull moment with Amie. She'd be the life and soul when we all went out.'

'What about your wedding? Was she the life and soul that day?' Time to pursue the line of inquiry that had opened up earlier.

Jamie looked momentarily downcast. 'To be honest, I think she was a little bit down. You know what weddings are like? Love is in the air, and all that. And Steve was just the latest in a long line of men who weren't up to scratch.' He frowned. 'But why are you asking about the wedding? Steve wasn't even there.'

'It's possible that Amie may have hooked up with someone at your wedding.'

He brightened. 'Well, yeah, she did, as a matter of fact. Eloise and me, we were really chuffed. Because Amie deserved somebody as special as she was. She totally wanted to settle down and start a family, but she wasn't going to settle for second best. She went through men at quite a rate.

Not that she was a slapper, or anything. She just had, like, really high standards and she was disappointed so often. So we really hoped that our wedding might have sprinkled a little bit of fairy dust on her love life.'

'So you knew who it was that she met there?'

He folded his arms again. 'Well, that's the funny thing. She messaged me the day after to say she'd met this lovely man called Mark and they'd really hit it off and he was a perfect gentleman and she was seeing him again. And how come neither of us had introduced her to Mark before. So I said to Eloise, "Who's this Mark, then?" Because the only Mark on my side was my cousin from Bingley and nobody, not even a blind person with a following wind, could call him a lovely man.'

'And what did Eloise have to say?'

'She said there were no Marks on her side either. There were a couple of people whose partners we didn't know, but if this Mark had come with somebody, then he wouldn't have been picking up Amie, would he?'

'I suppose not. Did Amie message you again about Mark?'

Jamie nodded. 'A few days after the wedding, he took her out for a curry.' He fiddled with his phone and brought up his messaging app. 'Look, see for yourself.'

He handed the phone to Alvin.

AMIE: You two lovebirds having FUN??? Hope Barbados is banging! Lovely Mark from ur wedding took me to gorgeous Indian restaurant last night, great food but even better company! He's a real sweetheart, I can't believe u've been keeping him from me! xxx

JAMIE: Not on purpose! We can't work out who he is. But fab that you've met some1 nice. X

AMIE: He says he knows El from work. Maybe he blagged his way in becoz u didn't ask him! xxx

JAMIE: Whatevs. Have a good time, babe, we're off for sunset cocktails then who knows?!? X

Alvin looked up. 'None of you was concerned that an apparent stranger was at your wedding.'

Jamie shrugged. 'Happens all the time. Ever since that movie, *Wedding Crashers*, it's a laugh. A bit of bants. I've heard some guys do it every weekend. There's no harm, it's just blagging a few free drinks.'

Alvin struggled with the carelessness of Jamie's attitude. He wondered if his disapproval was rooted in his length of service in the police, that he knew what was out there in the wild. Or was it more that he was over-protective towards his own? He'd never have been comfortable with the thought of complete strangers at a family gathering of his. 'Were there more messages?' he asked out of politeness, even as he thumbed the screen to look for himself.

'Be my guest,' Jamie said.

AMIE: Woo hoo, Dani from the Hunslett one stop shop is transferring into ours. She is 1 laff!

JAMIE: Top. Love that girl. You seen the Markster again?

AMIE: We went to this country pub with live music that was a bit zzzz but he was lovely. He makes me laff. Seeing him again on Tuesday. How's Barbados?

JAMIE: We are loving it large. El has gorgeous tan, I'm just pink.

AMIE: Fab night out with Mark, went for an ace Italian. He's only asked me to come to the Dales for the weekend. He's borrowed a cottage from a mate. How cool is that?

JAMIE: Ooh. Get u. Weekend in the Dales. Have u got wellies?

AMIE: Cheeky monkey. I've got walking boots, I'll have u know.

JAMIE: I'll hear all about it on Monday! Something to look 4ward to about going back to work. :(

AMIE: Promise u the full goss. Xxx

'And that was that?'

Jamie nodded. 'I couldn't work out why she wasn't in work without a word on Monday. I said to Eloise that her weekend in the Dales must have been even more of a cracker than she'd hoped.' He swallowed hard. 'I feel shit about saying that now.'

'You weren't to know,' Alvin said. 'We're going to need to see as many of the pictures taken at your wedding as you can get your hands on. Can you organise that for us?'

Jamie sighed. 'I suppose. Between us we've got phone numbers or emails for everybody that was there. I'll make sure they get the message. Everybody loved Amie.' His eyes glittered with tears. 'You need to catch the bastard who did this. She was lovely. She was like sunshine.'

Alvin bowed his head. 'Believe me, we are on it.'

33

By the time Kevin had reached Amie McDonald's flat in Leeds, West Yorkshire Police were already in possession. On the surface, there was nothing in their attitude that he could complain about, but since there was no sign of the man who had started dating her after Jamie and Eloise's wedding, there was nothing to be uncooperative about. There was no convenient paper calendar with dates marked on it; Amie presumably kept her diary on her phone and she hadn't backed it up on the tablet sitting on her bedside table. And the phone had presumably perished in the fire along with its owner.

Kevin took a quick look round anyway. The flat was the polar opposite of the one Paula had described. Where Kathryn had been tidy to the point of Spartan, Amie was a clutter queen. Clothes, magazines, make-up, holiday souvenirs, exotically coloured alcohol in oddly shaped bottles and what Kevin could only classify as 'junk' filled every room. Secretly, he was quite happy not to be responsible for searching the place.

'I'll leave you guys to it,' he said once he'd satisfied himself there was nothing obviously helpful to the investigation.

'We'll let you know if we find anything,' the sergeant in charge said. 'Apart from the definitive archive of *Heat* magazine.'

Since he was there, Kevin decided to try the neighbours. It was a purpose-built block of six flats, originally put up by the council in the mid-fifties, but long since sold for buttons under Thatcher's right-to-buy policy. Now their price tags were out of reach of first-time buyers but perfect for someone like Amie with a decent job, so long as they'd scraped together an eye-watering deposit.

No reply across the landing, which wasn't surprising in the middle of a working day. But Kevin thought he'd seen a net curtain on the ground floor twitch as he'd approached. There was a long pause after he rang the bell of Flat 1, but eventually the door opened to reveal an elderly man neatly dressed in grey twill slacks and a clean maroon knitted waistcoat over a blue shirt open at the neck to reveal a concertina of vertical skin creases. His face was lean and wrinkled with a scatter of brown age spots like a Golden Delicious left too long in the fruit bowl. He held an aluminium walking stick tight, arthritic knuckles bulging like marbles in a leather bag. 'Are you a policeman too?' he asked, every bit as forthright as cliché demanded of Yorkshiremen.

'I am,' Kevin said. 'Detective Inspector Kevin Matthews.'

'You don't sound like you're from round here,' the old man complained. 'Nobody lives where they come from any more.'

'I'm from Bradfield. Do you mind telling me your name, sir?'

'Why not? Costs nowt. I'm Harrison Braithwaite.'

'Nice to meet you, Mr Braithwaite. I wondered if I could have a word with you about one of your neighbours? Amie McDonald?'

His face softened in a smile. 'Amie? Lovely lass. Got herself into some bother, has she?' He giggled, a high-pitched sound that didn't match the rest of him. 'High spirited, that's Amie all over.'

'I'm afraid it's a bit more serious than that,' Kevin said gently. 'I'm sorry to have to tell you that Amie's dead.'

His watery blue eyes widened and his jaw sagged. 'Nay, lad. There must be some mistake. I saw her Friday after work. She popped in to say she was off for the weekend to the Dales, did I need owt from the shop before she went. She were fit as a fiddle. How can she be dead?'

'Could I maybe come in?'

Braithwaite nodded absently, pulling the door wider so Kevin could enter. The flat was overheated but smelled surprisingly of incense. There was a strange twittering sound coming from the living room at the end of the hall. Kevin followed the old man into a bright room, one wall of which had been caged in to make an aviary. There must have been two dozen small birds – budgies, canaries, parakeets and even a pair of lovebirds. Now the incense made sense – underneath its muskiness, there was a faint trace of ammoniac bird droppings. 'Wow,' Kevin said, going right up to the slender bars. 'I wasn't expecting these.'

'My pride and joy,' Braithwaite said, sinking into a threadbare armchair. 'They're not pets, they're companions.' There was neither stillness nor silence here. The fluster and chatter would have driven Kevin mad but Braithwaite clearly thrived on it. 'Amie loved the birds,' he said. 'But what happened to her? I can't take it in, nobody was more full of life than Amie.'

Kevin sat opposite him on the armchair's less worn twin. 'We found her body in a burned-out car on a back road in the Dales.'

'Oh my God,' Braithwaite cried out, stricken. 'Not burned to death? Not that?' He looked close to tears. 'I was a miner, I've seen what fire does.' He clapped a hand to his mouth.

'No, no,' Kevin said urgently. 'No, we think she was already dead when the car was set on fire.'

Braithwaite frowned. 'I don't understand.'

'There's no easy way to say this, Mr Braithwaite. We think Amie was murdered and her body set on fire in the car to cover the killer's tracks. What I'm trying to do is to build up a picture of Amie's life in the days before she died to see if we can find out where she crossed paths with her killer.' He paused, giving the old man a chance to compose himself.

'I can't credit what you're saying, lad.' He shook his head, wincing. 'Why ... I don't know why anybody would want to harm Amie. She had a heart of gold, that lass. I broke my foot last winter. I slipped on the step like a complete demmick. Amie did all my shopping for three weeks till I could get about again. And she still gets all my heavy stuff. Tinned tomatoes, bird seed, bottles of beer.' His face crumpled. 'What am I going to do now? Some weeks she was the only person I spoke to apart from my birds.'

Kevin let him have a moment. 'She sounds lovely.'

'She were. Unlucky in love, though. She was an eternal optimist. Every time she took up with a new one, she was sure he was the one. But they never lasted. She had standards, did Amie. Liked things done properly. And if they didn't match up? Well, what is it they say in America? Three strikes and you're out.' He shook his head, sighing.

'We think she might have met someone recently,' Kevin said.

'Aye. Happen you're right. She got rid of that waste of skin Steve Standish about three weeks back, but then she met a lad at a wedding, oh, it must be two Saturdays back. Mark, his name was.'

'Did she have much to say about Mark?'

'She thought he were the bee's knees. They'd been out two or three times since the wedding and she said he were a perfect gentlemen. Most men, she said, they were only after one thing. And they expected to get it on a first or second date. But she said Mark were different. He wanted to take things steady-like.'

'And was Amie happy with that?'

'She said she hadn't been out with somebody like that before. Somebody that seemed to want to get to know her for herself, not what she could do for him. She said he was widowed. Cancer.' He spoke the word as if it had power of its own. 'That's why he didn't want to rush into owt. Amie said he told her she reminded him of his late wife and that made him feel respectful. To tell you the truth, it was the first time I ever liked the sound of any of her men.' He pushed himself to his feet and went across to the cage. He pushed a finger through the bars and immediately, a blue budgie flew to it. He put his face against the cage and the bird rubbed its head against his wrinkled cheek. It was a curiously tender encounter. A moment passed, then Braithwaite gently withdrew and returned to his chair, composed again.

'So was it this Mark who did for her, then?'

'At this stage, we don't know anything for sure. Did Amie tell you more about Mark? A surname? What he did for a living?'

'He's a marketing executive with Tesco. Does a lot of travelling. He has to make sure the stores are displaying things properly. Something to do with promotions. You know? Buy one, get one half price. A hundred extra loyalty points on toilet rolls. That sort of thing. Not a proper job for a man, but you take what you can get. And he seemed to be doing all right for himself. Took her out nice places. Very well dressed too. I like to see a man taking pride in his appearance.'

Kevin struggled not to show the effect Braithwaite's words had on him. 'You actually saw him?' Deliberately casual, as if it didn't matter a damn.

Braithwaite nodded. 'When he took her out on Tuesday, they came back in a taxi. He got out with her and walked her up to the main door. Don't get me wrong, I wasn't spying or owt. I'm not a pervert. But I'd just that minute turned the telly off, so I was sitting in the dark. I like to listen to the birds settling themselves down for the night. Any road, they kissed goodnight. Nothing unseemly, but a bit of passion, you know? And he walked back to the cab while Amie let herself in. The cab waited while she came inside, then it drove off.'

'What kind of time was this?'

'Like I said, I'd just switched off *Newsnight*, so it would have been not long after quarter past eleven.'

'Could you describe him to me?'

Braithwaite tugged an earlobe in thought. 'Average height, maybe about five ten. Slim build, but not weedy, you know? Well made, you'd say. Dark hair brushed back in a bit of a quiff. He had them little round glasses with gold rims like that John Lennon used to wear. Granny glasses, we used to call them. Very nice suit, by the looks of it. He didn't get that from Tesco's.'

'You're very observant,' Kevin said, even though the description was no real use. But he was hoping for other fish to take his hook.

'I watch the birds in the garden as well as my own chaps,' he said. 'Telling the difference between different species, you learn an eye for detail.'

'Obviously. I don't suppose you noticed which taxi company they used?'

He nodded, showing a momentary flash of pride. 'I did, lad. Yorkie Cabbie. I remember particularly because I use them myself. They give pensioners a discount.'

Kevin knew it was the frailest of leads. But it was a lead. And there had been damn few of those over the past couple of weeks. He was bursting to pass the information on, but he knew he couldn't leap straight up and run for his car. Carol Jordan had always drilled into her team the importance of leaving the door open with witnesses.

Five minutes. That's what he'd give Harrison Braithwaite and his birds. And then he'd fly the coop himself.

34

They found Steve Standish using a painfully noisy machine to take a tyre off its alloy wheel. The tyre and exhaust centre where he was assistant manager was running at maximum capacity. All the bays and inspection pits were full and the mechanics juggled their tasks with a frantic air. Paula and Karim had sauntered in, apparently untouched by the bustle. They'd asked the first man in overalls they'd encountered to point out Standish. He'd jerked his thumb towards the machine. 'That's him. The one stripping the tyre off.'

They approached slowly, not wanting to obstruct any of the workers. Paula took the chance to size up Standish. He couldn't have been much more than five feet eight but he had wide muscular shoulders and his coveralls were cinched in at the waist with a broad leather belt. It was the tell-tale shape of a man who spent more time in the gym than on the sofa. But the physical element of his job meant his weren't just gym-bunny muscles. They were the real thing. He had a shock of dirty-blond hair, shaved close at the sides and a fraction too high at the back so he looked like he was wearing a wig that had slipped forward. They waited for him to free the tyre from the metal rim and turn off the machine, then Paula spoke. 'Steve Standish? We're from the Regional Major Incident Team.'

He whipped round at the sound of his name and his eyes widened in shock as he realised they were cops. 'I've not done anything wrong,' he said hastily. His voice was deep and assertive.

'Nobody said you had. I'm DS McIntyre and this is DC Hussain. Is there somewhere we can have a quiet word?'

He carefully placed the tyre iron on the ground at his feet. 'What's all this about?' he demanded, hands on hips, jaw thrust outwards, unconsciously making himself bigger.

'Trust me, you don't want to have this conversation in front of your mates,' Karim said.

'I've got no secrets. Anything you've got to say to me, spit it out.'

The two officers exchanged looks. 'When did you last see Amie McDonald?' Paula said.

Standish rolled his head in an exaggerated motion suggesting the question made his brain hurt. 'What is she saying? Look, I never touched her. OK, I threw the bloody teapot at the wall. I might have shouted a bit. But I never laid a hand on her. Why's she waited three weeks to call you lot? Has she got bored with her new life or what?' He leaned forward, hands bunched into fists.

'If you could answer the question, sir?' Paula was stony-faced. Already she was wondering what Amie McDonald had found so appealing in this man. Yes, he wasn't bad looking, but if this was his default mode, she wouldn't have wanted to be around him.

'I last saw her three weeks ago. She threw me out because I'd broken one too many of her stupid rules.'

'What kind of rules were those?' Karim asked.

'Don't leave the toilet seat up, don't put your feet on the

coffee table, put your dirty dishes in the dishwasher, don't leave your towel on the bathroom floor. All shit like that. Stupid crap. Like, stuff that would take her ten seconds to sort out. I mean, I did stuff for her all the time. Built her stupid bloody IKEA chest of drawers. Valeted her car. Picked her up from work. Like you do. Give and take. But no, fucking Amie was looking for Mr Perfect and, to be honest, she only just beat me to the draw. I'd had enough of her picking on me all the fucking time. So whatever she's said to you, it's bullshit.'

'So you weren't angry with her? You didn't want to get your own back?' Paula asked.

He shrugged his meaty shoulders. 'I was a bit pissed off. Nobody likes being given the heave-ho, do they? Especially not when they feel they're the one being hard done by. But I wasn't that bothered, to be honest. It's not like I was home-less or anything. I still have my own place, I wasn't daft enough to give it all up for a woman who's had more blokes than I've changed tyres.'

'So you didn't see her last weekend at all?'

He frowned, his forehead corrugating with the effort. 'This past weekend? Why would I see her? I never went near her after she chucked me out. I don't have to go begging any woman.'

Paula was aware that they were the centre of attention in the garage. The other mechanics were finding reasons to pass close by their conversation, and a couple of lads replacing an exhaust had given up any pretence of working and were ear-wigging for all they were worth.

'What were you doing this weekend?' Paula asked. 'Just for reference.'

'Is she saying I did something to her? Because I never laid eyes on her, never mind a hand.'

'This weekend.' Paula's voice had hardened. 'We can do this here or we can do it at the station.'

He snorted. 'I know my rights. You can't make me go to the nick unless you arrest me.'

Paula took a step forward into his space. 'You sure you want to push me down that road? Trust me, you will regret it. Does your employer really want his customers to see one of the staff being dragged out in cuffs? You think you'll have a job tomorrow?'

'Are you threatening me?' His voice had lost some of its certainty.

'No. Informing you.' Paula held his stare. He looked away first.

'Friday after work I went to the pub with the lads. They'll back me up. We went for a kebab after.' Once he started, there was no stopping him. 'I was home by eleven because it was my weekend on. I was here from eight till six on Saturday, then a bunch of us went into town. Same as before, except I picked up this lass at GlitteratLeeds. You know? The club down behind the station. I went back to hers, gave her what for, got her name and number off her and buggered off home around nine in the morning. Hardly had time to have a shower and get changed for work. I was here ten till four, then I went round my mam's for Sunday dinner. With my mam and dad, my sister and her bloke. I stayed till late – we watched *Match of the Day 2*. Then Joni and Chris dropped me off on their way home. That was my very fucking exciting weekend. So whatever that bitch Amie says I was doing, I wasn't.'

'Thank you, sir. I'll need a full statement to that effect, with the names and contact details of everyone who can corroborate what you've told us here. I'll have someone contact you and arrange a time for you to make your statement.' Paula gave a thin smile.

'Is that really necessary? All over some nuisance bloody complaint?' He had recovered his belligerence.

'Oh, it's necessary, sir.' Paula made as if to leave, taking a few tactical steps away that took her out of the range of his powerful arms. 'You see, this isn't some nuisance bloody complaint. We're investigating a murder.'

His face froze mid-sneer. 'A m-murder?'

'Yes, sir.' Paula wasn't given to shock tactics, but for Steve Standish she was willing to make an exception. 'Somebody murdered Amie McDonald. And you've got some serious questions to answer.'

35

Yorkie Cabbie operated out of what had once been the morning room of a Victorian villa in the no-man's-land between Headingley and Meanwood. Now the once-grand family home was home to a dozen small businesses. Stranded between a boxy three-storey sixties office block and a deconsecrated church that had been turned into a complementary healing centre, it looked like the interloper rather than the oldest resident. The street reminded Kevin of his Irish grandmother's frequent expression of disgust. 'Neither flesh nor fowl nor good salt herring.'

He pushed open a heavy front door that led to a scruffy hallway with cracked vinyl flooring and scuffed beige paintwork. A laminated sign on the wall directed him to the various tenants of the building and he made his way past Fone/Tablet Fast Repairs to Yorkie Cabbie. Kevin walked into a tiny cubicle with a door on one side and a counter at right angles. A metal grille separated him from the taxi office where a couple of women and a man were hunched over laptops, headsets clamped to their ears. The fractured mutter of their conversation was an aural palimpsest of projected journeys. Immediately behind the counter sat a sour-faced woman in her forties. She looked him up and down with an expression that said life had been a succession of disappointments and Kevin wasn't about to change that.

'You want a cab, love?' she said wearily, her voice dull and nasal.

Kevin flashed his ID and suddenly she seemed to perk up. 'Ooh,' she said. 'Regional. Not local. That sounds exciting. What can I do for you, love?' It was almost coquettish, which sat ill with the lines of misery on her face.

'I'm trying to track down some information about a fare one of your cabs picked up on Tuesday. I know people have to book their cabs through you. They can't hail them on the street, right? So I reckoned' – he leaned on the counter and gave her his best smile – 'you would be the one to talk to.'

'You got that right, at any rate. Nobody understands how this system works better than I do. What is it you need to know?'

'Tuesday evening. Around eleven p.m. I'm not sure where the pick-up was, but the cab made a drop at 43 Fulwell Crescent then went on somewhere else.'

'Ooh, now that makes it a bit more complicated,' she said, already abstracted as her fingers tapped the laptop keyboard. 'Let's see . . . '

Kevin couldn't quite believe his luck. He was accustomed to the low-level officiousness of almost everybody who ever tapped a keyboard. The knee-jerk reaction of 'Well, it's a data-protection issue,' when the information requested was completely innocuous and absolutely not covered by the legislation on the subject was one of the few things that provoked an irrational rage in him. To come up against someone who appeared not to give a damn about exerting petty power almost restored his faith in the public. 'I appreciate your help,' he said.

'I believe in helping the police,' the woman said, eyes still on the screen. 'Our Penny got attacked on the Chevin walking her dog last year and your lot couldn't have done a better job. The little shit got two years in the end but it wasn't the police's fault that the judge was a proper marshmallow.' She frowned. 'Here it is. Pick up ... Ooh, that's a lovely restaurant, our Jack took his girlfriend there to propose to her. Drop at Fulwell Crescent then ... Oh, that's a bit odd.'

'What's that?'

'Well, he picked them up in the city centre, went all the way out to Fulwell Crescent then came all the way back into town to drop him at the station. It would have made much more sense to do the station drop first. Not to mention being a lot cheaper.'

It might not make sense to the taxi dispatcher but Kevin saw exactly what was going on. The man called Mark was making sure Amie would have no reason to doubt anything he said about himself. And laying a false trail for her or anyone else coming along behind. 'I don't suppose the driver's on duty at the moment?'

'Let me check.' A couple of mouse clicks then she nodded. 'You're in luck, love. Barry Cohen. He came on at noon. Hang on.' She turned away and walked her chair across the floor to the nearest headset wearer. She tapped the woman on the shoulder and they had a muttered exchange.

'She's calling him in,' the dispatcher said when she returned to the counter. 'He's dropping up at Cookridge, he'll be back in ten minutes.'

Kevin's smile was a hundred per cent genuine. 'I really appreciate your help.'

'It's a pleasure. Why don't you wait outside for Barry? He's driving a silver Skoda Octavia. I'll let him know it's all right to talk to you.'

Barry arrived a few minutes later, jammed behind the

wheel of his taxi. Fat descended from his shoulders in waves. With his stubbled jaw, he resembled a bull seal who'd been washed up by the tide. Kevin couldn't imagine him getting out of the car and helping a passenger with luggage. He climbed into the passenger seat and introduced himself. 'We're pursuing a lead in a serious inquiry,' he explained. 'I need to talk to you about a fare last Tuesday evening.'

'Aye,' he grunted. 'Babs said. Is this going to take long?'

'That depends how much you can tell me,' Kevin said.

'Only, I'm working. I've got a wife and four kids to support.'

Kevin shuddered inwardly at the thought of how those children had been conceived. Stella would chide him for being judgemental, but sometimes it was hard not to be. 'Then the quicker we get started, the sooner you'll get back to work.'

Barry harrumphed. 'Easy for you to say, with your inspector's wages. Me, I'm always struggling. It's always the working man that loses out. I reckon you should pay me for the fares I'm losing.'

'That's not how it works.' Barry looked as if he might burst into tears and Kevin softened. 'I tell you what,' he said. 'Start the meter running and drive round the block.'

Barry didn't need telling twice. They moved into the stream of traffic and Kevin said, 'So, this fare on Tuesday evening. You picked them up outside a restaurant?'

'That's right. Nice little place. Not that I can afford to go there. Guadalupe, it's called. It's down an alley off Briggate, you can't drive down there. So they were waiting on Briggate itself.'

'How many passengers?'

'Just the two.' Barry moved over to the left lane and stopped at a set of traffic lights. 'A man and a woman.'

'Can you describe them?'

'Not really. I wasn't paying much attention, to be honest. All I'm bothered about is whether they're sober enough and if they look like they've got the money for the fare. I couldn't pick them out of a line-up or owt. What's he done then, this bloke?'

Kevin couldn't pretend he was disappointed. That had been a long shot. 'Did you overhear any of their conversation?'

'Wasn't listening. Have you any idea how bloody boring most people are? You hear folk taking the piss out of opinionated cab drivers, like we're stupid bigots. But bloody hell, you should hear the nonsense I have to put up with. So now I leave the radio on Smooth and try to tune them out. All I remember is they were quite chatty, so I reckoned they weren't married or owt.' The lights changed and they swung round the corner. Kevin hugged the door to avoid the ample flesh of his driver.

'Where did you drop them?'

'She got out at Fulwell Crescent. Not sure what number but it was a block of flats. He walked her to the door. I was keeping an eye on them in case they did a runner. People are tight bastards, especially late at night when they've had a drink and they think it'd be a laugh to rip off a cab driver. But he just gave her a kiss and got back in the cab. He was wearing glasses, now I think on. Big round ones like them hipsters wear.'

'OK. And Babs said you took him back into town?'

'Aye. That were a surprise. Why come all the way out of town to go straight back in again? I could have dropped him at the station easy enough ahead of taking her home. I never said owt, but I thought he had more money than sense.'

'You took him to the train station, then?'

'That's right.'

This was beginning to feel like a dead end. But Kevin plodded on. 'Did he say where he was going?'

'No. But here's the funny thing. He said his train was at ten to midnight. Only, us taxi drivers know the train times because we're always dropping people off. And I'm pretty sure there's not a train at ten to midnight out of Leeds station. I might be wrong, but I don't think I am.'

'I'll check it out.'

'You'll be wasting your time. Because here's the thing. I dropped him off at the station and he walked in the door. I didn't drive off right away, I stopped for a word with one of the other drivers. And bugger me if he didn't come straight back out the other door and walk away back into the city centre. So what was all that about, eh?'

If Tony was right and their killer was as careful a planner as they feared, this looked like another attempt to throw sand in their eyes. But perhaps he had miscalculated this time. There were few places in modern Britain quite so thoroughly surveilled as a mainline railway station in a major city. Kevin allowed himself a moment of satisfaction. This was something solid for Stacey to get her teeth into.

36

Tony only realised how long he'd been staring unseeing at his laptop screen when Flash padded through from the main part of the barn and dropped her head into his lap with a faint yip. He looked at his computer clock and pushed back from the desk, startled at how the time had slipped away. 'Sorry, Flash,' he muttered. 'You must have had your legs crossed.'

Five minutes later they were on the hill, Tony climbing in a series of wide zigzags, the dog flying hither and thither on the trail of whatever random scent caught her attention. There was a sharp breeze cutting across the moorland, alternately buffeting one side of his head then the other. The sky was the solid grey of impending rain. None of this impinged on his consciousness. Tony was digging deep inside himself in a bid to figure out what was going on under the surface of the double murder Carol's team were charged with solving.

Empathy lay at the root of everything he did, both as a clinical practitioner and a profiler. His ability to slip inside someone else's skin, someone else's brain, someone else's heart was uncanny. It had caused him a deal of grief over the years; there had been times when other people's pain had threatened to overwhelm his own defences. But he welcomed it. All those years when he'd believed he was only passing as human, that pain had been an anchor. And these days, now he was beginning to trust in the integrity of his own emotions, he still valued that identification with someone else's discomfort at the world.

He'd been scared of himself for so long because he knew how many of the boxes on the serial offender tick-list applied to him. A mother who failed to show him love and actively demonstrated her contempt for his existence. An overbearing grandmother who'd done most of the child-raising and had a punishment regime whose cruelty wouldn't have been out of place in the novels of Charles Dickens. A father so absent that Tony had known nothing of him till after his death. The target of bullying, verbal and physical, at school. And early sexual experience that had ended in mockery. His impotence still humiliated him; but sometimes he wondered whether these days he clung to it because it saved him from taking that final step towards Carol that would only end in yet another failure.

What had saved him – and it was something he thought of often now there was a dog on the fringes of his life – was that one person had showed him love when he was in deep adolescent despair. A dinner lady, of all the unlikely people. A dinner lady who had spotted his misery and pushed him into helping her look after her troop of rescue dogs. He'd seen her love for the animals and felt her concern for him and it had hit him at the precise point in his life where his despair might have taken him down a very different road.

He owed it to her memory to use his powers for good.

So now he was trying to feel his way to a sense of the significance that lay beneath these apparently meaningless crimes. 'You're not killing these women specifically,' he said aloud. Talking and walking always helped him to make sense of his cases. He used to pace the floor in his old study. Back and forth, back and forth for hours on end. Then he ended up living on *Steeler*, the narrowboat that had belonged to his father, and he'd begun to march along the canal towpath that led from the Minster Basin through a secret canyon that ran between tall city centre offices and hotels before it emerged in the scrubby hinterland of the inner city suburbs. And now, here he was, camping in Carol Jordan's dead brother's spare room, quartering the moorland behind the barn with a mad-eyed collie who was afraid of sheep. Tony had no idea how he'd ended up in this limbo. But he had to stay for as long as it took Carol to be easy with her new sobriety. Even if it made him wary and uneasy.

'They're ciphers,' he said. 'They could be anyone. You crash other people's weddings. Why? Do weddings have some symbolic meaning for you? Is it the wedding that matters, not the women?' He jumped over a marshy trickle of stream bravely forcing its way through the coarse moorland grasses.

'Or is it because weddings put lonely women in the right frame of mind to be picked up? Do you target weddings because it's an environment where women who are sitting on their own stand out? Easier to *identify* women on their own. Not like a club or a bar where women tend not to arrive alone. They go with their mates, in a group. But women will go to a wedding without a partner. They go because they're family, or they're friends, and it would cause offence if they didn't show up.'

He turned to survey the landscape and catch his breath. The dog bowled up to him and butted his thigh, as if to accuse him of laziness. Tony resumed his walking and Flash darted off, satisfied. 'So you turn up at the point in the day when the formalities are over and people are dancing and drinking, and you dress to fit in. You make yourself unobtrusive. You stand at the bar and pick up enough to pass yourself off as a friend of the bride or groom to the woman you choose.

'And then you move in on her. But you're not only acquiring her and killing her. That's not what this is all about. You've got a more sophisticated agenda than simply acquire and kill. You want them to love you. Or at least you want to be able to believe that they love you. You need to take them on dates so you can construct a fake reality. It's *The Truman Show*. They think they're in the real world, they think you're really attracted to them, they think you might be Mr Right. Because they met you at a wedding where Mr Right is on every woman's mind. And you use that to create an image in their head. You listen to them. You don't come on too strong.'

He frowned, wondering where this narrative was going. 'And then you kill them. You don't just kill them. You overkill them. You strangle them, you drive them to a remote roadside and then you set fire to them. You obliterate them.' He stopped again, hands thrust deep into his pockets. 'Who are you really killing?'

'It's a good question, Dr Hill.' The voice coming from behind him startled Tony so badly he jumped, stumbled and almost fell. If George Nicholas hadn't grabbed him, he'd have ended up on his knees on the boggy ground. 'Sorry, I didn't mean to startle you. I did call your name a couple of minutes ago but you seemed not to hear me.' Carol's neighbour let go Tony's arm and stepped back. He was dressed for the country in corduroy trousers, Hunter wellies and a Barbour jacket, a tweed flat cap on his head. His pink complexion was heightened by the wind and the effort of the climb, making him look a perfect caricature of the country gentleman.

Tony gave a lopsided smile. 'Sorry, I was thinking.'

'Aloud, by the sounds of it.' George smiled. 'I do that myself. After I lost my wife, I couldn't be bothered with anybody else's conversation.'

'It helps me put my thoughts in order,' Tony said, trying not to sound brusque. According to Carol, George had made her feel more at home in the valley than any other neighbour. He should try harder to like the man and not make snap judgements based on his wardrobe. But then, he'd spent his working life making judgements about how people chose to present themselves. He wasn't likely to stop now. Not for some land-owning toff who had let Carol get behind the wheel of her car when he must have known she was over the limit.

'How's Carol enjoying being back at work?' George asked, leaning on the shepherd's crook walking stick he carried.

'You'd have to ask her.' Tony knew he sounded abrupt, but what else could he say.

'This is a bit awkward . . . ' George looked embarrassed, his eyes on the far horizon.

'But?'

'But I think I ought to say something. I don't want Carol to be blindsided by more muckraking.'

Tony was immediately on the alert. 'You're going to have to explain that, George.'

'My staff are very loyal. You should know that upfront.' He sighed. 'The night Carol was breathalysed on the way home. There's been a woman asking around about the dinner party. Trying to find out who was working in the dining room that night. She tracked down Jackie, who runs the house for me. Asked her point-blank how much Carol had been drinking.'

The wind filled the silence between them. Then Tony said, 'What did Jackie say?'

'She said we didn't talk to the gutter press and even if we did, we understood the obligations of hospitality.' A sudden smile flashed across his face. 'And then she told her to fuck off.'

'If it's who I think it is, I can't say I blame her. Did she describe this woman?'

George nodded. 'Well dressed, well spoken, long dark hair. Unsuitable shoes, according to Jackie.'

'Sounds like Penny Burgess from the *Evening Sentinel Times*. She's wanted to bring Carol down for a long time. Thanks for letting me know.'

'I'm afraid there's a little more. One of the police officers who arrested Carol turned up yesterday. He spoke to Jackie. He asked her the same thing that the journalist woman had. How much had Carol been drinking. Jackie said she couldn't say for sure, that she hadn't been in the room the whole time but she didn't think Carol had had more than a glass of white and a glass of red over the whole evening.'

Tony knew that was a lie. So did George but neither was going to admit it. 'Did he go away?'

'He did. But I have a feeling he's going to go on asking. And it only takes one person to get cold feet when it's a police officer asking.'

Tony's heart sank. There would never have been a good time for this story to start stirring. But there couldn't have been a worse time. Not in the thick of such a crucial case. Not with the burden of guilt she was already carrying. Not when Carol was finally starting to get back on an even keel. He remembered the last time she had become embroiled in other people doing the wrong thing for the right reason and he didn't know how he was going to break this latest news to her.

37

Stacey flicked through the open windows on her half-dozen screens, checking what was still running and which of the programs she'd set in motion had come up with any results. There were routines that were straightforward – the algorithm she'd swagged from a friend which analysed data from the Automatic Number Plate Recognition system and projected driving routes based on camera sightings, for example. It was working backwards on any existing data on the cars of Kathryn McCormick and Amie McDonald, chugging away in the background, scavenging information from sources other than the official camera feeds. And there were other programs that were – how would she have put it? – not generally available.

One of those clandestine apps trawled social media accounts and classified contacts according to a wide array of criteria and attributes. It was based on a piece of code she'd written herself a few years before, so the developer who had pushed it to the next level had passed it on to her as a tip of the hat. She'd set it loose on Kathryn McCormick's Facebook, RigMarole and Twitter accounts, but it had been hard to develop any leads from them. Kathryn wasn't one of those women who was addicted to selfies and status updates. She'd used her social media sparingly, and mostly in relation to office-based social events. Most of her contacts appeared to be workmates or family members and the content was unremittingly dull to anyone outside those groups. A couple of new names had posted friend requests to her RigMarole account after the wedding, both saying how much they'd enjoyed meeting her, both tagging her in photos where she was on the sidelines. Kathryn had accepted the women and thanked them. But that had been the extent of their communication even though both women had posted comments about how great the wedding had been.

Stacey had checked them out. Tiffany Smith was a cousin of the bride, Claire Garrity was a bakery manager. Tiffany had been on RigMarole for years and had a reasonably static bunch of friends, adding new people every couple of months or so. Her feed was the usual – kids, dogs, cakes, holidays, karaoke, memes with varying degrees of funny. Claire used her account rather less frequently but she'd been a member for a couple of years. She'd posted a couple of photos of the wedding but hadn't tagged anyone. Based on her lack of activity, Stacey thought she probably didn't know how to. There was nothing apparently suspicious or even mildly questionable about either of them.

Looking at the screen now, Stacey noted the results from the trawl of Amie's social media were spooling down the page. New contacts were stuttering across the screen, the dateline on the end of each line. Two months ago, five weeks ago, two weeks ago. Two weeks ago. Right after the wedding. Stacey drew in a sharp breath. The final new friend on Amie's RigMarole account was Claire Garrity. Accepted the day after the wedding. Claire had commented on a photo that had caught Amie staring wistfully across the room, chin propped on her hand. 'Love you in this pic,' the comment read.

Amie had responded. 'I look like a wet weekend in Widnes.'

'No, you look dead romantic!!! Like, one day my prince will come.'

'LOL. Well, maybe he has already . . . '

'Hope so, you deserve it.'

And that was the end of it. But what was going on here? What were the implications of this? How could the same woman befriend two murder victims just after they'd hooked up with a man who was the most likely person to have killed them? The only logical answer was that this wasn't Claire Garrity. It was the killer himself, getting his kicks from infiltrating another corner of their lives.

She was halfway to her feet to share the new information with Carol when a thought occurred to her. Stacey went in through the back door she'd opened for herself years ago into the digital platform that housed the *Bradfield Evening Sentinel Times*. She typed in 'Claire Garrity' and found her answer in the personal columns. Claire Garrity had died in a road traffic accident ten weeks before. Nothing in the least suspicious about it – a lorry driver had fallen asleep at the wheel on the M60 and ploughed into her Fiat Punto. But presumably, because she scarcely used her RigMarole account, nobody had thought to close it down. And somehow a killer had accessed it and used it for his own twisted purpose.

Stacey stood up so abruptly her chair spun out behind her. She marched down to Carol's office. Only the courtesy ingrained by her parents stopped her from barging straight in. She knocked, waited, gripped the handle and shot inside as soon as Carol gave her the word. 'I think he friended them on RigMarole,' she blurted out. 'And he stole a dead woman's ID to do it.'

'I don't understand.' Carol looked baffled, as people often did when Stacey made her bald announcements. Patiently, she explained what she'd found. Carol's eyebrows rose. 'Why would he do a thing like that?'

Sometimes Stacey thought Carol spent too long listening to Tony Hill. In spite of the successes he'd helped them achieve in recent years, Stacey was still sceptical of his approach. Motive wasn't important in murder inquiries. Process was what counted. It didn't matter why the killer was messing with his victims. What really mattered was the opportunity it offered. What could they learn from his digital footprint? Where would this information take them? 'I've no idea,' Stacey said briskly. 'But RigMarole might know the IP address those messages came from.'

'Will they tell us?'

Stacey shrugged. 'We can try for a warrant, but they'll drag their heels even if we can get one. But I—'

Carol held up a hand. 'How many times do I have to tell you, Stacey? I don't need to know the intricacies of what you do.'

Which translated, Stacey thought cynically, to 'If you're going to break the law – what I don't know can't hurt me.'

'And besides,' Carol continued, 'there are practical avenues to pursue. There's a chance the killer knew she was dead because he knew her when she was alive. I mean, he would have had to crack her password to use her RigMarole account, wouldn't he?'

'Yes. Though it might have been something ridiculous like her husband's name, and he could have got that from the newspaper report. But these days, most people are a bit more savvy about social media passwords. Everybody knows somebody who's been hacked.'

'"I'm on holiday in Marbella and I've had my bag snatched, please wire me £200 to get home."'

'Exactly. So yes, maybe he did know her well enough to work out a more challenging password.'

'So we show the pics we've got to this Claire Garrity's nearest and dearest. And her workmates. And perhaps the gods will smile on us and someone will recognise him.'

'And just in case ... ' Stacey flipped a mock salute at Carol, 'I'll see what RigMarole can tell me. With or without their consent.'

38

As soon as he'd returned to the poky flat her betrayal had consigned him to, he'd flipped open the laptop and wallowed in the coverage. His first outing had been characterised as a curiosity, mostly ignored in the press but picked up online, especially once it had leaked out that Kathryn had already been dead when the blaze had started. But with a second similar incident in the same geographical location, everyone's ears had pricked up and the case had been upgraded to a mystery. The police weren't saying much, and nobody was acknowledging the fact that Amie hadn't died in the fire either. But everyone was absorbed by the odd circumstances of the deaths.

Nobody had made a connection between the killings and the weddings that had preceded them. Nobody was talking about new boyfriends or mysterious weekend trips to the Dales. That would come, though. He was sure of it. Now there was a genuine mystery to chase, the hacks would be all over the private lives of the victims. Eventually, friends would talk.

He didn't fear that moment. He wasn't afraid of being

caught because he didn't believe he would be. Didn't believe he could be. He'd covered his tracks so comprehensively. He'd researched the truth about forensics, as opposed to the half-truths peddled by TV shows and crime writers and he'd made a list of all the possible trace evidence he needed to avoid. So, no going back to their place for a coffee or sex. No giving them a lift anywhere. No messages that could be traced back to any of his electronic equipment. Never putting the batteries in his burner phones except when they were where he was supposed to be. Paying for everything in cash. Avoiding restaurants whose approaches were covered by CCTV. Making subtle but effective changes to his appearance, ones he could easily reverse so the people he had to see regularly wouldn't be freaked out by them.

When he'd first embarked on his mission of revenge, he was determined to avoid capture solely because that would interfere with his ultimate goal of killing Tricia. And he needed to kill her, to wipe her off the face of the world, to destroy her for what she'd done to him. The humiliation. The stripping of the things that mattered to him – having her by his side, on his arm; the luxurious home they'd made together; the business they'd built from scratch that was slowly disintegrating day by frustrating day; and the deep sense of security and achievement that possessing all that had given him. How could she turn on him like that? And not because he'd done anything wrong, but because she'd decided he didn't fulfil every bloody stupid romantic fantasy that magazines and movies had stuffed her head with.

Her disappearance had only fuelled his fury. Nobody would tell him a bloody thing. Not a clue. Then he had a brainwave. She might have closed down her social media accounts but there was no way she'd be able to give up that endless exchange of trivia with her friends. He'd put money on the fact that she'd have new accounts up and running in another name. And that under that other name Tricia would have befriended the women she trusted not to reveal her secret to him. If he could spy on their accounts, he was sure he could triangulate the identity Tricia was hiding behind.

But if he simply set up a new account, it would be obvious. He needed to weasel his way into an existing account so he could forge a connection to the women Tricia knew. But he had to find a way to do that without raising suspicions.

And then he had his second brainwave. So bloody clever it made him laugh out loud.

It hadn't been too hard to pull off and, so far, it was working. He'd managed to become RigMarole friends with two of the women Tricia was closest to. But it was taking forever. The more days that passed, the more his anger burned. Time was not healing these wounds. Rather, it was making them more agonising. He'd never be at ease with himself while she still breathed. He understood that very clearly. Her existence was an insult to him and everything he valued. But killing her would only be flawless if he walked away with clean hands. There would be no satisfaction in ending her life if it ended his too. And so when he decided to use other women as surrogates to give him some sort of relief from the rage that made his head hurt and his heart sore, he knew he had to perfect this act so that, although he'd be a suspect when Tricia died, he'd be untouchable.

The key, as always, was to consider every step of the process from all angles. What could go wrong? How could he guard against that possibility? What steps did he need to take to protect himself?

With the killing of Amie, he'd come to realise that the preparation was part of the satisfaction. It made him feel good. Not as powerful as the murder itself, obviously. But it gave him the comfort of control right down the line from first contact to the moment he lit the match.

And with his new RigMarole account, he'd been able to forge connections to his victims. He could spy on them, hugging his secret knowledge to himself. He could 'like' the photos from the weddings that their friends had posted. He could even 'talk' to them. And the beauty of it was that he wasn't putting himself in any kind of jeopardy.

The final part of the first stage, luring the women to his cottage in the Dales, was always going to be the riskiest part of his endeavour. He'd thought they might balk at not having the full address. He'd had an explanation prepared about the postcode not matching the actual location. But so far, neither of them had questioned it. When he'd told them the cottage couldn't be located on satnav, they'd both accepted it and fallen in with his suggestion that he meet them in a nearby pub car park – where he knew there was no camera coverage – then follow him to the cottage in their own cars.

The 'own cars' thing was a shrewd move, he thought. It would reassure them to have a means of escape if things didn't turn out the way they'd hoped. And it gave him the extra insurance of not ever having them shedding their DNA all over the interior of his borrowed car. It had been a brilliant idea, and it had worked perfectly in practice.

And then the sheer delight of leading them up the garden path. Two days of pandering to their every whim, of second-guessing what they'd enjoy. Of finding reasons to keep them indoors. Because he didn't want them to be spotted by some random hiker wandering around the landscape as if they owned the place. He hadn't been too worried about that in advance, though. Friday-night dinner with plenty of alcohol. Then bed and the most attentive sex he could manage. He hadn't found either of them particularly attractive, but there were ways round that. Fantasy, memory, and the sort of endless snuggly foreplay that women always appreciated.

He'd assumed that if the sex was good enough, they'd be

happy to spend Saturday in bed. Then cook dinner together. And that was exactly how it had gone with Kathryn. She'd been eager to please and thrilled by his attentiveness. He suspected she was so excited at the prospect of a new relationship that she was reluctant to make any demands of him. Really, she was a pushover. Easy to string along till, lulled by GHB-laced champagne on Sunday afternoon, he had put his hands around her neck and tightened his grip till her eyes had bulged and her face had turned from crimson to purple. It had been harder than he'd expected but imagining Tricia's face in front of him had been all it took to make him stick with it till she stopped struggling and making those terrible choking noises.

It had been so different the first time he'd killed someone. Then, it had felt unreal, like a video game. He'd had no idea it was so easy to kill someone for real. If he'd imagined it at all, he'd have thought it would be much, much harder to end someone's life. He'd been playing with Johnny Cape in the steeply wooded ravine between the terraced houses on Approach Street and the orchard behind the vicarage. They'd been wrestling on the ground, hot and sweating, their chewing gum breath in each other's faces. And Johnny had gasped, 'This is like how your mum is with the men she goes with.' Then he'd made the kind of animal grunts that were so familiar, so humiliating, so invasive.

A black fury had risen inside him and he'd grabbed at the first thing that came to hand. A fallen branch from an ash tree, about as thick as a toddler's arm. He'd smashed the branch against Johnny's head as hard as he could and when Johnny let go and fell back, yelping, he'd put the branch across Johnny's throat and leaned on it with all his weight, grunting with the effort. Just like the men who paid their rent did.

Johnny's heels had drummed on the forest floor, his eyes

swelled like a frog's, his tongue pushed out between his goofy teeth and his skin went a dark, dark red. Then he'd stopped. And everything in the wood was quiet. Even the birdsong was momentarily silent. Or maybe the ringing in his head wiped everything else out.

He'd staggered to his feet and run home. His mum had been in the kitchen, making cottage pie for their tea. He remembered the cottage pie. He'd said nothing and acted as though nothing had happened.

When the police arrived before bedtime, he'd acted shocked and upset. And yes, it had been an act. Because honestly? He hadn't felt much of anything at all. He told the friendly policewoman that he'd left Johnny in the wood, gathering sticks to make their gang hut look better. She asked if he'd seen anybody on his way home and he said yes, there had been a man walking along the path into the woodland. When she wondered what the man had looked like, he'd pictured the guy from the kids' club at the holiday camp they'd been at the summer before, and given a halting description of him. It had been ridiculously easy to fool everybody.

It had even been on *Crimewatch*. Nobody ever doubted his account. And nobody was ever arrested, which he was glad about. He'd have felt bad if somebody he had nothing against had been falsely accused.

And he'd carried on with his life as if nothing had happened. No nightmares, no bed-wetting, no panic attacks. To begin with, he'd missed having Johnny to play with, but he told himself that even if he'd still been alive, they couldn't have been friends any longer anyway, not after he'd said those things about his mother.

The difference was that this time he hadn't been able to run away from what he'd done. He could hardly bring himself to look at her after she was dead because the sight of her face reminded him that this wasn't Tricia. This was a poor substitute for the woman who really deserved to die. The killing had made him feel better, but the high hadn't lasted. He'd had to wait till darkness fell to carry her body out to her own car. He'd thrown a sheet over her so he didn't have to see her. It was only when he set fire to her in the car, obliterating her difference from the woman he wanted to kill, that the sense of control and power returned to him. And this time it lasted.

He wasn't worried about her DNA being all over the cottage. They'd never trace him back to this place. On paper, it was still owned by a company that had been defunct for five years, a company whose name he'd never been officially connected with. It had been Tricia who had briefly been on their board and who had done some shady deal where she'd got the cottage in exchange for not telling the VATman what had really been going on with the company accounts. It had been rented out off the books for years to an academic at Leeds University who used it at weekends, but she hadn't protested too much when he'd told her the arrangement was at an end a couple of months before. She knew she didn't have a leg to stand on. So there was no paper trail leading anywhere near him.

Still that didn't give him carte blanche to be careless. And it had been infuriating that things hadn't gone according to plan with Amie. She'd been a lot harder to please than Kathryn. On the Saturday morning, she'd insisted on going for a walk even though it was drizzling and the visibility was negligible. He'd tried everything to put her off, but she'd been determined. At least the rain meant they'd both had to put their hoods up. He didn't think any of the handful of walkers they'd passed could ever have recognised them again.

But once they'd returned, she'd gone on and on about the craft shops and tearooms they could visit the next day. All his careful planning was going up in smoke before his eyes.

However, he wasn't about to be defeated by an idiotic woman obsessed with finding some souvenir of their time together. He could think on his feet.

So he'd strangled her after dinner on Saturday instead. It had been easier the second time because he knew what to expect. The drugged passivity, the grunting gasps as the body struggled for air even in its unconscious state, the ugly colour of the skin as it suffused with blood. And beneath it all, the pure delight of imagining it was Tricia under him.

Afterwards he felt no guilt. Not least because Amie had begun to irritate him with her constant chatter about people he'd never met and places he'd never been. No wonder her relationships had never worked out. Everything was about her. There was a certain relief to her death, even though he didn't like having her body about the place all day on the Sunday. Ironically, he'd gone out for a long walk by himself to get away from her.

But it had all worked out in the end. And he felt fabulous. So fabulous he'd laid his plans for the next one. Manchester this time. Plenty of choice there. And hopefully it would be another Kathyrn, not another Amie.

39

Because it was a midweek match, it had been possible to buy a couple of tickets for Bradfield Victoria's game against Stoke City at the last minute. It was the best idea Tony could come up with after Paula had tracked him down in the shipping container he used as a library to tell him how worried she was about Torin.

He'd been catching up on his reading when she'd banged on the door, the muffled clang of something hard on metal making him jump. Nobody had ever visited him there before but Paula had once dropped him off outside, so he wasn't entirely surprised to find her on his doorstep. 'I was reading,' he said plaintively.

'Good for you. Can I come in?'

'There's only one chair.'

'Well, get your coat and I'll treat you to a coffee,' she said in the tone she normally reserved for children who'd witnessed something traumatic.

Obediently he grabbed the purple jacket and padlocked the container behind him, hurrying to catch up with Paula, who was already halfway down the street, coffee in her sights.

When he caught up, she gave him a sceptical glance. 'Are you wearing that for a bet?'

'It was in the sale,' he said. 'Carol said it suited me.'

Paula snorted. 'Carol just wanted you in anything but the disreputable brown thing.' She turned into the coffee shop and made for the counter.

'I think this is the last coffee shop in town where the barista isn't a hipster,' Tony muttered as they found a quiet table to huddle over their drinks. 'So what can I do for you, Paula?'

'It's Torin,' she said. And outlined their recent concerns and the discovery that he had apparently sold some of his mother's jewellery. 'And then he completely lost it with me. Ranted about me invading his privacy, told me I had no business sticking my nose into his life and that what he did with his own stuff was nothing to do with me.'

Tony sighed. 'Tell me you didn't go down the "my house, my rules" line.'

'I'm not entirely stupid,' she growled. 'I backed off. But the last couple of days, it's been like living in a "no comment" interview. He's silent and surly, he won't meet my eyes and I don't know what to do.'

'What does Elinor think?'

Paula fidgeted in her chair. 'I haven't told Elinor. I've hardly seen her since it all blew up between Torin and me and, to be honest, I'd rather bring her a solution than a problem right now. They're incredibly short-staffed in A&E and she's having enough of a struggle trying to make sure everything at work is covered.'

'And you don't want Elinor to think you can't deal with Torin,' Tony said. 'Because then she'll take everything on herself.'

'That too,' she acknowledged reluctantly.

'You want me to talk to him?'

'Would you? He trusts you. When you come round for dinner, it's like he relaxes.'

'It's a guy thing,' Tony said, clearly mocking himself. 'Seriously, though. It's mostly because I'm not in a parental role. It's always easier to talk to someone who's got less investment in you. There's not the same potential for disappointing them.

'He's going to be suspicious of me suddenly turning up out of the blue so soon after you've had this row.' Tony sipped his coffee and frowned in thought. 'It's got to be the kind of thing we do anyway.' And then he'd remembered the football. He'd taken Torin to a Bradfield Victoria match once before. They'd gone to the game then for a kebab afterwards. Tony thought it had gone well. The only reason he hadn't repeated it was that it was almost impossible to get tickets for the Saturday games now that the team were nudging that valuable fourth-place slot that would see them playing in the Champions' League the following season. He'd had to settle for watching his team on their dedicated TV channel.

So Wednesday evening found Tony and Torin riding the bus across town to Ratcliffe, the city's melting-pot suburb. Every colour and creed seemed to have migrated to the narrow streets of red-brick terraces over the years. Walking the pavement here, a man could hear the unfamiliar phonemes of twenty different languages within half a mile. But on match days, English reclaimed the air as the Bradfield Victoria fans were funnelled from tram halts, from bus stops and from car parks into the handful of cramped thoroughfares that led to the great cantilevered stands of Victoria Park. The bright yellow of the home strips seemed to bring sunshine into the dank streets and random chants broke out as the fans milled together towards the temple of their faith.

'We're going to be in the Vestey Stand tonight,' Tony said.

'It runs along the side of the pitch. Not like the Grayson Street stand where we were the last time. You remember?'

'Yeah,' Torin said. 'We were smack-bang behind the goal. We had a great view when Pavlovicz scored.'

'So we did. Do you know who the stand is named after?'

'No. Is it interesting?' Torin grinned.

'I think so, but then I'm an anorak.'

Torin snorted with laughter. 'No kidding. You can see that a mile off. You're well ready for a Prince revival.' He hummed 'Purple Rain' under his breath.

'You're too young to remember that,' Tony complained.

'My mum loved Prince.' His face clouded momentarily, but he recovered himself. 'So why is it interesting?'

'It's named after Albert Vestey. He was the Vics' centre for-ward – that's a striker to you – from 1929 to 1938. He scored one hundred and ninety-seven goals for the club and he won twenty-two caps for England. But he never scored a goal in open play for the national side. All three of his goals were penalties. Now, you've got to admit that's interesting.'

Torin gave him a gentle punch on the shoulder. 'OK. It's a bit interesting.' They approached the turnstiles leading to their section of the stand. 'Thanks for asking me to come. I really enjoyed it before.'

'I've not actually managed to get a ticket since the last time we were here. Otherwise I'd have asked you. But I watch the games on my laptop. I've got a sub to TVics. You can always come over to the boat and watch it with me if I'm in town.'

The boy nodded. 'But Paula said you'd moved in with Carol. So you're not going to be on the boat, are you?'

Tony pulled a face. 'I've not moved in with her, as such. It's more like keeping her company. And I'm still down in Minster Basin two or three nights a week. So next time there's a home game and I'm around, I'll message you.'

'OK.' They began the steep climb to their seats. 'Are you and Carol, like, a couple?'

'Start with the easy questions, why don't you?' Tony grumbled. 'We care about each other. But we're not a couple. Not in the conventional sense. We're more than best friends and less than lovers.' It wasn't something he'd ever had to codify for someone else. Why he was telling Torin, he wasn't quite sure. Except that he understood that the best way to provoke honesty was to offer it up.

They squeezed past fellow fans to their seats and settled in, studying the team sheet they'd picked up on the way in. 'Karabinits is on the bench again,' Tony said.

'So how come you never got it together as a couple?'

'It's complicated. Bad timing? Fear? Not wanting to spoil what works? All of the above. And I'm rubbish at romance.'

He was spared further interrogation by the referee's whistle. The first half zipped by. End-to-end play, a goal apiece, some dazzling passages of play. The crowd roared and seethed and sang and nobody cared that it started raining, a fine drizzle that the wind blew into the faces of those lower down in the seating tiers.

At half-time, half the crowd disappeared to stand in line for bad food and overpriced drinks. Tony reached inside one of his many pockets and produced a bottle of sugar-loaded energy drink and a bag of popcorn. He handed them to Torin. 'There you go. Saves us having to queue.'

'What about you?' Torin looked greedily at the snacks, too polite to dive in without checking.

Another pocket, a bottle of water. 'I'm fine.'

They discussed the first half, dissecting the problems with the Vic's midfield. As the stand filled up again and anticipation buzzed around the stadium, Tony said, 'So what's the problem, Torin?'

The second half kicked off and the noise from the fans

grew in a deafening crescendo. Paradoxically, it made the crowded stand a very private place to have a conversation. 'I don't want to talk about it.' Torin frowned and leaned forward, staring at the match below.

'We never want to talk about the difficult things. But if we don't they poison the good things in our lives. You've already fallen out with Paula. Where's it going to end? Are you going to fall out with Elinor too? With me? And for what?'

'You don't understand.'

'I understand shame. And I understand fear of loss, Torin. You've already endured the worst kind of loss and that makes you twice as scared of losing more.'

Torin licked his lips but said nothing.

'You're not going to lose us. We're not going to walk away from you. We're on your side. Trust me, there's nothing you could have done that would make us reject you. We want to help you. I want to help you. I remember what it felt like to be your age. Everything looms so large in your head. And it's never quite as bad as you think.' He gave a dry bark of laughter. 'And believe me, I had a completely shitty adolescence.'

Torin flashed a quick look at him. 'I can't tell you, Tony. I've let everybody down, I accept that. But there's worse to come.'

'So let's head it off at the pass. There's nothing out there that can't be mitigated. We can't fix everything, I know that, but we can find ways to deal with whatever the problem is. I've been dealing with people's problems all my professional life, and really, it's never as catastrophic as you think.'

'There's nothing that anybody can do.' His voice was dull, his shoulders slumped. 'I did one really stupid thing and it's going to ruin my life.'

If it hadn't been for Paula's insistence to the contrary, Tony would have assumed Torin had impregnated his girlfriend. 'What? You're throwing in the towel without a fight? That's not like you. The way you handled yourself after your mum died, that wasn't the reaction of somebody who caves in. Come on, Torin, whatever it is, it's not the end of the world.'

Torin's response was to get to his feet and push his way to the end of the row. Tony was seconds behind him, earning grumbles and complaints and curses. He ran down the vertiginous steps behind the boy and they emerged almost together in the broad concourse that swept round the back of the stand. Torin fell back against the wall and dropped down into a crouch, burying his face in his folded arms. 'I'm sorry,' he mumbled, so quietly that Tony barely heard him.

Tony hunkered down beside him. 'I know. But you're only going to start to feel better when you talk about it.'

'I can't talk about it.' His voice shook.

'I'm not going to judge you, Torin.'

'You don't need to, I can do that for myself.' He sounded disgusted. 'I don't know how I'm going to face anybody.'

Tony put an arm round the boy's shoulders and drew him close. 'Come on, mate. You know what I do for a living. After all I've heard over the years, I'm bombproof. You need to trust somebody and it might as well be me.'

Torin shivered then gulped. 'You got to promise you won't tell Paula and Elinor.'

'They need to know, Torin.'

'I won't say another word unless you promise.'

There would be a way round this, but it would have to come from Torin himself. In the meantime, what mattered was finding out. 'I promise. Cross my heart. Like you were a patient.'

'I was lonely. Paula and Elinor, they're great but . . . '

'They're not fourteen.'

'I post a lot on Instagram. I'm quite good at taking interesting pics. All sorts of people like my stuff, and sometimes they comment, you know?'

Tony knew. He didn't really use social media but he lurked

because he needed to know the kind of behaviours people engaged in online. Most predators found the anonymity invaluable, and it was the perfect environment in which to do bad things without taking too many risks. 'Somebody started commenting a lot? Really praising your stuff?' Torin's head moved in what Tony took to be a nod. 'A girl?'

'She was funny,' he said. 'She made really sharp jokes about stuff. And she liked the same bands and the same games I do.'

How hard would that be to find out? Even Tony could manage it with a few clicks and some search engine work. 'And you fancied her?' he said gently.

'Anybody would. She was gorgeous.' He let out a shuddering breath. 'I could hardly believe she liked me too.'

'And you took it out of the public arena? Into a private space?'

Torin raised his head and his eyes were damp. 'I was lonely. And she sent me photos. Then little videos. Sexy, you know?' His face was beseeching Tony to understand, to forgive.

A swell of sympathy rose in Tony's chest, tempered with the anger he felt at the heartless bastards who had exploited Torin. He could see what was coming and it made his heart ache. 'And she asked you to do the same.'

Torin dropped his eyes again. 'Yeah,' he croaked. 'So I did.'

Tony reached out and put a hand on his shoulder just as the noise from the stadium erupted and engulfed them. Bradfield had clearly scored. When it died down, he said, 'They blackmailed you. "Give us money or everybody in your contact list gets a copy."'

'Yeah. They wanted £500.'

'So you sold your mum's pendant?'

He nodded. 'I got £550 for it. And then Paula said it was up for £800, so whoever bought it, well, they were cheating me too. I'm a complete mug. But it's not going to stop. I got a message last week saying they want a grand by the end of the month or they'll distribute it to everybody I know and post it online.' His voice cracked with desperation.

'How did you pay them?'

'They gave me card details and told me to go into a bank and pay the cash on to the credit card. It was one of those cards you buy to load up with cash and spend with the card. Like when you go abroad. If anybody asked, I was to say it was for my cousin who was on his gap year and needed a top-up. But nobody asked.'

Probably untraceable, Tony thought. They needed to get Stacey on board with this. 'I'm sorry you've had to carry this by yourself.' He put an arm round the boy's hunched shoulders. 'I think we can sort this,' he said. 'But first you're going to have to tell Paula and Elinor.'

Torin pulled away, his face an accusation. 'You promised!'

'I know. That's why I said *you're* going to have to do the telling.'

40

Eileen Walsh sat on the stool in front of her dressing table removing her make-up with soft cotton pads. When she'd furnished her bedroom, the light bulbs surrounding the mirror were how she'd imagined a Hollywood star's dressing room would appear. She didn't mind the cliché; she wanted there to be one part of her day where she could feel like a star. Even if it was only the star of her own life.

That had been five years ago and nothing that had happened to Eileen had felt remotely starry. There was nothing glamorous about work. Being a nurse on the women's surgical ward in Manchester Royal Infirmary was to exist in a perpetual state of overwork with occasional moments of gratification when a patient you liked had a better outcome than expected, or when a family showered you with thanks and chocolates. But the constant exhaustion overwhelmed any sense of virtuous satisfaction at being part of a caring profession.

At one point, she'd dared to hope that marriage was going to rescue her from drudgery. Lovely, gentle Tim who had a good job with a major insurance company. They'd met when his mother had been in having her gall bladder removed and he'd inexplicably fallen for her. He wasn't the most exciting man in the world, but Eileen enjoyed his company and she could imagine a comfortable life with him. An end to loneliness, an end to financial worries. An end to dragging her weary body through endless shifts leading nowhere. She could do this, she told herself.

His mother made a good recovery, which Tim credited to Eileen's care. Two months later, after a succession of nights out at the cinema, an assortment of restaurants and a couple of gigs at the Apollo where they'd both been deafened by the volume, he'd proposed and she'd accepted. Her parents had been relieved as well as delighted; they'd been convinced that at thirty-five, she was definitely past her sell-by date.

Eight days later, he'd been waiting to cross Whitworth Street near the junction with Sackville Street when a roofer working on scaffolding right behind him had dropped a section of cast-iron drainpipe. It plummeted forty feet to the pavement below. And in those few terrible seconds, Tim lost all his remaining time.

Eileen's first emotion had been anger. One moment of heedlessness had cheated her out of the life that should have been hers. She was sorry about Tim. Of course she was. She wasn't some heartless gold-digging bitch. But she was more sorry for herself. He'd been her one chance to trade in an existence for a life. And now that chance was gone forever.

It was worse than being dumped because it wasted time. If some bastard gave you the elbow, you could put yourself back out there right away. But being bereaved meant you had to go through a respectable period of mourning. That was over now though. It had been seventeen months since the funeral and it was time to start looking again.

She'd been charm itself on the ward with anyone who might have a candidate in their life. Sons or brothers, single, divorced or widowed. She didn't mind. She'd put up with devotion to sport or oddball collections. Even an addiction to Jeremy Clarkson. She could squeeze herself into the mould of the woman they needed. But so far, there had been no likely candidates snapping at the bait. Time was running out and Eileen wanted off the ward and into a different life.

She wiped away the last of the make-up and leaned in closer to the mirror. There were shadows under her eyes, fine lines running through them. Still almost invisible, but they'd only get worse. And those faint brackets that appeared round her smile. They weren't going to disappear. Soon she'd become invisible. Just another woman sliding into middle age with a few extra pounds round her midriff and everything heading south along with her chances.

Maybe this weekend would be lucky. Eileen raised a coquettish eyebrow. She wasn't bad looking, not for her age. And weddings put a gloss on everybody. She'd seen it before. The celebration of matrimony turned love into an infectious disease. Surely a gay wedding would have the same aphrodisiac effect as a normal one? Surely Greg and Avram must know some straight men? OK, so she probably knew most of Greg's friends. They'd worked on the ward together for seven years, after all.

But Avram was a different matter. He worked at Media City. He was a radio documentary producer. He must know dozens of really interesting people. And statistically some of them must be single men of a certain age in want of a wife. And it was going to be a big wedding. A hundred and forty-three guests, according to Greg. She had to be in with a shout.

Eileen took the lid off her night nourishing cream and slathered it over her face. Only a few short days to go. Time enough for a lash tint and a manicure. There was no harm in making the most of herself.

Saturday could be the turning point. But if it wasn't, that was OK too, she told herself. She didn't mind her own company. She was doing all right on her own. She had friends from work, she had a life.

Who are you kidding? The voice in the back of her head was sardonic. And it opened the floodgates of fear again. The prospect of growing old and infirm all alone without the cushion of companionship and a comfortable income was terrifying. Her own parents were struggling with retirement, and they at least had each other. But she'd have no one. She'd be one of those smelly old women living in one room with nobody to visit her and no money to do anything except watch daytime TV. Surviving on baked beans and cheap white bread.

'Get a grip, Eileen,' she said sternly. Saturday would be her chance. She'd seize it with both hands.

41

Another week, another level of frustration for ReMIT. Some bright spark on a local paper had made the connection between the two deaths, in spite of Carol's efforts to keep the lid on the link between the circumstances. Now, as well as their colleagues looking over their shoulders, they had a daily media barrage demanding copy. Skenfrith Street was under permanent siege from a handful of determined hacks who were convinced the police were holding out on them.

The truth was very different. The morning briefing was bereft of new leads and none of the routine processes had led them anywhere. The CCTV from Leeds station had taken them no further; their target walked with his head bowed and never looked up. Stacey had been running ANPR results for all the major routes in and out of the Dales over the two weekends when their victims had been killed, but the handful of results had taken them nowhere. Every car number that turned up over both weekends had been accounted for.

'We've got forty-three locals going shopping or to football matches or to work. Thirty-one of them are men,' Stacey explained 'They've all got witnesses who confirm what they've told us and also alibis for assorted time slots over the weekend. None of them has enough time available close enough to the body dumps to have committed the crimes. And you can't get there by public transport.'

At her words, Tony looked up, head cocked to one side, frowning. But he said nothing.

'We've also got twenty-nine weekenders who have properties inside the camera-free areas we've marked out. Apart from one, they were all either couples or families and again, it's hard to see how any of the men could have popped out to seduce our victims and murder them.'

'What about the one?' Paula asked.

'According to the local police in Preston, where he lives, he's in the clear for both the wedding Saturdays. He's a tennis coach at the local club. On Saturday afternoons he runs three clinics. One for kids, two for adults. Both evenings, he was working behind the bar at the club during social fundraisers. His presence at the club is confirmed.' Stacey looked apologetic. 'So now Lancashire Police hate us as much as North and West Yorkshire for all the tedious alibi checking.'

'He'll be using hire cars,' Tony said, matter-of-factly. 'It's clear from everything to do with these cases that he has a remarkably high level of forensic awareness. He won't risk taking his own car anywhere near where he kills them or where he dumps them.'

'Still, we had to check,' Carol said. 'So, have we got anywhere with the wedding photos from either event?'

Alvin spoke. 'As we reported previously, we managed to track down all the wedding guests and compile copies of all their photographs and videos. Stacey came back to us with a CGI image of what the presumed killer looks like. We've shown it round the guests but nobody admits to recognising him.'

'And Karim and me have been doing the rounds of friends and families and workmates,' Kevin said. 'Apart from Amie's ex-boyfriend claiming he looked exactly like the guy who delivers Valhalla parcels to Amie's flat – which we checked out, and none of the delivery drivers looks remotely like the image – nobody recognised him. Guv, I think we should get his picture out in the media. What about *Crimewatch*?'

'I've been holding back because the software Stacey used to produce the image isn't tried and tested in court yet,' Carol said. 'I don't want to run the risk of some smart-arsed defence barrister accusing us of junk science down the line. But everything else seems to be a dead end, so I think we have to look at going public.'

Kevin groaned. 'Another mountain of false leads to chase down.'

'In the first instance, we'll use local bodies on the ground,' Carol said. 'I'll save you and Karim for checking out the ones that might go somewhere.'

'It's like terrorism,' Karim burst out. 'We know he's out there but we don't know where. It's like we're waiting for the next one, hoping he'll make a mistake. How do we stop this happening when we don't have a clue where to look?'

There was a moment's shocked silence. Finally, Carol spoke. 'Because it's what we do. We stop people like him because we keep hammering away at every possibility until we find him.'

Paula leaned across and put a hand on Karim's arm. 'You'll get used to feeling like this,' she said quietly. 'It happens every time. And we get past it.'

'We really do,' Kevin said.

Karim stared at the table, his left leg jittering beneath it.

Carol cleared her throat. 'Anybody have anything else?'

Tony stood up and began his familiar pacing routine. 'Stacey said something earlier. "You can't get there by public transport." But that means the converse is also true. The killer can't make his getaway on public transport. After Kathryn McCormick was killed, I thought he must be walking away. Or maybe jogging. I was going to suggest checking out all the properties within easy walking distance. Then I thought, what does that mean? Easy walking distance? I could easily walk five or six miles without thinking twice about it. But in the dark? Even on familiar terrain, that's a big ask. Because he couldn't walk on the road, could he? All it would take would be one passing car.'

Carol cut in. 'We did think about this, Tony. And we put it to one side for precisely that reason. We couldn't draw a radius that made any sense. For all we know, he could have left his car nearby at any point over the weekend and then used her car for their final journey.'

'That's true. And it's why I didn't waste your time. That was my reaction at the Amie McDonald crime scene too. How could we construct a meaningful search out of the little we knew? And then Stacey said what she said and all at once, something clicked and I understood what I'd been looking at.' He grinned triumphantly, not caring that he was met with an array of blank looks.

'You're going to have to tell us more than that, mate,' Alvin said. 'I don't think it's just me that doesn't have a clue what you're on about.'

'Carol, Paula? You remember that flattened grass and ripped-up earth I pointed out at the crime scene? Did forensics come back with anything?'

'No,' Paula said. 'There was nothing to indicate what it had been, except it had been heavy enough to make an impact and probably made of metal or sturdy plastic because it had scarred the ground.'

'Do we have the measurements?' Tony asked, taking out his phone and tapping at the screen.

'Let me check,' Paula said. 'The report only came in the day before yesterday . . . ' She crossed to her desk and pulled up the file. 'It's 716 millimetres long by 600 millimetres wide. They said the object was probably slightly smaller because it looked like it had skidded a short distance.'

Tony looked up from his phone with a beatific smile. 'A folded Brompton bike measures 585 by 565. If you chucked it over the ditch, it would probably skid a bit, wouldn't it? A thing that weighs that much?'

There was a moment's silence then Carol said, 'How did you work that out?'

'There are waymarked footpaths within a field or two of both of the crime scenes. You were all looking at the road because that's how he arrived.'

'We should have thought of that,' Paula said.

'Even if we had, we'd still have concentrated on the road,' Kevin said ruefully.

'That's brilliant,' Karim said, looking up with hope in his eyes.

'That's why we keep him,' Carol said. 'We're too busy looking at the trees. He sees the wood beyond. Paula, get on to Forensics and see whether there's anything on the crime scene photos that might be the impression of bike tyres. This changes things. We might have something solid to take to *Crimewatch*. If we can offer up a cyclist and the image, they might consider it worth going with. Anything else, anyone?'

Silence. 'Better get on with it, then,' Carol said wearily, heading for her office.

Tony caught up with Paula by her desk. 'Has he said anything to you yet?'

Paula shook her head. 'He was very quiet when you dropped him off after the football. And at breakfast, before Elinor came down, he apologised for losing his temper with me. And I said sorry for invading his privacy. What's going on, Tony?'

He sighed. 'I promised not to tell you,' he said. 'I can't risk losing his trust. Sorry. What if I come round tonight? Try to break the logjam?'

'Thanks.'

He nodded and grabbed his purple jacket on the way to the door. Paula messaged the crime scene technicians then leaned back in her chair. Spotting Kevin by the coffee machine, she decided now was as good a time as any and wandered nonchalantly across to join him.

'I thought you were back in harness for good, Kev,' she said.

'What's brought that on?' he hedged.

'Carol said you'd only agreed to come back till she could find another inspector she rated highly enough.'

He nodded. 'That's about the size of it. I was enjoying my retirement. I'm not one of those blokes who hankers after the thrill of chasing villains. I served my time and I was happy to settle into a new life.'

'But Carol tempted you back?'

He scoffed. 'Money tempted me back, Paula. She offered me my old rank. A step up from DS back to DI. She promised me that when she did find the right replacement, I'd go with a DI's pension. I won't pretend that wasn't a hell of an incentive. Me and Stella, we've got plans. And a bit more money will make things easier. Why are you asking?'

'She thinks I should go for my inspector's exams.' Paula studied his expression carefully. He didn't look very surprised.

'She's not wrong,' he said. 'What's holding you back?'

Paula shrugged. It wasn't that she lacked ambition but she feared what it might bring in its wake. 'I like doing what I do. I enjoy interviewing witnesses and suspects. I like being at the sharp end, not stuck in an office pushing papers and issuing actions to junior officers.'

Kevin shook his head. 'That's only what it would be like

if you were in a regular CID team. You know we do things differently here. You don't see me flying a desk much, do you? I'm out there doing the dirty work and asking the questions, just like I did when I was a DS. The only difference is that it's a bit easier when we're dealing with officers from the different forces we're working with. It's a lot easier to get cooperation when you're a higher rank.'

It was true. Even in these early days of ReMIT, Paula had noticed a reluctance to carry out her requests. And they had to be requests because she was often outranked by the officer she was asking something of. They didn't refuse outright, because they knew Paula could go up the ladder, which would mean they'd be shat on from a greater height. But they dragged their heels a bit, shared looks with their squad, made her feel like an interloper rather than one of the team. 'Does pulling rank really make it easier? Doesn't it wind them up even more?'

Kevin grinned. 'You don't have to pull rank, Paula. You just have to carry it. And it's about time you stepped up to where you should be. We all move on. Carol Jordan's going to have to retire one day. There needs to be somebody lined up to take her place.'

Startled, Paula gave a nervous laugh. 'What? You think I'm the person to do the boss's job?'

'Why not? You're a good detective and you're good with people. And you don't drag as many ghosts around with you as she does.'

A shadow passed across Paula's face. She had her dark places, albeit not as many as Carol. 'You've been spending too long in the sun on that allotment of yours,' she said, trying to sound light.

'And you need to take yourself a bit more seriously.' He finished making his coffee and walked away. Paula stood looking after him, a strange feeling stirring inside her.

42

Penny Burgess checked the clock on her phone for the third time in as many minutes. He was late. She was sitting at a grubby Formica-topped table in a motorway café that smelled of stale fat with something that claimed to be a flat white but tasted like hot milk that had once been shown a coffee bean. She'd have to wash her hair and probably take her coat to the dry cleaner at this rate.

She wondered whether PC Darren Finch was having second thoughts. She was used to having to warm up the cold feet of informants, but they had to show up before she could start the process. And he was nineteen minutes late for their agreed rendezvous. His suggestion of venue, not hers. She wondered at a traffic cop wanting to meet at a motorway service station. The very place where you might bump into a colleague, she'd have thought.

Maybe he was so limited that he couldn't imagine anywhere else. And they were technically in Lancashire, not West Yorkshire, the force he worked for, which gave him a margin of security, she supposed.

She couldn't help considering whether she'd adopted the

wrong approach. Finding the names of the officers who had arrested Carol Jordan had been easy enough now she had Sam Evans in her pocket. He'd looked up their names in the court records and found out where they were based. Penny had googled the two officers herself, and Finch had popped up, photographs and all, from a road safety programme he'd been fronting with sixteen-year-olds heading for their next birthday's driving lessons. She'd rung Halifax police station and asked to speak to him, hoping he was on duty or out on patrol. And she'd been obligingly told that he wasn't on duty until ten that evening. From what she knew of police shift patterns, she reckoned he'd be off duty at seven the next morning, so she'd risen early and had parked up opposite the back entrance to the station, where officers parked their cars.

At twenty past, she'd seen Finch leave the police station, chatting to a female officer. They'd separated and Finch had driven off in a black BMW. Penny set off behind him, keeping her distance since there wasn't much traffic that early in the day.

Finch drove straight through the centre of town and turned off into a maze of terraced streets, many of them one-way. Penny managed to keep him in sight as he zigzagged through the blackened stone rows, wondering if he'd spotted her tailing him and was trying to shake her off. Eventually he slowed right down, obviously looking for a parking space. She passed him and turned the corner, abandoning the car across the mouth of an alley.

She hustled back in time to see Finch squeezing into a space a couple of feet longer than his car. She was on the pavement waiting for him when he emerged. 'PC Finch?'

He looked startled. 'Do I know you?'

'Penny Burgess. *Bradfield Evening Sentinel Times*.'

'You're a bit off your manor,' he said. His voice was dark

and heavy, matching his looks. He paused and looked her up and down. 'What do you want with me?'

'I suspect you're as indignant as I am about the four drivers that walked free after you breathalysed them a few weeks ago.'

His face changed. Eyebrows lowered, jaw belligerently thrust forward. 'I've got nothing to say.'

'Off the record,' she said. 'I'm looking for confirmation, that's all.'

'Like I said. No comment.'

'So, what? It gets brushed under the carpet? Four people dead and we all shrug our shoulders and go, "Oh, well." And Carol Jordan gets to run ReMIT and tell your lads what to do? Not to mention that it makes you and your partner look pretty shoddy.'

He was still glaring, but he glanced quickly up and down the street. 'This isn't the time or the place.'

Penny slipped him a card. 'So you name the time and the place and I'll be there. It's not right that you lads are carrying the can for something much bigger than either of you.'

He'd taken the card and walked away without another word. But later that day, Penny had had a text from an unknown number setting the rendezvous where she was now waiting.

Had she pitched it wrong, appealing to his indignation and pride? Should she have banged the drum for justice instead? Was he more of an idealist than he appeared? She hoped not. If she was right about this, it was a helluva story. Front page in her own paper and picked up by the nationals and everywhere online. She wasn't ambitious in terms of moving to Fleet Street or TV, but Penny wanted a reputation that gave people pause when she called them up.

Her question was answered by a heavy tread behind her. She resisted the urge to turn around and waited for him to sink into the plastic chair opposite her. He was wearing a black puffa jacket over a black polo shirt and a black baseball cap pulled low over his forehead. He looked, she thought, like a low-rent rapper. He unscrewed the cap of a Coke Zero bottle and took a swig. 'Sorry I'm late,' he said. 'Shift over-ran. Had to charge some idiot with using his mobile while driving.'

'One less moron on the road tonight, then.'

'Aye. Now, before we get stuck in any further, I don't want to see my name in the paper.'

'We can keep your name out of it. That's not a problem.'

He glanced down at her phone on the table. 'And you're not taping this?'

Penny unlocked her phone and let him see that the voice recording wasn't activated. He didn't need to know about the second phone in her pocket that was diligently recording everything they said. 'You see, PC Finch? Or can I call you Darren?'

'Call me anything you like, except late for dinner.' He cracked a half-smile at the elderly joke. Definitely not the sharpest crayon in the box, she thought. 'Now, you wanted to talk to me about the breathalyser business?'

She nodded. 'It seems really dodgy: Carol Jordan getting away with drink driving just when she's about to be announced as the head of this new unit.'

'You think?' No mistaking the sarcasm.

'What's your take on it?'

'Word came down from on high,' he said.

'You know that?'

'What else could it be? There wasn't anything wrong with the breathalyser.'

'How can you be sure of that?'

He smirked at her, a man whose knowledge was infinitely superior. 'If you had a faulty breathalyser in your equipment locker, what would you do with it?'

Penny pondered her answer for a moment. 'Get it repaired? Or bin it?'

'Exactly.' Satisfaction in his smile. 'Now, on the night it happened, there didn't appear to be anything wrong with it. The four drivers we pulled over and breathalysed, they all had the smell of drink on their breath. There was nothing in the results that made us go, "Wait a minute, there's something not right." But here's the thing. That breathalyser was never taken out of commission. Not that night, not after the court kicked out those four charges. We're still using that same breathalyser.'

'You're kidding me!'

He shook his head. 'It's like nobody even bothered to do a cover-up. We just paid no never-mind. Carried on like nothing had happened.'

'That's so cynical. So where did the order come from?'

Finch shook his head. 'I don't know. Somewhere well above my pay grade.'

'You've no idea?'

He shrugged and took another long swallow from his Coke. 'All as I know is that when the case came up, the CPS solicitor stood up in front of the mags and said it was being dropped on account of the breathalyser had been discovered to be faulty. And that there were three other cases to be tret the same way.' He put a hand over his mouth and burped with surprising daintiness.

'What did you think at that point?'

He sighed. 'I thought maybe summat had come to light with the breathalyser. I hadn't been on duty the two nights previous, so I assumed nobody had got round to telling me. But when I went back to the station, duty sergeant said that were the first he'd heard about it. And there were nowt wrong with it so far as he knew. We even did a bit of a check on it ourselves. A couple of us blew into it and compared the results with one of the other machines, and it was bang on.'

Penny took a sip of her drink, even more disgusting now it had cooled. 'So what did you do?'

'Not much we could do. You can't start a fight when you don't know who you're fighting, can you? We only did it for our own satisfaction, like. But me and my partner, we wanted to cover our backs in case the shit hits the fan down the line. No way are we carrying the can if it all goes south. So I went and had a word with the housekeeper at that George Nicholas's house. I tried to get her to admit Jordan had been knocking it back, but she wasn't having it. She knows what side her bread's buttered. All she'd admit to was that Jordan had "probably" had a glass of white and a glass of red over a period of about four hours. Bollocks, she had.' His mouth curled to match his bitter tone.

It was a struggle for Penny not to show her delight at such a stonking story emerging from so unlikely a source. 'What do you think happened?'

'There's always people who've got insurance against the kind of shit that drowns ordinary folk. I've got no proof, mind, but I think somebody wanted Carol Jordan for ReMIT very badly.'

'As high up as the Home Office? ReMIT is their initiative, after all.'

Finch shook his head. 'I'm only a simple traffic cop, me. I know nowt about how things get decided. All I know is that five people would likely be alive today if those cases had gone ahead. And that's some price to pay so the bosses can slot somebody they want into a job.'

43

Tony rang the doorbell and waited. When Torin yanked the door open, he wasn't surprised. He'd texted from the end of the street to say he was on his way. Tony smiled. 'It's time, Torin. You've got to do this, mate. That's the start of sorting things out.'

'You promised.' The years fell away from him and he looked and sounded like a little boy, ready to burst into tears.

'And I'm keeping my word. You need to be the one doing the talking.'

'I can't. They'll be furious.'

'Not with you. They'll be hurt *for* you, not *because* of you. They're not going to turn their backs on you. I've known Paula a long, long time and I'd trust her with my life.'

Torin made to push past Tony and take off into the night but a voice called from inside. 'Who's at the door, Tor?' Paula. 'If it's the Jehovah's Witnesses, tell them we're lesbians.'

'It's only me,' Tony shouted back.

Paula appeared behind Torin. 'So why are you standing on the doorstep? Come in.'

'We were talking about the football,' Tony said. 'Didn't

want to bore you.' He stepped forward and Torin was obliged to move back to let him in. 'Don't let me down, lad,' Tony said softly as he came alongside.

They all shuffled into the living room, Tony tossing his purple coat over the banister as he passed. Elinor jumped up from the sofa and hugged him. 'Great to see you, Paula never said you were coming over.'

'I thought it was about time,' he said. 'I know Torin has something to say to you guys and I offered him my moral support.'

Torin's face showed the anger and betrayal he felt. 'You promised,' he spat. Elinor looked bemused.

'I did. I promised to let you speak for yourself.'

'Yeah, but you never said you were going to push me into it.'

'Nobody's pushing, Torin. I'm here to support you.'

Torin scoffed. 'Yeah, right. And now they know I've got something to hide.'

'We knew that anyway,' Elinor said quietly. 'We live with you. We can see there's something wrong. We love you, Torin. We want to help.'

'There is no help.' Torin threw himself into an armchair. 'I did a really stupid thing, right?' He sighed angrily. 'And now it's coming back to screw my life up completely.'

There was a moment's silence. 'I think you need to be a bit more specific,' Elinor said calmly. 'But before you are, I want you to know that whatever your stupidity, we are not going to turn our backs on you.'

'You say that now,' Torin muttered.

'I say it because it's the truth. You're part of this family.' She gave him her sweetest smile.

'Whether you like it or not,' Paula added. 'So you might as well get it over with.'

Torin glanced up, his eyes brimming. He dashed the back

of his hand roughly across his face, blinking the tears back. 'I was lonely, right? You two, you've been great. You *are* great. But sometimes it just feels a bit rubbish being me. And this girl, she started liking my pictures and then we started talking.' He squeezed his eyes shut.

'And it got to more than talking?' Elinor spoke softly.

'Not like you think,' he said quickly. 'It was all online.'

'They do things differently these days,' Tony said. 'So she sent you pictures of herself?'

'Yeah.' He gave Tony a pleading look.

'And they got a bit raunchy, right?'

Torin swallowed hard. 'That's a weird old person word. But yeah, they were ... you know? Sexy?' He shifted in his seat, crossing his legs tightly, rubbing a finger along his cheekbone. 'And she asked me to do the same for her, so I did.' It came out in a rush.

'Only human,' Paula said. She'd seen and heard much worse. She caught Tony's eye. 'But yeah, a bit stupid.'

'I know. And then ... ' Torin screwed his face up. 'Then she said if I didn't give her money, she'd mail the videos to everybody in my contacts. And post them on my social media accounts.'

'Oh, Torin, you poor boy.' Elinor was clearly on the verge of tears.

A single tear trickled from the corner of his eye. 'You tell them, Tony.'

Tony got up and sat on the arm of Torin's chair, laying an arm across the boy's shoulders. 'Torin didn't want to upset you guys. So he sold a piece of his mum's jewellery to pay the blackmailer. That's how the pendant you saw online got there, Paula.'

Elinor twisted in her seat to stare at Paula. 'What pendant? What is he talking about?'

'I'll explain later, it's not what this is all about.'

'But why am I only hearing this now?' Elinor asked, plaintive.

'Because you've been working and I didn't have the chance to sit down and explain. Later, Elinor.' Paula reached for her hand and held it tight. 'Tony?'

'And now the blackmailer is coming back for more. And we need to put our heads together and come up with a plan.' Tony rubbed Torin's shoulder, with no confidence that it would bring the boy any comfort.

'There is no plan,' Torin said, his voice flat and dull. 'I'm going to have to get used to my life being wrecked. Everybody will rip the piss out of me. No girl will ever come near me.' He hung his head. 'I'm glad my mum's not here to see this.'

'Your mum would have told you to stop feeling sorry for yourself,' Elinor said. 'She'd have told you you'd been an idiot but that was no reason to carry on being one.'

Torin looked up, shocked at Elinor's shift to briskness. 'What else can I be?'

'Like Tony said. We need a plan. And it's obvious where we start.' Three pairs of eyes stared at her, uncertain and unconvinced. 'For heaven's sake. We've got Stacey Chen. Somebody out there thinks they can mess with us, but they're not Stacey Chen.'

Later that night, when Tony had gone back to *Steeler* and Torin had finally fallen asleep, Elinor snuggled into Paula's side under the duvet. They lay skin to skin, each the other's shelter from the storm that had blown havoc through their lives.

'In the great scheme of being grateful for small mercies,' Elinor murmured, 'I am so glad we didn't have to look at those photos.'

'Me too. I know all about not being able to un-see things.'

Paula shuddered. 'It never even crossed my mind that this was what was going on.'

To her surprise, Elinor gave a soft chuckle. 'Of all the things I imagined our life would be, I never expected to find myself in the kind of tight corner where Stacey Chen was the answer.'

Paula kissed her. 'Me neither. But given the carnage she visited on Sam Evans, I think it's fair to say whoever thought they could fuck with Torin will be in for a nasty surprise.'

On the other side of Bradfield, another ReMIT member was awake. For once, Kevin was finding sleep elusive. He normally slept with the intensity of an adolescent, but there was something about this case that had deeply unsettled him. Cremating women in their cars was disturbing enough. But what lay beneath was something far more cruel. There was something callous, something dehumanising about what this killer had done. He had held out a promise to both his victims. He'd offered them romance. Love, even. And under cover of that promise, he'd won their confidence only to betray it. This twisted bastard wasn't satisfied with murder; he had to lace it with spite. He'd treated the women with scorn and contempt. Some people might think that was irrelevant, that the only thing that mattered was the killing itself. But for Kevin, the indignity the killer had inflicted by playing games with the women's emotions compounded the felony. If there were degrees of murder, in his mind this was one of the higher exemplars.

He lay on his back, staring into the dark, consciously still so as not to wake Stella. He ran through all of the actions they'd taken, looking for the loose thread to pull, to make the killer's careful planning unravel. Step by step, he went over what they'd done till his thoughts tumbled over each other in chaos.

He closed his eyes and breathed deeply, trying to calm the maelstrom in his mind. One more time, he tried to organise his thoughts. What were the forensic foundations of a case? There was no point in expecting anything from the body dumps, not after the fires.

He needed to come at this from a different angle. Think about the victims themselves as sources of forensic evidence. Their phones had gone in the fires. The killer had covered his tracks as far as his communications were concerned. He'd only ever been in touch—

And suddenly, a spark ignited a thought in Kevin's head. He remembered Harrison Braithwaite's words. 'They kissed goodnight. Nothing unseemly, but a bit of passion, you know?'

He must have held her. The killer must have held her. The mouth he kissed had been burned to ash. But the coat Amie McDonald had been wearing might still be hanging in her wardrobe. Hanging in her wardrobe with a killer's DNA all over it.

And Kevin had a witness who might be able to identify precisely which coat it had been.

PART THREE

44

Tonight, he was called Richard. Not Rick or Dick or Richie; Richard, he'd insisted to Eileen when she'd asked if his friends ever shortened his name. He'd spent the morning being himself – Tom Elton, magazine proprietor, briefing a series of freelances in Manchester for the articles he needed to fill the next tranche of magazines. None of them produced copy as good as Tricia, and he didn't have anybody on his books who could edit and rewrite the way she could. He knew the quality of his product was slipping inexorably and he knew who to blame for that.

That knowledge only sharpened his edge for continuing with his plan. Every time he carried it through, he learned some new refinement. And each time it was a little easier. As part of his forensic research, he'd read a paper recently by some guy called Dr Tony Hill, a clinical psychologist who did offender profiling for the police, about something called neural adaptation. Scientists had known about this in the physical world for a long time. When you pick up a pen, you're aware of how it feels in your hand but very quickly your nervous system tells you not to bother registering that sensation. But it turns out the same thing happens with dishonesty. The first time you lie or commit a particular crime, it's a big step and you're conscious of it all the way. But the more often you do that same thing, the easier it becomes. He'd always thought it happened that way because once you got away with something, you were less scared the next time. But apparently it was more than that. It was the brain adjusting itself. Wanting to be comfortable with the stuff that felt like crossing a line.

The things most people would classify as the bad stuff.

The same paper had pointed out that acting 'disreputably' raises the heart rate and the amount of perspiration the body produces. But taking beta blockers effectively overcomes those issues. It hadn't been hard to persuade his GP to prescribe beta blockers. Especially since he'd knocked back two double espressos immediately before the appointment. And now he felt even more in control.

He'd stopped at Waitrose in Otley to stock up with luxurious food and drink on his way to the pub where he'd told Eileen to meet him. It was a big roadhouse on the edge of the Dales, inside the ring of CCTV surveillance. The only cameras in the car park were trained on the entrance and exit to the pub itself. There really was almost no possibility of being spotted here. And besides, he wouldn't be getting out of the borrowed Merc, just in case.

That had been a stroke of genius too. He hadn't wanted to take any cars connected to him or the business anywhere near the Dales. At first, he'd decided to hire cars, a different one each time. But he'd have had to use his own driving licence and if the cops ever suspected him and started looking, he wouldn't be hard to find.

He'd racked his brains for an answer and it had been there under his nose all the time. Robbie Dawson. They'd been at school together and Robbie had advertised with Local Words since the beginning. He had a car dealership specialising in nearly new executive models with branches in Bradfield and Manchester. He'd borrowed a high-end Merc a couple of times to impress clients. Robbie wouldn't think twice if he bowled up and asked to borrow a car now and again. And so it had been. Robbie assumed he wanted to impress some bird, now Tricia was off the scene. A nod and a wink and it was done. No repeat sightings once he was in ANPR range. Every time he went to the Dales it was in a car that was forensically clean.

He parked under a spreading oak tree on the edge of the car park and waited, listening to the Bill Frisell playlist he'd put together from his Spotify account. And then, five minutes before the agreed time, her car nosed slowly into the car park. She drove a slow circuit and as she approached, he flashed his lights and drew out of his spot, coming to rest alongside her. He wound down his window and gave her his best smile. 'It's great to see you,' he said, meaning it.

Her smile was more tentative. As if she wasn't quite sure of herself. 'You too. Will I follow you, then?'

'That's right. We're going to have a great time.' Well, one of them was, he thought as he pulled round in front of her and set off into the night.

She couldn't fault him, Eileen thought as she lay sprawled by Richard's side in the king-sized bed that all but filled the tiny bedroom of the cottage. It was a setting made for romance. The cottage nestled at the end of a steep and narrow twisting lane. It was surrounded on two sides by dense woods that her headlights had barely penetrated as she drove round the back to park. The view on the other two sides, he assured her, was bleak but beautiful.

Inside, it was charming. She'd expected chintz and twee, based on her own experience of holiday cottages. But this was understated to the point of Spartan, yet it was both comfortable and comforting. He told her it belonged to a friend of his who owned a number of magazines. They'd known each other since they were kids, he said. Tom lent him the cottage half a dozen times a year. 'I wish I had a friend like Tom,' she said.

He'd raised his eyebrows and given her a cheeky smile. 'Maybe you will one day.'

Richard had taken time and trouble with everything. Dinner had been an exquisite spread of deli food – lobster and cooked meats and delicious French cheeses with grapes and dried fruits – and seriously good wine to go with it. He'd been attentive throughout the leisurely meal, asking her about herself and her work and apparently finding her answers fascinating.

The seduction had been nicely done too. No sudden lunges across the sofa or clumsy gropes as they cleared the table. Instead, he'd paused in the kitchen, meeting her eye and telling her she was the first woman he'd felt comfortable with since his Tricia died. That he'd been convinced he'd never find another woman to compare to her, but that Eileen had made it possible for him to close a door on his past and imagine a future. And then he'd taken her in his arms and kissed her with a fierce desire that was hard to resist. God, but it had been convincing.

Getting from the kitchen to the bedroom, never an easy transition, was a pretty smooth operation too, she reckoned. Subdued lighting, no unseemly fumbling with buttons or bra. Somehow it had been seamless, and then he'd shown as much attention to her body as he had previously to her conversation. He was considerate, imaginative and, frankly, successful, in spite of his protestations that he was out of practice. She'd laughed heartily at that point. 'If that's you out of practice, I can't wait for you to get back up to speed.'

His response had been to dive under the covers again and reduce her to a gibbering fool one more time.

And yet. Eileen was a natural sceptic. She lay there, sated and exhausted, having definitely had the seeing-to of her life, and still something in her held back. It all felt too good to be true. He was out of her league, that's what it was.

It wasn't that she was putting herself down or thinking she didn't deserve something so special. But Eileen had a pretty good idea of where she came in the girlfriend pecking order. She'd spent years on the wards, clocking what went on between patients and their visitors, watching the dynamic between couples and among families. It was important for the care of your patient to know where their supports and their stresses came from. And if there was one thing she knew, it was that water would find its own level.

And she was not on Richard's level.

Once the novelty of dating someone who reminded him so powerfully of his late wife had worn off, he'd see her for herself. Then, if she was lucky, it would be a gentle disengagement. But she was going into this with her eyes open. She knew this wasn't going to last for life. So she wasn't going to kid herself and fall in love with him, no matter how much he spoiled her. Because he was really trying to spoil the woman he'd genuinely loved, the one he couldn't have any more.

Eileen Walsh knew a good thing when she saw it. But she also knew a finite thing. So she resolved that she would enjoy the ride. Make the most of it while it lasted and walk away with a light heart because she'd been allowed to feel special for a while.

She had no idea how short a while that would be.

Getting through Saturday had been less difficult than he'd expected. They'd spent the morning in bed, drinking coffee and having sex. She definitely wasn't his type – he missed Tricia's toned body and hard muscles – but he supposed that years of nursing had taught her how bodies worked and he had to admit she knew some pretty nifty moves. No hardship there, then.

The afternoon had been less straightforward. What was it about these women and their obsession with walking in the Dales? He'd ended up taking her on a hike through the woods and up the tump beyond. It was a boring walk so he knew they'd be unlikely to run into anyone else. But the view from the top was dramatic enough for him to pretend that was the reason for the climb. She'd struggled for breath for much of the walk, and when they got back, she was desperate for a long soak in a hot bath. That suited him perfectly.

They cooked dinner together. Roast leg of lamb, dauphinoise potatoes, tender-stem broccoli. She made a surprisingly tasteless gravy with the remains of the first bottle of wine and some herbs from the kitchen window box. So no regrets about missing out on more of her home cooking.

Lots of wine – the lion's share for her – and then early to bed. He might as well make the most of a good fuck while it was there on tap.

Later, as she lay curled with her back to him, snoring softly, he began to feel anxious about what lay ahead. Not the killing itself; that had indeed become less difficult the more he did it. But in spite of himself, he liked this woman. She wasn't desperate and needy like Kathryn, or man-hungry like Amie. She seemed to be comfortable with herself and comfortable with him. If he spent much more time with her, he feared he might start to feel guilty about killing her. And that wouldn't do. Maybe he should bring things forward. Drug her at breakfast and then finish the job when she passed out. He knew now he could get through the day with a body in the cottage.

And then it occurred to him that killing her after breakfast would give him a chance at an alibi. If the police made the connection between his crimes, they'd soon figure out the victims were spending the whole weekend with their killer. But he could easily drive back to Bradfield and spend the afternoon in plain sight with people who knew him. 'Officer, I couldn't have been with Eileen Walsh that afternoon, I was in the Sportsman's Arms watching the football with five of my friends.' That had a certain beauty to it. He didn't have to set the fire till later in the evening so he could hang around after the game, narrowing the window of opportunity still further.

The other thing that struck him as he struggled to drop off was that he might not have to wait too long before he could deal with Tricia once and for all. He'd established a pattern of a killer who lured women away from their lives then left their lifeless bodies to burn in their own cars. If she died in the same way, it would look like she was part of a serial killer's sequence. All he had to do was place her at a wedding. That wouldn't be impossible. They were at an age where people were getting married every few months or so. Whatever stone she was hiding under, she'd emerge from it to see one of her friends walk down the aisle. Now he had found a back door into the lives of her friends, he'd have a heads-up on such an occasion. All he had to do was wait for a wedding, then he would be able to deal with the bitch. OK, he wouldn't be able to make the approach in public. But he'd find the right moment. It was what she deserved. She'd taken everything that mattered from him.

It would be a pleasure to do the same to her.

45

Harrison Braithwaite looked surprised to see Kevin on his doorstep next morning. 'I didn't think I'd be seeing you again,' he said, heading back down the hall to his birds. Kevin followed, lugging a heavy carrier bag with him.

'I wasn't sure whether you had a preferred brand of seed for your birds, but the man in the pet store said this was the best,' Kevin said, taking a large sack of mixed seed from the carrier bag.

Braithwaite frowned and looked at the sack. 'You bought birdseed for me?'

Kevin grinned, self-deprecating. 'Well, I was thinking the birds, rather than you. You said Amie shopped for stuff for you, and I thought this would tide you over till you sorted out other arrangements.'

Braithwaite sank down into his chair, his mouth working. He recovered himself and said, 'That's very kind. How much do I owe you?'

Kevin shook his head and sat down opposite the old man. 'Forget it. I was in the pet shop anyway, buying cat food, and

I thought it might be helpful, that's all. It's not a bribe, you know.' He smiled.

'Well, that's very helpful. I don't know what to say.' He roughly rubbed the back of his hand across his mouth. 'Thank you, lad.'

'There was something I should have asked you when I was here before but it didn't cross my mind.'

Braithwaite leaned forward, all attention. 'I doubt I have anything more to tell you, but ask away.'

'Could you tell what coat Amie was wearing that night when she came back with Mark in the taxi?'

Braithwaite tugged at his earlobe. 'It was her best coat. The one she always wore when she was going out on the town. It's a black-and-white houndstooth double-breasted coat with a high neck. Like a polo neck?'

Kevin couldn't believe his luck. It sounded distinctive. 'That's great,' he said. 'Can I ask you a favour? Can you come upstairs with me to Amie's flat and see if it's still there?'

'It should be,' he said. 'She was wearing her anorak when she went off on the Friday. So she could go walking up in the Dales.' He struggled out of the armchair. 'But I'll come up all the same and make sure.'

He followed Kevin upstairs, pausing on every step. On the doorstep, Kevin snapped on a pair of blue nitrile gloves. 'Please don't touch anything, Mr Braithwaite.'

The old man nodded. 'I watch those true crime pro- grammes on the telly, I know all about not contaminating the evidence.'

They stepped inside. Amie McDonald's coat rack extended along the wall behind the door. There was a black wool coat, a dark green raincoat and a grey-and-white tartan wrap. And at the end, the black-and-white houndstooth coat with the funnel neck that Harrison Braithwaite had described. Kevin wanted to do a little victory dance but he restrained himself.

'Is that it? The coat she was wearing when Mark embraced her at the door?'

Braithwaite nodded. 'Aye,' he said, his voice heavy. 'It brings it home, seeing her things hanging there. I'll never see her wearing them again. She were that full of life, I just can't get used to the idea that she's gone.'

'I'm sorry to put you through this,' Kevin said. He took a large evidence bag from his pocket, unfolded it and placed the coat inside, careful not to contaminate it with fibres from his own jacket.

'Happen he got his DNA all over her coat? Is that what you think?'

'It's a long shot, but it's possible.'

Braithwaite shook his head in wonder. 'Amazing what they can do nowadays. When I was your age, we thought fingerprints were as good as it could get. Now, they say fingerprints are a matter of opinion, not fact. It's all DNA now. How long will it be before that goes the way of fingerprints?'

It was a good question, Kevin thought. The further the technology went, the more confused the answers sometimes became. 'It's beyond me,' he said. 'But maybe those clever buggers in the lab will find an answer for us this time.'

'I see why that's got you all excited.' Braithwaite turned away, a catch in his voice. 'But that's all come too late for Amie. That lass didn't deserve what happened to her. You might catch who did it, but you can't turn back time.'

46

Even though it was Sunday, Stacey was already in her strong-hold of screens when Paula arrived at work bearing a box of six doughnuts. 'Cop cliché,' Stacey said when the box was proffered, but it didn't stop her going for the fudge custard one. 'What are you doing in on a Sunday when we've got no leads taking us anywhere?'

'I could ask you the same thing.'

'Well, unlike you, I have no life and no family outside work. It was either stay at home and wrestle with a bit of intractable code that I need to make work for a new app, or come in here and wrestle with the avalanche of pointless data this case is generating.' Stacey highlighted a section on one screen and moved it diagonally on to another. 'No, that didn't help.' She stopped fiddling with her trackpad and concentrated on her doughnut.

'Actually, it's family that brings me here. I swung by your flat first and when you weren't there, I reckoned you must be here.'

'On account of me having no life.' There was an unfamil-iar bitterness in Stacey's tone. Before Sam, her single-track life had always seemed sufficient. She had friends – Paula, and a few geeks who shared her fascination with data and programming – and she didn't seem to need more. If anyone had asked, Paula would have said Stacey was one of the few people she knew who was content with her life. Then Sam had infiltrated her heart and changed everything. Stacey wasn't given to sharing confidences, but what little she had told Paula indicated how stupid he'd made her feel. Whenever Paula thought of him, she felt the urge to slap him till his ears bled. She'd never do it, of course. She wasn't inclined towards violence. But any chance that came along to humiliate or damage him professionally? She'd take it in a heartbeat for the hurt he'd done to her friend.

'On account of everybody in this squad is obsessed by our cases,' Paula said. 'Only, like I said, this is family.' She dropped an iPhone on the desk and pushed it towards Stacey.

'It's an iPhone 6,' Stacey said.

'What it is, it's a ballistic missile that's blown a hole in Torin's life.'

Stacey's eyebrows flicked up and down. 'That sounds ... extreme?'

'It is.' Paula outlined the nightmare that had unfolded in their lives. Stacey showed no sign of shock or surprise.

When Paula reached the end of her narrative, Stacey nodded. 'This is nothing new, Paula.'

'I know that. I've read the stories. Teenagers committing suicide because all they can see ahead of them is shame and disgrace. Kids running away from home into who knows what because they feel like they've lost their future. Well, I'm not having that happening to Torin. Not on my watch.' Paula's face flushed with angry determination.

'I get that,' Stacey said. 'But you may not be able to stop the first part of that disaster. The making public of what he's done. But there are practical steps you can take that might make it harder for the attackers. There's a chance they might not have already raided all his contact lists. So what he has to do – and he has to do this today – is to delete all his contacts, one by one, from his phone. Then the same from all his social media accounts. One by one, manually, not some "delete all" command. Then he has to close down his social media accounts. Down the line, once all of this is over, he can set up new ones. But for now, he has to make himself invisible and stay invisible.'

'Will that stop it?'

'Honestly? Probably not. But it might make it so much harder that his attackers will move on elsewhere. Oh, and he needs to delete all his email contacts too. And I need you to bring his laptop in. Chances are they might have taken control of it and they're watching him all the time he's on it. In fact, text Elinor right now and get him to bring in his laptop and his tablet. I'll see what's on them and clean it up.'

Paula immediately did as she was asked. 'Can you not track who's doing this to him? And stop them at source?'

Stacey sighed. 'It's extremely unlikely. These cyber attacks come from places where governments allow anonymous servers that scrub clean all the source information from emails and messages.'

'What, like Russia?'

'More likely the Philippines. I'll do what I can but I don't hold out much hope.' Then, as a thought occurred to her, Stacey said slowly, 'How much money did they ask for?'

'The first demand was £500. Torin paid up then they asked for £1000. They've given him till the end of the month to pay.' Her phone pinged. 'That's Torin. Elinor's giving him a lift, he'll be here in about fifteen minutes.'

'It's not much return for all that work,' Stacey said. 'Usually demands start around the five-grand mark.'

'Horses for courses,' Paula said. 'A lad Torin's age might be able to raise a few hundred but he's not going to be able to get his hands on five grand very readily. Better to have some return than none at all. And if they're doing this to other kids, it's about the volume, not the individual amounts.'

'True. And they've got the footage of him. They can monetise that on a porn site,' Stacey mused.

Paula's eyes widened in horror. 'They'd put him up on a porn site?'

Realising the weight of what she'd said, Stacey hastily backtracked. 'Probably not. He's way too old for the paedos.'

But not for the perverts who liked adolescent boys, Paula thought. It was a grim notion.

'Look, I'll do my best. I've got a couple of contacts who walk the wrong side of the line. I'll see what I can drag out of them. And in the meantime we'll do what we can to minimise the damage.' She picked up the phone. 'What's his passcode? I'll take a look at this while we're waiting for him.'

'Three nine five two three nine,' Paula said. She'd insisted he give her the code before she'd left the house. She'd had to promise not to abuse it by going through his personal stuff. She supposed she'd deserved that caveat after her unauthorised search of his room. 'And I'm going outside to wait for them.' She could vape while she was waiting. What she actually wanted was a cigarette. But she'd kicked the habit hard and she wasn't prepared to put herself through that misery again. The occasional vaping would have to do.

Waiting for the lift, she sighed from the bottom of her lungs. She'd wanted Stacey to wave the magic wand she'd brought to their cases so often. But as with everything else to do with ReMIT, the old magic seemed to have deserted them.

47

After dinner, Carol was getting twitchy. She flicked impatiently through the lifestyle section of the Sunday paper. 'Who in God's name is trivial enough to read a piece about The Ten Best Plates for Outdoor Eating? Or "how to transform your wooden stairs by painting them to look like a stylish runner"?' Even as she spoke, she knew the answer. Somebody who wasn't trying to avoid thinking about a refreshing vodka tonic, or a glass of Pinot Grigio so cold it would make her teeth hurt.

Who was she trying to kid? Right now, she'd settle for a cheap Albanian white at blood heat. Or a break in her case to take her mind off the craving for a drink that was running like an electric current through her veins. The inside of her head felt like a swamp she was trying to wade through. How could she solve a case this complicated when her brain had stopped working properly?

Tony looked up from the journal article he was reading on his tablet. 'Someone who *has* stairs?'

'Very funny.' Carol glared at him and threw the paper aside. 'This case is killing me. How can there be nothing to get hold of? We're condemned to running endless streams of data through Stacey's systems in the hope that they'll pick up a cross-reference that'll give us something to latch on to. We're going to have to fall back on a media appeal.'

'Unless he sticks to his interval. If he keeps to a three-week cycle, tonight will be the night for another burning car. And every time he does it, we get closer to him. Because his patterns become clearer every time. The more we learn about him, the more possible it becomes to move ahead of him and stand in his way.' He rubbed his hands along the sides of his head. 'It grieves me, but my job gets easier the more he kills. It's the hardest part of what I do, Carol. The guilt I feel because I'm not good enough to latch on to the most important details from the start.'

'Nobody's that good. And if you thought about it honestly instead of using it as an excuse to beat yourself up, you'd acknowledge that and forgive yourself.' The warmth of her tone took the sting from her words. Carol reached across the corner of the table that separated them and enclosed one of his hands in hers. 'You're not omniscient.'

'No. So you end up having to fall back on a media appeal that drags up a net full of red herrings.' He shrugged. 'And maybe one genuine lead, if we can pick it out of the catch.'

'The way things are going—' Carol was interrupted by the ringing of her phone. She snatched it up. 'North Yorkshire,' she muttered, taking the call. 'DCI Jordan.'

'It's DSI Henderson. Control's been on the phone to me. I set up an alert on vehicle fires in the Dales so that any report comes straight to me. We've had a call from a group of bikers about a car on fire in a lay-by on the road between Blubberthwaite and Scarholme. Above Wharfedale.'

'Thanks for letting me know. Who's on the way?'

'Fire brigade and a patrol car,' Henderson said crisply.

'Can you speak to the fire chief and ask them not to put the fire out unless there's a risk to life or property?'

'I've already issued that instruction. I assumed that would

be what you wanted. Of course, we can't be sure at this stage whether this is a random car fire or part of your case, but I thought it best to take precautions.'

'Yes, ma'am. I appreciate you doing that. I'll be there with members of my team as soon as possible. If the patrol car officers can see a body in the car, can you arrange for a forensic team to be sent out to the locus?'

'I'm already across that too. I'll assign an SIO as soon as we know whether it's necessary and have them meet you at the scene.'

'Thank you, ma'am.' Carol ended the call and gave Tony a rueful smile. 'More data, by the looks of it. I need to change into something a bit more official-looking than jogging pants and a hoodie.'

'Where is it?' he asked, getting to his feet and walking to the bookshelf where Carol kept her maps.

'Wharfedale. Between Blubberthwaite and Scarholme. More ridiculous North Yorkshire names,' she added, crossing behind the screen that separated her sleeping area from the rest of the space.

Tony took out the Ordnance Survey Landranger map that covered Upper Wharfedale and spread it out over the table. He pored over it till he found the River Wharfe then traced its route back upstream to the places Carol had mentioned. Both appeared to be little more than a small cluster of dwellings without a church or a pub between them.

What there was, however, was a cycle track on the other side of the river from the road. And what looked like a couple of footbridges leading between the two. 'Carol,' he shouted. 'There's a bike trail right next to the road.'

She emerged from behind the screen, a loose grey jumper over black trousers. 'What?'

'Look, it runs right along the dale. If we're right about the bike thing, he could be on that trail right now.'

Carol leaned over his shoulder, instantly taking in what he was showing her. 'Shit,' she said, crossing to her phone and calling DSI Henderson back. 'We think he may be making his escape on a bike,' she said without preamble. 'There's a track runs along the Dale. There must be limited places on the trail where he can intersect with a parked car. Is there any chance you can cover those?'

To her credit, Henderson didn't miss a beat. 'I'll talk to our people and see what we can do. Though he may be long gone. Leave it with me.'

The line went dead and Carol stared across at Tony. 'Good police work,' she said.

He shrugged. 'We've been doing this a long time. We've rubbed off on each other. You come up with the psychological insights ahead of me sometimes too.'

'Nice of you to say so, but I'm not sure I'd agree. Are you coming with me, Sherlock?'

In the car, Tony leaned back in his seat, his head tilted against the rest. 'They won't get him,' he said.

Carol hammered through the lanes leading from the barn to the main road north. 'How can you be so sure?'

'Because he's too careful. He plans everything down to the last detail. He'll have worked out how long it takes the emergency services to get to the fire and how long it takes to get back to his car. But here's what interests me. Most serial offenders start to escalate in one way or another. Either the intervals decrease or the crimes become more violent, more elaborate. But that's not happening here. That's one important aspect of what's going on here. And another other thing? He's obsessed with leaving no traces that can lead back to him. Not because he's afraid of being caught, per se. That's not it. It's because he's on a mission. And if he's careless, if he gets caught because he's made a stupid mistake, he won't be able to complete his mission.'

Carol flashed a quick glance at him. 'Where did that come from?'

'You know my methods, Watson.' He grinned at her. 'It's the explanation that makes most sense of his behaviour, Carol. He's targeting weddings because it gives him the kind of victims he needs. A woman who's vulnerable to the promise of romance. But that offers no guarantee of a physical type, or even of an age range. He doesn't care about these women as individuals. It's what they represent to him.'

'And what do they represent?'

'The woman he wants to kill.'

'So why doesn't he kill her?' A long pause. Carol turned on to the dual carriageway and pushed the Land Rover a shade above eighty miles an hour. 'What's stopping him?'

'If I knew that ... Maybe she's dead already? Maybe she's beyond his reach for some other reason?'

'Maybe he wants to get it perfect before he does it to her?'

Tony mulled that over. He exhaled heavily through his nose. 'That doesn't feel right. Because he's got it pretty much perfect from the start.'

'Not necessarily.' Carol pulled out sharply to pass a delivery van. 'We're only seeing the end result. The body disposal. We don't have any idea what his ritual is before he kills them. That might be what he's trying to perfect.'

There was no denying it was a good point and Tony didn't even bother trying. 'You're right,' he said. 'See, I told you I wasn't nearly as good at this as I'm given credit for. We're only seeing the beginning of his process and the end. We've no idea what's going on in the middle. And that means we've got no idea at all who he really wants to kill.'

48

Stacey didn't do crime scenes. Not in a Stella McCartney suit and Nicholas Kirkwood loafers. Even if she'd been dressed appropriately, she still wouldn't have schlepped up to the middle of nowhere to stand around pretending to be useful. The place where she mattered was right where she was. So as flames devoured the interior of Eileen Walsh's seven-year-old Vauxhall Astra, Stacey sat alone in the office, waiting for fresh data to feed into her systems, hoping that this time someone would have salvaged something tangible for her machines to gorge on.

In the meantime, she had something to be going on with. Stacey always had something to be going on with while her official work churned on in the background. But tonight what she was focused on had a personal dimension that was usually lacking in her work. Some of her colleagues who knew her less well than they thought might have considered the personal would have scant impact on her.

They would have been well wide of the mark.

Stacey hated people who abused digital systems. It affronted her that they had fatally undermined the fundamental beauty and purity of the internet. They'd corrupted the most revolutionary invention of the twentieth century and turned it into an engine for triviality, for vitriol, for scamming and for undermining the very fabric of democracy. Her family had come from Hong Kong; they'd experienced the effects of tyranny and oppression at first hand, and it wounded Stacey that opportunists and idiots had taken so extraordinary a thing as the internet and made it ugly and exploitative. It was that anger that fuelled her police work as much as the licence it gave her to stick her nose in other people's data, an exercise of curiosity she justified as a necessary invasion of privacy. She was, after all, one of the good guys.

She'd spent much of the afternoon with Torin, scrubbing his various devices clean of personal data. He'd sat with a glum expression as they'd cleared out and closed down his social media. She'd tried to explain what she was doing and why but he'd cut across her with, 'I know. If I hadn't been a total dick you wouldn't have to wipe my life clean. I get it. So can we just get on with it, please?'

She got it too. She'd have felt equally gutted and miserable if she'd done something with such devastating consequences. Not the exposure part. That was survivable. But the scrubbing clean of all her connectivity? That would be killer. So she sympathised with the boy. 'When we set you up again after all of this is over, I'll show you how to put systems in place that'll stop anything like it happening again,' she'd replied.

'Can you do that?'

'Yes. Well, *I* can.'

'Thanks. I'm sorry.'

'You got unlucky. Most people, they manage to keep their screw-ups under wraps. But don't imagine you're the only one who screws up.' As she knew only too well. 'Grown-ups do it too.'

When they'd finished, he'd sloped off to catch the bus home, leaving his phone with Stacey. Now she had it plugged into her system. When – and it would be when, not if – his blackmailers contacted him again, she'd bring all her weaponry to bear to find out who was responsible and where they were hiding.

Sure enough, not ten minutes after the news had come in of that night's fire, a message had pinged on Torin's phone. Stacey imagined a web of filaments lighting up between the phone and the person who had set these wheels in motion as lines of numbers scrolled down the screen she'd dedicated to Torin for the evening. The IP address tracker she had running was working, following the signal back through cyberspace to the source.

Except it wasn't. As she had feared, the tracker had hit a dead end. The digital equivalent of a brick wall. Whoever had sent this message to Torin was net-savvy. They knew how to route their messages through a server that couldn't be identified remotely. Stacey studied the screen, running a couple of checks as she went. It was, as she had thought, a blind alley somewhere in the Philippines, a jurisdiction nobody could compel to identify its black-hat hackers, phishers and scammers.

Stacey breathed heavily through her nose. Not even she could bulldoze her way to this particular truth. She leaned back in her chair and frowned at the acoustic tiles on the ceiling, their pitted surface reminding her of lunar module photographs of the moon's surface. 'What is wrong with you?' she growled, cross with herself for such a frivolous thought at a time like this.

She straightened up, rolled her shoulders to free the tension and considered her options. Tracking the message had failed completely. But there was another avenue to explore, though the chances were that it would be no more successful.

Torin had paid the blackmail money into a prepaid credit card account. The issuing bank would have details of the owner of the account.

But getting those details would be almost impossible. Banks didn't hand out information like that. It was hard enough getting a warrant for that sort of disclosure when they were dealing with serious major crime, never mind working something off the books like this. Idly, Stacey did an ID check on the sort code attached to the card. To her astonishment, it was a branch of a high street bank in Bradfield. Someone had walked into a bank less than a mile from Skenfrith Street and bought a pre-loaded credit card.

Whoever had turned Torin over was no distant fraudster on the other side of the planet. It was someone a lot closer to home.

49

The car was still too hot to approach. Tony could feel the heat from twenty metres away. The occasional flame licked half-heartedly along the window frames but there was clearly nothing much left to burn. The smell was sickening. Burnt plastic and acrid chemicals from the upholstery and, underlying it, the stink of burned meat. The blackened skull, skin and flesh turned to ash, was discernible against the metal frame of the seat. He shuddered inwardly.

'You don't stay to watch,' he said so softly that none could hear him. 'It's not the fire that gets you going. It's the obliteration. Cremating them so there's nothing recognisable left of a human being. You're punishing someone but it's not them. They're just stand-ins.'

Carol left the knot of detectives and crime scene technicians who were lurking on the fringes of the scene. 'It's the same as the others,' she said.

'Not quite.' He walked to the end of the narrow lay-by, leaving her to follow in his wake. 'And there's drystone walls flanking the road here. They're over a metre high. And then you've got the river beyond that. To get to the cycle path, you'd either have to ride or walk, carrying the bike, for about five hundred metres till you come to a footbridge across the Wharfe.'

'So I need to organise a fingertip search along the verge here at first light,' Carol said. She hunkered down, angling her head so she could look back along the ground towards the car glowing against the night. 'Is that a bicycle tyre track?' she asked, pointing to a muddy blur a few metres back from the rear bumper.

Tony crouched beside her. 'It looks like it.'

Carol stood up. 'Can I have the CSM over here?' she called.

One of the white-suited figures detached himself from the group. 'That'd be me, ma'am.'

Tony winced. She hated that form of address and despised officers like DSI Henderson who cleaved to it as a marker of respect. 'It's old-fashioned misogyny,' she'd told Tony early on in their working life. 'It's a way of putting us in our place.' He'd understood exactly what she meant. It pretended to be a display of respect but it was really the opposite.

'DCI Jordan will do fine,' she said briskly. 'I'm not the lady of the manor, for God's sake. Now, squat down here and turn your head so you're at an oblique angle to the road. Speaking as an experienced Crime Scene Manager, would you say that was a bike tyre track? In that smear of mud behind the car.'

The CSM did as he was told. He moved his head around, trying to see what Carol had noticed. Then he stopped and said, 'Gotcha.' He straightened up. 'I think you might be right. We had rain this afternoon. It stopped about six, so it must have been made after that. And if I'm not mistaken, the heat from the fire seems to have baked it solid.' He tipped a mock salute at Carol with the first two fingers of his right hand. 'Well spotted. You think he's left the scene on a bike, is that right? I heard you'd ordered the exits from the bike trail covered.' He gave a tiny smirk. 'Trouble is, on a mountain bike, you don't have to stick to the main trail. You could be up and over Bicker Edge before we'd even had the emergency call.'

'It's not a mountain bike,' Carol said decisively. 'It's a Brompton, or something similar. We know that from the last crime scene. I want a fingertip search right along the verge as far as the footbridge as soon as it's light. If he rode along there, chances are he may have left some evidence.'

'Right you are, ma—Chief Inspector. I doubt we'll get much usable intel from the bike track. But you never know. We might get lucky and find he's got some visible damage on the tyre.'

'I doubt it,' Tony said. 'I can't see him overlooking something so obvious. Trust me, it's not his style.'

The CSM shrugged. 'If you say so. But we'll look anyway.' He rejoined his team, casting a swift look back over his shoulder at Tony and Carol.

'Made another friend there,' Carol said.

'I do my best.'

'I'm going to ask the fire investigator whether there's any trace of him using a fuse. I'm wondering whether he gave himself some extra time to make his getaway.'

Tony frowned. 'It's worth asking. But I don't think he'd leave anything to chance. He'll want to be sure the fire has taken hold because the last thing he wants is for someone to walk into his perfect set-up in time to stop it going up like an *auto da fe*.'

'A what?'

'Burning heretics at the stake. The Spanish Inquisition. Turning people into human torches.' He gave her a rueful smile. 'Sorry. You know my head is filled with inappropriate information.'

'It's not the information that's inappropriate, it's the time and place you trot it out.'

Before he could reply, Carol's phone rang. 'Kevin,' she said. 'What have you got for me?'

'Good news and bad news,' he said.

'As usual. Let's have it.'

'I've been liaising with the North Yorkshire teams tasked with monitoring the exit points from the cycle track along the riverbank. The team on the eastbound section were setting up in place to monitor it when a woman came past. She was out walking her dog.'

'Aren't they always? It's a constant amazement to me that Flash hasn't found me a corpse yet. So what did the dog walker have to say for herself?'

'She was heading home when she saw the cops. She told them that on her way out she'd nearly been knocked over by a cyclist coming down the path hell for leather on – and this is a quote – "one of them dinky folding bikes like that Hugh Bonneville had in *W1A*".' When she said nothing, he continued. 'It was a TV show, guv. Taking the piss out of the BBC.'

'I know what it was, Kevin. Bonneville rode a Brompton bike, like we think our killer might use. So, did she see anything useful?'

'She was a bit shaken, and angry at the way he was riding, so she turned to look back at him. And he left the path right where it enters the village. A couple of minutes later, she heard a car engine start up and drive off.'

'She didn't see the car?'

'Unfortunately not.'

'And what was the good news?'

Kevin cleared his throat. 'That was it, pretty much.'

'So we've got an unidentified car going off in an unidentified direction a bit before we got our teams in place?'

'Pretty much, yeah.'

'Did she get a look at him at all?'

'Yes, but it's not much use. He was wearing dark-coloured

lycra cyclist's gear, including a helmet and goggles. And he had a head torch as well as the bike lights. So she was pretty much dazzled.'

Carol sighed. 'Well, I suppose it's better than nothing. At least it confirms our theory that he's making his escape on a bike. Can you pass all this on to Stacey? She'll need to start feeding in all the ANPR data on cars hitting the main roads out of the Dales. Talk to you later, Kevin.' She ended the call and hung her head. 'Did you get that?'

'The gist of it. Dog walker saw our man, but not enough to give a description and she thinks he took off in a car?'

'Got it in one. Well, maybe Stacey can pick something up. A cross-reference to earlier ANPR info or something.'

'Unless he doesn't leave the Dales.'

Carol raised her head. 'You think he actually lives here?'

'It's possible. He clearly knows the area well. He knows where he can move around without triggering cameras. It's not hard to reach Bradfield or Leeds or – did somebody say this car tracks back to Manchester?'

'Not quite Manchester. It's registered to Eileen Walsh,' Carol said without having to think about it. She had a quirk of memory that meant she had total recall of anything she heard. It was sometimes more accurate than a recording. 'An address in Salford.'

'So it's not unreasonable to think he might live in the area. Or maybe he has a weekend cottage. That way he can go back to his bolthole and stay put till Monday morning, when he becomes one more commuter heading out from the Dales to wherever work is. I'm not sure that helps at all, but . . . '

'But it's another hypothesis to throw into the pot. You've said often enough that when it comes to sexual homicide, murder isn't usually where the criminality starts. So what do you see as the gateway offences here?'

'Let's walk,' Tony said. His head always worked best when

he was on the move. They skirted the crime scene and set off down the road in the opposite direction to the one the killer was assumed to have taken. The heat died away quickly, making him glad of his new anorak. The night was clear and chill and the plumes of smoke that drifted across the sky looked like a blackboard duster drawn across a child's impression of the stars.

'It's not going to be the usual stuff. Not the animal cruelty, petty vandalism, minor sexual offences. This isn't sexual homicide as such,' he said, waving his arms as he spoke. 'He's having sex with them, I suspect. He's set up this scenario that's all about romance and wooing and chances are it ends up in bed. Like I said before, he acquires them at a time and place where they're open to the idea of love. He takes them out on dates and he clearly doesn't set their alarm bells ringing because they agree to go out with him repeatedly. They trust him enough to agree to spend a weekend in the Dales with him. It's completely atypical of serial sexual homicide.'

'Maybe it's all an act. Once he gets them here, maybe that's when Mr Nice Guy disappears and he rapes and tortures them?'

Tony realised his hands were cold and stuck them in his pockets. 'That's possible,' he said. 'And it's hard to argue against since we have no witnesses to their behaviour towards each other. Except that the fact there are no witnesses suggests it was completely normal to the point of dull. No scenes in restaurants, no rows in the street, no complaints to friends. All we hear about him is what a gentleman he is, how attentive he was, how he was still getting over the tragic death of his wife.'

'What about the wife?'

'Wife, girlfriend, whatever. I don't think she's dead. I think she's the woman he wants to kill. He's a man obsessed and he's determined to see his obsession through to the end.'

'And the end is, what? Actually killing the woman he used to love?'

'He still loves her but she doesn't love him. I thought at first that the reason he might not be able to kill her was that she was dead already. But the more I think about it, the less sense that makes. Dying just *feels* like desertion to the ones left behind. If she was dead, I think he'd be taking out his revenge on whoever he could find to blame. Doctors who couldn't cure her. The police officers who didn't protect her. The driver who—' He stopped suddenly, remembering who he was talking to. 'Anyway, he'd be looking for someone that fitted the blame frame. That's not what these women represent in his head.'

'So you've decided they're definitely surrogates?'

'Yes. And killing them gives him a degree of comfort. The reassurance that he can control his world. Because she took that power and control from him when she walked out.' Tony stopped in his tracks. 'He's planned this with infinite care. He knows he's got to get this right because he needs to stay free until it's safe for him to kill her. Whoever she is. And somewhere down the line, he will kill her. Because we can't stop him. So until then he'll keep on doing this again and again and again.'

As soon as he'd spoken, Tony realised the mistake he'd made. He could see it in her eyes. The guilt she was carrying over Dominic Barrowclough's victims was bad enough. But now she had the added weight of guilt because she wasn't able to catch a killer. In Carol's eyes, he knew, the world was simple. Her job was justice. All she had to do was to catch violent criminals and put them away. Doing that one thing saved lives. Every day, people went about their lives – cooking, shopping, sleeping, laughing, loving – because she'd done what she was supposed to do. But he'd just told her she wasn't good enough. None of them was good enough to catch this killer.

50

Paula hadn't been able to stop yawning on the drive into work. It had been after two by the time she'd driven home from Wharfedale and her body ached in surprising places from having slept on the sofa. There was no spare room now that Torin was living with them, and Paula hated to disturb Elinor's sleep, given the long and erratic hours she worked.

She stopped at the doughnut shop again on her way to the office. The cheery familiar greeting of the Estonian lad who did the early shift gave her a moment's pause. When the staff behind the doughnut counter knew your name, it was time to break the habit. She'd noticed a thickening round her waist lately. She was heading towards the age range where it was infinitely easier to put it on than take it off, and Paula liked the feel of her body when it was fit too much to want to kiss that goodbye for the sake of fried dough and sugar. This, she promised herself as she paid for a dozen box, would be the last time.

Kevin, Ambrose and Karim were already in the office, the smell of fresh coffee heady in the air. The men fell on the sweet treats like starving waifs. Caffeine and sugar, that was what everyone craved after a murder. 'Where's Stacey?' Paula asked, surprised to see her office door closed and the lights out.

'No idea,' Alvin said. 'She wasn't here when I got in.'

'Maybe Sam kidnapped her,' Kevin said through a mouthful of Strawberry Creme Dreme. 'Holding her hostage till she sorts out his fucked-up financial status.'

Paula groaned. 'Don't even joke about it. How come none of us really grasped what a slimeball he is when we worked with him?'

'He's a clever slimeball,' Kevin said. 'He never felt like a mate, but I didn't think that made him a creep.'

'So, seriously, nobody knows where Stacey is?'

'She'll be doing something mysterious with a silicon-based life form,' Alvin said. 'So by my reckoning, that means I'm legally entitled to her doughnuts.'

'How do you work that out, big man?' Kevin reached for a Coconut Coco Sensation.

'I am the big man so I need more fuel.'

The door opened and Carol came in, the dog at her heels. She looked as if she hadn't slept, Paula thought. She glared at the box and shook her head, disapprovingly. 'Bad influence.' Then she plonked herself down at the table and reached for a coffee-glazed ring. 'I need coffee,' she said, finding a smile from somewhere deep inside.

Paula jumped to it. Old habits died hard, and she'd been devoted to Carol from the first day they'd worked together. Even now, when Elinor was the principal focus of her devotion, she still liked to do whatever she could to make Carol's life easier. 'Do you know where Stacey is?' she asked, heading for the coffee machine.

Carol turned to stare at the closed door. 'No idea. I assumed she'd be here. Is Tony not in?'

Kevin and Alvin shared a quick glance of surprise. 'No,

boss,' Karim said. 'And it's not like we'd miss him with that purple coat.'

Carol looked puzzled. 'He set off twenty minutes ahead of me.' It was the first time she'd publicly acknowledged the change in their domestic arrangements. Paula knew already because Tony had told her, and she'd shared the information only with Elinor and Stacey. For Carol to break her perpetual habit of personal discretion must mean something, but Paula wasn't sure what.

'Perhaps they've run off together,' Kevin said.

'There would be a certain communicative symmetry to that,' Carol said with an edge of acid. 'But with or without them, we need to get the day moving. We think the dead woman is Eileen Walsh, a nurse at Manchester Royal Infirmary. GMP are dealing with tracking down her dentist. As soon as we have a confirmation, we'll be all over her life. Just as we were with the last two victims. And maybe this time we'll get a break. God knows we need it. But for now, we have to sit on our hands.' Her tone was heavy. Paula passed her a cup of judicial-strength coffee and sat down.

'Can we not make some discreet inquiries?' Karim said.

'No. Not while there's a chance it's not her. The last thing we want is to freak out someone who happened to lend her car to her pal for the weekend.' Carol sipped the coffee and winced at the heat. 'The fire investigator was on the scene pretty much from the start so if there's anything significant to discover, he's better placed to find it.

'One thing we can do, though – Paula, I want you to follow up the Claire Garrity lead that Stacey dug up from social media. Go and see the widower and see whether the pics we've generated ring any bells with him. The rest of you,' Carol continued, 'there's not a lot we can do except go over the ground we've already covered—'

Before she could say more, the door opened and James

Blake marched into the squad room in full dress uniform. The chief constable was a big man, but his uniform was tailored to make him look powerful rather than fat. 'Marvellous,' he said, his voice dripping sarcasm. 'Three women dead in identical circumstances, and our crack squad are sitting around eating doughnuts and drinking coffee.'

Karim scrambled to his feet, but everyone else stayed in their seats and gave Blake the cold stare of dumb insolence. Carol wiped her sticky fingers on a napkin to buy a little time, trying not to show her anger and distress. Her stomach burned with acid as anxiety kicked in. 'Good morning, sir,' she said. 'Have you come to join our briefing?'

Blake scoffed. 'Briefing? From what I hear, you've nothing to brief. It's been six weeks since the McCormick woman was murdered and as far as I can see, you haven't developed a single viable suspect. That would be bad enough, but then there was the girl in Leeds. And now I'm told another one from Manchester has been found burned in a car. What's the problem, DCI Jordan? Is your team not up to the job?'

'We're dealing with a very sophisticated killer. He's clearly forensically aware,' Carol said. She could feel her throat tightening, as if tears were close. She couldn't let herself fall apart in front of Blake, never mind her own team. Under the desk, she drove her fingernails into the sensitive flesh on the inside of her knee.

Blake strolled imperiously around the room, studying the evidence boards that were jammed with crime scene photographs and the whiteboards covered with apparently random notes, some written by the squad officers and others by Tony. 'There's no order or method in this,' he complained. 'If we sent in a review team to assess what you've done so far, they'd struggle to make any sense of this.' He turned back, shaking his head. 'You've got another week to make some progress, DCI Jordan. You and your ragtag and bobtail team. Then I'm going to demand that we have oversight. A full-scale audit and analysis of what you've done. So in the interim, you'd better make progress. And you'd better have your case notes in the kind of order that a proper copper can make sense of.'

There was stunned silence as he walked out. 'Fuck,' Paula said. 'We are so screwed if we get a review team.'

'Why?' Carol demanded, her voice harsh.

'Because we don't always do things exactly by the book,' Kevin said. 'It makes us vulnerable.'

'We'll just have to make sure we get it sorted, then.' Alvin's bass rumble was, they all knew, a false reassurance. But Carol could see it made the others relax a little. It only served to make her feel even more inadequate to the task.

Then Kevin leaned forward. 'Well,' he drawled. 'I might have something to take us in the right direction. According to Amie McDonald's neighbour, Harrison Braithwaite, the man we think killed Amie gave her a passionate kiss on the doorstep. And it dawned on me that it's hard to snog somebody without getting your DNA all over their coat. And it turns out that Amie's good coat is quite distinctive. Mr Braithwaite picked it out from her coat rack right away. So I bagged it and tagged it and drove out to the lab with it myself. If the gods are smiling, we'll get DNA. And if there's one thing I've learned from Tony, it's that serial killers don't start off with homicide. Seems to me his DNA is a dead cert for the offender database.'

Carol had visibly perked up at Kevin's report until he reached the end. She shook her head. 'Great work, Kevin. But Tony thinks it's possible he's not got the usual kind of form. We talked about gateway offences last night and Tony reckons he's all about being in control. If he's shown up on the radar at all, it'll be for getting into a ruck with a police officer, or a confrontation with a bartender who wouldn't serve him an after-hours drink.'

'Doesn't matter though, does it?' Karim said eagerly. 'Whatever he's done, we'll make the connection if he's on the database.'

'It's not that simple,' Paula said. 'It's a coat. Amie will have come into contact with lots of people. On that night out alone. She'll have taken a taxi into town. There's a megadose of stranger DNA right there. One of the waiters could have taken her coat. More fresh DNA. The taxi back to the flat, more of the same. And we don't know whether she wore that coat between their date night and now. So yes, we might get lucky and it's better than no shot at all, but it won't give us any kind of definitive answer.'

Carol sighed. 'There are times when I think DNA is more trouble than it's worth.'

Kevin chuckled, still feeling pleased with himself. 'What? Are you hankering back to the days when we could just give them a good slap in the interview room?'

'Hardly. But I do sometimes wonder whether the technology has de-skilled us as detectives. How long before we've got algorithms for questioning? Before skills like Paula's are deemed to be redundant.' Carol wiped her mouth and threw her crumpled napkin at the bin, missing by inches. She stood up. 'God, listen to me. Ignore me, guys. We are going to get this bastard, believe me. We are going to get him.'

She walked to her office, head up, shoulders back, dog tailing her. They all looked at each other. In spite of her body language, not one of her squad believed she believed her own words.

51

Tony had gone to bed convinced he needed to do something to shake Carol out of the redoubt of guilt she'd dug herself into. When they'd got back from the crime scene in the small hours, she'd stood talking to him outside the barn in the chill night air while Flash tore around the rough pasture behind the barn, celebrating her liberation from guarding the house.

It broke his heart to hear her piling blame on herself for deaths that were not her responsibility. The five people who had died because a drunk driver had been allowed to walk free on her account. The victims of a killer she hadn't caught after his first excursion into murder. These were the burdens she had assumed to add to the demons she'd kept at bay for so long with alcohol. Her dead crowded the shadows of her heart and her mind. Her brother Michael and Lucy, the woman he'd loved to distraction. Officers she'd been responsible for who had encountered killers far more ruthless than their hunters. And all the victims she believed she'd let down with delayed justice.

None of it was her fault. But it was eating away at the slender rope of her well-being and self-confidence. He'd tried talking to her in therapeutic mode but she saw through that in about two minutes and stomped back indoors to make a cup of fruit tea. He'd whistled the dog to his side and followed her in. This time he tried talking like someone who cared about her. She told him not to patronise her and suggested it was time he retreated to his end of the barn.

He'd slept badly, worrying about her. He'd known plenty of addicts in his time, both patients and colleagues. He knew how fragile her hold on sobriety was right now. He'd seen her driven almost mad with rage and with grief, but he'd never seen her so close to the edge of herself. In the morning when he woke, he'd known he had to do something to change the direction of her emotions.

Ten minutes on Google and he had the makings of a plan. By the time he'd showered and wolfed some toast and coffee, she was out with the dog. She'd mentioned a ReMIT briefing, but he had other ideas. He made sure he left well in advance of her so she couldn't see that instead of turning left at the end of the lane, towards Bradfield, he turned right towards Hebden Bridge and Halifax.

The house he parked outside was a handsome detached Victorian villa with a pair of tiny turrets on the corners of the frontage. The pale York stone had been stained with the smoke and soot of the area's dark satanic mills. Some of the other houses in the leafy lane had been sandblasted back to their original creamy yellow but the Barrowclough family home wore its industrial heritage like a badge of honour. He sat in the car for a few minutes, persuading himself again that he was doing the right thing. Not everyone would agree, he knew. But for Tony, trying to rescue Carol from herself was a greater priority than negotiating some moral quagmire. She was the person he owed a duty to, not the one he was about to deceive.

The woman who answered the door had the haggard look

of someone who had lost a lot of weight too quickly. Her dark hair fell lifeless to her shoulders, a line of white showing at the parting. She was dressed carelessly; her clothes were clearly expensive and stylish, but nothing matched and her long cardigan was inaccurately buttoned.

'Mrs Barrowclough?' She nodded. 'I'm Dr Tony Hill. I'm a specialist in the psychology of risk. I work with the police. I know you've suffered a terrible shock lately and you have my sincere condolences. But I can't imagine anyone having a better idea of what Dominic was like. And I hoped you might be willing to talk to me.'

She looked blank, as if he'd spoken in a language foreign to her. 'It won't bring him back, will it?'

'No. But it might help us understand more so that we can try to stop what happened to Dominic happening to someone else.'

'Nicky. We called him Nicky, not Dominic.'

'I'm sorry. Perhaps we could talk about him over a cup of coffee?' He felt bad for playing her, but Carol was more important to him even than a grieving mother. He was taken aback to realise, after all these years, that there was apparently a hierarchy of empathy.

Mona Barrowclough had no resistance. She stepped back and allowed him to enter. She led the way down a panelled hall painted in a pink-tinged grey that probably had a name like Rabbit's Nostril. The carpet underfoot was a rich burgundy that swallowed their footsteps. At the end of the hall they entered a vast kitchen warmed by a four-oven Aga. It opened into a conservatory filled with well-established flowering plants. *Wasn't this how one of the Raymond Chandler novels opened?*

She waved vaguely at a pine refectory table surrounded by captain's chairs well supplied with comfortable-looking cushions. Tony sat down and while her back was turned filling the kettle, he double-checked that his phone was recording.

She fussed with the cafetiere, the mugs and a tin of ground coffee but eventually they were sitting at the end of the table with china mugs full of weak coffee in front of them. 'You didn't know Nicky,' she said. 'He was a lovely boy. So loving. He never went out the door without giving me a hug and a kiss, still. But he was always wild. He had that streak in him from a toddler.'

'I imagine it's like a light has gone out.'

She sipped her coffee, her eyes sad and ancient. 'That's it exactly. A light that's gone out.'

'That's hard. And a shock too.' He led her gently into her story, his eyes on hers, his expression filled with concern. Tony had spent years learning how to draw out the hurt and damage in people. But it had never felt more important than today.

She sighed, long and deep. 'A shock, maybe. But not a surprise. It's a funny thing to say about your own child, but I never thought he'd make old bones. He was always reckless. He'd throw himself at things without a thought. God knows, we tried to teach him to take more care, but we might as well have saved our breath. He had so many accidents when he was a child, we had social services at the house.' She made a noise halfway between a laugh and a cough. 'It wasn't funny at the time, mind.'

'Had he had accidents in the car before?'

'He'd scraped it and banged it into things through not paying attention. In car parks and the like. But he'd never had a proper accident. Nicky loved speed but he was a good driver. He knew how to handle a car. But that girlfriend of his, Casey? I blame her. She wasn't content with going out in town. She always wanted to be off to Leeds or Bradford or else some pub up on the moors with live music. So then

Nicky would take a drink … ' Her voice tailed off and her eyes filled with tears.

'And when he took a drink?'

'He thought he was indestructible.' She turned her head and stared into the conservatory. 'I half-hoped he'd get caught. I was daft enough to think that would put a stop to the madness.'

'But he did get caught.'

Mona gripped her mug tightly. 'And much good it did him. When we got the call from the police the night he was arrested, we decided not to go and pick him up. We thought a few hours in the cells among the low-life drunks and druggies might make an impression on him.'

Not likely, Tony thought. Not for someone like Dominic who believed the rules simply didn't apply to him. 'And did it?'

She seemed to slump further into her chair. 'Not a bit of it. He said it wouldn't make any odds to him. Even if he got banned, he said, he'd still drive. "I'll change cars, get something they're not looking out for," he said.'

Tony's heart leaped. That was what he needed to hear. The sentence that might take away some of Carol's guilt. Dominic Barrowclough would have carried on drinking and driving regardless of any ban handed down by the court. He was an arrogant, irresponsible arse; nothing could have altered his self-imposed fate.

Mona was still talking and Tony forced himself to pay attention. He had to see this through to the end. 'His dad was raging. He said if Nicky got banned and carried on driving, he'd throw him out of the house and out of the business. He worked for his dad, you see. He's an estate agent, my husband. And you need to be able to drive, obviously. I was that upset, I didn't know how Nicky would manage.'

Generation Y man-child, Tony thought. Men in their

twenties whose parents still let them dodge responsibility. 'But he didn't get banned?'

'No. There was something wrong with the equipment, they said in court. So they had to drop the charges.' She shook her head. 'I didn't know what to feel. Nicky'd got away with drinking and driving, but at least he still had a roof over his head and a job. We sat him down after the court case, me and his dad, and we gave him a good talking to. But he just laughed. He said he was safe behind the wheel. He said nobody was going to stop him driving. Not the police, not the courts, not his dad.' She crossed her arms across her stomach, hands gripping her elbows. 'I don't know what we did wrong. We did our best, but he was always a law unto himself. I don't know where he got it from. We're not impulsive people, me and my husband.'

'You shouldn't blame yourself,' Tony said. 'There are so many factors that shape the way we turn out. Did Nicky ever have a head injury when he was a child?'

She looked startled. 'How did you know that? He fell off the top of a kiddies' slide when he was a toddler. He'd not long turned two. He knocked himself out. He had to stay in hospital for two nights for observation but the hospital said he was fine. Is that what made him the way he was?'

'It may have had an effect.' Tony touched his forehead. 'This part of the brain here, the frontal lobe? It's the part of our brain that controls impulses. Sometimes a head injury can change people's behaviour quite dramatically. You mustn't blame yourself, Mrs Barrowclough. The work we're doing on what affects our attitude to risk is turning up more and more evidence that physical brain injuries are more common than we think and they have a more profound impact than we'd previously realised.' That was mostly bullshit made up on the hoof, but he hoped it would stop her wondering later why on earth he'd come to see her and asked the questions he had.

'So all those times we tried to make him see sense, he wasn't ignoring us out of badness? He couldn't help himself?'

'To some degree, yes. When he said to you he'd keep on driving regardless, that was probably a manifestation of his poor impulse control. It ran counter to logic and sense, but they didn't matter enough. Did he say anything else about his determination to keep driving, regardless?'

She thought for a moment. 'He kept on insisting that nobody had the right to tell him what to do. That he was safer behind the wheel even with a drink in him than most idiots were when they were sober. When I think about that, it makes me so angry.'

'I understand that.' Tony's voice was gentle.

'I can't walk down the street in this town any more. I feel so ashamed of what Nicky did. Four other people died because of him. Four other families devastated, but it's worse for them because they don't have the guilt. I'll never get past this, Doctor. Even though you tell me it was something inside Nicky's brain that made him the way he was, I'll never be able to let myself off the hook.'

Tony believed her. The rest of Mona Barrowclough's life would forever be shaped by the manner of her son's death. There was no comfort he could offer that would alter that. But at least he'd given her something to cling to when the guilt threatened to engulf her.

More importantly, he had a recording on his phone that might offer Carol a slender crack of light in the gloom of her guilt.

52

That the prepaid credit card Torin had loaded with £500 had come from a local bank branch offered Stacey options she hadn't expected. Usually, if it couldn't be done digitally, it didn't feature on her radar. But for once, she decided she needed to get out from behind her screens and do what needed to be done in person.

She wouldn't have done it for just anyone. But Paula was her friend. Over the years they'd moved from mutual wariness to mutual loyalty. If Stacey had needed proof of that, the support she'd had from Paula over Sam's betrayal had settled the matter. So because this was about Torin, and because Torin owned a place in Paula's heart, Stacey was willing to do what it took.

She'd stayed up into the small hours, partly because there were search parameters coming in from the crime scene, but mostly because what she was planning was extremely risky and she wanted to be sure she'd done everything possible to cover her back.

By three a.m., she'd done her research and prepared all

the materials she reckoned she'd need. Unusually for her, she'd slept badly and woken feeling edgy and nervous. For someone accustomed to being in command of herself and her environment, what she was planning was actually terrifying. Kevin was right about their methods making them vulnerable. It never bothered her when it came to her digital exploits; she knew she could outsmart any investigator the job set on her tail. But going into the field was a very different matter. She didn't want to count up the potential offences she was about to commit. It was, frankly, scary.

Stacey unearthed an old box of kava tea that she'd bought when she first started seeing Sam, a period of her life when she'd felt in a permanent state of anxiety. Two strong cups made no appreciable difference. She was going to have to screw up the courage to go through with her plan all by herself.

And so at half past nine, palms clammy and damp, she walked into the Campion Way branch of the Northern Bank and asked to see the manager. She met with some initial resistance, not having an appointment. But the production of a warrant card wore down the gatekeepers and within fifteen minutes she was seated opposite a man with a plaque on his desk that told her he was Patrick Haynes, Branch Manager. He had the smooth skin and perfectly groomed hair of a man who spent too much time looking in the mirror, but his shirt let him down, Stacey decided. It probably sat perfectly when he was standing up admiring himself, but seated, it strained and gaped across the beginnings of a pot belly. 'So, what's this all about?' he asked. He was almost cordial, but anxiety seeped through his words.

'I'm Detective Constable Xing Ming,' she said, presenting ID that was not that of ReMIT. 'As you can see, I'm attached to the Anti-Terrorism Unit.'

Haynes looked confused. 'I don't understand?'

'Perhaps this will help?' Stacey produced an envelope from her businesslike handbag and passed it to him. She put the bag on the desk nonchalantly.

He extracted two sheets of paper which, to anyone unfamiliar with such things, appeared to be a warrant authorised under the Prevention of Terrorism Act by a District Judge, requiring the bank to provide all details relating to a prepaid credit card, number listed below. He frowned as he read it through to the end. 'I still don't understand,' he said.

'I'd have thought it was perfectly clear. Pursuant to our inquiries under the Act, we have come into possession of certain information that may indicate that this card has been used to make purchases relating to the preparation of acts of terrorism. A warrant has been obtained and you are obliged to tell me who bought that prepaid credit card and when.' Stacey delivered her little speech with a chilly authority that completely disguised the racing of her heart and the trickle of sweat on her spine.

'And that's it? I just have to hand over the information?'

'Yes. It's that simple.'

'I think I need to speak to head office about this,' he said uncertainly.

She glanced at her watch. 'Be my guest. But they'll tell you the same thing as me.' She leaned forward slightly and said with a confiding air, 'Look, we've done this in the most low-key way possible. With this warrant, I could have come in mob-handed and closed down this branch while I served it. How would that play in the media? Northern Bank allegedly implicated in the financing of terrorism. Your head office would love that. This is a matter of some urgency.' She fixed him with her steeliest glare. 'If there is a problem, my team are five minutes away. I promise you, they don't give a shit about the reputation of your bank.'

He opened and closed his mouth, looking pained. Then

self-preservation kicked in. 'Well, this paperwork all seems to be in order, Detective. Give me a moment ... ' He pushed back from his desk.

Her heart hammered harder. She couldn't let him leave and talk this through with a colleague. 'Do what you have to do here,' Stacey said briskly. She gestured to his computer. 'You have access to the systems.' She leaned across and turned his screen so she could see what he was doing. 'It's a question of security. No more people involved than absolutely have to be.'

He cleared his throat and started hammering his old-fashioned keyboard. 'Of course. I'm just taken aback,' he jabbered. 'I can't believe ... '

'Nobody ever can,' she said briskly, her eyes on the screens. She couldn't quite believe she was getting away with this.

'That can't be right.' Haynes frowned. 'I know this customer. He's not a terrorist. He's a plumber. He took out a loan with us last year to expand his business.'

Stacey pulled out her phone and snapped a photograph of the details on the screen. Norman Jackson. An address in Harriestown. 'I appreciate what you're saying. And there may well be a completely innocent explanation for the intelligence that has come to us.' She stood up. 'I appreciate your assistance. Please don't discuss this conversation with anyone.' She flashed a quick smile. 'Nobody understands security like a banker, right?'

Haynes' smile was uncertain. 'Absolutely.' He got up and walked round the desk to show her out. Stacey leaned across to get her bag, making sure her body shielded her slipping the fake warrant into it. Pulse racing, she walked past the manager and carried on across the lobby and into the street.

Stacey let out a long sigh of relief as she turned the first corner she came to. She leaned against the cool brick wall, eyes closed, waiting for her breathing to return to normal. She'd done it. She'd abandoned her screens. She'd gone out into the field and fooled a man who should have known better.

And now she knew who had tried to blow a hole in her friend's life.

53

There was nobody home at the well-maintained between-the-wars semi that Sean Garrity had shared with his late wife Claire. Paula walked round to the other half of the house, which looked distinctly scruffier. A glance through the bay window of the living room revealed a chaos of children's toys and folded clothes. She rang the bell and heard a child's wail in response. The door opened to reveal a young woman, blonde hair in an untidy ponytail, a whimpering baby on her hip and a sticky-faced toddler clinging to her leg. She looked about ready to join the baby in its tears. 'What?' she demanded.

Paula held out her ID. 'I'm looking for Sean Garrity. There doesn't seem to be anyone home.'

'Well, there wouldn't be, would there? He'll be at work. Lucky bastard.' She jiggled her leg, unsuccessfully trying to shake off the toddler who was staring at Paula as if she was a creature from another galaxy.

'And where is work? Do you know?'

'He manages that gastropub in Kenton Vale. What's it called ...?' She screwed up her face in an attempt to remember.

'The Dog and Gun?' Paula vaguely recalled reading some-thing in the paper about the revamping of the traditional local into something more upmarket.

'Yeah, that's it. He invited us to the opening. I only had the one then ... ' She looked dreamy for a moment, then a full-scale howl from the baby brought her back to reality. She shushed the baby ineffectually. 'You'll find him down there. Thrown himself into it, you might say. Since Claire died. You know his wife died? Is that what this is about?'

'Thanks, you've been very helpful.' Paula backed away, glad to escape the aura of sour milk and stale flesh that clung to the harassed woman. She drove off, car window open so she could vape. God, but she missed smoking. Vaping made her feel like the toddler clinging to its mother's leg. There was something infantilising about the cigarette substitute that made Paula feel she probably needed to knock that on the head too.

She reached the Dog and Gun ten minutes after opening time. It was all faux distressed wood and antiqued tables. The heritage it was channelling was the Yukon gold rush rather than Bradfield's industrial past. The hipster behind the bar perked up at the sight of her, clearly thinking she was the first customer of the day. His face fell when she showed him her ID and said she was looking for Sean Garrity. 'He's through the back,' he said. 'I'll go and get him. Is this about that twat that drove into Claire?'

'If you could just fetch Mr Garrity?' Paula softened her words with a genial smile.

Sean Garrity appeared moments later. He was a lanky six-footer with a shaved head and a full beard. It was a look that Paula found faintly ridiculous. He wore a checked shirt but-toned to the neck and low-slung skinny jeans. A pair of silver skull earrings completed the image. But there was nothing fashionable about the dark shadows under his eyes or the tumbler of rum in his hand. 'You're a cop?' he said, aggression in his stance and his tone. 'Is this about that tosser who killed my wife? Are you actually going to charge him with something?'

'Can we go somewhere more private?'

He gestured to the far corner of the bar where a trio of high-backed booths were clustered. 'That do?'

Paula nodded and followed him. His gait was a little unsteady and as she drew closer to him, she could smell alcohol in his sweat. This was a man who was dealing with his grief through the medium of drink. Never helpful when it came to eliciting information.

He threw himself into the booth and glared belligerently at Paula. 'Well? What's happening?'

'I'm not on the team investigating what happened to your wife,' she said, keeping it slow and calm. 'I'm with the Regional Major Incident Team.'

He snorted and took a swig from his glass. 'What happened to Claire. That was a major fucking incident, don't you think?'

'I'm sure that's what it was for you, Mr Garrity. But I can't comment on it because I don't know the circumstances.'

'So what are you doing here if you're not interested in Claire?' Another swallow and the glass was empty. 'Norrie,' he shouted. 'Bring me the bottle.'

'Did your wife do much on social media?'

'What's that got to do with anything?'

'We think someone hacked Claire's RigMarole account after her death, and we're trying to find out who and how.'

The barman scuttled over with a bottle of artisanal rum with a ridiculously over-designed label. Garrity waved him away and poured three fingers into the glass. 'What kind of sick fuck does that?'

The kind who gets a kick out of fucking with his victims. 'We believe this may be connected with a series of serious crimes. Do you happen to know what Claire's password on RigMarole was?'

'Yeah. It was Claire890714. Her birth date in reverse. The fourteenth of July 1989. But she hardly ever used RigMarole. She couldn't be arsed. She liked talking to people, not sending stupid messages to people she'd never met.'

It wouldn't have taken much to work out that password, Paula thought. All the information the killer needed would have been there in Claire's death notice. Stacey was right. People were depressingly stupid about passwords. She took the photo from her bag and laid it on the table. 'Do you know this man?'

Garrity peered at it. 'I don't think so. He's not one of our friends and I don't recognise him from in here. Norrie?' He summoned the barman again. 'He'd know better than me.' He waved the photo at Norrie when he arrived.

The barman studied it. 'He's definitely not a regular. Other than that, I can't say. Has he done something we should know about?'

'He may have hacked Claire's RigMarole account after she died.'

Norrie's mouth curled and his eyes screwed up in an expression of disgust. 'That's sick.'

'Maybe you should go round to Freshco.' Seeing Paula's frown, Garrity continued. 'Where Claire worked. She was the bakery supervisor. It might be one of the weirdos who work there. Most of them, I wouldn't give them houseroom in here.' He clambered out of the booth, almost tripping over his own feet. 'So if that's it, we've got work to do. Right, Norrie?' And he stumbled away, trying to straighten up and look sober but failing.

'He's taken it hard,' Norrie said. 'He used to be a really nice guy, you know? He totally worshipped Claire.'

'Get him some help,' Paula said. 'You're not doing him any favours colluding in the drinking. Trust me, I've seen colleagues go down that road.'

Freshco in Kenton Vale was a ten-minute drive away. It took Paula almost the same length of time to find a parking space then walk back to the store. As usual during the day, the aisles were busy with shoppers. All human life is here, she thought, dodging a dozy-looking man in drooping sweat pants and stained T-shirt, only to step into the path of an elderly woman pushing a trolley containing a loaf of bread, a bottle of milk and a tin of beans.

Two hours later, she emerged into daylight, feeling dazed and frustrated. The HR department in the superstore had insisted on consulting head office before they would even look at the photograph she was toting. But once they got the go-ahead, she had to admit they'd been helpful. She'd been introduced to Claire's workmates in the bakery and when none of them admitted recognising the man in the picture, the helpful HR boss had taken her on a tour of every department, showing the picture to every member of staff they encountered. And nobody showed any sign of knowing who he was. One check-out operative said she thought he might have come through her till a couple of times, but her colleagues rolled their eyes and said, 'Stop showing off, Varya.'

It was a bust. The HR woman had made copies of the photo and promised to put it up in the staff room and on the various department noticeboards. But Paula couldn't feel even the faintest stirring of hope. Another lead going precisely nowhere. She'd never known a case like it. Usually there were frustrations a-plenty in any investigation. But at the heart of it, there would be something that finally broke in their favour. A moment of carelessness by the killer. A chance encounter that broke an alibi. A forensic breakthrough.

But this man was too sharp for that. Too sharp for them, which was unnerving. Carol Jordan, Tony Hill and Stacey Chen were, in Paula's view, the best in the business. And the rest of the team were the coppers she'd hand-pick herself if she was building an elite squad. Yet they'd hardly advanced the case an inch in over six weeks.

Blake was a bully but he'd meant what he said. He was longing to turn on them because Carol Jordan had out-flanked him in the past. But there were other chiefs without a personal agenda who wouldn't be slow in following suit. Sooner or later, the bosses were going to turn on them. If they didn't deliver something soon, it wouldn't be long before they were consigned to the scrapheap.

54

He'd never been busier. Even when the business had been going gangbusters with Tricia, he'd had more time to call his own. But executing his careful plans to perfect his revenge took time. It wasn't simply going on the dates with the women, it was preparing the ground. He only ever sent them texts or spoke to them using the burner phones. And to cover his tracks, he only ever made the calls from the cities the women lived in, then removed SIM cards and batteries. The only time those calls would show up in Bradfield was when he was courting a victim in Bradfield. So as well as running his business, he was running around chasing women. Luckily he often managed to roll the two things up together and text his next target in between meetings in other cities.

He'd been listening to a Bradfield Victoria football match in the car driving to Liverpool the other evening when he'd heard something that he liked. The commentators were talking at half-time about football chants and the inventiveness of fans. One mentioned a chant he'd heard from the terraces of a team on a losing streak: 'You're nothing special, we get beaten every week.' It had made him think about the final showdown with Tricia and what he could say to her. 'You're nothing special, I've done this too often to count,' perhaps? That wasn't bad, but something snappier would come to him, he was sure.

That morning, he'd already supervised the layout for two different magazines and spoken to a couple of key advertisers demanding circulation updates. The latest figures had not left anyone feeling happy; he was going to have to cut the rates both advertisers had been paying. And now he had a meeting with Carrie McCrystal, a businesswoman who ran a chain of beauty spas across the North. He hoped she was going to offer him a juicy slice of advertising revenue to stave off the problems coming at him from all sides. He might even be able to afford to hire someone to take on the editorial work Tricia had done so effectively.

She arrived right on time, a walking advertisement for her business. Her hair flowed to her shoulders; dark, glossy and well-kempt. Her make-up was flawless, emphasising slightly eerie pale blue eyes and full lips. She wore a well-fitting business suit with a pencil skirt and nude heels. He couldn't help a buzz of admiration at her style. He took care with his own appearance and always appreciated it when others did the same. It showed respect for the people you dealt with. Tricia had always maintained an impeccable façade, however. And look how that had turned out – the perfect mask for her insincerity. So he wasn't going to take Carrie McCrystal at face value.

They met in a small conference room that he used for team briefings. It was plain but smart and gave nothing away. He poured coffee and let her witter about the weather and the traffic till finally they sat facing each other across the table. 'I expect you're wondering why I asked for this meeting,' was her opener.

'I assumed you wanted to talk about an advertising deal.'

Her smile reminded him of a cat. 'Oh, Tom, if that was all I wanted, I'd have dealt with Marianne in advertising. We've always managed to come to a satisfactory arrangement in the past. No, I have bigger fish to fry today.'

He leaned back in his chair, head cocked to one side. 'I'm listening,' he said.

'A little bird tells me that your business partner has left the building.' She let the words hang in the air.

He struggled to keep his anger in check. The idea of other people discussing his private life enraged him. Was that to be Tricia's legacy? To make him look inadequate in other people's eyes? 'People move on,' he said, managing to keep his voice even and pleasant.

'Tell me about it. We're business people, we understand that nothing is forever. But it occurred to me that you might be interested in bringing another partner into the business. Now, I've no direct experience of running magazines but I have a brilliant press and PR person who has a background in precisely that. Melanie was the editorial manager of *Leeds Alive* before I snapped her up. I think she could do wonders in this business and I have lots of promotional ideas to bring to the table.' She gave him a brilliant smile. Teeth that would glow in the dark, he thought. All the better to eat you with.

'That's a very interesting proposition, Carrie,' he said. A lifeline for the business he'd spent so long building. A chance to salvage what Tricia had so nearly destroyed. But did he really want to put his fate in the hands of someone else? And how the fuck was he going to get his hands on Tricia's shares? He couldn't sell what he didn't have.

She opened her substantial handbag and took out a thin cardboard file. 'I've taken the liberty of putting a financial proposal together. Obviously, I don't have access to your commercially sensitive information, but I've been taking a long hard look at what you do and even taking into account that slight but noticeable dip in quality recently, I think this is a great little business.' She pushed the file across to him. 'Tell me whether I'm wide of the mark.'

He opened the file. At first, the figures were a blur but he forced himself to focus and he had to admit, she'd done a remarkably thorough job. He almost wondered if she'd picked Tricia's brains before coming to him. But no, he told himself. This was not a conspiracy. He couldn't start thinking like that. This was a report that could have been assembled by anyone with enough business experience who knew where to look. He took his time, going through the pages line by line till he came to the end. Her estimate of what his business was worth and her proposal to buy into it.

He was momentarily stunned. He'd resigned himself to the fact that his business was going down the tubes. He knew the content was suffering, he knew he'd been too busy chasing editorial to keep a tight grip on design. The gradual decline of his magazines was something else to lay at Tricia's door, and that quantum of blame had added fuel to the blaze of his determination and anger.

But Carrie McCrystal was offering him an alternative ending to one part of the catastrophe that Tricia had inflicted on him. Her financial offer was a reasonable starting point. He'd have to meet this Melanie and see her work to decide whether she was good enough to make a difference. But it was a potential reprieve, no doubt about it. The only question was whether he wanted to be saved or to go down in flames to make a point.

It was no contest. He looked up from the papers and met Carrie's level gaze. 'I think this is the start of a very profitable conversation,' he said.

Not that it would let Tricia off the hook. Quite the

opposite, in fact. If he was going to sell her share in the business, it would be a lot easier if she was dead. That way she couldn't contradict his version of events when he said she'd signed the shares back over to him when she'd left. Now killing her wasn't for revenge alone. It was for solid business reasons.

55

Dr Dave Myers was no stranger to most of the ReMIT team. He and Paula had known each other since her earliest days in CID when much of modern forensics had been a pretty bare-bones science. He'd worked on DNA analysis in the old Home Office facility in Bradfield, and when the government had privatised the Forensic Science Service, he'd been recruited by one of the new providers to run a private lab. When the former Bradfield MIT had been up and running, he'd been their first port of call whenever a case demanded the expenditure associated with forensic analysis. Chief Constable James Blake had fought a constant battle with Carol Jordan over the cost of using Dr Dave and his team, arguing that cheaper services were available.

Carol had dug her heels in, insisting on the 'you pay peanuts, you get monkeys' principle. More often than not, she won the day because of Blake's fear that somehow the press would find out he'd insisted on cutting corners on a murder inquiry. Sometimes, a man's vanity could be used constructively.

One of the conditions Carol had placed on her acceptance

of the ReMIT job was that they'd have access to Dr Dave and his lab when they deemed it necessary. So when Kevin had picked up Amie McDonald's coat, the obvious destination had been the state-of-the-art lab that lurked behind the anonymous façade of a prefabricated warehouse on an industrial estate on the edge of town. He'd emphasised the importance of the coat in a multiple-murder investigation, and Dr Dave had promised his best efforts, though he'd looked dubious.

Usually, the lab would transmit their results digitally, flagging them up with a phone call to the investigating team. So it was a surprise when Dr Dave himself walked into the Skenfrith Street squad room. Paula looked up from her computer screen where she'd been bringing her case paperwork up to date and grinned with delight when she saw him shamble through the door with his perpetually casual gait. Outside the lab, stripped of his protective overalls, he looked nothing like a scientist for whom precision was the stock in trade. His big brown hands appeared more suited to manual labour than the delicate work he performed constantly. With his baseball cap, his soul patch, his baggy chinos and the glasses perched on the end of his nose, he always made Paula think of a non-conformist academic. They'd been friends for years, linked by common tastes in music and comedy. When they'd both been single, they'd regularly kept each other company at comedy clubs and small-scale music venues. Even now, they met up in a foursome with their partners for a gig every couple of months.

Paula left her desk and gave Dave a hug. 'What are you doing here?' she asked.

He gave a mock-frown. 'So much for the, "Hi, Dave, great to see you."'

'Coffee?'

'Sure, why not? Is Kev around?'

'No, he's gone to brief the media team about the latest case,' she said, heading for the coffee station. 'By the way, this is Karim Hussain, our new boy.'

Dave sketched a wave at Karim, who hadn't taken his eyes off the new arrival since he'd walked in. 'Hi, Karim. I'm Dave Myers.'

'The king of forensic DNA analysis,' Paula added as she prepped an espresso for Dave.

'Not so much today,' Dave said. He folded his long body into an office chair and walked it over to Paula's desk. He took an envelope out of his pocket and placed it next to her keyboard. 'Kev brought in a coat belonging to Amie McDonald. He thought there might be usable DNA on it.'

Paula put his coffee next to him and eyed the envelope. 'And was there?'

'There was DNA all right. Trouble is, there was way too much DNA.'

Paula groaned. 'Mixed samples?'

'Complex mixed samples,' Dave said. 'I don't know whether Amie ever had her coat dry-cleaned, but if she did, it wasn't recently. Kev asked me to concentrate on the arms and the upper back, where you'd hold or hug somebody if you were kissing them. He brought in her toothbrush so we could eliminate Amie's DNA, but that was no help. Even taking her out of the equation, I'd estimate we've got at least six or seven different DNA traces on the outside of the coat in the key regions.'

'Can you not tell when they were left there?' Karim asked. 'Like, are they not in layers, one on top of the other?'

Dave shook his head. 'That's not how it works. They're all jumbled up together. They could have been deposited in any order. It's like making soup. You can't tell from the finished bowl whether the carrots went in ahead of the onions. And if you've put it in the blender, you can't even be sure whether it's onions or shallots.'

Karim looked bemused at the analogy but Paula was more accustomed to Dave's style. 'If we had a suspect, could you pull his DNA out of the soup?' she asked.

'Maybe, but it's a long way off a definite.'

'Didn't I read somewhere that there are new computer programs that could figure out the separations of complex mixtures?' Paula asked.

'People have been working on it,' Dave said. 'The idea is that they have a set of complex algorithms that predict the likelihood of different sequences based on statistical analysis. Probabilistic genotyping, they're calling it. It sounds great. They've been doing some clinical trials in the US. And it has huge problems. You take the same mixed sample and run it through two different programs, and the answers that come out of the other end are completely different. The researchers sent the same mixed sample to a random bunch of analysts and all the responses were different. So no, I would not pin any hopes on a conviction based on that evidence.' He tapped the envelope. 'It's all in there. Kev was very insistent that it was top priority so I wanted to come in myself and explain the results, in case there were questions.'

'I appreciate that, Dave.' Paula sighed.

'Sorry to piss on your chips.'

'Not your fault. But this case is killing us. It's got more dead ends than a seventies housing estate. Every time we turn a corner we hit a blank wall.'

'Much as we'd like to help, it's not *CSI* and we can't work miracles.' Dave stood up. 'Resolving mixed samples is coming down the road, but it's not going to get here in time for your investigation.'

Paula sighed. 'Oh well, maybe in years to come, some brilliant cold-case detective will get Dave Myers 2.0 to apply the new techniques and solve our case.'

'Don't give up hope. You're a good detective, Paula.

Sometimes the old ways are what you need to crack the case. It's like I tell juries when I get the chance. If you've got an absolutely clear fingerprint and half a dozen eye witnesses, you really don't need to sweep for DNA. Good luck.' He waggled his fingers in a wave as he walked out.

Karim stared after him. 'We're fucked, aren't we?'

'Probably,' Paula said. 'But that's no reason to stop plugging away.' Before she could say more, Stacey marched through the door with the air of a woman on a mission.

'Oh good,' Stacey said. 'You and me have somewhere to be, Paula.'

'We do?'

'We do. I'll explain in the car.'

'What about me?' Karim said plaintively.

'Hold the fort and do your paperwork,' Stacey said.

'Where will you be if the guv'nor asks?'

'Fighting crime,' Stacey said firmly, heading back out the door.

Paula shrugged and spread her hands wide. 'I have no idea what's going on either. But experience tells me not to mess with Stacey. See you later.'

56

C arol stepped off the Minster Basin wharf on to a prettily painted narrowboat whose name, *Steeler*, unfurled along a painted gold-and-black banner. The deck shifted under her feet as her weight transferred itself to the water. This was Tony's domain, as the barn was hers. He'd inherited it from the father he'd never known and, to her surprise, he'd transformed himself from a squirrel who lived among piles of papers and books into as neat a boatman as it was possible to imagine. To live in so confined a space imposed an order and rigour she would never have believed he could adapt to. It helped that he had colonised a shipping container with his books, turning it into a library that would have given Carol claustrophobia inside an hour. And of course, he still had his office at Bradfield Moor Secure Hospital, which presumably provided him with all the cluttering possibilities he needed.

She had no idea why he'd messaged her to meet him at the boat rather than come into the office. She'd put the question in reply but he'd ignored her so she had no option but to leave the station and head for the canal basin. The old Grosvenor

Canal ran parallel to Skenfrith Street, invisible between high buildings, but there was a narrow alley that led to the towpath which led to Minster Basin. Five years before, it would have been a foolhardy person who would have ventured alone along the towpath even with a dog at her heels. But European money had paid to refurbish the towpath, installing a flagged walkway and proper lighting that dispelled the dark shadows of the undercrofts that carried the canal beneath the streets. Local businesses had put their hands in their pockets and paid for landscaping. Now it was a pleasant shortcut across the city centre.

Flash darted back and forth along the bank, never leaving Carol for long. When the path opened out on to the basin, she knew exactly where she was going and bounded across the cobbles and sat next to *Steeler*, ears pricked and tongue lolling. In spite of herself, Carol couldn't help feeling grateful to George Nicholas for virtually forcing the dog on her.

As she boarded, the collie leaped on to the narrowboat roof and settled there, head between her paws, eyes scanning the basin for any threats to her mistress.

Carol meanwhile knocked on the hatch before sliding it back and descending the steps into the main cabin. Tony was sitting at the table, a book in front of him. 'Don't get up,' Carol said. 'I'm coffee'd out.' She slid on to the buttoned bench seat opposite him. 'You missed the briefing this morning.'

'I know. Sorry, I had something more pressing to deal with.'

'So, why am I here? What's so mysterious that we can't talk about it in the office?'

'Not mysterious,' he said. 'Private.'

Anxiety clenched Carol's stomach. *Private* spelled ominous to her these days. Another nightmare was more than she could take at the moment. She straightened in her seat, clasping her hands on the table in front of her. 'What now?'

'I've been worried about you,' he said. 'The way you've let guilt eat into you.'

Carol snorted. 'It wasn't a matter of choice. What's happened is a matter of fact. You'd have to be a monster not to feel guilty.'

'I agree. Some guilt would be inevitable. But it's swallowing you up, Carol, and you need to fight it.'

'Christ, what is this? A therapy session? I'm not one of your bloody patients.'

'No, you're my friend. My best friend. For years, you were probably my only friend until I started to get the hang of it. So I can't sit on my hands and let you be consumed by remorse. You're condemning yourself for things that no reasonable person would blame you for.'

She shook her head. 'Five people dead, Tony. Because I wanted to reclaim my place in the sun.'

'I'm glad you brought that up,' he said. 'I know it's eating away at you but it really isn't your responsibility. Connection isn't the same as causality.'

He was making no sense. How could those deaths not be laid at her door? 'You're wrong,' she said.

Tony took his phone from his pocket and laid it on the table in front of him. He fiddled with the screen for a moment. 'I went over to Halifax this morning. That's why I missed the briefing. I went to talk to Mona Barrowclough. Dominic's mother.'

'Why? Don't you think she's had enough to cope with, without you stirring everything up again?'

'We had a very interesting conversation. You can listen to it all if you like, but there are a couple of things I need you to hear.' He raised one finger to silence whatever she was about to say. 'Please. Just listen, Carol.'

He pressed <play> on his phone. The tinny sound of a strange woman's voice filled the cabin:

He said it wouldn't make any odds to him. Even if he got banned, he said, he'd still drive. 'I'll change cars, get something they're not looking out for,' he said. His dad was raging. He said if Nicky got banned and carried on driving, he'd throw him out of the house and out of the business. He worked for his dad, you see. He's an estate agent, my husband. And you need to be able to drive, obviously. I was that upset, I didn't know how Nicky would manage.

Then Tony's voice. *But he didn't get banned?*

No. There was something wrong with the equipment, they said in court. So they had to drop the charges. I didn't know what to feel. Nicky'd got away with drinking and driving, but at least he still had a roof over his head and a job. We sat him down after the court case, me and his dad, and we gave him a good talking to. But he just laughed. He said he was safe behind the wheel. He said nobody was going to stop him driving. Not the police, not the courts, not his dad. I don't know what we did wrong. We did our best, but he was always a law unto himself. I don't know where he got it from. We're not impulsive people, me and my husband.

Carol felt dizzy. She couldn't quite take it in. 'Play it again,' she whispered. And he did.

'You see?' Tony spoke gently. 'It was nothing to do with you. Even if Dominic Barrowclough had lost his licence that day, he'd still have been driving drunk the night he ploughed into that Mini. It's not your fault, Carol.'

She couldn't help the tears. She was angry at herself for her loss of control but there was nothing she could do about it. Mona Barrowclough's words didn't absolve her, but they lifted the burden enough that she could see a chink of daylight in the darkness of her guilt.

'You should listen to the whole thing,' Tony said. 'In case you think I pushed her into it.'

'That's not your style,' Carol said shakily. 'Thank you.' She cleared her throat and wiped her eyes with the back of her hand. 'And now I need to go back to the office and see whether anybody's come up with a set of dental records for Eileen Walsh.' She slid out of the booth and turned to go.

At the last moment, she turned back and took three steps that brought her to Tony's side. She leaned forward as he looked up in surprise and she planted an awkward kiss on his forehead. 'I don't deserve you,' she said.

'It's not about what we deserve. It's what we earn.' Their eyes met. Confused by a surge of emotion, Carol backed away and climbed back into daylight. 'See you later,' she said, far from certain what later would bring.

57

Paula fastened her seat belt and put the car into gear. 'Speak to me, Stacey. You have to tell me where we're going or else we'll be sitting here in the car park till it gets dark.'

'Harriestown. 71 Camborne Street.'

'That's just round the corner from ours. Why are we going there?' Paula pulled out into the traffic and set a mental course for Camborne Street.

'They've got a problem with their boiler.'

Paula groaned. 'You know, if you want people not to fall into racial stereotypes, you really need to give up on the whole inscrutable thing. Why are we interested in the boiler at 71 Camborne Street?'

'We're not.' Stacey gave Paula a quick sidelong look. 'OK, I'll take pity on you. As you know, I got absolutely nowhere trying to track the IP address of the bastard who's blackmailing Torin. That left the prepaid credit card that he deposited the money on to. Now, normally that would be an equally dead end. I honestly expected the sort code to correspond to some slightly dodgy private bank in a tax haven with

Byzantine privacy laws. Which would have been as inscrutable as you accuse me of being.'

'And it wasn't?' Paula stopped at a red light and glanced across at her friend. 'That's why we're chasing boilers in Camborne Street?'

'Not only was it not a dodgy bank, it wasn't even in a tax haven. It was a Bradfield branch of the Northern Bank.'

'No way!'

'Way. Campion Way to be precise.' Stacey grinned. 'Sorry, you walked into that one.'

'OK. So this is a local blackmailer?'

'That's the inescapable conclusion. But it's still got very strict rules about customer privacy and the old chestnut of data protection.'

A slow smile spread across Paula's face. 'You did a bad thing, didn't you?'

'I did. I pretended to be an officer in the Anti-Terrorism Unit.'

Paula's mouth fell open and her foot momentarily slipped off the accelerator, provoking a loud hoot from the car behind. 'You did what? You pretended to be a spook?'

Stacey shrugged, not an easy manoeuvre to pull off while wearing a seat belt. 'Kind of. I faked up ID.' She giggled. 'I called myself Xing Ming. That's Mandarin for "first name, surname".'

Paula gave her a look of incomprehension. 'That's a joke, right? You prepped a fake ID that was a joke?'

'I took a chance that a bank manager called Patrick Haynes wasn't going to have Chinese heritage,' she said severely. 'The joke was to make me feel relaxed, not to take the piss out of the Anti-Terrorism Unit. I take what they do very seriously. So, I made the ID and I did a fake warrant for disclosure.'

'Tell me you're making this up. Because I can see both our careers disappearing in smoke at this point.'

'I'm not making it up. There's nothing that tracks this back to me.'

'Except that you're the only Chinese female officer in Bradfield and they presumably have CCTV?'

'I kept my head down. And I put on my posh Radio Four accent. But there won't be any blowback, I promise. I put the fear of God and the Official Secrets Act into Mr Patrick Haynes. And he dug out the details on the card. Purchased by one Norman Jackson five months ago. I couldn't see the balance and transactions on that screen, only his name and address. He's a plumber.'

'Hence the boiler?'

'Got it in one. Hence the boiler. I called his number this morning and asked where he was working so I could drop off a part for a job I'd booked in with his office girl. I was able to reassure the bank manager that the nice plumber he'd loaned thirty-five grand to wasn't going to use the money to buy guns or bombs to start his very own Harriestown jihad.' She frowned, considering. 'I don't think he'll take it any further. I think I struck the right note of authority plus holy terror.'

'I imagine you did. I'm amazed, Stacey. Jeez. All the same, I don't think you should get out from behind your desk too often. You missed Blake's grandstanding performance this morning. Basically, he's coming for us. And as Kevin pointed out, when we bend the rules and don't get results, we put ourselves at risk.'

'But I got a result, Paula.'

'You did. A plumber in Harriestown. Where did that come from?'

'It's weird but it's not as scary as a bunch of gangsters on the other side of the world. This guy lives three streets away from you. He's married, he's got his own little business. He employs three other guys and he's rated four stars on Google.

He's probably some lone weirdo who crossed paths with Torin and created this whole fantasy relationship in his head.'

'One for Tony to explain to us,' Paula said, taking the right-hand fork that led them into Harriestown. 'People are weird.'

'You have to promise not to thump him.'

Paula had a sudden thought. 'But what are we going to do? We can't arrest him. I don't want Torin dragged through the courts.'

'I've been thinking about that,' Stacey said. 'I think we threaten him with arrest. Offer to throw the book at him. Then we talk about restorative justice. Pay Torin his money back and never do anything like this again or we'll give you a taste of your own medicine and plaster it all over social media and the local press that he's a blackmailing pervert. Between us, I think we can scare the living shit out of him.'

'Is that enough, though? What's to stop him going after somebody else? How do we know he isn't already targeting other people?'

Stacey looked startled. 'I thought this was just about Torin?'

'Well, yes, it was, but I don't want this guy thinking he can get away with it with other people.'

They drove in silence for a few minutes. 'Torin's still a minor, right?'

'Yeah, he's fourteen.'

'I'm thinking we could caution him and put him on ViSOR. Torin doesn't have to come into it at all. With a caution, it's only about him admitting the offence. There's no court case, no reporting of it. But we thoroughly bugger his life up.'

She had a point, Paula thought. With a caution, Jackson could be put on the sex offenders list for two years. He wouldn't be able to move house or change his job or his bank details without reporting to the police. 'You're getting worryingly good at buggering people's lives up.'

'It's a digital world, Paula. I own that space. No more Ms Nice Guy.'

There was a white van in the driveway of 71 Camborne Street, JACKSON PLUMBING emblazoned on the side. Paula found a parking space a hundred metres away and the two women walked back down the pavement. 'I'm channelling Cagney and Lacey right now,' Paula said with a swagger.

Stacey groaned. 'That means I'm stuck with Harve, right?'

They turned into the driveway as a heavy-set man in battered jeans and a checked shirt emerged from the side of the house and made for the van. His sleeves were rolled up, revealing complex intertwined Celtic tattoos on his forearms. He glanced at them briefly and carried on sliding the door back. He looked to be in his mid-forties, strands of grey in his untidy brown hair. He had the florid complexion of a man who drinks too much too often and a soft belly to match.

'Mr Jackson?' Paula called. 'Norman Jackson?'

He withdrew his upper body from inside the van and looked them up and down. 'That's me. How can I help you, ladies?'

Local accent, genial tone, friendly smile. First impressions, Paula knew, could be deceptive. He didn't look like someone who was due a good kicking. 'I am Detective Sergeant McIntyre and this is Detective Constable Stacey Chen. Norman Jackson, I am arresting you on suspicion of blackmail and of possessing indecent images of a minor. You do not have to say anything. But it may harm your defence if you do not mention when questioned something which you later rely on in Court. Anything you do say may be given in evidence.'

She'd barely got past the introductions when he started spluttering. 'What the— I don't— What do you mean— Bloody hell, what is this? Blackmail? Indecent images?

You've got the wrong bloke. I haven't a bloody clue—'

'Is there somewhere we can go to talk about this?' Stacey cut in. 'Or would you rather accompany us to a police station for questioning?'

He looked stunned. 'This is a mistake.' He looked around wildly. 'Is this a wind-up?'

'You're under arrest, Mr Jackson. What's it to be? Here or at the station?' Paula kept her voice level.

He bit his lip. 'The house owners are at work. We can talk inside. But you're making a terrible mistake. I've no idea—'

'Save it,' Stacey said. They followed him into a kitchen where the cupboard under the sink stood empty, the U-bend missing. Tools were scattered on the draining board. They sat at a small dining table, the two women facing Jackson. Stacey took out her phone and set it to record. She identified everyone present and the time and place of the recording. Then she silently held out a sheet of paper with the card details laid out in thick black letters.

He frowned. 'What's that?'

'You don't recognise this information?' Paula laced her voice with disbelief.

'No. What is it?'

'A sum of money was extorted from a fourteen-year-old boy. It was paid on to this prepaid credit card.'

He shrugged. 'What's that got to do with me?'

'The card was originally purchased from your bank account. It's registered to you. You are the legal owner of the card that was used to extort money. The money was paid to prevent you posting indecent images of an underage boy online,' Stacey said.

Paula leaned forward, getting in his face. She could smell the rank coffee breath. 'There's no hiding place. We have you bang to rights.'

But their words were having the opposite effect to the

one they expected. First he'd looked relieved, then as Stacey had continued, he'd looked upset. Not afraid, upset. 'I don't understand,' he said. 'I did buy a card. I put fifty pounds on it. But it wasn't for me. It was for our lass. She was going on a school trip to London and she didn't want to take cash.' Then his face cleared. 'She must have lost it or had it stolen. She'd have been too embarrassed to admit to it.' He beamed at them. 'See, I told you it was all a misunderstanding.'

'You must think I came up the River Brade on a bike,' Paula said. 'Is that the best you can do?'

'It's the truth.' He looked at his watch. 'Look, it's nearly dinner time. We can go over to the school and talk to Elsa. My daughter. She'll be able to explain.'

Paula and Stacey exchanged glances. 'Are you sure you want to involve your daughter in this? These are very serious charges,' Paula said. 'If this goes to court, on the evidence we've got, you'd be looking at five years. Maybe more. But if you're willing to admit the charges, we would consider a caution. That would avoid your victim having to testify in court. You'd go on the sex offenders register for two years. But nobody would have to know. Unless you committed another offence, obviously.'

'Are you not listening to me? I've not done anything wrong. I'm not admitting to something I didn't do. Go on the sex offenders register? You must be mad! I've read the kind of things that happen to people on that list. Dog shit through the door, graffiti on the house, broken windows. I'm not having that. Not for something that's nothing to do with me.' There was a rising note of indignation in his voice and his colour was heightening. He looked like he might stroke out before they could charge him.

But Paula's heart was hardening against him. What kind of creep tried to hide his sexual offences behind his daughter? She wasn't keen to put Elsa Jackson through this, but if that was the only way to nail Norman Jackson, she'd do it in a heartbeat after what he'd done to Torin. 'Let's go, then. Cuff him, Stacey.'

'What? You can't do that.'

'You're under arrest. That's what we do with people who are under arrest,' Paula snapped.

'Don't humiliate Elsa in front of her mates. Look, this is all a misunderstanding, but mud sticks. Have some common decency.' He looked as if he might burst into tears. But then, criminals were capable of weeping too.

Stacey caught her eye and gave a tiny shake of the head, as if to remind Paula that this wasn't a real arrest. Paula sighed. 'OK. But one wrong move, and I will taser you. Which, believe me, will be a lot more humiliating than wearing a pair of plastic cuffs.'

They walked him out to the chequerboard-patterned police car and put him in the back seat. Paula leaned in. 'Where is Elsa at school?'

'Kenton Vale High.'

Paula felt a high ringing noise keening in her head. Kenton Vale High was the school Torin attended. This crime was coming closer and closer to home. And she might be skating on very thin ice.

58

When the phone rang, Alvin was the only person in the office. Carol had gone to North Yorkshire for a press conference, Kevin was canvassing wedding guests again. Karim had gone for a bite of lunch with his cousin who was visiting from Glasgow and Paula and Stacey were on the missing list. Alvin was desperate for lunch himself but he'd have to wait till one of the others came back. That was the trouble with a small team; you had to cover each other's backs. So while his stomach rumbled, he tried to distract himself with going through his notes yet again to see whether he'd missed anything.

Alvin was conscious that he was the person on the squad with most to prove. Paula, Kevin and Stacey had been on Carol's previous MIT here in Bradfield. They'd worked together for years and cracked a series of horrifying cases in the city and elsewhere. Karim was only a beginner; he could afford to make the occasional mistake and have it chalked up to his lack of experience. But Alvin had been in the job for as long as Paula. There was a level of performance expected of him, even though he'd come to Bradfield from a much smaller force. Fewer than five murders a year on average, and you could rely on most of them being domestics or drunken young men careless of the damage they inflicted. It hadn't been hard to be the best detective sergeant there. Nobody had been more surprised than Alvin when helping Carol's team out on a case had ended in an offer to join the new ReMIT.

But with the best will in the world, re-reading his notes was getting him nowhere. Hopefully they'd soon get a call from the lads in Leeds to say they'd positively ID'd Eileen Walsh and then they could get properly stuck in. When the phone finally rang, he was convinced that was what it was, so it took him a few seconds to work out what he was actually hearing. 'I'm sorry, could you say that again?'

'I'm Denise from Customer Services at Freshco. I'm ringing about the photo.' The voice was nasal, the accent broad Bradfield, which didn't make Alvin's comprehension any easier.

'What photo is that, please?'

'Am I talking to the right person? Is this ... the Regional Major Incident Team?'

'That's right, I'm Detective Sergeant Ambrose.'

'Lovely. Only, a Sergeant McIntyre left a card saying if anybody recognised the photo they should give her a call. Is she there?'

'Sorry, she's out of the office right now, but we're working on the same case. Is this the Freshco where' – he searched his brain – 'Claire Garrity worked?'

'That's right. Well, the thing is, I came on for my shift and I took one look at it and I thought, "That's him."'

'"That's him?" That's who?'

'The man who complained. I told you, I'm on Customer Services.' She spoke as if he was a toddler to whom she was explaining the self-evident for the third time. 'He complained there was a foreign object in his bread. I had to bring Claire across to talk to him. She ran the bakery, right? So he was demanding to know how a child's sock got into his stone-baked San Francisco sourdough.'

'A child's sock?' Alvin had the sense that this conversation was getting away from him.

'He kicked off good and proper. I mean, you can't blame someone for that. You don't expect to find a child's sock in the middle of a loaf, do you? Especially when there's no way of telling if it's clean or dirty and you've already eaten three slices off the end. He was livid. He said his girlfriend had been so horrified she'd thrown up her breakfast. And that's not the way you want to start your day, is it?' Clearly, Denise was not going to fall into the category of reluctant witness.

'No,' he said weakly. 'So this man in the photo DS McIntyre left? You're sure he's the one who complained about the bread?'

'As sure as I can be. He wasn't wearing glasses when he came in, but it looks like him. I remember him so well because it was an interesting complaint. Mostly it's the same old, same old. A mistake on the till. Shoddy stitching on the own-brand clothes. Food gone off before the sell-by. But a sock in a sourdough loaf? That was a day to remember. And of course, when he came back in, well, that was soon after Claire died. You knew she'd died, right? Well, anyway, that made it even more memorable because of course he wanted to talk to Claire. To thank her. And I had to tell him she'd passed away so tragically.'

She paused for a respectful moment and Alvin grabbed his chance. 'Let me get this straight. The man in the photo came in to complain there was a sock in his bread and Claire Garrity spoke to him about it?'

'That's what I said. She was very apologetic. She said she'd leave no stone unturned to find out what had happened. Obviously she gave him another loaf and said she'd have head office get in touch about compensation. Anyway, it turned out the sock had fallen into the dough mix by accident. One of the bakers had bought some kids' clothes earlier and nobody really understands how it happened but it did. Anyway, he came back in a while later to thank us for taking him seriously. Head office had been on to him and he said they were giving him compensation and he wanted to thank Claire personally. Only he couldn't, could he? Because she was dead.'

'Very tragic.' And now for the $64,000-dollar question. 'Do you have a note of this man's name, by any chance?'

'It'll be on file. I can look it up. Is there a reward?'

Alvin rolled his eyes. 'Sorry. You get to feel good about doing your civic duty, but that's all, I'm afraid. So, can you look it up for me? This man's name?'

'Oh well, it was worth asking,' Denise said with a sigh. 'Hold on a minute.' The clatter of a phone being put down, the rattle of a heavy-handed typist on the keyboard, the mutter as Denise talked herself through what she was looking for. Then a pause. 'Hello? You still there?'

'I am. Any luck?'

'It's right here in front of me, on the screen: Tom Elton, 426 Minster Tower, Walker Wharf, Bradfield.'

Alvin couldn't quite believe it. He scribbled the address as fast as he could.

'There's a mobile number too, if you want it?'

'Please.' More scribbling as she read it to him. 'You've been incredibly helpful, Denise. Do you mind telling me your surname?'

'It's Chowdhry.' She spelled it out. 'My husband's family's from India.'

'I'm going to have an officer come round to Freshco to take a statement from you. All you've told me already, plus anything else you might remember. When does your shift end?'

'I'm on till eight.'

'Great, I'll organise that right away. Thanks very much, Denise. You've been amazingly helpful.' Alvin felt a kind of joy rising in him as the import of her words sank in properly. This could be the single piece of evidence that broke the case wide open.

'You're welcome,' she said. 'This'll be another day to remember.'

Alvin put the phone down and jumped up. He was doing a mad little happy dance when Karim walked back in, a look of amazement on his face at the sight of Alvin showing off his fancy footwork round the squad room desks.

'Nice moves,' Karim said, doing a little shimmy with his hips and a Bollywood dance move with his hands.

Sheepishly, Alvin stopped. 'We finally caught a break, man,' he said, slightly out of breath. 'I need you to go over to Freshco in Kenton Vale and take a statement. I think we might have put a name to our killer.'

59

Lunch break at Kenton Vale High; swarms of teenagers milling around in groups as discrete and organised as bees. But there was a distinct slowing of movement and stilling of conversations when the police car drove into the staff car park. Hundreds of eyes watched the trio of adults who walked into the main block, then, with nothing solid to fuel speculation, they returned to whatever had obsessed them previously. One or two speculated that the man might be Elsa Jackson's dad, but they were too far away to be certain.

Paula had phoned ahead and spoken to the head teacher, explaining that they needed to interview Elsa Jackson as a witness and they were bringing her father with them to act as appropriate adult.

'Thanks for not embarrassing her,' he'd said brusquely.

Paula didn't explain that she wasn't trying to spare his daughter; it was simply that they were so far down the road of unorthodoxy that there was nothing for it but to keep going in the hope that they'd find an acceptable destination. She hoped Lorna Meikle wasn't around. The last thing she wanted was for Jackson to clock that she was responsible for a fellow pupil of his daughter. Because that would get very messy. 'So long as you don't start prompting her,' she said. 'You start coaching her answers and you're out of there.'

Once the two women produced their IDs, the school receptionist directed them to the head teacher's office. Luckily, in a school with fifteen hundred pupils, only Torin's teachers were likely to recognise her as a parent. Their footsteps echoed on the vinyl floor of the side corridor. Nobody was going to creep up on this woman, Paula thought. The door at the far end stood ajar and when Stacey tapped on it, a deep Scottish voice invited them to enter.

Dr Anna Alderman stood up as they walked in. She was in her forties, tall and sturdy, dressed in a black V-neck sweater and a grey tweed pleated skirt. As she made the introductions, Paula thought not for the first time that Dr Alderman would have made a formidable hockey player. 'I've put Elsa in one of the guidance rooms,' she said. 'I told her someone needed to have a word with her. As you asked. Can you give me any more information as to what this is about?'

'It's all a misunderstanding,' Jackson blurted out. 'The sooner we sort it out, the better.'

'As my colleague said, Elsa is a witness,' Stacey said repressively.

'Very well. I suppose since Mr Jackson is here . . . I'll show you the way.'

They followed her back through reception to a long corridor, empty apart from a couple of lanky boys with prefect's braid heading towards them. 'Where are you boys going?' Dr Alderman demanded as they drew closer.

'Mr Merton asked us to set up the experiment for this afternoon's lab,' one said.

'Nevertheless, you shouldn't be in this corridor at lunchtime, as you very well know.' They mumbled apologies and hurried off. 'Sorry about that. We have strict rules about where students are allowed to be during breaks.'

'Good to see you run a tight ship,' Paula said.

'One has to. They're teenagers. They'll run rings round us, given half a chance.' She paused at one of the closed doors that lined the corridor. 'Elsa is in here.' She waited expectantly, her fingers straying towards the door handle.

'Thank you. We'll take it from here,' Stacey said firmly.

'If you're sure. This does seem a little . . . '

'You've been very helpful,' Paula said, grabbing the handle and interposing herself between Dr Alderman and the door.

'If you need anything, I'll be in my office.' She walked off, giving one last look over her shoulder.

Paula opened the door and walked in, followed by Jackson. Stacey brought up the rear and closed the door behind her, standing with her back against it.

Elsa was sitting at a table, dark head bowed over her phone. She looked up at the sound of the door. Confusion then consternation crossed her face as she registered her father's presence. Then she took in the two women. Paula produced her ID and got as far as, 'I'm Detective Sergeant McIntyre—' before the girl burst into tears.

Jackson started forward but Paula grabbed his arm firmly. 'Leave her.'

Elsa sobbed for a few moments, covering her face with her hands. Then gradually she subsided. She looked at them, a piteous expression in red-rimmed eyes. 'I'm sorry, Dad,' she gulped.

'Your dad's under arrest,' Paula said. 'For blackmail, among other things. We need to ask you some questions.' She pulled out a chair opposite Elsa and gave her a hard stare. This was not the Paula McIntyre who gentled criminals into confession. This was an angry woman defending one of the people she loved.

Elsa gave her father a beseeching look. She ran her hands through her short spiky hair, clutching the side of her head. 'You can't do this. You've got it all wrong.'

'There's some misunderstanding going on,' Jackson said. 'Just answer their questions and we can get it all sorted out. Tell them what happened to the credit card I bought for you. That you lost—'

'Enough,' Paula snarled. 'You've been warned not to interfere, Mr Jackson. Any more of that and we'll be doing this down at the station with social services sitting in instead of you.' It was amazing how inventively unpleasant she could be once the rules were relaxed, she thought. 'Now sit down and be quiet.'

He obeyed, wringing his hands, his tattoos contorting as his muscles twisted. 'Just explain, Elsa, love.'

'Elsa, do you have the credit card your father bought for you?' Stacey asked, softening her voice. Good cop to Paula's bad.

'Yes.' It was barely a whisper.

'No, that can't be right,' Jackson said, jumping to his feet. 'Check your wallet, you must have lost it or it was stolen or something.'

'Mr Jackson,' Paula thundered. 'I'm not going to warn you again.'

'It was me, Dad.' Elsa's eyes were brimming with tears again. 'I'm so sorry. I never meant it to go this far.'

Jackson fell back into his chair as if his muscles had failed. An expression of utter bafflement slowly spread across his face. 'I don't understand,' he said.

'You blackmailed Torin McAndrew,' Paula said flatly. 'Is that what you're saying? You forced him to pay you five hundred pounds so you wouldn't spread indecent images of him all over the internet?'

Elsa nodded. 'I wanted to humiliate him like he did to me.'

'Wait a minute,' Jackson said, suddenly indignant. 'What do you— How did he— Where did you get indecent images of this lad from? If he's sending dirty pictures of himself to my Elsa, how come he's not the one you're arresting?'

'He was conned into sending the images. He thought he was engaged in an online relationship, but the truth is your daughter used sexual images of another girl to trick him into thinking she was someone quite different,' Stacey said. 'And we will be questioning him about the images, you can rest assured on that point. There may be wrongdoing on both sides in that respect. But Elsa is the only one who's been engaged in extortion. Five hundred pounds is a lot of money.'

'So where did this lad get his hands on that kind of money? He doesn't sound so lily-white, does he?' Jackson was becoming belligerent now.

Paula turned on him. 'Where did he get the money? He sold his dead mother's jewellery. She was murdered a few months ago and he inherited the few bits and pieces she had. And he had to sell her favourite piece to pay off your daughter. Because she was threatening to destroy his life.'

A long moment of silence. Then Stacey said, 'Why did you do this to Torin, Elsa?'

The girl screwed up her face. 'I really like Torin. I wanted him to ask me to the prom. But he didn't. Everybody was pairing off and he hadn't asked anybody yet. I tried being subtle, but he wasn't taking the hint.' Once she started, she found her momentum and her worlds tumbled over each other.

'So this day we were all hanging out under the library bridge and I kind of went, "Hey, Torin, you'd better ask me to the prom since I'm the only cool girl left." And he looked at me like I was a piece of shit and went, "No way." Can you imagine how totally humiliating that was? He could have made a joke out of it, or whatever, but no, he had to say something that made me look like an utter dog. And every-body was laughing at me. It went on and on for days. Stupid girls going, "Hey, Elsa, I hear Jimmy Barker from the special needs group wants a prom date. Better get in there quick, girl." And so on and so on. You have *no* idea how completely crap he made my life. So I decided to get my own back.'

'So you stalked him online and made this poor lad think a beautiful, sexually experienced young woman wanted to be his lover?' Paula knew she was being harsh but she didn't care.

'All this over a stupid prom date?' Her father was incredu-lous. 'Over some dickhead who didn't fancy you?'

'I didn't mean it to go this far,' Elsa wailed. 'I didn't think he'd go through with getting hold of the money. I thought he'd just beg for it to stop.'

'You could have stopped it any time, Elsa. But you didn't. That boy was almost suicidal because of what you did to him.' Paula was giving no quarter.

'I'm sorry,' she whimpered. 'I'll give the money back. I promise I'll delete all the pics and the videos.'

'Videos?' Her father sounded as if he'd be the next one in tears.

'That's not how it works,' Paula said. 'You've broken the law. You can forget about going to university and having a good career. You're going to have a criminal conviction.'

'DS McIntyre?' Stacey interrupted her. 'A word outside?'

Reluctantly, Paula followed her, aware that father and daughter were leaning towards each other, exchanging low bitter words. As the door closed, Stacey said, 'You're getting a bit carried away, Paula. We can't charge her. We've broken every rule in the PACE code. Not to mention a formal charge means Torin being dragged through the courts. And as Mr Jackson astutely pointed out, technically he's guilty of com-mitting the offence of distributing indecent images. Plus, at some point Jackson or his daughter is going to see you at a parents' evening or a careers fair and realise you're related to Torin. And then it'll go tits-up and we'll be hauled before the Internal Complaints Department.'

Paula leaned against the wall, squeezing her eyes shut. 'I got carried away.'

'You did,' Stacey said.

'But she's got to pay.'

'I know. And I think I've figured out a way to see that she does.'

60

Stacey had been back at her desk for half an hour by the time Karim returned with Denise Chowdhry's formal statement. Long enough to have made a start on discovering who Tom Elton was. But she was interested in whether Karim had anything to add that would make her work any easier.

He was already at the multi-function printer, scanning in the written statement. He glanced up. 'I've got a digital recording as well,' he said hastily.

'I sent you the photograph from Elton's driving licence. In a six-pack. Did you get it in time to show Mrs Chowdhry?'

He nodded. 'It's all in the statement. We uploaded the six-pack on to her office computer so she could see them properly. And she picked Elton out straight away. Not a moment's hesitation. But bloody hell, that woman can talk. I thought I was never going to get out of there.'

'Observant, though.' She turned to go back to her research.

'Is the boss coming back?'

'On her way. So's the rest of the team.' Apart from Paula, who would be having an interesting conversation with Torin round about now. Stacey settled in front of her screens and carried on researching the digital footprint Thomas Jonathan Elton had generated. She already had the obvious ones – driving licence, the cars registered to his company, current address (which, interestingly, was not the same as the one he'd given to Freshco), details of his company and its finances, and a handful of media articles about the company that mentioned Elton and his business partner, Tricia Stone. The dossier was growing; by the time Carol got back from North Yorkshire there would be something worth presenting to the team.

Kevin and Alvin were not far behind Karim. Having first checked that Elton was out of the office, Kevin had posed as a garden centre owner considering advertising. In the course of the conversation, he'd gleaned a little about Elton which he proceeded to type up for the file. Alvin had been back to visit Kathryn McCormick's workmates. Almost all of the half dozen who had claimed to have seen the man called David had picked Tom Elton out of the six-pack. Slowly but surely, the circumstantial was building. Tony ambled in, peering over people's shoulders as they worked, gleaning what they had gathered.

When Carol finally swept in, everyone except Paula was ready and waiting. 'Brilliant work, everyone. Getting a name is a huge step forward.'

'We've got a lot more than a name now,' Kevin said, ebullient as he always became when the chase grew hotter. 'We've got a man whose business is looking a bit wobbly since his business partner walked out on him about three months ago. She was also his live-in girlfriend, so his life's had a bit of an upheaval lately.'

Tony perked up at this revelation. 'I've been wondering who he really wants to kill. You might have answered my question.'

Kevin consulted his notes. 'Tom Elton runs a company

that produces glossy magazines with a very precise local circulation. There's a handful here in Bradfield. *Harriestown Huddle. The Vale Voice. Chevin Chatterbox.* They come through your letterbox for free. A couple of local columnists, a few recipes, gardening tips, restaurant reviews, that sort of thing. In our house it goes straight in the recycling. Anyhow, they're paid for by advertising. And Tricia was the one who smooth-talked the advertisers and also organised the copy. Even wrote some of it herself. She joined the company when Elton was starting out six years ago and they got together as a couple about four years ago.' He looked up with a cheeky smile. 'The lass in advertising didn't need much encouragement to gossip. Nobody in-house knows what happened between Tricia and Elton. One Monday, she just wasn't there any more. She came in when Elton was out seeing clients, and emptied her office. She told her team it was time for pastures new. And that was that. No forwarding address or anything. And she changed her mobile number too.'

Stacey scribbled a note on her tablet. 'I'm on it,' she said.

'Well done, Kevin. So what does Elton do in the business?'

'He does the design and layout and deals with the printers and distributors. He used to take care of some of the advertisers, the ones who had been with him since the very beginning. But now he's having to do all of that, plus the editorial, so he's a very busy boy.'

'That'd annoy you, if you'd got things set up so your workload felt comfortable,' Tony observed. 'Another reason to resent Tricia.'

'However.' Kevin raised one finger in a cautionary gesture. 'Apparently he had a meeting this week with some local businesswoman and afterwards he was very chirpy. He said things would be looking up soon and somebody else could worry about content.'

'Bloody hell, Kev,' Alvin said. 'I'd always wondered how

you got your Stella to marry you, but you've obviously got a hidden chat-up line to charm the birds out of the trees.'

Kevin grinned. 'I wouldn't waste it on you, Alvin.'

'Excellent,' Carol said. 'We need to talk to Tricia Stone, I think. If you can track her, Stacey, maybe Paula ... ' She looked around, puzzled. 'Where is Paula?'

'On her way,' Stacey said. 'She had something to take care of.' Her fingers flashed over the keyboard but nobody paid any attention. Stacey was always tapping and swiping and scribbling. She hit send on the urgent message to Paula, warning her to get into the office asap. Torin was important, for sure. But murder trumped everything in their private lives.

'Another thing, now we have a name?' Tony chipped in. 'If you remember, I said that if he was this forensically aware, he wouldn't be taking his own car anywhere near his killing zone. Stacey, I'm assuming you've got his driving licence details?' She nodded.

Carol picked it up. 'Karim, check with every car-hire firm in the Bradfield area. We know the dates when he saw the women. Tie him to hire cars on those dates and we're another step closer.'

'We've already got positive six-pack IDs that put him in contact with Claire Garrity, the woman whose account he stole to mess with his victims on RigMarole. He knew she was dead, so he could assume her ID.'

'And according to her husband, her password would have taken a small child about five minutes to crack,' Stacey said.

'And I've picked up positive six-pack IDs from five people at the wedding where he called himself David and picked up Kathryn,' Alvin added.

Carol smiled, her eyes lighting up as they hadn't for a long time. 'This is all good intel,' she said. 'Stacey, do you have a little treasure trove for us?'

'He's forty-four and he's a Scorpio.' A chuckle rippled through the group. 'November sixth. Born in the Simpson Wing of Bradfield Cross Hospital to Doris and Kenneth Elton. She died two years ago of breast cancer and Kenneth now lives in Eyam in Derbyshire.'

'The plague village,' Tony said.

'What?' Carol, distracted, stared at him.

'The plague arrived in the village carried by the fleas in a bolt of cloth from London. The vicar persuaded them to cut themselves off from the outside world to prevent it spreading further.' He gave an awkward smile. 'Sorry.'

Carol groaned. 'Stacey?'

'Elton did a degree in graphic design at Manchester School of Art. He got a job in Dundee working on a range of magazines, came back down here to work on the *Dales Living* magazine, and also worked with a community magazine in Leeds called *Chuffin' Heck*. Then just over six years ago he started Local Words magazine company. He's got seventeen titles based in Northern cities. He targets prosperous areas that like to think of themselves as having a "village feel".' They could all hear the quote marks and the disdain. Stacey thought there was nothing clever about living in a village when you could choose a city.

'Until recently he was living in one of the high-rise executive blocks down by the canal basin.' She glanced at Tony. 'He could probably have seen your boat from his balcony. When Tricia left the company, he had to move out because the lease was in her name and she cancelled it.'

'Why was it in her name?' Carol wondered.

'Probably a tax dodge,' Alvin grumbled. 'Maybe the company sub-let it off her or something.'

'So, now he's moved to a rather less cool address. Still a nice modern flat though, only it's at the back of Central Station, not overlooking the canal basin. The downside is that he has underground car parking, which makes it hard to stake out. If we were to need that option?'

Carol shrugged. 'We'll take it as it comes. What else?'

'The company leases four vehicles. As far as I can tell, he uses the BMW. They've also got two VW Passats and a small Peugeot van, which are all insured for Elton and five of his staff. He's got a clean driving licence, no criminal record and a credit score of 775, which is close to excellent. But he gave Tricia Stone thirty per cent of the company three years ago. He'll want to buy back those shares or get her to sell them to a third-party buyer otherwise he'll be handing over a chunk of his profit to her for nothing in return.'

'More fuel to the fire,' Tony muttered. 'In his head, he's got all the reasons in the world to hate her. Who gets the shares if she dies?'

'I don't know,' Stacey said. 'Not everything is available, you know.'

'Which really pisses you off,' Kevin teased.

'Right now, his debt levels are not worrying but if his profits keep falling, they could become troublesome. According to a couple of brief trade press articles about the company, his hobbies are watching football and listening to jazz.'

'Not cycling?' Tony asked.

'People who are into cycling don't tootle around on a Brompton bike,' Kevin said.

'Maybe not, but you'd have to be reasonably comfortable on a bike, not to mention reasonably fit, to make your getaway back to where your car is parked. I thought he might be a proper cyclist.'

'More likely he's got a stationary bike in his bedroom,' Carol said. 'Anything more, Stacey? No property in the Dales?'

'Not that I've found. I'll keep looking, though.'

'OK.' Carol leaned back in her chair. 'We need to talk

to Tricia Stone. She might be able to shed some light.' She looked around again with a sharp sigh. 'Where the hell is Paula? Stacey, can you trace Tricia Stone? I want Paula to talk to her. So, we're a lot further forward than we were. We've still no confirmed ID on Eileen Walsh but the pathologist thinks he might be able to extract some usable DNA. We have an ID for our mystery man, but it's all circumstantial. We need a lot more than we have now.' She stood up and walked over to the incident board where all the tenuous elements of their investigation were laid out. 'I think we should sleep on it. See what Paula can extract from Tricia Stone. And if we can't come up with anything else, tomorrow we bring him in. Shake the tree and see what falls out.' She gave a little snort of derision. 'Knowing my luck, it'll be a poisonous tree frog.'

61

Paula was waiting at the kitchen table for Torin when he got home from school. 'Grab a drink and sit down.' It wasn't a request. She cradled her coffee mug in her hands, running over what she would say as he fixed himself a tumbler of fruit squash. He was so nervous the ice cubes clinked and tinkled like a percussion section against the glass.

'Good day?' Paula asked.

He shrugged. His eyes met hers then slid away. He stared out of the kitchen window at the garden beyond.

'Only, I haven't had a very good day, as it happens. Thanks to Stacey, however, we now know who conned you and blackmailed you. At first we thought it was the usual gang of cyber-scum because Stacey tracked the messages back to a blank-wall IP address in the Philippines. But she doesn't give up easily. So she took a look at the payment card you paid the money on to. She thought that would be another dead end. Some private bank in a tax haven with secrecy laws that make Switzerland look expansive. But it turns out, the bank card was issued right here in Bradfield.'

Torin's face crumpled in bewilderment. 'I don't understand. You mean, this is somebody local?'

'Exactly. Somebody very local. Somebody three streets away from here.'

He was clearly baffled. 'How? I mean, why? Who'd do something like that? Is it somebody I know?'

'It's somebody you upset, Torin. See, here's one of the things I know about being a teenager. You don't always have a sense of proportionality. That idea of the punishment fitting the crime? It doesn't always happen like that in the adolescent brain,' Paula said bitterly. 'So when you hurt somebody's feelings, sometimes they go completely overboard in response.'

He shook his head. 'I've not upset anybody enough to justify this,' he protested. 'I'm one of the good guys. I don't pick on anybody. Honest, Paula. I'm not just saying it. I'm not like that.'

Paula sipped her coffee, studying him over the rim. He really didn't get it. He'd drifted right past the embarrassment and humiliation he'd inflicted on Elsa Jackson without even noticing. She put her mug down. 'Elsa Jackson.'

His eyes widened and his mouth opened in shock. 'Elsa? What am I supposed to have done to Elsa?'

'You humiliated her in front of her mates.'

'I did?' He frowned. She let him hang in the silence. At length, he cocked his head and said slowly, 'Is this about when she asked if I'd go to the prom with her?'

Paula nodded. 'And you said "No way", Torin. In front of everybody. Not very nice, was it?'

He shook his head, not in sorrow but in denial. 'That's not how it went. She didn't let me finish what I was saying. I was going to say, "No way, I wouldn't be seen dead at a lame gig like that." But she took off after the "No way" bit. She was off like a hurricane. I like Elsa,' he said plaintively. 'If I was going to go to a crap night out like the school prom, she's probably the one I'd have asked. And she did this to me? She fucked me over till I wanted to die? I sold my mum's necklace because some stupid self-obsessed girl thought I'd treated her like shit? Bloody hell, Paula, I hope you're going to throw the book at her. That's totally irrational. Jeez. How could she be so vile to me?'

'Because she was hurt and she lashed out. I agree, her reaction was totally out of proportion to the perceived offence, but she genuinely thought you started it.' Now she could see the misery in his face and she reached out for his hand and squeezed it.

'But she's not getting away with it, right? You arrested her?'

'Actually, it was her dad I arrested, because it was him that bought the card.' She grinned. 'It was all a bit of a cock-up. But I'm not throwing the book at her.'

'Paula!' he protested.

'Hear me out. If we'd arrested and charged her, there's no doubt it would have ended up in court. The CPS would have definitely prosecuted. You'd have had to go to court and testify. And even though the news media couldn't report your names because you're minors, do you imagine there's any way that it'd not be round the school like wildfire? It'd be worse than Elsa originally threatened. Which, by the way, she's adamant she wasn't going to do. She wanted you to sweat and to suffer and then she was going to back off. But you paid up too quickly. Ironic, isn't it?'

He sighed. 'It's not fair.'

'There's another thing. OK, she blackmailed you, but you had actually sent her the pics and the videos. And technically that makes you guilty of distributing indecent images of a minor.'

'What?' He pushed back in his chair, astonished. 'But it was my own pictures.'

'It doesn't matter. Under the letter of the law, you committed an offence. Which is something that Elsa's dad spotted right away and jumped all over. If we'd arrested her, the defence would have argued that the original offence behind all of this was yours, and it's possible you'd have ended up in court. And me and Stacey weren't willing to take that chance.'

He slammed the palms of his hands down on the table. 'So she gets away with it? She tortures me, she blackmails me, and nothing happens?'

'Calm down. Don't you know me better than that? It's not, "nothing happens, business as usual". We did a deal with the Jacksons. Bev's necklace is still up for sale on the website. They've agreed to buy it back, even though it's a lot more than you sold it for. You'll get it back. That's the first thing.'

His eyes filmed over with tears. He struggled not to shed them. 'Thanks,' he managed.

'And there's more. Stacey was surprised that a fourteen-year-old girl could navigate the web and its systems the way Elsa did. She talked to her about her interest in the digital world, and it turns out Elsa is pretty precocious in the whole IT sphere. Stacey kind of sees herself in Elsa. So in future, Elsa's going to be spending three hours a week with Stacey, developing her programming skills.'

Torin pulled a face. 'That doesn't seem fair. Why should she benefit from this? I'm the one who's the victim here.'

Paula laughed. 'You think it'll be fun? Do you have any idea what a slave-driver Stacey is? This is going to last till Elsa leaves school. Think of it as a three-year detention, Torin. She made your life a misery for a few weeks. Stacey is going to inflict pain on her for years. And yeah, she'll come out of it at the end in a better place than she is now. But I think you've learned something too.'

'Don't trust the internet,' he grunted.

'That too. But I hope you've learned to think about the effect of your words before you blurt them out.'

'I never—'

'I know you didn't. But people don't always take things the way we mean them. So avoid ambiguity and think before you speak.' Whatever else Paula was going to say was cut off by a text buzzing on her phone. 'Oh, bloody hell, the boss has noticed I'm on the missing list.' She sighed and got to her feet, grabbing her bag. 'Elinor should be back around seven, there's a tub of Bolognese sauce from the deli in the fridge. Be kind and grate the parmesan for her, there's a love.' She rounded the table to wrap him in a hug, kissing the top of his hair. 'It'll be all right,' she said. 'We made it out alive, kiddo.'

'Not everybody gets to say that,' he mumbled. 'Thanks.'

62

Paula made it back to the office in time to hear Carol's words at the end of the briefing. 'Sorry, boss,' she said. 'I had to take a couple of hours' personal time.'

'In the middle of a murder inquiry?' Carol said, her face cold and her voice icy to match.

'Yes.' Paula stood her ground. She'd always been a bit sniffy about women officers who used their children as a tool of privilege. But since she'd taken responsibility for Torin, she'd learned the uncomfortable truth that sometimes crises wouldn't wait till you could get home. 'It was time-sensitive. Nothing was moving here and I was on the end of a phone at all times.'

'Well, something is moving here, now.' A slight thaw, but Carol's tone was still clipped. 'We've got a name to go with the face. Recognised by some of the guests at the wedding where he acquired Kathryn McCormick. And he'd met Claire Garrity through her job. All the details are in the updated case file that Kevin has put together. I want you to talk to his ex. Stacey's tracking her down.' Carol turned away and headed for her office.

'Consider me bollocked,' Paula muttered at Kevin out of the side of her mouth.

'Bad timing. You should know better than go awol when we're in the thick of it.'

'It was my work at Freshco that caught us the break.'

'And she knows that. But this isn't the time to piss around, especially not if you're serious about going for promotion. You know she's not been at her easiest since she got ReMIT up and running.'

Paula looked penitent. 'I think I preferred it when she was still on the sauce.'

Kevin's eyebrows shot up. 'She's on the wagon?'

'Yup. Tony told me he gave her the hard word after she got nicked and she's been sticking to it ever since.'

Kevin gave a low whistle. 'No wonder she's driving this case so hard. Talk about having something to prove to herself.'

Paula nodded. 'I was such a bitch when I quit smoking for vaping, so I do get some of what she's going through. Anyway, I'd better see what Stacey's got for me.'

Thanks to the miracles of modern technology, the fact that Tricia Stone had relocated to the hills above Marbella didn't mean she was beyond the reach of ReMIT. Stacey had tracked her to the editorial department of an English-language magazine for ex-pats. Within the hour, Paula had managed to set up a Skype call, which Stacey had set up to record.

The webcam of a laptop never did favours to anyone, but even with that distortion, Paula could see Tricia Stone was a woman who made the best of herself. She wasn't drop-dead gorgeous, but her make-up and hairstyle emphasised the elfin shape of her face and gave her a witchy look about the eyes. 'Thanks for talking to me,' Paula began. 'Do you mind if I tape this call? To keep the record straight?'

'Be my guest, I've got nothing to hide. But what's all this about? What's Tom done? Your message was quite evasive.' She was brisk and businesslike, her Yorkshire accent almost buffed clean.

'We think Tom may be able to help our inquiries into a series of crimes. I'm sorry, I can't say more at this stage.'

'I don't know whether I can help. I haven't seen him or spoken to him for the best part of three months.'

'You wanted a clean break?'

She pulled down the corners of her mouth. 'No point in dragging things out once you've made your mind up.'

'So it was you who broke it off?'

Tricia looked curious. 'Why are you interested?'

'I'm trying to paint a picture. What Tom's like. What his state of mind might be.'

She gave a sardonic laugh. 'Pissed off. That would be his state of mind. I did break it off, which he was not happy about.'

'Do you mind telling me why you left?'

'I don't see what this has to do with anything.' Even on Skype, the challenging look was obvious.

'I appreciate that. But it would be helpful if you could fill me in.' Paula smiled. 'I'm sorry, we often find ourselves asking what seem to be pointless and intrusive questions, but sometimes it's really helpful when we're trying to make sense of scattered bits of information.'

'And you won't tell me what he's done?'

'At this point, we don't know that he's done anything.'

A sudden smile. 'You're not going to tell me, are you? So it's a question of whether I trust you or I end this call?'

Paula could see why Tricia had been successful in persuading journalists to write for their publications, and business to advertise. She had an air of friendly candour. Time to match that. Or at least the appearance of it. 'That's about the size of it. But I'm guessing from the lack of contact between you since you split up that you don't actually feel you owe Tom Elton anything. So why not help me out?' She counted the seconds while Tricia considered. Eight, nine, ten, eleven—

'Why not? OK. I ended it because it dawned on me that I didn't actually have to put up with his shit any more. Don't get me wrong. He was never physically violent towards me. He threw things but never at me. There was one wall in the flat we had repainted three times because he lost his temper. Once it was a Thai takeaway, once it was a bottle of Baileys and the last time it was a jug of sangria.'

'A man with a temper, then?' A gentle push, to see where it took them.

'Volatile, I would say. He lost his temper quickly but it was like a flash flood. Once the anger was gone, he'd get straight down to cold, hard planning to make sure whatever it was that had made him angry wouldn't happen again. It was an amazing driver in business. He didn't lose it with staff or clients in the room, but he'd let rip later, in private. And then he'd work out how to screw them over.'

'Not the easiest thing to live with.' Keeping the flow going, encouraging more revelation.

'No, but I suppose I got used to it. The other side of Tom is that he can be very charming and considerate. Especially when it gets him what he wants.'

'So what precipitated your departure?'

Tricia smiled. 'You're persistent, aren't you? You'd make a great journalist.'

'Except I can't write for toffee. What finally made you leave?'

'It sounds stupid when I say it.' She sighed. 'I went to a friend's wedding by myself because Tom couldn't be bothered spending time with people he didn't much like.' Already, alarm bells were ringing in Paula's head, but she kept quiet and let Tricia continue. 'Anyway, I got chatted up by this lovely guy. Smart, funny, and only single because his girl-friend had refused to relocate to Spain with him when he bought a bar over here. He was only over for the wedding, but we kept in touch online. And it dawned on me that while Gary – that's his name, Gary – might not be Mr Right, Tom was very definitely Mr Wrong. I realised I needed to get out, that being with Tom was turning me into someone I didn't want to be. Always watching what I did, guarding my tongue, acting like a UN peacekeeper half my life. So I started looking for a job opportunity over in Spain. Not to be with Gary. I wasn't about to jump from the frying pan into what might be the fire. But to give myself a second chance. When this job came up, I took a deep breath and got out.'

'Wow. That takes real nerve,' Paula said. Her admiration was genuine. She hadn't always been so clear-eyed herself in the past. 'When was this?'

'Almost three months ago. We'd been away for a weekend walking in the Peak District. Tom had had one of his explo-sions because the hotel had cocked up the booking and we ended up in a poky twin room. And I thought, enough. On the way home, he was outlining how he was going to demol-ish their reputation on TripAdvisor and Facebook. Something snapped in my head and I thought, now or never. I got him to pull over into the next lay-by and I told him it was over. I know I should have waited till we were home, but I'll be honest, I thought this time he might throw something at me instead of the wall.'

'How did he react?'

'He refused to believe me. He said I didn't know what was good for me and I'd think differently in the morning. Because I'd come to my senses and realise I could never be happy without him. And then he started the car and drove home.' She shook her head, as if she still couldn't quite believe it.

'So what happened next?'

'I was supposed to be out on the road seeing clients the next day. So I set off early, as usual. I took the car to a dealer who used to advertise with us and traded it in for a van. I bought a load of archive boxes at the stationery store. Then I went back to the flat after Tom had left and packed up all my stuff. Clothes, books, CDs. I was out of there by mid-afternoon and on the south coast by late evening. I checked in to a motel and in the morning, I took the ferry to Santander.'

'Forgive me, but that's a pretty extreme strategy. Were you afraid of what he might do if he realised you were serious about leaving?'

'The truth? Yes. I thought he might try to stop me.'

'Were you afraid he might be violent? Even though he'd never hurt you before?'

'I didn't put a name to what I was afraid of. All I knew was that I needed to get out and I didn't want to be caught up in Tom's reaction to that.'

'Did he contact you?'

She gave a wry smile. 'I ditched my phone and got a new Spanish mobile. He showered me with emails and social media messages to the point where I closed all my accounts. How did you find me, by the way?'

'My colleague is the mistress of cyberspace,' Paula said, always evasive when it came to Stacey's skills.

Tricia drew in an apprehensive breath. 'But if that's how you found me, he might too.'

Paula gave a reassuring smile. 'I don't think that's at all likely. We have access to databases that Tom could never penetrate.'

'Really? You're not just saying that?'

'Really. So when you closed down all your regular communications, how did you communicate? About the lease on the flat, about your shares in the business?'

'Via my lawyer. He's a very old friend who would never sell me out to Tom in spite of his efforts to persuade him otherwise. Tom has a pathological need to get his own way and when the world contradicts him, it's not pretty. But don't get me wrong. This isn't a daily thing, because he's also very good at getting the world to bend to his will. That's the charming side, which is all most people ever see.'

Now that she felt she had a handle on Tom Elton's character, Paula decided it was time to change tack. 'You said you'd been walking in the Peak District. Did you do that a lot, then?'

'Not as much as we'd have liked. Work was always a big demand on our time. But yes, we loved the Peak District. And of course Tom's dad lives there, in Eyam, so he could kill two birds with one stone. So maybe once a month we'd go down.'

'What about the Dales? Did you head up there?'

'Hardly ever. It's closer, as the crow flies, but it's actually really quick with the motorway network to get down into the Dark Peak and those high moorland edges.' She sighed. 'That's one good thing about this part of Spain. There is decent walking in the hills behind Marbella.'

'So Tom didn't spend time in the Dales? Walking, or cycling?'

'Not at all. What's the big deal about the Dales?'

She'd find out soon enough if she had even rudimentary internet search skills. 'No big deal, only curious. Have you heard anything from mutual friends about Tom's reaction to you leaving?'

Tricia gave a little snort of laughter. 'Plenty. Mostly that he's pissed off and affronted rather than distressed. Also that he's outraged I went off without a word. He's hopeful that I'm having a miserable time in a bedsit in some gloomy Northern town. Luckily, I can trust the few people who know where I am to keep their mouths shut.'

Paula had run out of questions. Given there had been no contact between them for three months, there was no point in asking about changes in behaviour or schedules. And she'd gleaned enough about Tom Elton's personality to find it credible that he might be their killer. Tony might have a different view, but she doubted it. 'Thanks for talking to me, Tricia. I appreciate your time and I'm sorry if this has meant revisiting painful memories.'

'Not really painful. It's early days yet, but things are going well with me and Gary. And I totally love my new job. I made the right choices, Detective. I've no doubts about that. I'm not even sorry I stayed with Tom so long. Even though he was scary sometimes. I learned so much working for Local Words. I couldn't have done this job without that experience. Anyway, good luck with whatever it is you're investigating.'

'Thanks. I hope things continue to go well for you.' She signed off and leaned back in her chair. Tricia had dumped him in a lay-by after meeting an interesting new man at a wedding. Really, she couldn't have come up with a better match if she'd tried. Yet another brick in the wall.

63

After Paula had outlined Tricia Stone's revelations, Tony had retreated to his boat. He wanted peace and quiet to consider. What Paula had learned was almost too neat a fit. But sometimes obvious was also authentic. Not everything had to be sublimated and translated into a different formulation. A man deprived of the direct route to his satisfaction – in this case, killing the woman who had so comprehensively spurned him – might well be inclined to perform a cathartic act as close to the original scenario as possible. Especially since these cases weren't sexual homicides. The way sexual offenders behaved often had complex codification that placed the killer's acts at some remove from the events that had provoked him. This was different. And that was why Tony needed time and space to think about the perpetrator. The Wedding Killer, as he'd come to think of him.

There wasn't much room on the boat for pacing. Ten steps, turn. Ten steps, turn. But it was room enough. Especially if he took his time. He began with the opening paragraphs that always preceded his profiles, stepping out the rhythm of the words. 'The following offender profile is for guidance only and shouldn't be regarded as an identikit portrait. The offender is unlikely to match the profile in every detail, though I would expect there to be a high degree of congruence between the characteristics outlined below and the reality. All of the statements in the profile express probabilities and possibilities, not hard facts.

'A serial killer produces signals and indicators in the commission of his crimes. Everything he does is intended, consciously or not, as part of a pattern. Discovering the underlying pattern reveals the killer's logic. It may not appear logical to us, but to him it is crucial. Because his logic is so idiosyncratic, straightforward traps will not capture him. As he is unique, so must be the means of catching him, interviewing him and reconstructing his acts.'

Well, that was as true of the Wedding Killer as it was of any sexually motivated murderer. The first question he had to ask himself was whether that distinction was real. Given his experience over the years, he thought it was. Sexual homicide was about sexual satisfaction. Whether the perpetrators acknowledged it or not, the act of killing and the ritual surrounding it had the sole aim of satisfying their desire. Usually that desire had been perverted and distorted by their experiences. But murder and sex had wound round each other as inseparably as a barley sugar twist; the one had become a replica of the release that the other offered people whose lives hadn't been fucked up irredeemably by what had been done to them.

These three murders, he believed, were not about sexual release. The pressure they relieved wasn't sexual but emotional. If he was having sex with his victims – and on balance, Tony thought he probably was – it wasn't at the heart of what he was doing. 'It's another way of charming them,' he said. 'Another step on the journey of falling in love.'

Even before he'd heard what Tricia had to say, he'd been convinced that the victims were not sexual surrogates. Men who were killing for sexual reasons tended towards victims who had similarities. These women – the first two for sure, and if they were right about Eileen Walsh, also her – had far more dissimilarities than they had common ground. Looks, occupations, lifestyles, preoccupations; all different.

'You're looking at a different kind of surrogacy,' he said, pausing at the door to his sleeping cabin. 'Tricia walking away destroyed your plans. She took your home away. She threatened the business you'd built. And she exposed you to people either feeling sorry for you or going, "I told you she was too good for him". You wanted to kill her. But you're smart. Even if you'd known where she'd gone, you knew you couldn't kill her. Not now. You'd be the prime suspect. The man who'd been spurned, the man who wanted revenge.'

So he'd constructed an alternative plan. A macabre rehearsal for what he wanted – no, *intended* – to do to Tricia when the time was right. And he went about it with meticulous care. He'd obviously spent long hours researching current forensic techniques to learn how to avoid leaving a trail for detectives to follow. He'd mapped the location of the cameras he needed to avoid. He'd understood how to change his appearance in small, temporary ways. He thought he was cleverer than all of them. He thought he could outsmart the best.

The one time he'd slipped was stealing Claire Garrity's identity. And it was exactly the kind of mistake that overweening arrogance made time after time. He couldn't resist the urge to make himself part of the story, even in disguise. He'd made the effort to research a dead woman's life enough to figure out her password. And he'd squeezed into his victim's lives undercover and made them be his friend twice over.

Unless that hadn't been part of the plan. Maybe stealing Claire's identity had been part of his wider plan to track down Tricia? Friending her friends in another person's clothes, hoping to triangulate the whereabouts of his ex? But the possibility of inveigling himself into the world of his victims had been too delicious to resist.

This was a man who craved admiration and love. He'd become powerful enough in his own small universe to believe he'd achieved that. Tricia had smashed that illusion and now he was rebuilding it.

'I can't profile you,' Tony said, stopping in his tracks. He could have made a stab at a profile a day or two ago. But now there was a suspect, his process was contaminated. One of the central tenets of offender profiling was to avoid any knowledge of a specific suspect. The danger lay in the temptation to incline the profile towards the person in the crosshairs. If two or more options offered themselves up, it was hard to resist coming down on the side of the choice that fitted someone who was already in the frame. Every profiler remembered a notorious case in the early nineties, where a killer had remained on the loose to murder more women because police and profiler were too eager to follow their first suspicions.

So, no profile. But that didn't mean he couldn't be useful. He could use this time to think and to work out the strategic advice he wanted to give Carol before the interview with Tom Elton in the morning. If indeed that was still on the agenda after everyone had slept on it.

It would be Paula and Carol there in the interview room, he was sure of that at least. Paula because nobody was better at the subtle dance of interrogation. She probed weaknesses and undermined strengths. She knew when to provoke to incautious anger and when to soothe into unexpected confidences. The Wedding Killer – or Tom Elton, as he must now think of him – might be her match but Tony doubted it. And Carol would be second chair because it was always good to put two women in the room against a man. They either felt insulted at not being taken seriously enough or they relaxed because they felt sure of themselves against such opponents. It was very seldom that they acted as if they were going into battle against an equal.

Good cop/bad cop remained a cliché because it still worked sometimes. In this case, Tony thought Paula could profitably play up to Elton's idea of himself while Carol could undercut it at every opportunity. Where Paula took for granted that women would be attracted to him, Carol could play the sceptical, even incredulous role. When Paula could admire the killer for his forensic nous, Carol could rubbish the notion, pointing out the endless stream of forensic revelation in podcasts and TV shows. And when Paula patiently plodded through places and times, looking for alibis that probably weren't there, Carol could sneer and point out that it'd only take one piece of forensic evidence to nail him. And that everybody makes a mistake eventually.

He sat down at the saloon table and started drafting his notes for Paula and Carol. 'And finally, when he thinks you've exhausted all your ammunition, when he's about to get to his feet and leave, Carol reveals that Paula has spoken to Tricia. He won't know what's been said; he won't know which part of the rug is about to be pulled from under him.'

And that, Tony knew, was when mistakes were made.

Tony wasn't the only one brooding over what the morning might bring. High on the moors above her home, Carol was also hoping the rhythm of walking might bring some discipline to her thoughts.

She'd come back to policing because she thought it was her rock in a stormy sea. The job had always been a haven, the place where she could lose herself and let her abilities shine. When she looked around at the women she knew from school and university, she envied nothing about their lives. Not their men, not their marriages, not their children. She'd never craved those things. Her commitment to justice had always been the only thing that really mattered to her. Her feelings for Tony, her friendships with colleagues like Paula and John Brandon – they were all bound up with her identity as a detective.

And now it felt as if that was all slipping away from her. She'd become what she'd spent her adult life hunting down. She was a drunk, and because of that, innocent people had lost their lives. She'd conspired in an act of supposedly noble corruption, but really, how did that make her different from every other bent cop who'd ever tried to justify their criminality? Her team despised Sam Evans for the relatively trivial offence of leaking to the press. What would they think of her if they knew who she really was? And her own slide into indiscipline meant she'd kept turning a blind eye when her team took shortcuts and bent the rules.

Maybe – just maybe – she could live with that if she was still doing what had once been second nature to her. But she wasn't even managing that. There was a man out there killing women apparently at will. Seven weeks of tireless plodding and they had next to nothing. Their failure offended her. She'd lacked the inspiration to send her team down a line of inquiry that might produce a result. And now all these chickens were flocking home to roost.

The single tenuous connection they had tying Tom Elton to the three murders would normally have provoked some optimism in Carol's heart. But this time, all there was inside her was bleak despair. She didn't believe they could stop this man. They didn't have enough to crack someone who was clearly confident and assured. But they didn't have time to dig deeper. Blake and his cronies were on her back and clearly what drove them was nothing to do with justice, whatever the words they used.

Her instincts told her to wait, to drill down into every aspect of Tom Elton's life. But she knew if she trusted those instincts it could be too late for her guys. A review squad would be all over them, their nitpicking fingers turning over everything they'd done, finding fault wherever they could. She'd plucked her team out of positions where they were doing good work with the promise of something more challenging, more fulfilling, something that might change the shape of national policing. She couldn't just shrug and walk away from that commitment.

Whatever she did next, she had to protect them. If that meant falling on her own sword, then so be it. She'd walk into the interview room with Paula in the morning and give it her best shot. And if that didn't work, she'd have to make some hard choices about what to do next.

64

Alvin and Kevin were waiting by the lift doors outside Local Words' fourth-floor suite when Tom Elton stepped out. He gave them a curious glance but didn't break stride as he headed for the office. Alvin stepped forward to obstruct him. Elton flashed him an angry look and moved to sidestep his bulk. 'Mr Elton?' Alvin sounded the soul of politeness.

Elton paused, gave Alvin closer scrutiny, allowed himself a faint frown of curiosity and said, 'Who wants to know?' in the most nonchalant of tones.

'Detective Sergeant Ambrose of the Regional Major Incident Team.' He produced his ID as Kevin moved to his side.

'And I'm Detective Inspector Matthews. Same unit.'

Elton raised his eyebrows, nostrils flaring slightly, his expression verging on the supercilious. But his voice was neutral. 'Really? What brings you to my door?'

'We'd like to ask you some questions in an ongoing inquiry,' Alvin said. As he spoke, the lift doors opened and a couple of young men emerged carrying takeaway coffee, shoulder bags slung across their bodies, each with beautifully barbered facial hair.

'Hey, boss,' one said.

Elton glanced at him and grunted, 'Morning. I'll be there in a minute,' he added as one of them swiped his card, opened the door and held it open expectantly. Elton waved his hand distractedly and the two disappeared inside. 'You'd better come in, I suppose.'

'Actually,' Kevin said, 'we'd like you to come to the station. Easier all round. Saves awkwardness in the office. And everything's to hand if we need you to look at anything or provide any samples.' Chin up, cool blue stare meeting Elton's eyes.

'Samples? What is this all about?'

'If you don't mind, we'd prefer not to discuss that here.'

'And what if I do mind?' The first hint of a challenge in the words, though his voice was warm, almost jokey.

'We can do this the friendly, low-key way, or we can not. It's up to you, sir.' Kevin took a step closer.

'And what's the unfriendly way? Is that where you wrestle me to the ground, slap on the handcuffs and drag me from the building?' Now he was quite clearly taunting them. Kevin flushed.

Alvin didn't. 'We'd simply arrest you. We only do the other stuff if you're dumb enough to resist arrest. Which we don't mind at all, because it gives us something incontrovertible to charge you with.' He smiled. 'Shall we go?'

'Do I need a lawyer? Isn't this what people say at this point? And don't you go, "If you've done nothing wrong, why would you need a lawyer?"'

'It's up to you,' Kevin said. 'You can decide on the way to Skenfrith Street.' He gestured towards the lift. 'After you, sir.'

Carol and Paula were in the squad room with Tony. The rich smell of strong coffee filled the air. Carol looked at her watch for the third time in as many minutes. 'I thought they'd be here by now.'

'Traffic,' Paula said.

A second later, Kevin walked in.

'Traffic,' he said, then looked puzzled when they all laughed, an easy release of tension.

'How did he take it?' Tony asked.

'Tried to be a bit of a joker, but when he realised we weren't playing, he got serious. Spent all the time in the back of the car making calls. Lawyering up, cancelling meetings.'

'Who's he got?' Carol asked.

'Who do you think?' Kevin said, the vicious edge in his voice telling Carol what she didn't want to hear.

'Bloody Bronwyn Scott,' Paula lamented. Bronwyn Scott was the nearest thing to a celebrity lawyer that Bradfield possessed. The standard joke was that if you hired Scott, the police knew you were guilty and the jury believed you were innocent. There was some truth behind the cynicism. Scott had crossed swords with the Bradfield MIT more than once, but she'd also been the person they'd called on to defend one of their own. She didn't mind who paid the piper; she'd find a tune that everyone could dance to.

'The same,' Kevin said. 'She's in court, but she'll be here within the hour. I've put Elton in an interview room with a uniform to keep him company. Alvin's gone down to the canteen to get him a coffee.' Because, although ReMIT had probably the best coffee delivery system in any UK police office, it was for those who upheld the law, not those who might have broken it.

Carol could hardly bear the thought of another hour. Her body felt electric, her brain heavy. Sobriety was supposed to make you sharper; all it made Carol feel was that she'd been born two drinks under par. She caught Tony's eye and exchanged a rueful grin. 'I know it's tough having to wait. It puts us all on edge. But it's tougher on Elton. We know what we've got and where we're going. He has no idea.'

'How did Karim get on with the car-hire firms?' Kevin asked.

'He drew a blank,' Paula said. 'And we're still waiting for ID on victim three. No joy with dentists so we're reliant on the lab managing to extract some DNA.'

'I really hoped we'd get something on the car hire,' Tony said. 'He has to have access to another vehicle we don't know about.'

Carol stared at the incident board, eyes dark and heavy. 'Christ, I hope we haven't gone with this too soon.'

Less than forty minutes had passed when Alvin came to tell them Scott was in the building, conferring with her client. 'Though what they've got to confer about at this stage, who knows?' Paula muttered as they made their way down the hall to the interview room. Tony and Kevin peeled off into the observation room, Paula adjusted the earpiece that nestled unseen behind a wing of hair, and on Carol's nod, they walked in.

Scott looked as expensive and brittle as ever, her fitted black jacket snug over a white shirt, the long points of the collar like knife blades against the narrow lapels. 'DCI Jordan,' she said. 'Amazing to see you in harness again.'

'Ms Scott. Always a pleasure.' Carol took her time over her first appraisal of Elton. He looked more like his driving licence picture than the photofit Stacey's software had generated but with a pair of glasses on the thick bridge of his nose, he'd definitely be identifiable. He seemed calm and there were no obvious physical tics to signal nervousness. That was unusual enough. Most people in his position were twitchy at the least. Citizens who had committed no crime had a habit of freaking out in a police interview room, probably because they'd watched too much TV drama.

'And DS McIntyre. Still a sergeant, Paula?' Scott was clearly in abrasive mood.

'Happily, yes. I've managed to avoid being demoted.'

Scott's smile was sharp enough to cut a well-done steak. 'Why are we here?' It was a reasonable opener.

'Because we would like to ask your client some questions.' Paula was taking the lead, as agreed. Carol was happy to concede; she acknowledged Paula was better at this than she was.

'Are we allowed to know what about? I presume that since you are ReMIT now, we're not talking unpaid parking tickets?'

'We are investigating a series of murders.' Elton didn't move a muscle at Paula's words. 'The bodies of three women have been incinerated in their own cars at various locations in the Yorkshire Dales. All three were already dead when they were set on fire. The post-mortems indicate probable strangulation.'

'Fascinating. And this involves my client how, exactly?'

'We believe he may be able to help us with our inquiries. Mr Elton, have you even met a woman called Kathryn McCormick?'

He frowned and shook his head. 'Not that I can recall.'

'Or Amie McDonald?'

'You mean the singer?' It was almost a smirk. 'I don't move in those sorts of circles.'

'Not the singer. A council employee from Leeds.' Carol chipped in.

'Definitely not. I've never met anyone who worked for Leeds City Council.'

Paula slid an enlarged print of the photograph taken at the bar of the wedding where the man called David had connected with Kathryn McCormick. 'Is this a photograph of you, Mr Elton?'

He leaned forward to study the photograph. 'I don't wear glasses,' he said. 'So it's not me.'

'It looks very like you.'

He glanced at Paula with disdain. 'The hairstyle's completely different.'

'Glasses, hairstyle. That's very superficial. The jawline, though. The ear. The shape of your mouth. I'd say they're pretty much identical.'

Scott intervened. 'Oh, please. On a blown-up photo that's obviously been taken on a mobile phone from some distance away? I don't think so.'

Paula took out the next photo, from the wedding where 'Mark' had encountered Amie McDonald. 'And this? Is this not you either?'

This time, the look was cursory. 'Hardly. Again, I don't wear glasses. And that's a ridiculous hairstyle and the colour's all wrong.'

'Big deal,' Carol said. 'Like you couldn't make those changes in a matter of minutes.'

'It's not me.' Elton didn't raise his voice. He simply stated his denial as if it was self-evident.

'Where is this going?' Scott demanded. 'Where were these photographs obtained?'

'They were taken at two weddings, three weeks apart. That's where the first two victims met the man who killed them.'

'You know that, do you?' Scott came straight back at Paula.

'We know they were both picked up by a man posing as a wedding guest but who was unknown to bride or groom. They met him again on a date on more than one occasion. Then they arranged to spend a weekend with him. And the next time they were seen was in a blazing car by the side of the road in a remote location. So yes, I think we can safely assume that the man who picked them up had murder in mind from the start.'

Scott chuckled. 'Quite an assumption. Any evidence? I can

already think of several alternative explanations, were my client to need them.'

This was not going as well as either detective had hoped. There was no sign that Elton was even mildly discomfited, and there was no prospect of diverting Scott from her focus. Time to go down a road she hoped would be unexpected enough to throw Elton off his stride. 'You say you'd never met Kathryn McCormick or Amie McDonald. But you have met Claire Garrity.'

He looked puzzled. He opened his mouth to speak but Scott cut across him. 'Is this your third victim?'

'No. We don't have a confirmed ID on the third victim as yet. Claire Garrity met Mr Elton in her professional capacity as bakery manager at Freshco.' Paula paused.

And on cue, he filled the gap. 'That's right. She dealt with a complaint I made.' A little laugh, false as the bottom of a smuggler's suitcase. 'I found a child's sock in a loaf of bread.'

Paula spread a pair of screenshots in front of them. This time, Elton shifted in his seat, but his face didn't change. 'Claire Garrity posted a picture of Kathryn McCormick at the wedding on her RigMarole page and invited Kathryn to be her friend.' She paused. Scott's expression shifted, revealing a shred of uncertainty. 'The thing is, Claire wasn't a guest at the wedding either. Just like the mystery man.'

'Wedding crashers, obviously,' Scott said, the line a casual throwaway.

More screenshots. 'Three weeks later Claire Garrity also posted a photo of Amie McDonald at the wedding she attended on *her* RigMarole page and asked to be her friend. She's the only person who made friend requests to both women associated with the weddings they'd attended.'

Bronwyn Scott leaned back in her chair, looking bored. 'Frankly, it looks to me as if the person you should be questioning is Claire Garrity from the Freshco baking department.'

Paula thought she saw a transient moment of shock in Elton's eyes. 'There's only one problem with that,' she said mildly. 'Claire Garrity's been dead for nearly three months. Which your client knew, because the customer service representative at Freshco told him.' Paula paused, but Elton's expression never varied.

'So?' Scott moved swiftly from back to front foot. 'It's not exactly a state secret, is it?'

'Whoever posted those photos stole Claire's identity to do it. The only person who would have understood the relevance of those two friendship requests is the killer. And even as we speak, we are pursuing the IP address those communications came from.' This time she saw the fleeting change of expression in Elton's eyes. And his shoulders relaxed fractionally.

Paula heard Tony's voice in her ear. 'He's covered his tracks on that one.' But she'd already worked that out for herself. She didn't need him telling her to let it go.

Now it was time for Carol. She folded her arms across her chest and glared at Elton. 'You can lie all you like, Tommy boy. But we can put you with these women. We've got photographs. We have you using different names and attempting to disguise yourself. You're the only link between Claire Garrity, these weddings and these women. We are coming for you and, make no mistake, we will have you for these crimes. Keep lying to me, Tommy. Because the more you lie, the more we demonstrate you're nothing but a liar.' Hands on the table, leaning forward, in his face. Then Paula's hand on her arm, restraining her.

Prearranged, of course. Scott sat up straight and gave a slow handclap. 'You're wasted here, DCI Jordan. You really should be on the stage.'

Carol ignored her, reaching for Paula's folder and pulling

out another two sheets of paper. 'We know you did this. We know you're lying. So give us some more lies. Here's a list of dates and times. Fill it in, Tommy.' She had a way of spitting out the diminutive of his name that made it sound like an insult. 'Every last one of them.'

'How do you expect me to remember where I was—' He pulled it towards him. 'Five weeks past Tuesday?'

'You're a modern man,' Carol said. 'Get your phone out and start going through your diary.'

'I must protest,' Scott said. 'This is a fishing expedition. We're out of here.'

'I don't think so,' Paula said. 'Either do this willingly or I will arrest your client and close your options right down. And you know what a leaky sieve this station is. Give us some cooperation. Show me he really is the injured innocent he's playing right now. Mr Elton, we'll give you some time to go through it with Ms Scott here.' Paula stood up. 'Take as long as you like. We'll have some coffee and sandwiches sent in.'

Scott looked up. 'Your coffee, Sergeant. Not that crap they serve in the canteen.'

'I don't think so,' Carol said. 'You don't deserve anything more than the rank and file drink.' She got to her feet. 'Best handwriting, Tommy.'

'Now,' came Tony's voice in Paula's ear. 'Hit him now.'

She gathered her papers and gave Elton an up-and-under look. 'Tricia says you've got a violent temper.'

Now she won a reaction. Elton reared back in his chair like a man seeing an apparition. 'What?'

'She says she had to have the living room wall repainted three times because you threw things at it when you were pissed off.'

'That's a lie.' He struggled to keep his face under control.

'She told me how she met a man at a wedding you didn't

want to go to with her. A man who made her realise precisely how wrong for her you were. A bit of a pattern there. Lone woman at a wedding meets a man who reminds her what romance is.'

His face had darkened, his jaw set, the muscles bulging.

As she reached the door, Paula stopped and turned. 'Oh, and she told me where she dumped you as well. You got burned in a lay-by, Mr Elton. Just like your victims did.'

65

Carol stood in her office, blinds drawn, forehead against the cool glass of the window. 'We went too soon,' she said.

'You had to make a move. Even if you don't have enough now, you've shaken him up,' Tony said.

'You saw him. Did he look shaken to you?'

'At the end, yes. When Paula delivered the sucker punch, he looked appalled. Then furious. What else could you do?'

She pushed back and turned to face him. 'Turns out I could have waited half an hour and had Eileen Walsh's identity confirmed. The team's out there now, Alvin and Kevin and Karim, combing her life for traces of him. And maybe they'll find something.'

'And then you can charge him.' He went to pat her arm but she flinched away from him.

'I had a nightmare last night,' she said. 'Michael and Lucy.'

She didn't have to say more. Tony himself had occasional flashbacks to that blood-drenched scene of horror. He'd often wondered whether returning to the scene of the crime had been wise, even though Carol's mission had been to strip the barn to its bare bones, to remove every trace of what had happened there. Underneath the façade she'd constructed, the skeleton of a murder scene remained, the ghost of its history still in the air. He felt it sometimes when he was there; he couldn't believe it wasn't part of her day-to-day. The miracle was that she didn't have nightmares more often.

Or perhaps it was simply that she didn't admit to them. The idea of PTSD had crossed his mind from time to time. She'd certainly seen and experienced enough trauma, both personal and professional, to take many people over the edge. But he was a professional. She couldn't have kept that from him, could she?

'I'm sorry,' he said. 'Does that happen often?'

She shook her head. 'Less and less.' She gave a wobbly smile. 'Maybe having you around has helped. God knows, you've got to be good for something apart from gaming.'

'I've not been much use this time round.' He moved away and leaned against the filing cabinet. 'You get a second crack at him over the alibis, though.'

'More circumstantial evidence, nothing else. I need something hard, something solid, and it's not coming. You saw him when we said we were tracing the IP address for the Claire Garrity messages. He relaxed. He's got that covered. He'll have found the last internet café in Bradfield and used that. Or the library. Or somebody else's office.'

Tony sighed. 'Probably. He's very savvy. So go for that nerve. Suggest he's not as smart as he thinks he is.'

'I think he's too hardcore for that. Hitting him with Tricia unsettled him, but he's got to know she doesn't have anything on him from the last three months.' Carol aimed a vicious kick at the wastepaper bin, sending it skittling across the floor, shedding its contents in an arc. 'Oh, fuck,' she moaned, crouching down and picking everything up.

Like the good girl she was, Tony thought. Always trying to

be the best, that was the cross Carol carried. Adamant for justice, but also adamant that she was the best person to deliver it. She never made it easy on herself.

Paula used the break to talk to Elinor. They met in the Starbucks opposite Bradfield Cross Hospital, their regular rendezvous when they both managed to escape for twenty minutes.

They'd discussed the outcome of Torin's disastrous foray into online relationships the night before. Elinor had agreed with Paula, shaking her head with a wry smile at the prospect of having to spend three hours a week under Stacey's rigid supervision. 'Elsa will end up a software millionaire,' she pointed out.

'Then she can lavish Torin with penance gifts.'

But that had been yesterday, and the two women had a policy of not dwelling on matters settled. Not for them the chewing over of decisions already reached, the revisiting of resolutions. Sufficient unto the day was good enough for them. Now it was time to move on to that day's fresh hell.

Paula slumped in her seat, stirring her flat white into submission. 'We've got nothing on this guy. We know it's him, and all we have is gossamer.'

'Very poetic,' Elinor said. 'Have you been sneaking sonnets when I'm not looking?'

In spite of herself, Paula found a smile. Elinor's perpetual gift to her. 'Every spare moment. But I'm really worried about this one. He's quietly confident. Not cocky, just sure of his ground. Unless we get something solid on victim three, he's going to walk out with a spring in his step, feeling like he's king of the world.' She sighed. 'And more women will die.'

'Maybe he'll take fright. Stop while he's still free and clear.'

'His sort never do. They start off tentative but pretty soon they can't do without it. It's the ultimate power trip. It's not love that's the drug, it's power. And there's nothing more powerful than taking somebody's life and getting away with it.'

'You're beginning to sound like Tony.' Elinor squeezed her hand.

'I've been listening to him for years. It would be surprising if nothing had rubbed off.'

'You've had cases before that stayed on the books. You know you can't always put the bad guys away.'

'I know. But those failures came in the context of a lot of success. This is ReMIT's first official major outing, and we're under the spotlight. There are a lot of people with vested interests in us failing. You don't think they're rubbing their hands with glee right now?'

Elinor sighed. 'Pitiful. What kind of person puts their own petty ambition ahead of saving lives? Oh no, wait, I've met surgeons . . . ' She grinned. 'You have to rise above it, Paula. You have to be better than them. You have to go into that room and give it your best shot. And if you fail? What is it they say? "Try again. Fail better." I know it hurts. I've lost enough patients in my time. But it doesn't diminish you. Now go back in that room and do the best you can. And whatever happens, I will still love you.'

Paula inclined her head in acceptance. 'I know. And I'm the lucky one. I have you to come home to. No matter how hard Tony tries to make it otherwise, Carol only has the inside of her head.'

Elton and Scott looked as relaxed as a couple of acquaintances waiting for afternoon tea when Carol and Paula returned. The sheet of paper had been annotated in neat block capitals. Scott passed it over to Carol. 'There you go.

As you will see, on almost all of these occasions, my client has no human alibi. He was either at home or in a hotel in another city.'

'Worthless, then,' Carol said, lip curling in a sneer.

'Not exactly,' Elton said. 'My car has an onboard computer. It will tell you where the car was on the evenings in question. If need be, I will give your people access to that computer which will show that I didn't drive off to meet strange women on those evenings.'

'But since you have no substantive evidence against my client, we're not going to volunteer that. You'll need to get a warrant. And good luck with that,' Scott said.

'And as you can see, last Sunday, I was in the Sportsman's Arms watching Bradfield Vic get taken apart by Chelsea. With a group of friends.' There was nothing defiant about Elton. He spoke conversationally, as if he was telling a mate what he'd been up to at the weekend.

'Plenty of time to get back to the Dales and murder Eileen Walsh,' Carol said.

'Another woman I've never heard of,' Elton said nonchalantly.

'So if you've nothing further, DCI Jordan, my client and I will be leaving now.' Scott gathered her notepad and her slim silver Tiffany pen and stowed them in her slim leather shoulder bag. 'This has been a comprehensive waste of time. If you want to speak to my client again, you'd better have something more than a computer-generated image and a Freshco complaint. Otherwise I'll be the one making a complaint of harassment.' She glanced at Elton as if to encourage him to leave.

But he remained seated. 'If I was the person who had done this, I'd be laughing myself sick.' His voice dripped contempt. 'You're so bereft of ideas and evidence that you're grasping at the slightest coincidence and trying to build a case against an innocent man. While the real killer is out there, probably planning his next murder, not a stain on his character.' Now he stood up.

'I thought you lot were supposed to be the elite? I remember the news stories when you were formed. Top guns, they said.' He scoffed. 'Top bums, more like. If I was your man, I'd be dancing in the streets. With you lot running the show, anyone could get away with murder.'

66

Carol sat on the sofa, elbows on her knees, head hanging. 'He fucking laughed at us.' She'd been saying the same thing at regular intervals for the past hour. As far as Tony knew, she'd been saying them to herself all the way home in the Land Rover too.

'Think of it as a spur to action.' It was a weak response but the only one he could come up with.

'I don't need a "spur to action". I need some bloody evidence. The team have been all over Eileen Walsh's life this afternoon and so far it's another big fat zero. A few notes on a wall calendar with a defunct pay-as-you-go phone number. Richard, this time. So far, not even a glimpse on a photo. He's not becoming careless, Tony. He's getting better at this.'

'So what are you going to do?'

'What can I do? I've ordered up full surveillance on Elton. There'll be teams on him twenty-four seven. If he's stupid enough to think he can keep doing this unmolested, he's very wrong.'

I think he'll expect surveillance. I think you'll bust your budget long before he puts a foot wrong. Tony knew better than to voice his thoughts. Which were the thoughts of a clinician as much as a friend. Right now, Carol needed to believe a positive outcome was possible. The alternative wasn't something he wanted to contemplate.

The moment was broken by the doorbell. 'What now?' Carol grumbled, getting to her feet and dragging weary steps to the door. She looked through the spyhole. 'Bloody Penny Burgess.' She turned her back and leaned against the door, as if barricading it against an invader.

'If you don't talk to her here, she'll only ambush you somewhere else. Probably in the most public place she can manage.' Tony sprang up and hurried to the door. 'Let me do the talking.' Gently, he pushed her aside and opened the door, his foot behind it to prevent the reporter getting a good look inside. 'Penny,' he sighed wearily. Let her know she was a pain in the arse. Albeit an elegant one.

'Dr Hill. I find you here again. How very cosy. And is Carol here too or are you home alone?'

Carol stepped into her line of sight. 'I'm here. I live here. What's your excuse?'

'I've come to do you a favour. We're running a story and I wanted to give you a heads-up. And to get a quote, obviously.'

'I've got nothing to say to you,' Carol said. 'I don't discuss ongoing cases with the press. You need to talk to the media office.'

'It's not about the case. Though three murders does seem a lot to be going on with. And no prospect of an arrest, I hear.'

Tony and Carol remained silent. They were both too experienced to be so easily baited.

Penny grinned. 'Worth a try. No, what I'm here about – and I'm sorry to keep banging on the same old drum – is the mystery of the drink-driving bust that wasn't. Since we spoke last, I've been making further inquiries. When five people die needlessly, after all, I don't think we should just forget it and walk away. Do you?'

Again, silence.

'OK, I'll cut to the chase. According to what the CPS told Calderdale magistrates, the breathalyser that you and four other motorists blew into that gave you all criminal alcohol breath levels was faulty. Am I right?'

'That's what the court was told, yes.' Carol was cautious but saw no point in disputing a matter of record.

'I have a problem with that,' Penny said, pushing a stray strand of hair aside that the wind had blown into her eyes. 'You see, the breathalyser in question was never withdrawn from use. Never repaired. Not even so much as serviced and recalibrated. Next shift, it was out on the road. Still is. How does one make sense of that?'

Stony-faced, Carol said nothing. But Tony could feel the tremble in the arm that touched his back. 'Not DCI Jordan's job,' he said.

'But it is mine,' Penny said. 'According to my sources, the officers who breathalysed you and arrested you and brought you to Halifax police station – incidentally, walking your lovely dog—' She glanced down at Flash, whose head was against Carol's thigh. 'Those officers are pretty disgruntled about what happened. They are convinced they made a right-eous arrest, using equipment that has not subsequently been found fault with.'

Time to go on the front foot. 'So what?' Tony said. 'Coppers spend half their lives being disgruntled for one reason or another. That's not news.'

'Maybe not. And we'd all have to swallow it as a strange anomaly but for the fact that I've got a witness who says DCI Jordan was drinking wine all evening. That she had at least five glasses of strong red wine followed by a glass of port.'

Silence so absolute they could hear the dog's breath.

'It doesn't sound like a faulty breathalyser to me.' Penny's tone was deceptively light. She'd delivered a killer blow and she knew it. 'Who put the fix in, Carol? It can't have been James Blake. He may be chief constable of Bradfield but he hasn't got the clout for that. And anyway, everybody knows he hates you. So who was it, Carol? Did it go all the way up to the Home Office? Your old boss John Brandon's in their pocket these days, isn't he?'

'You're so wide of the mark, Penny,' Tony said. 'Maybe you should be looking at the other people who got off that night. Maybe this isn't some giant conspiracy to exonerate Carol. Maybe it's local corruption. A senior copper doing a favour for a friend or a bit on the side, not expecting any blowback. He'll be shitting it now, waiting for the other shoe to drop. Did you think about that?'

For a moment, she looked disconcerted. Then she laughed. 'Good try, doc. But no cigar. Even if it did play out the way you suggest, I've still got a witness to the fact that Carol was well over the limit when she got behind the wheel that night. And that's all I need, really. Let the readers join up the dots.'

'Why are you doing this?' Tony asked. 'Why are you so determined to destroy a good detective's career? You go ahead with this and people will die because you've taken the best cop in the region off the streets.'

Penny's eyebrows rose in a perfect arch. 'Plenty of people have already died on her watch. There's a trail of bodies in your wake, the pair of you. But despite that, I'm not pursuing any kind of vendetta. This isn't personal. This is about who guards the guards. This is about Caesar's wife having to be above reproach. Once you start playing this kind of game, Carol, where does it stop? Once you become the one who matters, what happens to justice? Where's the justice for the five people who died when Nicky Barrowclough got pissed and got behind the wheel?' Her voice rose with passion. Flash gave a low growl deep in her throat.

'No comment,' Tony said and closed the door. He turned and wrapped Carol in his arms. She allowed the embrace for as long as it took Penny Burgess to stop leaning on the doorbell and leave. Then she pulled away and smashed the side of her fist against the door.

'That's it,' she shouted. 'I'm done. Thanks to Penny fucking Burgess, I'm going down in flames.' She squeezed her eyes shut and jerked her head to one side in an angry gesture. 'She's going to ruin me. There'll be no ReMIT left by the time she's done. They'll all be tainted by association.' She crossed the room and threw herself into an armchair. 'I'm finished, Tony, I'm finished.'

He stood by the door, uncertain whether to go to her. 'She'll never run it. Her editor won't have the balls to take on the police, the Home Office, whoever.'

'She'll take it somewhere else, then. She's got a cracking story and she won't walk away from it. She's got form, you know she has. I am truly fucked.' Head in hands, she rocked to and fro in her chair. Belly to the floor, Flash crawled to her side. Cautiously, as if he was playing Grandmother's Footsteps, Tony also approached. When he reached her side, he crouched down and put a hand on her knee.

'Nobody will believe it,' he said.

'They will.' Her voice muffled by her hands. 'I've been turned into a star by the bosses. My team's been boosted as the elite. And there's nothing people like more than seeing the likes of us brought low.' Carol raised her head. 'If it was just me, I'd say, fuck it, and walk away.' A sharp sigh. 'But it's not just me. It's the rest of them. Paula, going for her inspector's exams. No chance. Kevin, who only came back for me, out in the cold. Alvin, who moved his whole family up to Bradfield because of what ReMIT offered him. Karim, the best and the brightest of his intake. He'll be stuck at the bottom of the CID pile forever now. Stacey? Without me to protect her, she'll either end up in jail or she'll walk away too. And the force loses the best digital analyst in the country. And you. You'll be tainted too, you and what you do. It's a bloody disaster.'

She jumped up again and started pacing. 'And that piece of shit Tom Elton? He's already laughing at us. Whoever they bring in to replace us, he'll run rings round them. And he's going to keep on doing this. OK, on the law of averages, some dumb traffic cop will eventually stop him when he's got a dead woman in the car. But how many more women will die before that happens? What about Tricia? Who's going to keep her safe over in Spain? I can't take it, Tony. I can't let this happen. No more blood on my hands, I can't—' She pounded her fists against her chest.

She was coming apart in front of him. He'd have known what to do if he'd been inside the high walls of Bradfield Moor Secure Hospital. He'd have had her sedated then dealt with her pain when it was less acute. But this was her home. A home she'd opened up to him too. He had to be her friend, not her doctor. So he went to her again and tried to hold her. But she fought free and turned on him, panting, her mouth a snarl, her hands fists.

'I'm not going to stand for it,' she growled. 'I've got nothing left to lose, Tony. I'm going to put a stop to him. I'm going to follow him to the next fucking wedding.' She took a deep breath. 'I'm going to follow him and then I'm going to kill him.'

67

They argued late into the night. They only broke off so Carol could check in with the surveillance teams she'd set on Elton's tail. But nothing Tony said could even dent Carol's conviction that her solution was the only reasonable one. Nothing gave her pause. 'I'm history, whatever happens now. So I'm going to do one good thing on the way down.'

'You don't know for sure that Elton's guilty,' Tony tried. 'You think he is, but—'

'All the circumstantial points to him. Psychologically, he makes complete sense. You said that yourself after you listened to Paula's interview with Tricia. And you saw the way he reacted when Paula mentioned her name.'

'That might be nothing more than shock at hearing you'd managed to contact her when he couldn't.'

Carol shook her head in exasperation. 'What about the photographs? It's him. We'll bring in expert witnesses who can match up all the micro-measurements.'

'So do that. Prove it.'

She shook her head. 'We'll never get that far. The CPS won't even consider a prosecution without at least a fifty per cent chance of success, you know that. And juries hate that kind of evidence, it makes them feel like they're being blinded by science.'

Tony paced the floor in front of her. 'I don't believe you'll do it. You couldn't kill someone in cold blood. You've not got it in you.'

She gave him a cold, calculating look. 'If you say so.' Her tone denied her words.

His final throw of the dice was, he knew, a high-risk strategy. 'I've tried really hard to be your friend tonight,' he said, keeping his exasperation at bay with difficulty. 'But now I need to be the doctor here.'

'What? I need a doctor? You think I'm sick?' Her voice was filled with exhaustion and hurt.

'I think you might be suffering from PTSD. Post-Traumatic Stress—'

'I know what bloody PTSD is. And I'm not a victim.'

'There's no shame in it, Carol. It's not a comment on your brilliance or your bravery or your commitment. It's as real as breaking a bone and there's no shame in it.'

She scoffed. 'You think? Tell that to all the soldiers invalided out these past few years. You don't see them walking into top jobs and running the world, do you? Anyway, that's irrelevant. I'm not suffering from PTSD.'

'In my professional opinion, you probably are. You should be on sick leave, having treatment.'

'You think? So what are my symptoms, *Doctor*?' she sneered.

'You told me yourself you've been having nightmares. That's a classic.'

'If that was the criterion for going on the sick, you'd hardly have a single member of the emergency services in work. We all see appalling things and we all revisit them in the night. Don't you dare lecture me about bad dreams and not sleeping.

By your own admission, you've hardly had a proper night's sleep in years. It was one of the first things you told me when we were working our first case together.' She jumped to her feet again and started on circuits of the room. Flash looked up momentarily then let her head fall to the rug again. She'd had enough pacing for one evening.

'There's a difference between general insomnia and the onset of nightmares.'

'Having bad dreams doesn't make me special, Tony. Call Paula, ask her how she sleeps. How Elinor sleeps after a bad shift in A&E. Is that it? Is that what you're basing your diagnosis on?'

'You're talking about killing someone as if that was a normal, acceptable solution to a problem.'

'You think that's an easy decision? Something I take lightly? Tony, I have devoted my life to the pursuit of justice. Now, that life is imploding. Penny Burgess and the other jackals are going to take what I value most from me. I'm going to sink without trace. If I'm going to live with myself, I have to make it mean something. Saving other lives is meaningful. You can't deny that.'

'But turning yourself into a cold-blooded killer isn't the way to do that. I know what it is to take a life. It took me years of therapy to recover from that, years of sitting with Jacob and letting him help me heal.'

'That was different, Tony. You didn't mean to kill. You were defending yourself against someone who was intent on killing you. What I'm talking about is different. It's about justice. It's about saving lives, not taking one.'

'This isn't justice, it's vigilantism.' His voice rose in a heartfelt plea. 'Listen to yourself, Carol.'

'There is no other way. There's no fucking evidence. How many times do I have to say it? How else do we stop him? He's got carte blanche to carry on murdering innocent women whose only crime was to go to a wedding, and he knows it. You saw him today. That confidence. That arrogance. If I don't stop him, he'll keep on doing it. There's nothing more to be said. So what other symptoms do I allegedly have, according to you?'

It was like talking to a wall. No, a barricade of rubber tyres, because whatever he said was bouncing right off. 'You will become what you've devoted your life to preventing. You'll be a murderer. A vigilante. You'll be despised. Nobody will see what you've done as righteous.'

Carol turned away. 'Next.'

'Carol—'

'I'm done with this so-called symptom. What else have you got?'

'You're quick to anger and your temper flares much more than it used to.'

She burst out laughing. 'And whose fault is that? You've pushed me into giving up drinking. Cold turkey. My whole system is screaming for a drink most of the time, especially running a case like this. Of course I'm short-tempered. It would be bloody amazing if I wasn't.'

Tony threw his hands up in frustration. 'You were edgy long before I helped you get to grips with your alcohol dependency. I think you've been clinically depressed since Michael and Lucy died. Maybe even before that. But I've been too close to you to see it. Because you're nearly OK when you're with me. Being with me is a safe place for you because I always, always make it possible for you to behave exactly as you need to.' His voice was raised now. 'I've been your co-conspirator, Carol. Your enabler. I've greased the wheels for you. Because I love you, I have not been good for you.'

The words spilling from his mouth silenced them both. He'd broken the unspoken understanding that there were things better left unsaid between them: that there existed bridges better left uncrossed for fear that what lay beyond might make it impossible to retreat. He looked away first. He always looked away first. Because she needed him to.

'I think you'd better go.' Carol's voice was cold and hard. 'There's nothing more to be said.'

68

The days trickled by and the ReMIT squad repeated the same actions for Eileen Walsh's murder as they had for the previous two killings, with the same fruitless results. Carol spent most of her time bunkered down in her office, reading and rereading the reports that landed in the system. Stacey grew more frustrated with every passing hour when all the digital avenues she sent her bots down turned out to be dead ends. When Alvin came into the office, he couldn't get out fast enough. Karim had begun to look haunted, his eyes hollow and his hair unkempt. Paula was interviewing Eileen Walsh's workmates, a task that seemed endless because of the arcane shift patterns of the NHS. And nobody knew where Tony was. On the single occasion he'd turned up in the office, Carol had taken one look at him and walked straight out. 'Like one of those weather prediction things,' Paula said. 'The little wooden houses with a man and a woman on the opposite ends of a stick, and when one goes out, the other goes in.'

Kevin, in theory, had the most potentially productive task. He was supervising the surveillance teams tasked with watching Tom Elton's every move. Two teams of two on six-hour shifts. On day one, Elton had gone to work, to lunch with a woman they'd identified as Carrie McCrystal, the owner of a chain of beauty salons, and to a late afternoon meeting in York, where he'd stayed for dinner before checking into a local hotel. Day two, he drove to Leeds where he had coffee with two men in business suits then drove back to Bradfield. The rest of the day in the office then to the pub across the street with a couple of people from the office. A single bottle of overpriced exotic beer, then home. No movement till morning when he'd driven to work, gone to lunch with a board member of Bradfield Victoria. After work, he'd gone bowling with a group of people from work. And that was all they knew because on Friday evening, the surveillance was pulled.

The trouble had started with a phone call from John Brandon to Carol that morning. These days they didn't even bother exchanging meaningless pleasantries. Brandon simply came straight to the point. 'Are you making any concrete progress?'

Carol squeezed the bridge of her nose in the hope it would ease the headache she'd had for two days. 'It's difficult,' she said. 'We're dealing with someone who has a very high level of forensic awareness and is smart enough to stay beneath the radar.'

'That would be a no, then?'

'It's slow.'

She could hear him breathing. He wasn't finding this easy. Good, because neither was she. 'A significant part of the reasoning behind ReMIT was economies of scale,' he said. 'And you've got a full-scale surveillance operation – sixteen officer-shifts per day – on a man against whom you have, by your own admission, nothing, except a smattering of circumstantial evidence and a couple of coincidences.'

'Elton's good for it, sir. I know he is.'

A sigh. 'Good though your instinct is, Carol, I've got six chief constables breathing down my neck. They share the costs of your operations, you know that. And they're squealing at what you're doing to their budgets.'

'We shouldn't be putting a price on lives,' she snapped.

'Of course we shouldn't. But we do it all the time. We have to. Fewer front-line officers, reclassifying certain crimes to make the crime stats look good, rationing forensic tests to the bare minimum. None of us wants to do the job like this but the politicians push us into a corner time and time again.'

'What are you saying?'

'I'm under pressure from the chiefs to close down your surveillance on the grounds that it's nothing more than a fishing expedition. That you're trying to make the suspect fit the crime, not the other way round. And we all know how badly wrong that can go.'

'It's not like that,' Carol protested.

'Nevertheless. They wanted it stopped with immediate effect, but I have managed to buy you a little time. Might even be a reprieve. The senior prosecutor from the Bradfield CPS office is going to come over to Skenfrith Street this afternoon and go through what evidence you have. He'll give his considered opinion as to whether this is proceeding in a direction that's likely to lead to a prosecution. And based on that . . . '

'So I've got, what? Four hours to find something?'

'I'd say so. I'm sorry, Carol. It's a shame your first official case had to prove such a difficult one to nail.'

'Wasn't that supposed to be the point of us? The difficult ones, the intractable ones?'

'I thought so. We're not masters of our fate, Carol.'

Oh yes, we can be, she thought as they wound up the call. She'd spent three days examining her decision from every angle, all the while waiting for Penny Burgess to cry havoc and unleash the dogs of war on her. She'd even thought about telling Brandon about the sword of Damocles hanging over her. But he couldn't protect her from the press, and revealing something that might not even happen would only give the brass a reason to accelerate closing her down.

Nothing had changed. If they didn't stop Elton, other women would die. She was certain of that. Men like him didn't stop until they were stopped. Without sufficient evidence to prosecute, there was only one option.

Her weapon of choice would be a knife, she thought. A sharp kitchen knife, easy to conceal in her shoulder bag. Straight up under the ribs into the heart. Pull it out, a second stab to the guts. It wouldn't be easy to overcome her residual ties to obedience of the law. But the act itself would be easy, she thought. She'd seen the end result too often to believe it was a complicated thing to do.

And afterwards? She'd go to jail, obviously. Maybe, in the ultimate irony, she could get Bronwyn Scott to represent her. Just so long as nobody suggested she was suffering from diminished responsibility and got Tony in the witness box yammering on about PTSD. She had no desire to diminish her responsibility for what she was about to do. She'd face the consequences.

Prison. A career cop, she'd have a rough ride. Except that killing a man who was victimising women might earn her some prestige. But not enough, she suspected. She'd be on the vulnerable prisoners' wing, spending most of the time locked in her cell. That wouldn't be so bad, all things considered. She could read, sleep, listen to the radio. She's be housed, clothed, fed. Better off than the sixty per cent of the world's population without access to toilets or clean water.

Carol believed she could do it. She'd spent six months more or less on her own when she'd quit the job before. She'd stripped the barn of everything that Michael and Lucy had installed and rebuilt the interior from scratch. After that, she reckoned there wasn't much she couldn't get through. With luck and a compassionate judge, she'd be out in less than ten. Her life would be far from over. She could sell the barn, put the cash on deposit and buy somewhere new, start over when she got out.

She'd miss the dog, though. She was damned if she'd ask Tony to take Flash, but she knew he'd offer and she'd let him. And he'd visit her. That was one thing she could be certain of.

Really, none of this was insurmountable.

Peter Trevithick, the CPS solicitor, had the slightly harried air of a man who has too much to do in the time available. He was in that middle period of a hard-pressed man's life when his looks offered no clue as to where he sat between thirty-five and fifty-five. His suit was baggy and crumpled but his shirt was clean and pressed, his tie neat over the top button. He had the faint remains of a West Country accent but there was nothing rustic about his mind. Carol had worked with him a few times and she admired his analytical ability.

'They want me to give you a bit of a doing over this investigation,' he said, as soon as they were alone in her office. 'But you knew that, right?'

Carol nodded. 'I know the answer they want you to come back with.'

'Which is plainly different from the outcome you want.' He took off his jacket and draped it over the back of his chair. 'I have to be honest, Carol.'

'I know.'

'But I will try to lean in your direction. I know what a good copper you are. You don't take the lazy or the obvious route. Unlike some of your colleagues. So, why don't you take me through it from the beginning?'

Which she did. Step by laborious step, dead end by frustrating dead end. He listened keenly and jotted indecipherably in a Moleskine notebook. When he was uncertain, he asked questions. Occasionally, he made comments but she had no clue which way he was going to jump.

When she finally ground to a halt with an account of Eileen Walsh's final day, he nodded sympathetically. 'I entirely see why you think as you do,' he said. 'But as things stand, this is in no sense contestable by my department. There's nothing to prosecute with. I'm so sorry, Carol. You know how we work these days – fifty per cent chance of success or nothing happens. As this stands, I'd give it about fifteen per cent if you had a jury who loved you.' He looked genuinely miserable. 'The bitch of it is that I actually think you're right. He smells all wrong, this Tom Elton. But that's not what your bosses want to hear.'

'You're going to recommend that they pull their officers off surveillance, right?'

Trevithick nodded. 'Nothing else for it, I'm afraid.' He stood up and thrust his arms into his jacket. 'But I tell you something, Carol. I'm bloody sure this isn't going to be the last I hear of Tom Elton.'

You have no idea how right you are. 'Thanks, Peter. I'm sure this case will bring us back together, one way or another.'

'I do hope so, Carol. Good luck with closing it down.'

69

Parking was always difficult on the quiet Halifax street where Vanessa Hill had chosen to live. It was a mix of detached houses from the thirties, post-war semis and a single row of terraced houses of indeterminate age. Not many of the houses had driveways wide enough for modern cars, so visitors struggled. It wasn't a problem Tony had often had. He seldom visited his mother; she never visited him.

But for once, he thought talking to her might be useful and so he had put to one side his deep distaste for the woman who had given birth to him but had chosen to sidestep the obligations of motherhood. Tony – 'your little bastard' – had mostly been raised by his autocratic and frequently violent grandmother while Vanessa had dedicated herself to getting on in the world. The fact that she had a child at all had often come as a shock to her colleagues and, later, her employees.

Worse still, she had refused to tell him anything about his father. Tony had had no idea who his father had been until Edmund Arthur Blythe had died and left him his entire estate. A substantial house, a wedge of cash and the boat he now called home. Even then, Vanessa had tried to trick him out of his inheritance.

To say the two were estranged would be to imply a greater emotional engagement than actually existed. The therapy Tony himself had undergone to enable him to treat others had left him with an understanding of his mother but no desire to include her in his life. He'd worked at a studied indifference and that was how he wanted to keep it.

Then events beyond the control of either of them had placed them in each other's path the best part of a year before. A killer seeking revenge on Tony had mistakenly thought he could hurt the son through the mother. He'd been wrong on both counts. Vanessa had proved herself infinitely better at inflicting damage than he was; and even if he had succeeded, Tony's suffering would have been eminently bearable.

The encounter had driven them no closer, but what Tony now knew of his mother had brought him to her door tonight. Vanessa had acted in self-defence, technically. But she had prepared for what might happen; she had considered an outcome where she'd had to take the law into her own hands. He wondered how that had gone, what it had felt like. What he might learn that would help Carol.

He sat in his parked car, staring down the empty street, trying one more time to make sense of what Carol had seemed determined to do. Had she really meant it? He couldn't be certain. There was a twisted logic to what she had said. She'd always been driven by the urge for justice. He'd been the beneficiary of that himself in the past. And Carol was right that if Penny Burgess published her story, her career was over. She might even face conspiracy charges herself.

But to consider murder as a reasonable corollary to disgrace? That was the step he couldn't follow. Either she had spoken wildly, with no intention of carrying it through, or else she must be ill. It was the only answer he could find. He'd been blind to all the signs, but the more he thought about it, the more he'd grown convinced that she was suffering from PTSD. It wasn't surprising, after all she'd been through herself, never mind what she'd witnessed.

It would be no consolation to make that argument after the fact, however. Even if there was a raft of experts singing from the same hymn sheet, even if they persuaded a court that the balance of her mind had been disturbed, she'd still be branded a killer.

Whatever she said to the contrary, he didn't think Carol could live with that.

Somehow he had to stop her. She'd placed herself at a distance from him to prevent him from doing precisely that. But he couldn't let that continue. He had to put himself in a position where he could forestall what she had in mind. Whatever it took, he'd have to save Carol from herself.

He looked up at his mother's house. The curtains were drawn, but through a chink he could see the fluttering light of the television. Vanessa would be stretched out on her luxurious sofa, glass in hand, watching some TV drama, alone in a room designed for one. He'd come tonight to break the habit of a lifetime and seek something from her. He wanted to draw on her experience, to ask her what it had been like for her to kill someone. To slide a knife through flesh and feel the life drain from another human being.

Even more than that, he wanted to know how she felt afterwards. He'd held a knife that someone else had been impaled on and he knew how he'd struggled to cope with the emotional fallout, even thought it had been a case of kill or be killed. But he was a scientist. He wanted more than a sample of one. And it wasn't really something he could ask his patients, not for this purpose.

But now that he was here, on the brink of that discovery, he found that he no longer wanted to know. What could Vanessa say that would have any relevance here? She was one of a kind, and whatever the aftermath of her exercise in self-defence, it could have no parallels now.

He was about to start the engine and drive away when his phone rang. Paula, he saw. She was his friend, he reminded himself. So he answered. 'Hi, Paula.'

'Tony, they've called the surveillance off.'

'You're kidding.' He felt his heart contract. While there were watchers on Elton's back, Carol knew there was no need for her to step up to the plate; any move he made would be picked up and pounced on. Chances were it would remove any need for her to act.

'No, Peter Trevithick from the CPS came round and reviewed the case file and advised Brandon that the surveillance wasn't justified. So all bets are off after this evening's shift. It's a nightmare.'

'What's Carol saying?'

'That's the thing. She's convinced he's going to a wedding tomorrow. It's the pattern, you see.'

'Yeah. The Saturday after he kills, he acquires his next victim. So what's she got planned?'

'She's going to follow him, and as soon as he makes a move on a single woman, we're going to arrest him.'

'We?'

Paula sighed. 'Yeah, she wants me on it with her. Two cars, so he doesn't spot the tail. And so I can be there with her for the arrest.'

No. She wants you there to make the arrest after she kills him. 'I need to be there with you, Paula.'

'How come she hasn't got you on board with this? Are you two not speaking, or what?'

He didn't want to burden Paula with the truth. 'We had an

argument. You know how touchy she's been since she quit the booze.'

'Right. Anyway, the reason I rang is that I agree with you. You should be there. We'll need your advice to make sure it doesn't all go tits-up.'

'What's the arrangement?'

'Six a.m., stake-out. She's in the lead car, I'll be a couple of streets away ready to tuck in behind her. I thought you could ride with me? In the back seat so it's not so obvious?'

'Of course. This is crazy, you know.'

'I know, but she's determined he's not going to kill anybody else. So can you be at ours at half past five? I'll have the coffee on.'

He didn't have to think twice. This was probably the only chance he would get to save Carol from herself. He couldn't live with himself if he stood by while she destroyed herself. 'I'll be there. How's Torin, by the way?'

'Getting better. Thanks for what you did. I owe you. Actually, we all do. You're a star, Tony. Carol doesn't know how lucky she is to have you in her corner.'

Tony started the engine and with one last look at his mother's house, he drove off. He had a terrible feeling that something very bad was coming his way. Something that would be impossible to side-step even if he wanted to.

70

Tony huddled in the back seat of Elinor's car. Paula had chosen it because it was more nondescript than her own personal car. 'How in the name of God does Torin get in here?' he grumbled as he tried to find an unobtrusive position. Every way he turned, the contents of one pocket or another of his purple anorak dug into part of his body.

'With difficulty.' Paula yanked a dark blue beret over her blonde hair and put on her driving glasses. It worked for Elton, Tony thought. It might work for them if their target caught sight of her. 'OK, so Carol's borrowed Kevin's Stella's car, which is a silver Toyota Prius—'

'Borrowed,' Tony exclaimed. 'Not hired, Paula, borrowed. Elton lives by advertising contracts. He must have car dealers on his books. People he's got a long-standing relationship with. Men who will lend him wheels with a nod and a wink. That's why Karim couldn't find a car-hire firm who'd rented him a vehicle. He borrows a different car every time, that'll be how it goes.'

Paula groaned. 'Of course. He's exactly the type who has a boys' network. I bet you're right. Anyway, his block's got underground parking and she's set up down the street. We're going to be one street over at six a.m., just to be sure. But you're going to have to be quiet because we'll have an open phoneline on speaker. With us not having radio cars.'

'You won't know I'm here.'

'It's not me you have to worry about.'

A couple of minutes before six, they were in position, sipping strong coffee and eating bacon sandwiches. One thing about working with cops was that you were never short of comfort food and coffee, Tony thought. He'd lost count of the number of times he and Carol had sat hunched over a curry in their favourite Indian restaurant in Temple Fields, discussing cases and colleagues. He wondered whether they'd ever do that again.

The phone rang and Paula answered it on speaker. 'Morning, boss. You all set?'

'I am. Nothing to see yet. You might as well hang up, listen to the radio or whatever. I'll call you back when he stirs.'

Paula ended the call. 'So what did you guys fall out about?'

'Something and nothing,' he said. 'We're both of us too accustomed to our own company. I've been staying out at the barn a bit lately, just to give her a bit of moral support with setting up ReMIT.'

'And giving up the booze,' Paula said.

'And giving up the booze. Anyway, Carol and me, we always think we play better with others than we do in reality. We need our own space, and living under the same roof . . . well, let's say it wasn't always plain sailing for either of us.'

'So you're giving each other some space?'

He sighed and shifted his position again. 'Yeah. Something like that.'

'So no actual falling out?'

'No wonder you get the interview room results you do,'

Tony teased. 'No, no actual falling out. A difference of opin-ion, that's all.' He couldn't tell Paula the truth, much as he longed to. It would be unfair to burden her with the knowl-edge. And after all, Carol might have spoken wildly. Or she might have changed her mind on reflection. Any reasonable person would.

But maybe Carol wasn't entirely reasonable any more. 'You never told me the full story about Torin's blackmailer,' he said, trying for a deft change of subject.

And so she did. Then they talked about Elinor's career prospects, and the inspector's exams that Carol was so eager for Paula to take. 'I don't know,' she said. 'I'm not sure if I want the rank.'

'I don't suppose it would make much difference in terms of your job as long as you stay with ReMIT. It would mean more money, a better pension. And that's not something to be sniffed at.'

She sighed. But before she could say more, her phone chirped with a text. 'That's interesting,' she said, reading it. 'It's from Elton's ex, Tricia. She wants me to give her a ring. Not urgent, she says.' He could see her pulling a face in the rear-view mirror. 'I'll call her later, I don't want to be in the middle of talking to her and miss the boss telling me it's time to move.'

'Use my phone,' Tony said.

'Good idea.' Paula reached behind and he put it in her hand. She tapped in the number and they both listened to the long intermittent tone of a foreign number ringing out. Then the voicemail clicked in.

'Hi, this is Tricia. Leave a message and I'll get back to you when I've got decent reception.'

'Hi, Tricia, this is DS McIntyre. I got your text, sorry I've missed you. I'll try again later.' She hung up. 'Bugger.'

'She did say it wasn't urgent.'

'Let's hope she's right.'

It was several tedious hours, three more attempts to contact Tricia and two fat Saturday newspapers later when Carol finally called back soon after three. 'He's just come out of the front entrance of his block,' she said. 'He's looking up the street as if he's waiting for someone ... Ah yes, here's a cab. It's a black Skoda, City Cabs logo ... Elton's on board ... Heading south towards Kempton Road.'

Paula waited for a gap in the traffic then swung the car round. 'I need to get over behind you, this street doesn't go that far.' She did as she'd promised and they found themselves four cars behind Carol. 'I can see you, boss.'

'Turning left at the junction,' Carol said.

Soon they were on the inner ring road, heading out towards the motorway. Near the entry slip road was a string of car dealerships, and Elton's taxi turned off on to the loop that circled past them. Tony enjoyed a moment of quiet satisfaction when Elton got out at the reception entrance of a dealership specialising in nearly new executive cars. 'What's he up to here?' Carol asked.

'Maybe he's borrowing cars from clients, not hiring them,' Paula said hesitantly, turning to poke her tongue out at him.

Carol tutted. 'Brilliant. Why didn't we think of that? Of course, he's got contacts in all sorts of areas. Good thinking, Paula.'

Elton emerged a few minutes later and walked to the back of the lot. The car he drove away in was a dark blue Mercedes coupé. 'You take him now,' Carol said. 'I'll tuck in a few cars back.'

They hit the motorway and soon they were racing down towards the M62. The Mercedes was cruising effortlessly in the fast lane while Paula struggled to keep up, shifting between the middle lane and the fast lane, occasionally even drifting over to the inside lane when there was little traffic around. They headed west along the M62. 'Looks like Manchester or Liverpool,' Paula said.

'I'd guess Liverpool,' Carol said. 'He did Manchester last time, he won't want to chance being spotted in the same city so soon after Eileen Walsh.'

And she was right. They swapped lead cars again and Carol tailed him to the waterfront, where he pulled into a multi-storey car park next to the Philharmonic, a new hotel in the heart of the redeveloped docks. The dark red-brick building had once housed a massive tobacco warehouse, but only the façade remained of what had been. 'I'm betting that's where his target wedding is,' Carol said. 'Park on the street and be ready on foot for when he comes out. I'll park up inside. If he takes the lift, I'll take the stairs. And vice versa. Be ready.' The call ended abruptly.

'Bloody hell, where am I supposed to park round here?' Paula grumbled.

'There's some meters back down the street,' Tony said, pointing over his shoulder. 'You get out, I'll park the car and catch you up.'

'I don't—'

'Just do it.'

With a worried look over her shoulder, Paula did as he told her. Tony struggled with the unfamiliar car but managed to do a three-point turn without annoying too many other drivers. By the time he'd parked and hustled back down the street, he could see Elton cutting into the hotel entrance. Paula was a few metres behind, hanging back till she was sure he was properly inside. Then Carol emerged from the car park.

There was no possibility of escaping her notice. Not in the purple anorak. 'What the hell are you doing here?' she demanded as soon as he came within range.

'If your head's still full of crazy ideas, what the hell is

Paula doing here?' he threw straight back at her. 'You make her complicit, you destroy her as well as yourself.'

'Don't be stupid. She's not complicit. She's here to make the arrest after I stop him.'

'You can't do this, Carol.'

'I will, Tony. You can't stop me.' She pushed past him and joined Paula at the hotel entrance. Together they walked inside.

He thought about phoning the police. And saying what? The head of ReMIT is about to commit a murder? He could imagine the laughter in the control room. He couldn't tell Paula because then he'd be the one making her complicit if they couldn't stop Carol.

There was nothing else for it. The only person who could stop Carol from destroying her life was him.

He'd never felt less heroic.

71

Heart in mouth, Tony followed the two women up the steps and into the foyer. Blond wood and grey granite were the keynote materials, offset by receptionists in sombre dark-grey unisex Nehru jackets. Splashes of colour came from the dresses, shoes and fascinators of young women moving through on their way to another part of the hotel. The men blended in better, except for the occasional startling tie.

A large plasma screen over to one side revealed the events of the day and their locations. The only wedding was in the first-floor Lennon & McCartney ballroom. Carol and Paula stood to one side of the screen, heads close, conferring. Nothing for it but to approach them.

'What's the plan, then?' he asked genially as he drew close.

'One that doesn't include you,' Carol said.

'I'm the only one he hasn't seen before,' Tony said reasonably.

'You're not a police officer.' Carol turned away, her face rigid with anger.

'But I can observe. I can alert you when he makes a move.'

'He's got a point,' Paula said.

'Go away, Tony,' Carol said.

'Fine. See you later.' He smiled and walked away. Up the wood and steel staircase to the first floor.

Carol watched Tony climb the stairs with a growing sense of dismay. What the hell did he think he was playing at? This was hard enough without having to factor in whatever interfering plan he had cooked up. For there would be some plan, she knew him well enough to realise that. Her blood was already beating in her veins, her palms damp. 'We can't let him get in the middle of this,' she said. 'Come on.'

By the time the two women had climbed the stairs, Tony was handing in his purple anorak to the cloakroom. Underneath, he was wearing his best suit. It wasn't most people's idea of a wedding suit; it had been fashionable briefly about ten years before. But it was a suit and his tie didn't clash with his shirt. His shoes were polished for the occasion. He'd even had a haircut. Carol couldn't remember a time when he'd looked better. It pierced her to the heart. She knew that what she was about to do would grieve him more deeply than he'd ever be able to admit. She would be drawing a line between them forever. But high as it was, it remained a price she was willing to pay to avoid having more death on her conscience. There was no going back now. Carol drew in a sharp breath and stepped in front of him.

He smiled again. 'I think you and Paula are a bit underdressed for this.' He gestured at their smart casual outfits. 'It's a wedding, you know. Look, why don't I slip in and keep an eye on Elton? We already know how he operates. Let's wait till he's made a move on his victim and brought her out of the reception to talk to her privately in the bar. Then you can move in on him. Because by then he'll have given her a false name and spun her the same set of lies that we know he told the other women. The dead wife, the "let's take it easy" line.'

'It makes sense, boss,' Paula said. 'It'd be a lot easier to arrest him in a quiet bar rather than in the middle of a wedding reception. And do we really want to wreck some innocent couple's wedding?'

Carol looked from one to the other. It was hard to argue against them because it was exactly the strategy she'd have employed if she'd been considering arrest rather than the alternative. They looked at her expectantly and she made up her mind. The very circumstances that would make arrest easier would also simplify what she had in mind.

'OK,' she sighed. 'But keep your distance. Don't do anything to make him suspicious. And call me as soon as he makes a move on a woman. You are not a police officer, Tony. Don't try to act like one. We'll find a quiet corner out of the way for now.' She watched him walk down the hallway to the ballroom. 'Wait here,' she told Paula, setting off after Tony.

Carol slowed as she approached the double doors of the ballroom. They were thrown wide and she could see from the detritus on the tables that the wedding meal was over. The long drapes had been pulled over the windows and the DJ was warming up the room with the Brian Eno remix of 'Congratulations'. She kept moving and found a ladies' loo at the end of the hallway.

She locked herself into a cubicle and felt inside her bag. The handle of the knife was still perfectly aligned to her hand. It was a six-inch rigid boning knife, one of a set she'd bought to equip the new kitchen in the barn. She'd never actually used it. Cooking wasn't something she did very often, and when she did, it never required filleting a piece of meat. But the set had looked good in its brushed steel block and, it turned out, it was more practical than she'd ever have imagined.

Her mouth was dry, her stomach fluttering. She hadn't been able to keep food down since the day before and there was a dull ache at the base of her skull. But she could do this, Carol told herself. She wouldn't think twice if she was protecting someone she cared about. Paula, say. Or Tony. Why should that be any different from the lives of strangers? Didn't they deserve their lives as much as people who happened to be dear to her?

Carol leaned her forehead against the cool marble wall of the cubicle. It was too late for cold feet now. It was only a matter of time before Penny Burgess brought her life crashing down around her ears and then it would be too late. She'd never get anywhere near Elton again and he would kill and kill again. How many women would he murder before he was finally caught? She couldn't let that happen.

She had enough on her conscience. The guilt stopped here. It was time for a good death.

Tony ambled across the ballroom, a genial smile here, a nod of apparent recognition there, a little wave to a small child who looked startled. He leaned on the bar and ordered a pint of bitter, letting his gaze drift down the bar. There, halfway down, was Elton, jacket over his shoulder, tie loosened, drink in hand. He was talking to the man standing next to him. Probably gleaning a few details about the bride or groom to help him with his mission.

He wasn't the only one with a mission. Tony felt faintly sick at the thought of what was to come. However he did it, he had to stop Carol from killing this man. It would be an unsurvivable event for her, he was convinced. She had drawn on extraordinary strength to hold herself together all these years, but even Carol Jordan had to run out of sheer determination somewhere. And this, he thought, was probably the time and the place.

The DJ was running the repertoire of sure-fire dancing tracks. ABBA, Madonna, Rod Stewart, as well as more modern stuff Tony couldn't put a name to. The dance floor was crammed with bodies. Not everyone was dancing, however. Some of the older guests were in little knots and huddles of conversation. The parents of small children were chasing after them, whooping and laughing. The men who wouldn't dance were mostly crowded round the bar. And a couple of women sat alone, gazing intently at their phones, pretending not to mind.

And then Elton made his move. He approached one of the women, pulling out a chair to join her. Even from that distance, Tony could see he was employing a deal of grace and charm. Tony took out his phone and called Paula. Not Carol. 'He's found his target,' he said. 'Thirty something. Long blonde hair, red dress. I'll call back when they're on the move.'

It took no more than fifteen minutes. Elton jumped to his feet and pulled the woman's chair back as she stood. They walked to the door, heads close in conversation, his hand cupping her elbow. Tony called Paula again. 'Coming your way,' he said.

He left his untouched pint and hurried after the Wedding Killer and his latest acquisition.

There was a dimly lit cocktail bar at the far end of the corridor. Its smoked-glass windows offered a view of the Albert Dock that almost made it look glamorous. Paula and Carol had chosen a table as far away from the door as they could get, tucked round the corner of the bar. They could see the heads and shoulders of people walking in. And right on cue, moments after Tony had made his second call, Tom Elton walked in with a woman. He was paying attention to her, not to his surroundings, as he steered her towards an empty table only a dozen metres from Carol and Paula.

He solicitously arranged a chair for the woman and was about to sit down when he glanced across and saw the two women. An expression of shock flickered over his face but as he composed himself, Carol got to her feet and moved towards him, her hand reaching into her shoulder bag.

Paula right behind her.

Time slowed. Carol's hand inched out of her bag. A gleam of metal. Then Tony's voice, urgent; loud. 'Mr Elton.'

Elton turned. Tony appeared to embrace him, something black sliding between them.

Paula's hand on Carol's wrist, twisting it so hard the blade fell back into her bag.

Then Elton on the floor, gasping like a landed shark, scarlet spreading across his shirt front. A woman screaming.

And Tony standing, arms loose at his side, a black blade dripping red.

Epilogue

One phone call. That's all it would have taken. One short phone call to change so many lives. Tom Elton would still have been alive. DCI Carol Jordan would no longer have been a warranted police officer. And Dr Tony Hill would not have been sitting in a room beneath Liverpool Crown Court awaiting sentence.

Not a day passed without the newly promoted Detective Inspector Paula McIntyre cursing the delay in returning Tricia Stone's call. If she'd been able to get through, she would have learned about the cottage in the Dales that Tom Elton had access to, that Tricia Stone had forgotten to mention when they'd spoken previously. That knowledge would surely have been enough to stay Carol Jordan's hand.

When Paula eventually got hold of Tricia two days later, she'd already heard about Elton's death and was full of apologies for not having remembered the cottage in the Dales. 'I never went there,' she said. 'When I left my last company, I swapped my shares for it. My lawyer dealt with everything. There was a sitting tenant, an academic. We only realised she moved out a few days ago when she rang up about some archive boxes she'd left in the loft. And then I remembered you asking about the Dales.' Too late, Paula thought bitterly as she listened. Too bloody late.

Tricia's information opened up an Aladdin's cave of forensic evidence. The DNA of all three of Elton's victims. The Brompton bike he'd used to leave each scene. A cache of burner phones. Three boxes of packets of crisps. All the evidence they'd have needed to put him away for murder three times over.

And her friend Tony wouldn't be about to receive a life sentence.

Remarkably, things had not descended into chaos after the stabbing. Paula somehow held it together. She had arrested Tony, who meekly sat in a chair until other officers arrived. She'd told the barman to close the bar. She'd quietly told Carol – who was apparently paralysed with shock – to shut the fuck up about the knife in her own bag. 'Nobody saw it,' she'd hissed. 'If anybody remembers you reaching into your bag, it was your warrant card you were going for.' Carol had nodded, mute with stupefaction.

Then routine had taken over. Paramedics, cops, crime scene techs had staked their claim to the event. Paula had given a statement and had finally been cut loose in the small hours of the Sunday morning. Nobody would tell her what was going on or where Carol was, so reluctantly she went home. She had no recollection of the drive back to Bradfield. Elinor found her asleep at the kitchen table later that morning, a half-drunk tumbler of whisky next to her.

When she turned her phone back on, she found a deluge of messages from the ReMIT team. She couldn't face any of them. There was one voice message from Carol, which she listened to. 'I'm so sorry,' was all she said.

They charged Tony with murder. Of course they did. Carol refused to discuss with Paula what had happened. Numb and shocked, the team pulled together the evidence against Elton, which came in handy for Tony's defence team. But the fact that your victim had himself killed three others and was on the way to number four wasn't a defence to murder. Nothing more than a speech in mitigation. Somehow, between them, the defence team and the Crown Prosecution Service had parlayed the charge down to voluntary manslaughter. Still, it would be a heavy sentence. The use of a knife made sure of that.

Paula had visited Tony several times during the eight months he'd been on remand. The first time, she asked him why he'd done it. He'd given her the saddest smile and said, 'So she wouldn't have to.' He refused to say anything more except to point out the irony that the black commando knife had been a joke leaving present from the Home Office task force on offender profiling that he'd led years before. 'Like mother, like son,' he'd said. As if she needed reminding about Vanessa's track record.

Tony looked up as the door opened, expecting his lawyer with a final burst of optimistic but entirely unrealistic reassurance. Instead, Carol walked in, her face a pinched mask of misery. It was the first time he had seen her since his arrest and he wasn't in the least surprised that his heart still gave a spasm of joy at the sight of her. Ridiculous, but undeniable.

He jumped up and moved towards her, stopping a couple of feet short. 'It's wonderful to see you.'

'I didn't think you'd ever want to see me again. But Bronwyn said ... '

'I've missed you. I wanted to write but I didn't want to compromise you.'

She nodded and sat down on the bench that ran along one side of the cell. 'I've been so angry with you. For doing this to yourself. For doing it because of me.'

A crooked smile and a half-shrug. 'I knew you couldn't do the time. So I stopped you doing the crime.'

'You've ruined your life. Your career. Everything.'

He sat down next to her, turning so he could see that face that was always there when he closed his eyes at night. 'I'll be OK. Because I pleaded guilty to voluntary manslaughter with provocation, my brief reckons I'll get somewhere between five and ten years. I won't be in maximum security. I can do the time, Carol. I can finally get down to that book I've been supposedly writing for years about offender profiling and my experience in the field. I can help other prisoners who don't get enough therapy in the system.'

'Stop being so bloody noble. You know you shouldn't have done it.'

'No point in thinking like that. Paula tells me you've still got ReMIT to keep you occupied.' His brow wrinkled in a frown. 'What happened to Penny Burgess's story, by the way? It never appeared.'

Carol sighed and shook her head. 'She never ran it. The papers turned ReMIT into heroes after Elton. You how the *Daily Mail* loves a vigilante. There was no mileage in trying to make us the bad guys. So I get it all, Tony. Freedom, respect, applause.' The bitterness burst through her attempt at levity.

'Good. So make the most of it. Otherwise all this was for nothing.'

She took a deep breath. 'You were right. About the PTSD. I should have listened to you.'

He said nothing. There was nothing to be said.

'I'm seeing someone.'

His face was stricken, eyes wide with hurt.

She gave a dry little laugh. 'For therapy, you idiot. Actually, I'm seeing Jacob Gold.'

'Jacob?' Tony was startled. 'My Jacob?'

'Yes. I remembered you saying how much he had helped

you over the years. So I went to see him. I didn't want to go through official channels. For obvious reasons.'

'He's very good.'

'I hope so. Because it's the hardest thing I've ever done.'

'It works.' He stood up. 'You should go now. They'll be taking me up for sentencing any minute.' He paused, drinking in the sight of her looking up at him. 'Come and visit me?'

She stood up and touched his arm. 'As often as they'll let me.'

'And look after *Steeler*. I'll need somewhere to live when I come out.' A single tear trickled from the corner of her eye. He lifted a hand to her face and gently brushed it away. 'That time I said I loved you?'

She nodded, swallowing hard.

'I meant it.'

'I know. I love you too, Tony.' Then she turned away and was gone.

Dear Reader

I am about to presume on your goodwill. Now that you have reached the end of *Insidious Intent*, I believe you'll understand the favour I'm about to ask you. I hope that the ending of Tony Hill and Carol Jordan's tenth outing will have taken you by surprise. I like to think that although it may seem shocking, it makes a terrible kind of sense, given what we know of their character traits and the experiences both have endured at my hands.

Nevertheless, I believe it is not predictable. And for that reason, I'm asking you not to say or write anything that is a spoiler for that ending. I really want other readers to experience that moment of indrawn breath for themselves. Remember the disapproval showered on the people who revealed the twist in *The Sixth Sense* and spoiled it for the rest of us? I don't want that to happen here.

I'm sorry if this sounds self-important, but I've had twenty years of readers telling me how invested they are in these characters, and I want them to enjoy this book as much as, I hope, you have.

Thanks for your time and your continued support.

All the best

Acknowledgements

Like journalists, writers of fiction are only as good as their sources. And I am very lucky with mine. Professor Niamh Nic Daied gave me valuable tutorials on fire and packets of crisps. Professor Dame Sue Black demonstrated how easy it is to break a hyoid bone. Professor Jo Sharp aided and abetted me in various ways.

As always, I have a great team at my back who work with me to make the books the best they can be. My publisher David Shelley, my editor Lucy Malagoni, my American editor Amy Hundley, my agent Jane Gregory and editorial expert Stephanie Glencross are my first readers and they all have wisdom to offer. My copy-editor Anne O'Brien knows Tony and Carol better than I do and nobody could deal more effectively with the detail where the devil resides. Laura Sherlock keeps the show on the road with a smile (in spite of the car . . .), and the Little, Brown sales and marketing teams get the books into readers' hands with flair and diligence.

Kudos to Kathryn McCormick, Amie McDonald, Eileen Walsh and Lorna Meikle, who made generous charitable donations to see their names in print. Only the names are the same!

And then there is my family. I couldn't do this without their love, patience, GSOH and support. Jo and Cam, you are my rocks in a stormy sea.

It's been thirty years since my debut, *Report for Murder*, was published. I never imagined I had so many books in me. I'd like to take this opportunity to say thanks to all the readers, booksellers, festival organisers and reviewers who have helped to make it so rewarding and so much fun. Let's hope there's many more years and many more books to share.

Read on for the opening pages of
Broken Ground,
the new Karen Pirie novel from
Val McDermid.

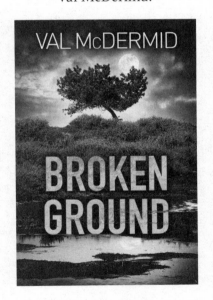

Available December 2018.

1

1944 – Wester Ross, Scotland

The slap of spades in dense peat was an unmistakable sound. They slipped in and out of rhythm; overlapping, separating, cascading, then coming together again, much like the men's heavy breathing. The older of the pair paused for a moment, leaning on the handle, letting the cool night air wick the sweat from the back of his neck. He felt a new respect for gravediggers who had to do this every working day. When all of this was over, you wouldn't catch him doing that for a living.

'Come on, you old git,' his companion called softly. 'We ain't got time for tea breaks.'

The resting man knew that. They'd got into this together and he didn't want to let his friend down. But his breath was tight in his chest. He stifled a cough and bent to his task again.

At least they'd picked the right night for it. Clear skies with a half-moon that gave barely enough light for them to work by. True, they'd be visible to anyone who came up the track past the croft. But there was no reason for anyone to be out and about in the middle of the night. No patrols ventured this far up the glen, and the moonlight meant they didn't have to show a light that might attract attention. They were confident of not being discovered. Their training, after all, had made clandestine operations second nature.

A light breeze from the sea loch carried the low-tide tang of seaweed and the soft surge of the waves against the rocks. Occasionally a night bird neither could identify uttered a desolate cry, startling them every time. But the deeper the hole grew, the less the outside world impinged. At last, they could no longer see over the lip of the pit. Neither suffered from claustrophobia, but being that enclosed was discomfiting.

'Enough.' The older man set the ladder against the side and climbed slowly back into the world, relieved to feel the air move around him again. A couple of sheep stirred on the opposite side of the glen and in the distance, a fox barked. But there was still no sign of another human being. He headed for the trailer a dozen yards away, where a tarpaulin covered a large rectangular shape.

Together they drew back the canvas shroud to reveal the two wooden crates they'd built earlier. They looked like a pair of crude coffins standing on their sides. The men shaped up to the first crate, grabbing the ropes that secured it, and eased it off the bed of the trailer. Grunting and swearing with the effort, they walked it to the edge of the pit and carefully lowered it.

'Shit!' the younger man exclaimed when the rope ran too fast through one palm, burning the skin.

'Put a bleeding sock in it. You'll wake up the whole bloody glen.' He stamped back to the trailer, looking over his shoulder to check the other was behind him. They repeated the exercise, slower and clumsier now, their exertions catching up with them.

Then it was time to fill the hole. They worked in grim

silence, shovelling as fast as they could. As the night began to fade along the line of the mountains in the east, they attacked the last phase of their task, stamping the top layer of peat divots back in place. They were filthy, stinking and exhausted. But the job was done. One day, some way hence, it would be worth it.

Before they dragged themselves back into the cab, they shook hands then pulled each other into a rough embrace. 'We did it,' the older man said between coughs, pulling himself up into the driver's seat. 'We fucking did it.'

Even as he spoke, the *Mycobacterium tuberculosis* organisms were creeping through his lungs, destroying tissue, carving out holes, blocking airways. Within two years, he'd be forever beyond the consequences of his actions.

2

2018 – Edinburgh

The snell north wind at her back propelled Detective Chief Inspector Karen Pirie up the steady incline of Leith Walk towards her office. Her ears were tingling from the wind and tormented by the grinding, drilling and crashing from the massive demolition site that dominated the top end of the street. The promised development, with its luxury flats, high-end shops and expensive restaurants, might boost Edinburgh's economy, but Karen didn't think she'd be spending much time or money there. It would be nice, she thought, if the city council came up with ideas that benefited its citizens more than its visitors.

'Grumpy old bag,' she muttered to herself as she turned into Gayfield Square and made for the squat concrete boxes that housed the police station. More than a year on from the bereavement that had left her unmoored, Karen was making a conscious effort to breach the gloom that had fallen across her life like a curtain. She had to admit that, even on a good day, she still had a fair distance to go. But she was trying.

She nodded a greeting to the uniform on the front counter,

stabbed the keypad with a gloved finger and marched down the long corridor to an office tacked on at the back like a grudging afterthought. Karen opened the door and stopped short on the threshold. A stranger was sitting at the usually unoccupied third desk in the room, feet on the wastepaper bin, the *Daily Record* open in his lap, in one hand a floury roll trailing bacon.

Karen made a theatrical show of stepping back and staring at the door plaque that read 'Historic Cases Unit'. When she turned back, the scrappy little guy's face still pointed at the paper but his eyes were on her, wary, ready to slide back to the newsprint with full deniability. 'I don't know who you are, or what you think you're doing here, pal,' she said, moving inside. 'But I know one thing. You've left it way too late to make a good first impression.'

Unhurried, he shifted his feet from the bin to the floor. Before he could say or do more, Karen heard familiar heavy footsteps in the hall behind her. She glanced over her shoulder to see Detective Constable Jason 'the Mint' Murray bearing down on her, trying to balance three cups of Valvona & Crolla coffee on top of each other. *Three* cups?

'Hi, boss, I'd have waited for you to get in but DS McCartney, he was gagging for a coffee so I thought I'd just ...' He registered the frost in her eyes and gave a weak smile.

Karen crossed the room to her desk, the only one with anything approximating a view. An insult of a window looked out across an alley on to a blank wall. She stared at it for a moment then fixed the presumed DS McCartney with a thin smile. He'd had the good sense to close his paper but not to straighten up in his seat. Jason gingerly stretched at full length to place Karen's coffee in front of her without getting too close. 'DS McCartney?' She gave it the full measure of disdain.

'That's right.' Two words was enough to nail his origins: Glasgow. She should have guessed from his gallus swagger. 'Detective Sergeant Gerry McCartney.' He grinned, either oblivious or indifferent. 'I'm your new pair of hands.'

'Since when?'

He shrugged. 'Since the ACC decided you needed one. Obviously she thinks you need a boy that knows what he's about. And that would be me.' His smile soured slightly. 'Hotfoot from the Major Incident Team.'

The new Assistant Chief Constable. Of course she was behind this. Karen had hoped her working life would have changed for the better when her previous boss had been caught up in the crossfire of a high-level corruption scandal and swept out with the rubbish. She'd never fitted his image of what a woman should be – obsequious, obedient and ornamental – and he'd always tried unsuccessfully to sniff out the slightest improprieties in her inquiries. Karen had wasted too much energy over the years keeping his nose out of the detail of her investigations.

When Ann Markie had won the promotion that brought the HCU under her aegis, Karen had hoped for a less complicated relationship with her boss. What she got was differently complicated. Ann Markie and Karen shared a gender and a formidable intelligence. But that was the limit of their congruence. Markie turned up for work every day camera-ready and box-fresh. She was the glamorous face of Police Scotland. And she made it clear at their first meeting that she was 110 per cent behind the Historic Cases Unit as long as Karen and Jason cracked cases that made Police Scotland look modern, committed and caring. As opposed to the sort of idiots who could spend a month searching for a man reported missing who was lying dead in his own home. Ann Markie was devoted to the kind of justice that let her craft sound bites for the evening news.

Markie had mentioned that the budget might stretch to an extra body in HCU. Karen had been hoping for a civilian who could devote themselves to admin and basic digital searches, leaving her and Jason to get on with the sharp end. Well, maybe sharp was the wrong word where Jason was concerned. But although he might not be the brightest, the Mint had a warmth that tempered Karen's occasional impatience. They made a good team. What they needed was backroom support, not some strutting Glasgow keelie who thought he'd been sent to be their saviour.

She gave him her best hard stare. 'From MIT to HCU? Whose chips did you piss on?'

A momentary frown, then McCartney recovered himself. 'Is this not your idea of a reward, then?' His lower jaw inched forward.

'My ideas don't always coincide with those of my colleagues.' She picked the lid off her coffee and took a sip. 'As long as you don't think it's a holiday.'

'Naw, no way,' he said. Now he straightened up in his seat and looked alert. 'You get a lot of respect from the MIT,' he added hastily.

Karen kept her face straight. Now she'd learned one useful thing about Gerry McCartney – he was a good liar. She knew exactly how much respect her unit had with detectives who wrestled with intractable crimes in real time. They thought HCU was a doddle. If she nailed a historic perpetrator, she was a media hero for a day. If she failed? Well, nobody had their beady eyes looking over her shoulder, did they? 'Jason's working his way through a list of people who owned a red Rover 214 in 1986. You can give him a hand with that.'

McCartney's lip twitched in faint disgust. 'What for?'

'A series of violent rapes,' Jason said. 'He beat the last lassie so badly she ended up brain damaged in a wheelchair. She died only a couple of weeks ago.'

'Which is why our new evidence turned up. A former street girl saw the story in the paper. She didn't come forward at the time because she was still using and she didn't want to get on the wrong side of her dealer. But she had a wee notebook where she used to write down the cars that other women got into. Amazingly, she still had it, tucked away in an old handbag. The red Rover was around on all of the nights when the rapes took place.'

McCartney raised his eyebrows and sighed. 'But she couldn't manage to get the number. Is that not typical of your average whore?'

Jason looked apprehensive.

'Something you might like to take on board, Sergeant? We prefer the term "sex worker" in this unit,' Karen said. It wasn't a tone of voice people argued with. Gerry sniffed but said nothing.

'She did get the number,' Jason said brightly. 'But the bag was in the attic where she lives now and the mice have been at it. The edges of the pages have all been chewed away. All we've got is the first letter: B.'

Karen smiled. 'So you guys have got the fun job of going through the DVLA records and tracking down the owners from thirty years ago. Some clerk in the driving licence office is going to love you. On the plus side, the lab at Gartcosh have managed to extract DNA from the evidence that's been sitting in a box all these years. So if we find a likely lad, we could get a nice neat result.' She finished her coffee and binned the cup. 'Good luck with that.'

'OK, boss,' Jason mumbled, already focused on the task. Setting a good example, Karen thought. The boy was learning. Slowly but surely, he was learning.

'Where are you heading?' McCartney asked as she made for the door.

She wanted to say, 'None of your business,' but she decided it was probably worth trying to keep him more or less on side. For now, at least. Till she had the full measure of him and the closeness of his connection to Ann Markie. 'I'm off to Granton to talk to one of the conservators who thinks she might have seen a stolen painting in a private collection.'

Again that slight twitch of the lip. 'I didn't think that was our thing. Stolen paintings.'

'It is when a security guard got a face full of shotgun pellets in the course of the theft. Eight years ago, and this is the first sniff we've had of where the painting might have ended up.' And she was gone, already planning the route in her head. One of the many things she loved about Edinburgh was that it was easier to get places on the bus and on foot than it was to wrangle a pool car out of the division. Anything that avoided the petty exercise of petty power was a plus in Karen's book. 'Number sixteen,' she muttered as she headed for the bus stops on Leith Walk. 'That'll do nicely.'